SPECIAL MESSAGE TO READERS

THE ULVERSCROFT FOUNDATION
(registered UK charity number 264873)
was established in 1972 to provide funds for
research, diagnosis and treatment of eye diseases.
Examples of major projects funded by
the Ulverscroft Foundation are:-

- The Children's Eye Unit at Moorfields Eye Hospital, London
- The Ulverscroft Children's Eye Unit at Great Ormond Street Hospital for Sick Children
- Funding research into eye diseases and treatment at the Department of Ophthalmology, University of Leicester
- The Ulverscroft Vision Research Group, Institute of Child Health
- Twin operating theatres at the Western Ophthalmic Hospital, London
- The Chair of Ophthalmology at the Royal Australian College of Ophthalmologists

You can help further the work of the Foundation
by making a donation or leaving a legacy.
Every contribution is gratefully received. If you
would like to help support the Foundation or
require further information, please contact:

THE ULVERSCROFT FOUNDATION
**The Green, Bradgate Road, Anstey
Leicester LE7 7FU, England
Tel: (0116) 236 4325**

website: www.foundation.ulverscroft.com

Nina Stibbe was born in Leicester and now lives in Cornwall with her partner and two children. *Man at the Helm* is her first novel.

MAN AT THE HELM

Not long after her parents' divorce, heralded by an awkward scene involving a wet *Daily Telegraph* and a pan of cold eggs, nine-year-old Lizzie Vogel and her sister and little brother are packed off to a small, slightly hostile village in the English countryside. Their mother is all alone, only thirty-one years of age, with three young children and a Labrador. It is no wonder that she becomes a menace, a drunk — and a playwright. Worried about the bad plays — though more about becoming wards of court and being sent to the infamous Crescent Home for Children — Lizzie and her sister decide to contact, by letter, suitable men in the area. In order to stave off the local social worker they urgently need to find someone to be the new man at the helm.

NINA STIBBE

MAN AT
THE HELM

Complete and Unabridged

CHARNWOOD
Leicester

First published in Great Britain in 2014 by
Viking
an imprint of
Penguin Books
London

First Charnwood Edition
published 2015
by arrangement with
Penguin Books Ltd
London

A catalogue record for this book is available
from the British Library.

ISBN 978–1–4448–2496–4

Published by
F. A. Thorpe (Publishing)
Anstey, Leicestershire

Set by Words & Graphics Ltd.
Anstey, Leicestershire
Printed and bound in Great Britain by
T. J. International Ltd., Padstow, Cornwall

This book is printed on acid-free paper

To A. J. Allison

PART I

A Menace and a Drunk

1

My sister and I and our little brother were born (in that order) into a very good situation and apart from the odd new thing life was humdrum and comfortable until an evening in 1970 when our mother listened in to our father's phone call and ended up blowing her nose on a tea towel — a thing she'd only have done in an absolute emergency.

The following morning she took a pan of eggs from the lit stove and flung it over our father as he sat behind his paper at the breakfast table. He screamed like a girl — expecting it to be hot — and fell off his chair. It wasn't hot (she wasn't insane). He remained on the floor for a few moments until we all looked away, which we did out of decency. Then he went towards the coffee. Before he could lift the pot, our mother launched herself at him and, slipping on shards of wet *Daily Telegraph*, they both went down and began rolling around in the mess. It seemed mild enough to begin with, and quite play-groundy, until his great white hands circled her neck and one of her shoes came off as it might in a murder or fairy tale. I willed her to throw him off, judo-style, and tread on his throat with the remaining shoe, but in the end Mrs Lunt had to intervene and prise his fingers apart.

And then by coincidence it was 8.30 and our father's driver (Bernard, who lived in a chalet on the grounds) tooted outside in the Daimler and took him away to the office — furious, with scruffed-up hair and a wet shirt. Our mother smoothed herself down with her hands and poured a Scotch and ginger ale. She didn't come to the breakfast table, she didn't smile or cry or exchange looks with us, but instead stood at the sideboard, thinking, in a world of her own and in the one shoe.

We had tea-biscuits for breakfast, everything else having been caught up in the riot (Mrs Lunt's words). In those days you didn't have endless supplies in the larder. You got it in daily. Mrs Lunt did.

As I say, our mother stood leaning on the sideboard thinking, and after swallowing down her drink she visibly had an idea and rushed into the hall. We heard her dialling the telephone and, because of everything that had gone on, we all listened intently, wondering whom she might suddenly want to speak to. Mrs Lunt didn't babble to shield us or protect our mother's privacy but froze with an ear to the doorway. She even put a finger to her lips.

I thought it might be the police or this man called Phil. But actually she just cancelled the coal.

'So, that's it, then,' she said, in a brave but broken voice. 'I'll settle up at the end of the week.'

And I was disappointed again. I think we all were.

Our parents had always liked a fire in the grate and only a heat wave prevented it. Our father particularly liked a coal fire and would gaze at the steady orange glow until his cheeks mottled and his eyes stopped blinking. Our mother preferred wood — tiny flames dancing along a collapsing log-type thing. She didn't like coal, its wet blackness twinkling in the gaping bucket. And hated the ash it produced — the kind that remained in the air after Mrs Lunt had cleaned the hearth — as opposed to more obedient wood-ash. We knew this because she'd written a poem containing all these images. Plus she'd taken against the coalman since seeing him pee onto a flowerbed. She wouldn't have minded except he'd targeted a clump of calendula with his forceful stream and battered it down. She hadn't included that image in the poem but complained about it to our father, who'd said, 'The chap needed a pee — big deal!' and then he dragged Mrs Lunt into it for his own amusement. 'Have you ever had the good fortune to see the coalman relieving himself, Mrs L?' he'd said. And Mrs Lunt had gasped like a lady in a sitcom and rushed away muttering.

So, that was it. The coalman didn't come any more and we went over to logs from the milkman, who drove his whining float right up the drive and circled it like a fairground ride with everything sliding sideways. Better even than that, he whistled through his teeth and made a fuss of Debbie, our Labrador.

Mrs Lunt said it was all very well but logs required a certain amount of stacking and keeping dry (though not too dry) and that things liked to live amongst them and give you a heck of a fright. Whereas coal was simple and uninhabitable and you knew where you were with it. Our mother reminded her about the coalman peeing and stuck to her guns.

And I thought the switch to logs would be the long and the short of it. But my sister didn't think that. She worried about our father's continuing absence and pestered me from time to time to see if I had started to worry yet. As if I was bound to, sooner or later. She was very keen to drag me into it.

'Mother will go 100 per cent crazy on her own,' said my sister. 'Let's pray he comes home soon and they don't split up.'

'They won't split up,' I said.

'I bet they will. They have nothing in common — they're chalk and cheese,' said my sister. I didn't agree. I thought they were just different types of cheese (or chalk).

They seemed to me to have plenty in common. They looked alike, both adored toast, they had the same walk (heel down first), loved Iris Murdoch and had a habitual little cough as if they were saying 'Come in' very quickly. Truly the list went on and on but I didn't mention those things because it didn't seem to add up to much — listing it like that.

I did say, 'They both love sitting by a blazing fire.' And then we were back to the coalman.

Our mother tried to break the news of their separation as painlessly as possible.

'I want this to be as painless as possible,' she said, soothingly. 'Your father and I have decided to split up and get a divorce — Daddy has gone to live in the flat.'

But the mood changed when my sister accidentally said, 'Oh no! Poor Daddy.'

And our mother erupted, 'Poor Daddy? Poor Daddy is over the fucking moon.' And she sobbed — great comical sobs — and I didn't dare look at my sister for fear of laughing. The way you do at times like that.

I couldn't understand how my sister, with all her apparent worrying about our mother, had managed to blurt out, 'Poor Daddy.' I honestly couldn't.

My sister immediately wrote to our father on her special peach-blossom writing paper with matching envelope and implored him to rethink the separation. It was a brief note, to the point, and included the line 'Lizzie and I have some concerns about the future', and although he didn't write back he telephoned and spoke to her about the situation and warned her that his chauffeur, Bernard, was going to call in and collect his small belongings. Upon hearing this, our mother told us to be vigilant re Debbie — as she wouldn't put it past the chauffeur to snatch her.

Bernard arrived the next day and took a few things, such as a painting of a gun dog with a dead bird held softly in its mouth, a gentleman's case containing assorted hairbrushes, and the toaster. My sister had made a pile of other things ready — including a cushion he apparently liked — but Bernard wouldn't stray from the list, except for a blanket to wrap the painting in.

I kept Debbie on the lead for the duration and felt relieved when the Daimler drove away dogless.

You might think our mother would have been glad to be rid of our father (and all his awful hairbrushes). Not just because he was now in love with Phil from the factory but also because, even before that, he hardly ever came out of his den except to have dinners (though never teas or lunches). And when he did show himself he seemed to be nothing but a tall irritant. For instance, we'd be halfway through our dinner, deep in conversation about whether or not we agreed with the modern tendency to cover everything with breadcrumbs, when he'd appear with his hair combed and ask our mother to put her cigarette out. And then, turning on us, say we weren't holding our knives and forks correctly. And though our mother would undermine him with her expression, I always felt I should obey. And I'd struggle to eat using the pronging method with the fork in my left hand when I much preferred the Scandinavian way of scooping with the fork in the right hand. And he'd finish his food and say, 'Right, I've work to do.' And leave us alone again and we'd go back to scooping and discussing the breadcrumbs.

Often our mother would murmur 'idiot' or similar and Little Jack, my brother, would defend him, run after him and then come back, sad and in no-man's-land.

And to begin with, after the split, I thought I was quite glad to be rid of him. But actually, I missed him — his dinnertime appearances being

8

better than nothing and his mild disapproval suddenly seeming quite important. And hearing about his love affair — which we did via the short play-act our mother wrote recalling her discovery of it — my opinion of him changed. It was exciting and unexpected. He was flesh and blood all of a sudden, whereas before he'd seemed like a dusty old statue, to be driven around and avoided.

Even my sister — who was furious about the split and very worried about the future — was thrilled by the affair. 'I just can't imagine Daddy like that, you know, kissing etc. with another man,' she said. 'It's amazing.' And we agreed. It was.

Maybe that's why our mother was so upset. Perhaps, like us, she began to see him in a new, romantic light. Let's face it: she'd actually heard the loving whispers on the phone. And now he was gone.

> (*Adele holds telephone receiver to ear. Hand over mouthpiece.*)
> Roderick: (*quietly*) I want you.
> (*Adele grimaces silently.*)
> Man's voice on phone: When?
> Roderick: Meet me in half an hour at the flat.
> Man's voice: Bring the toaster.

'You won't be lonely, Mum,' I said. 'You've still got Mrs Lunt.'

'I don't need Mrs Lunt. Mrs Lunt is a cunt,' she said, and seemed pleased with the rhyme.

'Well, you've got us three anyway,' I chirruped,

but she recited a line from a poem called 'Lonely in a Crowd', which illustrated that strange problem with the image of a plastic parsley garnish on a hungry person's plate.

My sister did finally get me worrying — as big sisters do — about our mother's loneliness by going on and on about the possible outcomes. She was eleven and I was nine, she knew better than I did, and I was forced to admit loneliness probably was one of the top-ten worst things imaginable and might easily turn into unhappiness and play-writing and that was definitely to be avoided. But I still wasn't as bothered as she was and could only spend so much time on it — a position my sister felt was unkind.

Defending myself, I listed the many other people our mother might count on to help ward it off (the loneliness). And it was a long list. There was her family for starters — she had some older brothers (though not sisters, which would have been a million times better — especially in those days). I didn't count her mother, her being an unloving woman who liked to rub salt into wounds. But there were some nice aunts and a few cousins dotted around.

I had to admit that our mother's lack of a proper best friend (or any friend really) put her at a disadvantage (the result of being sent away to boarding school in a far-away place and then marrying at nineteen before she'd got going properly on adulthood). But on the plus side there was an assortment of family friends she'd known all her life — well-mannered posh people who had little cocktail parties and so forth that would be perfect to ward off feelings of loneliness.

More immediately, there were our neighbours. Such as the blousy Mrs Vanderbus and her driver, Mr Mason, whose big old house shared our D-shaped drive and who had daytime naps and would shout at us from an upstairs window ('Myself and Mr Mason are goink for our siesta, so shut up your noises') and we would tiptoe about dramatically and stay as quiet as possible until she reappeared at the window and shouted, 'Wakey, wakey,' meaning they'd got up again.

We loved Mrs Vanderbus — I'm writing an extra line about her because of it. She often brought us home-made Dutch sugar cakes in pretty tins, which she always wanted back (the tins). And who, when she found a grass snake in the crocosmia, called us to see it and lifted it like a true expert even though she'd only ever seen one on the telly before and suffered a delayed panic attack approximately one week later and had to see Dr Hillward for a pill.

Other nice neighbours included Dr Hillward and Mrs Hillward (who was named Marjorie before margarine had become the norm, she said, and wished either she hadn't or it hadn't). The Hillwards were charmed by us and brought their sweet puppy, Bimbo, to meet our sweet puppy, Debbie, when they were still puppies and after. And they helped us with our fireworks one year when our mother was afraid of the danger aspect and our father was tied up at the factory.

There was Mrs Lunt, who, whatever our mother called her, was always helpfully around and though definitely not in the nanny role (for she hated children and said they gave her the horrors) was a comforting presence and made wonderful little jam tarts, with different-coloured jams, which we called pot-dots. 'There's nothing quite like a jam tart to cheer a person,' she used to say, and although that was the only nice thing she ever said, it was nice and she said it often.

I didn't count the nannies as possible warders-off of loneliness (apart from one very nice one called Joan, but she was in the past by then). The rest never stayed long and never seemed quite to be on our wavelength (unlike the cunt Mrs Lunt who'd been with us for years and knew us inside out). Our mother would begin by trying to befriend the nannies and behave informally until they showed signs of not wanting to be friends and then she'd go chilly on them like a schoolgirl. The whole performance seemed, even to me, uncomfortable. They just wanted to be left alone with a small cash float. After the third one left, our mother hardly had the heart to contact the agency for a fourth — the agent being a judgemental cow and a friend of my grandmother's. But she did and we got Moira who had amber eyes — like a wolf — and it was hard to look at her. Our mother knew not to try to befriend Moira. For one thing she had ointment jars on show on the bathroom ledge and for another she went to bed early to read and these things irritated our mother no end.

Ignoring amber-eyed Moira, I pointed out to my worried sister, there was a marvellous group of people on hand and I didn't see how our mother could be lonely for a moment. My sister disagreed and quoted that poem ('Lonely in a Crowd') so that I knew she'd been speaking to our mother on the subject.

'Look,' I said, 'I know about the plastic parsley — but, in real life, she's got plenty of friends and acquaintances and so forth who will all rally round and do their utmost.'

'No, they won't, that's not what happens,' said my sister, sounding horribly grown-up at only eleven years old. 'That only happens when someone dies and, even then, not for long. If a lone female is left, especially if divorced, without a man at the helm, all the friends and family and acquaintances run away.'

'Do they?' I asked.

'Yes, until there's another man at the helm,' she said.

'And then what?' I asked.

'Then, when a new man at the helm is in place, the woman is accepted once again.'

2

We moved to the country. Our father bought a house for us in a village fifteen miles from the city — so we could grow up in a small community and with fresh air. Fifteen miles away from our neighbours and their dogs and biscuits and niceness.

When our mother told us this news we didn't think it very important, as you often don't with important things until you realize. We mistook it for good news or, at worst, nothing to worry about and didn't really take it in. By the time we had (taken it in) it was upon us and three strong men from Leonard's of Leicester were loading our furniture — via a bouncing ramp — into a lorry that Little Jack called 'the blue whale', due to its colouring and size, and two less strong men were wrapping pictures and mirrors in acres of creamy paper and marking them with a red pen, meaning 'fragile'. Some paintings and a chandelier had gone the week before and we hadn't noticed. The piano had gone earlier too because of it needing to settle down after a move and our mother wanting it at the new place, ready for her to play all the tunes that women like her played (Chopin, Beethoven etc.) plus the lesser-known but much nicer Clementi.

Soon we left the brick dust and fumes of the city and all the people we'd known. We didn't see Mrs Vanderbus ever again. She herself didn't

14

drive and her chauffeur, Mr Mason, had had his leg amputated and she couldn't afford to keep two (chauffeurs).

We drove away in our mother's old Mercedes, Gloxinia, following the blue whale. Then, somewhere just beyond the smart garage doors of the nice suburb (and its thousand bendy saplings), our mother stalled the engine on a roundabout and the whale floated on without us and Little Jack's lip began to quiver. He'd had enough of being left behind.

'Shit,' said our mother, but Gloxinia started up again and somehow knew the way and we carried on past the rusty corrugations of the less nice suburb and into the fringes with warehouses and badly built shelters and then the countryside and the cheaper villages with abundant bus stops. Then, in the greenest loveliness we'd ever seen, we caught up with the whale again as it bashed its way through unruly hawthorns on its way to our new home. My sister stuck her head out of the car window and said, 'Smell the fresh air.' So we did. It didn't smell of anything but no one said so.

On entering the village my sister read the sign. 'This is our village,' she said delightedly, and our mother said, 'Jesus fucking wept.' But we took no notice of her mood. The sign read: FLATSTONE — HOME OF THE FLATSTONE MUNTIE. We discovered later that munties were greasy little mutton pasties traditionally served on Flatstone Day, a day in June when the children of the village would hide coins and pasties under flat stones in ancient gateways for soldiers travelling

15

homeward from old wars.

As we entered the village the Leonard's of Leicester lorry clipped a tree and brought down a low-hanging branch in a great destructive crash. It had to be dealt with before we could go on and all of a sudden the quiet street was lined with grey curly-haired people with angry eyes and wellington boots. But we ignored that too and stayed delighted.

For a few dreamy days we had no idea of the sadness this little village was going to cause — more than all the uncomfortable nannies, homosexual fathers, unloving grannies, absconding family and non-existent best friends put together. It was going to stare at us in the Co-op and never want to make friends with us and our little family would be worn ragged trying to please it. But we didn't know that then; we still had a few days of discovery and all the fresh air we could possibly want.

Typically, and to our dismay, our mother straight away began on a play. Before she'd even unpacked, explored or knocked on any neighbours' doors to say hello etc. The play, called *The Vicus*, illustrated her misgivings about the immediate situation as well as addressing some old and persistent themes. That was how the play(s) worked.

Adele: I'm not sure this village is the best place for us.
Roderick: Nonsense, it's the countryside and very good for children.
Adele: But it's stultifying for me.

16

Roderick: Yes, but villages are the best place for children.

Adele: I'm not sure I know how to conduct myself in a village.

Roderick: To signify that one has finished eating, place the knife and fork at the five o'clock position.

Adele: What if I haven't finished but I'm having a cigarette break?

Roderick: If one is still eating, the fork must be placed at the eight o'clock position and the knife at the four o'clock.

It was just the four of us in the end because Moira the amber-eyed nanny had decided at the eleventh hour she wanted to remain in the city and not have the fresh air.

'Why didn't Moira come?' I asked quietly, so my brother wouldn't hear.

'She doesn't want to live in a village,' said our mother.

'Why not?' I asked.

'She's obviously not as stupid as she looks,' said our mother.

I was secretly pleased. I had my own list of things I didn't like about Moira (pulling at her top lip, saying 'Lordy' and always going on about calcium). Also, being nanny-less always felt as though we might have more adventures (and less milk) — which I preferred. I'd love to say more about Moira but she's not in the story, so I'll leave it there.

Little Jack — who loved Moira and hated change (especially enormous change at the last

17

minute) — didn't notice her absence until the next morning. And then, in his troubled state, he made the prediction that a crab was going to rap at the door, pincer us and gobble us up. It was troubling to hear, because his predictions almost always came true in some way or another. He was like one of those people in a film who say hysterical things that no one wants to hear. Things that then happen.

Only moments after we'd translated Little Jack's messy and hesitant words (he had a stammer when upset), a loud buzzing noise made us all freeze and look at each other.

'It's the crab,' stammered Little Jack in all seriousness. But it wasn't. It was the Liberal candidate, Mr Lomax, at the door. Mr Lomax also happened to be the builder who had come to put the finishing touches to one or two jobs on behalf of the vendor.

'We thought you were going to be a crab,' said my sister, to explain the delay in answering the door and the fearful faces that had greeted him.

'No, no, I'm human,' said Mr Lomax, and that made me like him and my sister offered him a cup of tea. He said he'd prefer a mug of hot water and I stopped liking him. I think you should just have what's offered or say, 'No, thanks' — otherwise you're being demanding. Anyway, Mr Lomax got on with the jobs with the radio going and went to the toilet twice, once for about twenty minutes.

As soon as Mr Lomax had completed the little jobs and gone, we set about putting our mother's books onto the wall of shelving in her sitting room. They were to be arranged alphabetically as in a library, she instructed. And hearing that made it seem like fun. It wasn't though, because it's difficult arranging things alphabetically if you don't even know the alphabet, which my sister apparently didn't as she kept asking questions about J, K and L and the later letters and then it turned out that Little Jack — who, like most stammerers, very much *did* know the alphabet — had been ordering them by author's first name. This came to light when I noticed Arnold Bennett and Arnold Wesker next to each other on account of the Arnold and that was doubly bad because we'd been instructed to make separate shelves for plays.

Anyway, there we were, up the sturdy library ladder that came as part of the shelving system, when the buzzer went again and this time it was Mrs Longlady, a villager. Mrs Longlady had solid curls set into her beige hair and you could see quite a lot of scalp. She didn't say exactly who she was or why she'd come, only that she basically ran things in the village and she'd wanted to say, 'Welcome to Flatstone.'

Our mother came into the hall looking pretty with a headscarf tied at the back. She looked as though she'd been unpacking though she'd actually been writing a play. Mrs Longlady said, 'Welcome to Flatstone,' and they shook hands. Mrs Longlady peered in at the activity around the bookshelves.

'Ah, books,' she said. 'Goodness gracious, have you read all those, Mrs Vogel?'

And our mother, who hated people saying

'Goodness gracious' (thinking goodness or gracious on their own were enough) and asking pointless questions, replied, 'A few of them.'

Mrs Longlady told us she lived on the other side of the bakery and we should get in touch if we needed any accountancy work done because her husband did the accounts for the village and also had an interest in fruit trees, wood and bees, should we need advice in those areas. She also issued an invitation for us to go and have 'a short supervised tea' at their house with her twin girls at some point in the near future.

Our new house was nice — formerly three tiny cottages, now one charming family dwelling (as on the property particulars) with a newly crafted curving staircase in rare timber that had been featured in a magazine. Not that the interesting staircase was of any interest to us, but we did love the stables with their doors in half — exactly as they were on our farm set — and the great corner mangers. We loved the bigness of the pear trees bang in the middle of the paddock. We loved Merryfield's bakery which sent nice bun smells wafting over the wall.

Best of all I liked the miles of fieldy vistas beyond the paddock. And the plywood platform that some previous person had put up in one of the pear trees — from where you could make out feudal hillocks in the agricultural patchwork, the squat grey tower of a Saxon church (that we would later visit at least three times each with school) and ancient trees whose lines marked out old lanes. Tweeting birds filled the hedgerows and trees from dawn to dusk, and cattle grazed behind and sometimes stood near a muddy trough and we'd look at their kind eyes as they queued for water.

The new house was — adventure-wise — a vast improvement on the old one, which had offered only things that adults might admire (such as a grapevine in an old glass lean-to) but not children, only a pissy sandpit and deep, dark cellar. Though the new house was nice and the fieldy vistas enthralling, we soon began to notice that hardly anyone in the village liked us. It was plain to see. People looked at us but no one smiled or stroked Debbie, our nice-looking Labrador. And we looked away and that probably made us seem furtive, but then again *not* looking away would have made us seem mad. And though I felt sure they'd warm up given time, my sister said they never would (like us, or stroke Debbie) until we had a man at the helm.

Sure enough, the months went by and Brown Owl from the Scout and Brownie hut, who seemed a reasonable woman, never called to say our names had reached the top of the list, even though our mother called in and made enquiries. And, apart from Mrs Longlady's theoretical tea, we were never invited anywhere. We weren't asked to take part in the Flatstone Day parade and never saw, let alone tasted, a mutton muntie. No one wanted to play with us — their mothers didn't want them to. Gradually I gathered (from mounting snippets) that the problem was — exactly as my sister had warned — our mother's divorcedness. That she, and therefore we, were not to be trusted. Mrs Longlady herself, who'd come round that second day asking about our mother's books and saying her husband was an accountant, gave us suspicious looks from her Hillman. Also, one of Mrs Longlady's twins, Miranda, claimed that an old woman had been forcefully evicted from one of the three cottages that made up our house and now lived in misery in a hovel with mushrooms growing on the stairs. My sister said she was talking rubbish and that hovels didn't even have stairs.

And, to add to the sense of us being untrustworthy and manless, our father soon got over us (and his love affair with Phil from the factory) and married a handsome woman from London with a perfectly symmetrical face and fluffy hair, and we weren't invited to — or even told about — the wedding. Their picture was in the *Mercury* and it gave my sister a stomach-ache. And they started having children straight away. Which, in a way, was exciting to hear about, but, in another, felt like we were being painted over with a brighter colour. My sister said she supposed we should be pleased for him and glad that in the future we'd have a whole new set of people to call on at Xmas time and Easter. And that has certainly been the case.

And, worse than all of that — day-to-day-wise — Mrs Lunt wrote a card saying she wouldn't be able to be our help any more, blaming the price of petrol. But wishing us happiness in our new home. Our mother was brave about Mrs Lunt, but we knew it was a terrible blow because on reading the card she'd let out a tiny cry of sad surprise that made us all look up. She covered it up by saying, 'Ha! The Lunt has got the message at last.'

I was disappointed because I'd been looking forward to making Mrs Lunt a cup of tea, a thing I'd learned to do since the move, and had kept imagining presenting her with her favourite cup (plain white with a yellow rim) brimming with tea and saying, 'Tea, Mrs Lunt?' and her saying, 'Well, I never.'

Finally, albeit chronically (and as predicted), our mother's family did indeed seem happy to let her slip into lonely abandonment. It was fair enough, they weren't bad people — they were/are very nice, actually — they just didn't want her embarrassing them — manless — at their get-togethers and little cocktail parties. And word spread among them that she'd become a menace and a drunk. And so she did (become a menace and a drunk) and, worse than that, she dug her nails into the soap and settled into her play-writing.

And our mother was pretty much all alone and unhappy and only thirty-one years of age and with us three and a Labrador in a small, slightly hostile village. It was no wonder, when you put it like that, that she became a menace and a drunk and a playwright.

Adele: I see you've remarried.
Roderick: Yes, a more accomplished woman
    with a nice tinkling laugh.
Adele: But plumper?

23

Roderick: Well, not a boyish stick like you.
Adele: But you like boyish sticks.
Roderick: Not any more. I now prefer accom-
   plished pears.

It wasn't long before I was forced to admit to my sister that she had been 100 per cent right about things, which I thought a decent thing to do. Not satisfied with that, my sister then informed me that our mother's unhappiness and manlessness and play-writing could have further damaging implications for us unless we managed to nip it in the bud (which could be tricky as it might be way past the bud stage by now, thanks to my denial of the problem). She explained that children of the chronically unhappy (particularly the manless and unhappy) often became wards of court, and children who became wards of court had their skin pinched day in, day out by the people who should be caring for them and only had spaghetti on toast for tea and sometimes not even on toast but with Jacob's Cream Crackers broken up and sprinkled on top as a toast substitute. And I could really imagine the unpleasant combination and the disappoint-ment (toast being the best thing about anything on toast) and it hit home. And that wasn't all. My sister went on: in addition to the constant pinching, there was no chance whatsoever of having a pony, a dog or even a guinea pig.

   I said I'd probably cope with the ponylessness and the pinchings — a small part of me excited by the thought of an ongoing battle with a pinching carer (and secretly not wanting my own pony anyway) — but my sister had heard true tales from the dreaded Crescent Homes (the children's home two villages away) and she assured me that wards of court were always dragged into sadness, however sunny their disposition at the start of it.

So, we agreed that our main aim in life would be to find a new husband for our mother. Not only for her happiness but to keep ourselves from being made wards of court and ending up in the Crescent Homes. We were realistic about it — we didn't expect her to be going out with a new man every week, we knew the dating game was tricky — we'd read enough magazines. In between times we'd have to find other bits and bobs of happiness to be going on with in a bid to lure her away from her play(s) and help her enjoy real life for a moment or two, with a view to it becoming the norm.

We decided we'd contact, by letter, the suitable men in the area and invite them to have a drink with her and hope that it would lead to sexual intercourse and possibly marriage. Obviously one at a time. My sister asked me to name the top three qualities I'd look for in a husband. It was difficult because I knew so little about men, only really that they loved fires and omelettes and needed constant snacks.

I began by saying I'd look for an enthusiastic television watcher. And was about to say I'd want someone 'down-to-earth' but could see that my sister wasn't listening. Like all people who ask for your favourite or top three things, she was merely waiting to tell me hers. When I'd noticed other people doing this, I'd always thought it might be better if the person asking just said, 'May I tell you the top three things I look for?' And that way you're not wasting time thinking up your top three things (just so they feel justified in saying theirs). The worst offender in this regard was Little Jack, usually over Roman emperors or pies.

Anyway, my sister began on her top three qualities in a man. She felt strongly that we needed a man who would answer the front door and generally be authoritative, and someone who really loved animals and would nurse a sick one back to health by hand, and possibly a landowner.

Little Jack joined in and said he liked a man with deep pockets. Not meaning it metaphorically but literally — him having just gone into pocketed trousers himself and thrilled at the possibilities. He also wanted someone with an interest in owls and Romans.

We devised a vetting process based on a list of questions with yes/no/don't-know answers, mainly pertaining to a man's appreciation of animals and television, his susceptibility to certain ailments — in particular catarrh, which our mother couldn't stand, even the word (or any form of sinusitis or nose blowing) — and a good swimmer (likely to want seaside holidays). And pockets.

Once Little Jack was out of the way, we compiled a list of possible men. When I objected to one or two that my sister had included, she said, 'Let's not rule anyone out at this stage.'

'But Mr Longlady is married,' I said, 'to Mrs Longlady.' I mentioned his wife, Mrs Longlady, by name because being married to Mrs Longlady was a lot more serious than being married to anyone else.

'They're all married,' she said, 'except for Mr Lomax, and he would be married except he's slightly retarded and no one probably would want to.'

We were silent for a moment. I thought it a bit unfair to describe Mr Lomax as slightly retarded and then my sister expanded on the subject. 'We don't want too many unmarried candidates, they might not have the necessary.'

'The necessary what?' I asked.

'Experience etc. If they haven't experienced the hell and high water of family life, they might go to the bad with the shock of it,' she said.

'But what about the wives?' I asked.

'You've heard the saying 'All's fair in love and war', haven't you?'

I had, and though it was a lot to take in, I had to agree (all was fair in love and war). The Man List was established and it looked like this:

Mr Lomax — Liberal candidate
Dr Kaufmann — doctor
Mr Dodd — teacher (avoid if poss)
The coalman — too far away?
Mr Longlady — accountant and bee lover
Mr Oliphant — posh farmer
Our father

3

As luck would have it, just a day or two after we'd compiled the Man List and made our solemn pledge, our mother made an appointment to see Dr Kaufmann, the village doctor, who was already on the list. My sister and I thought we might as well make a start with him and it gave us both butterflies thinking about it. We knew doctors were a sought-after group, man-wise.

The plan was: after our mother's consultation with Dr Kaufmann, my sister would follow up with a short letter to him on the peach-blossom writing paper (which was quite sensual in appearance with pink peaches in the top right-hand corner), inviting him for an evening drink. As it turned out, I accompanied our mother to the doctor so she could show him my clickety shoulder, and it was a good job too because I knew straight away that Dr Kaufmann wouldn't dream of having sex with our mother. He wasn't the type to exploit the abandoned or fragile — however pretty. I could tell this by the way he spoke to us and the way he regarded us, a mix of seriousness, compassion and concern — I'd never seen that type of look before, or many times since. In fact, it was my opinion that an advance on Dr Kaufmann might be counter-productive (i.e., he might see it as a sign of her unsuitability, thereby bringing us closer to being made wards of court). Actually Dr Kaufmann seemed to have the same set of practical worries as my sister and he gave her a pep talk right there and then, in front of me.

'Mrs Vogel,' he said, 'you are the captain of your ship — you have people depending on you. People whom you must care for and be *seen* to care for.' He nodded at her encouragingly and went on. 'You must look after the children and you must pay your rates on time. It is imperative that you do these important things and you must try to — '

Our mother butted in there and said, 'Yes, all right, I'll try,' before Dr Kaufmann had even finished listing the things that were imperative. He paused, then continued doggedly with his list.

'You must prepare the children for school and you must keep your doors and gates closed. This is a village after all, Mrs Vogel, not a town, people notice things. You must eat well yourself, too — you're clearly underweight,' he said. 'It is imperative.'

He may as well have said, 'Or the children will be made wards of court, Mrs Vogel.'

He may as well have, because that's how I interpreted it.

Certain things were imperative. And hearing it all from the doctor made me commit 100 per cent to the quest for our mother's happiness. Because to be honest, even though I'd already pledged on it with my sister, I hadn't fully accepted the imperativeness until I'd heard Dr Kaufmann say so. That's the thing about

29

doctors, I find. Everyone believes them. Maybe that's why they're sought-after.

So when I got home, I told my sister all and we thanked God for my clickety shoulder and crossed Dr Kaufmann off the list. We were not put off finding a man, however, and decided to strike while the iron was hot and that instead of the doctor we'd make a start on Mr Lomax, the Liberal candidate and handyman. He was top of the list after all and a good bet as he'd already been to the house.

My sister wrote to him straight away. She didn't seem able to call up our mother's turns of phrase as well as I could, which was frustrating, and eventually I had to intervene to make it authentic. It was my sister's writing paper and envelope, though, and her idea in the first place, so I suppose you could say it was a joint effort.

Dear Mr Lomax,

How silly of me! I realize now I didn't get around to thanking you properly for all the little odd jobs you so kindly did when we moved into the house. I feel it's imperative to thank you properly. So would you like to come and have a drink some time — hot water or Bell's or whatever you fancy? Perhaps we could discuss more jobs. Please telephone to make a date.

Yours truly,
Elizabeth Vogel x

We delivered the letter by hand and later told our mother that Mr Lomax had rung up on the phone asking how everything was going — house-wise.

Our mother was irritated by this and said, '*House*-wise?'

And my clever sister, quick as anything, said, 'For goodness' sake, Mum, he likes you and wants to see you.'

And our mother shrugged and said, 'Christ.' But seemed pleased.

Then a couple of days went by and we hadn't heard from Mr Lomax and thought that was probably that, so my sister asked our mother if she might ring him.

'Why on earth would I ring Mr Fucking Lomax?' she asked.

And my sister said, 'Because he wants to see you.'

Then, only a moment later and to our amazement, the phone rang and we heard our mother say, 'Well, then, I suppose Friday would be lovely.' Albeit rather sternly.

On Friday at six p.m. Mr Lomax parked his van at a funny angle on the grass verge and clambered out in his work overall and chunky light-tan boots. He said he'd parked on the verge like that so as not to block any exits. And I think I realized then that he wasn't going to be our mother's cup of tea. She couldn't care less about exits being blocked and would rather people had other things on their mind.

Our mother asked Mr Lomax what he'd like to drink and he asked for a mug of hot water and

31

our mother, who already had a glass of Bell's on the go, said, 'Hot water — really? What kind of a drink is that?' She made a face and ran the hot tap. Mr Lomax asked if he might have it boiled from the kettle and our mother looked exasperated.

They sat at the kitchen table and Mr Lomax talked a lot about the difference in drinking quality between water from the water tank, water from the mains supply and water from a heated tank or boiler. He talked about the house and its condition. He was concerned about the possibility of pests, with us having chickens and the closeness of the bakery over the wall. He felt pests were 'almost inevitable'. He was concerned about the positioning of the boiler and the lack of space for ventilation and the looseness of the stair banister.

Our mother offered him another drink. He had more hot water and our mother questioned him rather rudely about the drink choice. Mr Lomax explained that he'd had a recurring fissure and it was necessary to stay hydrated to avoid a relapse. Our mother probably realized then she had nothing to lose and we ended up acting a bit of her play for him. We often acted bits of the play(s) but not usually with an audience, and that made it quite nerve-racking, albeit exciting.

It was a scene where the separating couple fights over custody of a young Labrador.

Roderick (*played by our mother*): I'm taking Debbie.

Adele (*me*): No, no, you're not. Debbie is
   devoted to me.
Roderick: You've got the children.
Adele: I want Debbie (*she holds Debbie in
   her arms*) — you've got the toaster.
Roderick: You're hurting Debbie (*pulls
   Adele's arm*).
(*The couple tussles.*)
Adele: You're hurting me!
Roderick: Give him over.
Adele: No.
(*Roderick submits and leaves the stage. Adele
   cuddles Debbie.*)

Our fight over Debbie had been vigorous and
a bit exhausting, and after acting the scene we
had a short break so our mother could have a
cigarette. During the break I pointed out what I
thought was an error in the script (Roderick
refers to Debbie as 'him' when Debbie is actually
a bitch and therefore the line should have read
'give her over') but our mother claimed she'd
written the error in — to reinforce the point that
Roderick was not on intimate terms with the
Labrador, he was just being an awkward bastard.
Our mother stubbed out her cigarette. It was
only half smoked and it snapped at the filter and
the white part carried on smoking thickly. I knew
she was ready to continue so I announced the
next act, 'My Husband Has Gone', but before
we could begin it Mr Lomax said *he* had to go.
   As he struggled into his anorak he said he
knew of a man, an ex-plumber, who needed
work due to losing his Confederation of

Registered Gas Installers certificate and might be more suitable for what she had in mind, and that he'd drop his card through the letter box. And then he strode away to his van on the verge.

'Strange chap,' said our mother, and I had to agree.

'Retarded,' said my sister, who loved saying that word.

'Crab,' said Jack, who'd called him that before and rarely changed his mind.

★　★　★

There's not going to be a better moment to explain the play(s). At the time of her separation from our father, our mother had experienced only one success in her whole life. Just one, and it had been the writing of a play entitled *The Planet* when she was sixteen years old. She'd thought it up and written it by herself and then entered it into a competition. She'd won first prize and the play had been put on at a theatre in one of the universities and acted out for a whole week by drama students (that was the prize).

Our mother hadn't enjoyed writing the play that much and, in spite of the exciting title, the subject had been mundane and gloomy (her words) but, by coincidence, mundane and gloomy plays were all the rage then and the judges had been overwhelmed by her maturity and insight. And though a gloomy mood pervaded the play, she enjoyed all the attention of people saying she was a genius at writing plays and brilliant at dialogue and structure etc.

Therefore, as time marched on and her life was just a long grey smear with no relief — only staring at flames, giving birth and drinking whisky — she would often try to re-create that time of recognition and acknowledgement. After our father left, play-writing became a daily thing. And it was mostly just the long, ongoing play of her life with snippets expanded, exaggerated, explained or remedied. The Play. Occasionally she might write a classical version or a poem, but it was essentially the same story. Hers.

Sometimes writing the play warded off misery and she'd bounce around with staging ideas and on those days we hated the play because it was those days she'd beg us to enact it when we'd rather be watching Dick Emery. Other times, she didn't have the energy to write (usually because she'd not started early enough and was too drunk) and on these days we longed for the play.

Our mother was the main character and was always played by me because I could really play her and had her exact voice and mannerisms. Our mother always took the role of our father or the significant man because she was taller than us and this proved important. This meant she and I often fought or tussled and shouted at each other (in role). My sister, who was less dramatic than our mother or me, always played the other characters such as teachers, neighbours and so forth. My little brother Jack had only occasional, tiny (albeit important) parts such as an ambulance man or a judge and, once, a pharmacist.

Although I had mixed feelings about performing the play, I had to admit it was well written. Clever, sometimes funny and always worldly — as good as anything you saw on telly or on stage except perhaps for Terence Rattigan, who didn't do as much explaining and yet revealed so much. Our mother did rather spell things out and her characters occasionally broke the fourth wall, which I considered cheating. The play didn't bother me as much as it bothered my sister. Except that what bothered her bothered the rest of us in the end.

4

In the post-mortem following Mr Lomax's visit my sister and I were self-critical and rightly so. Our aim had been that they should have a drink and then have sex in her sitting room and do it enough times until they got engaged and then married. But we'd let him slip through our fingers with bad planning and shoddy execution.

And though we agreed Mr Lomax wasn't the ideal, we evaluated our efforts as if he had been, even though he most definitely hadn't. It had been a mistake, we agreed, not to have offered any snacks or put on any music, and this might have led to Mr Lomax feeling uncomfortable and probably peckish and if there was one thing I knew for definite about men it was that they cannot perform sex if hungry. We also agreed that doing the play had only made things worse — especially that particular scene with Debbie and her being a bugger to lift. It wasn't surprising that it freaked him out.

We didn't let it put us off, though. My sister consulted the Man List, crossed off Mr Lomax and added Bernard, our father's chauffeur. I objected, saying he and our mother hated each other's guts, but my sister mentioned the very fine line between love and hate (i.e., that you're more likely to want to have sex with and marry someone you hate than someone you don't care one way or the other about). Which, when I

37

thought about it for long enough, made sense. Worryingly.

With that in mind we added a semi-retired mechanic called Denis who offered a taxi service in his Ford Zodiac — whom our mother also hated.

I wondered if it might be simpler just to instigate a reunion with our father. My sister disagreed. In her opinion they were still chalk and cheese. Also, he'd begun to fade as a notion. It was the way with divorced fathers in those days. They tended to keep out of the picture from sheer politeness and convenience. Ditto non-divorced fathers, except with divorced ones you actually never saw them except for the odd Sunday lunch or to trudge across a field with a picnic. They were absent from your private life and this was hard on leftover boys like Little Jack because there was no man at home to show them how to make the noise of an explosion or tell them that West Germany were better than Ecuador. Not that our particular father would have been able to do either of those, but it was the principle of the thing. And, worse than that, they were absent from your public life, never attending parents' evenings, sports days, school plays, and never seeing nature displays or topic books. They never saw you perform, excel, try, succeed, fail, and this was hard on my sister because it meant he never got to hear about her extraordinary cleverness in school and therefore couldn't possibly admire her as much as he should. She did occasionally tell him about it but it always sounded boastful and far-fetched and it sickened all concerned, so she stopped.

I was the least bothered by our father's private and public absence. Probably because I was certain he'd have been a fine father if it hadn't been for the divorce. I somehow didn't need his reminders to save lolly sticks in case of a sudden urge to make a model of Leicester Prison as he had done as a boy (albeit with matchsticks). I had a good memory and had heard plenty of his advice on life. Neither did I need his seal of approval. I just happened to think that, compared with everyone else on offer, he was the nicest and the best and, more importantly, the wellest known. He remained on the Man List, theoretically, but (before you get any ideas) there was never a romantic remarriage, there wasn't even a try-out; we decided it was all just too tangled and unlikely, not to mention the travel.

For the time being though, we decided we shouldn't invite any of the other men on the list to meet our mother until we'd done more research and honed a routine. In the meantime we devised some in-between projects to cheer her up and hopefully prevent the writing of the play. My sister's ideas were quick fixes — getting another foal or going to the theatre fifteen miles away or building a feed-shed. She even toyed with the idea of pretending something really bad had happened and then saying it was a false alarm so our mother could experience the sense of intense relief that makes a person count their blessings. But I thought it risky.

I preferred longer projects with multiple outcomes — planting a line of poplar trees like they have in France as a barrier against strong, hot winds, for instance, or trying to befriend someone like Mrs C. Beard across the road, who seemed like the only nice person in the village and who told us off for littering but only if we *were* littering, and if we weren't she'd smile and sometimes even wave for some reason.

My best idea, though, bearing in mind our mother's under-weightness, was a cookery spree, seeing as we were sick of toast and parsley sauce anyway. My sister considered all my ideas either too ambitious or 'unlikely to bear fruit', meaning they might never make it out of the idea stage. Or, in the case of the cookery spree, too unrealistic, seeing as our mother hated food almost as much as she hated the chauffeur (her worst word in the English language being 'portion').

And my sister, being far more practical than me, came up with a good and simple idea, which she introduced so naturally I hardly noticed it when it popped out. We were in our mother's bedroom. She had a heavy four-poster bed with ugly drapes and a few pieces of awkward walnut heartwood furniture whose open-grained appearance I hated and which I would have painted a pretty greeny-blue. We liked being in her bedroom nevertheless. It smelled nice and had a feeling of things before the split — the same linens, the same little bottles of scent etc. She even had her Ophelia in oils hanging above a cold hearth. Other old paintings had been dumped in the loft and replaced by abstract shapes in orange and yellow and quaint old signs from market stalls advertising motor oils and digestive powders.

'I think we should start going to church,' my sister said, looking into our mother's magnified eyes via the dressing table mirror. (That was her good and simple idea.)

I spoke up in surprised agreement — reminding them both that the church, being handily situated across the road, would be easy to get to. Our mother didn't respond for a while. She looked as if she were preparing to leave the house — a drop of Eyedew in each eye and pale lipstick dragged across her stretched lips. She didn't use much make-up, preferring to look natural. Her hair was plain and long, and her brown face was bony and scattered with a few tiny square freckles which looked like pieces of a broken plant pot. She was uncluttered, which I thought impressive when so many others were so done up.

'You can go to church if you want,' she said eventually, with a sniff of sarcasm, gazing at herself.

'No, I meant us as a family,' said my sister, 'to get to know people in the village.'

'I wouldn't be seen dead in the place,' said our mother, 'not after the visit from that idiotic little vicar, and his ridiculous little speech.'

'What did he say?' I asked.

'He said we were more than welcome at church,' said our mother, 'but I wouldn't be permitted to join the Mothers' Union on account of being divorced.'

'Well, then, we're 'more than welcome' — we

41

should go,' I said, opening my hands in a gesture that means 'you see', which was funny because it looked like a prayer book.

'No, Lizzie, when people say you're 'more than welcome' it means you're not welcome at all,' said our mother.

'Does it? What do they say if you *are* welcome, then?' I asked.

'They don't say anything,' she said, 'you just know.'

My sister looked a bit crestfallen, her idea having been so thoroughly rejected, but then Little Jack piped up with an idea, which was strange because we never included him in our planning, him being a worrier and too young for the whole truth. It just showed how clever and perceptive he was. And not only did he have an idea, he had a leaflet about it.

★   ★   ★

Little Jack's leaflet gave details of the Easter Fancy Dress Parade and he was very proud of it. Jack was not interested in the parade per se, but loved waving the leaflet around. He always picked up leaflets. They weren't as prevalent then as nowadays and there was some novelty value, if you can believe it. And he was particularly pleased with this one because of getting so much attention for it — that being the purpose of most things with youngests.

We followed our mother downstairs and huddled together on the chesterfield at the chilly end of the kitchen and discussed the parade and the fancy dress competition. Our mother wasn't going out after all: she was writing a one-act play called *The Female Vixen* about the wife of a huntsman who tames a wild fox just to prove she can and is then stuck with a tame fox that can't ever be returned to the wild and gets addicted to Shredded Wheat. Which sounded quite exciting.

The thing was, though, by the time that leaflet appeared my sister and I had already grown to hate the village and I am not keen on villages to this day. Having said that, I must also admit that more than anything I wanted us to fit in and belong and be liked by the village. The tiniest gesture of friendship, however lukewarm, would have made things seem so much better and I was quite prepared to do whatever necessary to be included.

In theory you could join one of the village clubs or groups and there were some good ones, only you needed to be nominated, seconded or have your name reach the top of a list and therefore you were always at the mercy of someone in charge. For example, our mother tried to join the choir but was told it was full of sopranos like her and they'd contact her when someone died or lost their voice or got ill. My sister — a true bird lover — was keen to join the Young Ornithologists but she was too old for the juniors (eleven) as they were full except for under-eights, but when Little Jack said perhaps he'd join and we rang the man, suddenly the under-eights had become the under-sevens and therefore he was too old too.

In reality — apart from going to church, which had been ruled out because of the idiotic little vicar saying we were 'more than welcome' and our mother having the intelligence to translate it into its true meaning — opportunities to join in were fairly limited and depended on already being happily integrated. However, the Easter Fancy Dress Parade was open to all and something we could join in with no waiting list, hoops or hurdles.

'The judges will be particularly looking for unusual and timely home-made costumes,' Little Jack read out in his machine-gun voice.

I say 'no hoops or hurdles' though there was the small hurdle of my sister and me deploring those kinds of things (fancy dress parades). She, because she hates being on display, and me, because I hate it that you only win if you're in a brilliant costume and it's quirky and timely and you need to have a quirky, timely idea and still have the time and materials and skill to produce the costume itself. Or a mother who will. And it's always the same lucky few who can rise to the occasion, when actually it would be nice if someone else won for a change.

My sister refused to even consider dressing up and I'd almost given up on it when our mother came up with a quirky idea that was so brilliant and timely I almost fainted and thought I must be dreaming. I honestly think it was the best idea she'd ever had or ever would have. Even she said so. It was better than the award-winning play she had written in 1957. Better because that was just an accident and

44

this was a good *idea* and they're almost impossible to have. I was to be Miss Decimal.

Our mother set to work and got the whole outfit made in an hour. A plain white crêpe-paper dress with a giant Bacofoil-covered cardboard fifty-pence piece stuck on to the front of it. The idea was so up-to-the-minute it was still in the news even. Decimalization had only occurred in the February and there I'd be, on Easter Monday, a walking, talking fifty-pence piece. I felt sure this parade would be the start of our being embraced by the community, not least because of our mother's fantastic and timely decimal idea, but also its simplicity and lack of ostentation.

I made this observation and badgered my sister to agree, which she did reluctantly, and our mother offered to construct a simple outfit for my sister called the Divorce Reform Act, which had also come into effect that year and would therefore be timely (and home-made).

'What would the Divorce Reform Act look like?' I asked, feeling slightly that it might trump Miss Decimal.

After a few moments our mother said, 'I'd start with a simple calico dress, pin-tucked at the bust and embroidered with words of love and bound with a red sash. But the skirt would be rudely shredded and the embroidery unpicked with threads hanging . . . '

'And the hair all messy and smudged mascara,' I added.

'No thanks,' my sister interrupted.

Little Jack decided that he'd like to enter the

45

parade, but not as the Divorce Reform Act and our mother, being in the right mood, got to work on a simple John Lennon outfit.

The day of the parade dawned and Jack and I got into our costumes and trotted hand in hand to the vicar's garden by the church. Mrs Longlady, our almost neighbour, was one of the judges and she spoke into a microphone to the entrants and their mothers. Seeing her there in her role as boss of the village, she seemed tall and important — like her name. And she kept saying 'thrice', which seemed important too. I'd never before heard anyone say 'thrice' and it became my favourite word.

'The entrants will be viewed thrice,' she announced to the entrants and their mothers in her echoey mic voice, 'walking, standing and close up, before we adjudge who is to be awarded the prizes.'

I was in the under-twelves class and we were the first to be looked at. We had gathered in a huddle under the chestnut tree and a helper came along and unhuddled us so that the judges could view us (thrice). I was bang in the middle of the line. To my left was Bo-Peep with a fluffy sheep under her arm and to my right a boy in his swimming trunks with a flap who I guessed was Mowgli. I tried to talk to my fellow contestants, but they turned away from me when I spoke. A couple of them smirked at my costume and one said, 'What's she come as?' and another answered, 'Ten bob!' and the whole line laughed.

Then the judges, Mrs Longlady, Mrs Worth

from the toy and hardware shop, and Mrs Frink from the hunt, came along and looked thrice at Bo-Peep, smiled and asked if she'd helped her mum make the costume and if she'd lost her sheep. They walked straight past me. They didn't look once, let alone thrice.

They didn't smile or say what a clever idea. They didn't ask if I'd made the costume myself. Neither did they look carefully at my clogs, on to which we'd stuck plastic coins, even though I waggled them a bit to draw attention to them. Partly they just didn't like me — me being me and a member of a family with no man at the helm. But equally they hated decimalization and saw it as a nuisance foisted on them by London, a no-good, pointless change they'd never asked for. They were angry about the rounding-up of the ha'penny or the rounding-down of it. Shopkeepers like Mrs Worth felt the shopkeeper was losing out and wives like Mrs Longlady felt the housewife was being cheated. And there I was, the living personification of the thing. Bacofoil-covered.

They didn't even look; they glanced, winced and moved straight on to Mowgli. Mrs Worth mistook him for an American swimmer called Mike and complained that there hadn't been a single medal for Britain in the 1968 Olympic Games. Mowgli explained he was Mowgli and, looking thrice or more, the judges adored him, said how much they loved *The Jungle Book* and so on.

A mermaid in a bikini top won first prize. She had a padded tail, the flipper end being her out-turned feet. Her bikini top was two of those shell ashtrays that are thoughtfully placed in the waiting areas of takeaway restaurants and never quite come clean in the washing-up due to the ridges. Anyway, she won, though I couldn't see how it was timely. Still, the judges liked the bikini top and the clever use of a wheelchair borrowed from the Pines old people's home.

Soon the younger class was all lined up on a platform, the committee thinking, rightly, that the audience particularly like to see the little ones in costume. Little Jack was King Farouk of Egypt, which wasn't quite so timely and up-to-the-minute as Miss Decimal, Farouk having stopped reigning twenty years beforehand and gone into exile, but Little Jack had been given a fez by our much-travelled father. And on seeing the fez, the image of King Farouk popped into our mother's head and she switched him from the planned John Lennon with the wire-rimmed specs to the well-known, albeit old and probably dead Egyptian king. Little Jack was fine about it. I mean, who wouldn't want to be a king?

Little Jack didn't appreciate the close-up part of the thrice viewing and kept edging away from the judging trio until he fell off the platform and his fez rolled away in circles like a dropped toffee. And though Little Jack didn't win his class, the judges didn't totally ignore him either, especially after his tumble. They loved his little curled-up moustache and the fez (which everyone was captivated by) and they loved laughing at his foreignness of course. Plus he was little and a boy and so had that bit more going for him. In fact, the judges pulled him forward with another younger Bo-Peep and Jiminy Cricket (both in costumes hired from Pinocchio's in Leicester) and for a moment it really looked as if Jack might get a rosette — the judges were pointing at him (him looking so podgy with his cushion tummy and regal with his recovered fez at a funny angle). Then, at the last minute, Mrs Longlady asked, 'Are you King Hussein of Jordan?' and Little Jack shook his head and the audience laughed and Mrs Longlady said, 'Well, who are you, then? Could you tell us, please?' and Little Jack stammered, froze on the K and looked desperate, so I rushed forward in my crêpe dress and explained that he was actually King Farouk of Egypt, now deceased, and they laughed again.

With that information, the judges shooed Little Jack back into the line and beckoned forward Lady Godiva and she got the rosette for third place. They were most tickled (Mrs Longlady's words) by the use of the real-live pony and the flesh-coloured body-stocking. And that was doubly galling because we'd said we should *not* involve our ponies, due to a family rule about not seeming ostentatious.

It would have (might have) changed everything if Little Jack had won that yellow rosette. We might have felt differently about the village. I think we would. But he didn't and we didn't and we trudged home and I went upstairs and looked in the mirror and felt utterly bereft and humiliated. I didn't dramatize it. I didn't stamp on my fifty-pence piece or rip it to shreds. I was mature for my age: I made a cup of tea and said what bitches the judges were and Little Jack nodded.

Our mother was bitterly disappointed. I say bitterly because it goes so well with the word disappointed. In fact she was just a bit disappointed and annoyed and like me thought the judges were bitches, especially the way they snubbed me in my decimal outfit, it being such a timely idea.

My sister said we'd been fools to enter and that we'd both looked ridiculous and she'd been ashamed. I loved her then. I knew she'd always be honest with us and it was most reassuring, her scathing response being a silver lining of sorts.

Our mother's play about the parade was the least entertaining she'd ever written.

Judge: So, what have you come as?
Adele: I'm the village.
Judge: But you look like a distressed high-court judge.
Adele: It's my interpretation of the village.
Judge: Is the costume home-made and timely?
Adele: Yes, except for the periwig, which I bor-rowed.
Judge: Make sure to return it.

All that entering fancy dress parades had got us nowhere with our quest and nowhere else besides and we decided it was time to crack on. So we were discussing the Man List one day with some urgency — the relative merits of Bernard the chauffeur and Mr Oliphant the local farmer type (though not an actual farmer) — and racked our brains for more candidates — when our mother drifted into the kitchen in a caramel dress of an almost triangular shape that ended below the knee in a sharp point. She wore it with a metal belt and white sandals and looked like a slice of Portuguese pudding in two shades of sugary brown and a three-pronged fork on a thin white plate. We asked where she was going and she said she was going to see Dr Kaufmann again to get a prescription for a few pills to make her feel better, and strode off as quickly as the narrow skirt would allow.

A few pills to make her feel better: it sounded like such a brilliant idea that when she slammed the door behind her, I punched the air. It was a simple solution to all our problems (and so much easier than painting furniture or traipsing off to church once a week) and it meant we might not have to pull the next ideas out of our metaphorical sleeves.

My sister said we shouldn't get carried away because even if the pills came up trumps we'd still desperately need a man at the helm in order to regain a few shreds of respect — however happy or normal our mother became.

'We need a man, Lizzie, and until we find one, we're as good as lepers,' she said.

Little Jack pressed his face against the window. 'Where's Mum gone?' he asked, and started banging on the window after her. She always forgot to tell him things, and so did we, and he

51

was often left in the dark or banging on windows.

'She's just gone to get some pills from Dr Kaufmann,' I said, 'to make her feel better.'

And feeling a bit better ourselves we made a jug of Lemfizz — our special secret drink that used to be banned by Mrs Lunt for making a sticky mess and making us do sick burps, both of which she hated.

To show that I appreciated the limited expectation of the pills, I joined my sister in looking at the Man List and tried to think up new men for our soon-to-be-happier mother and, inspired by the Lemfizz, we suddenly remembered the idiotic little vicar whom our mother detested. Recalling the fine line between love and hate previously mentioned, we added him to the list of men and said he'd be next.

★   ★   ★

I must admit the idea of the pills made the Man List seem less important to me. I felt sure they were going to do us all a power of good and in spite of my sister's words I thought we might not even need the list. I had one more attempt at coaxing my sister round to my view, but she gave me a look of disappointment and spoke to me gravely.

'How many times do I have to tell you, Lizzie?' she asked. 'The pills are *not* a substitute.'

She looked hard at me for my response. 'Right,' I said, 'but they should make her feel better, shouldn't they?'

'Yes, they should. But feeling better can become a problem in itself, feeling better can become *the* problem.'

'But if they make her feel better . . . that's good, isn't it?' I said, feeling a bit exasperated by the whole thing, to be honest.

'They might make her feel *too* better,' explained my sister, 'so much better that she loses the will to even find a man. That's why she's going to need so much help from us.'

'*Too* better?'

'Yes, *too* better, *too* happy, *drugged*.'

'I see,' I said, though I couldn't imagine why that would be a problem.

It sounded like happiness to me.

★   ★   ★

OK. I tried to put the pills right out of my mind and to stop being so optimistic. And when our mother returned from the doctor, having come home via Mr Blight the pharmacist, I didn't even mention them, and when she put them on the sideboard I looked away and focused only on the Man List.

'Why do you hate the vicar so much?' I asked.

'I don't hate him,' she said. 'I'm sure he's a perfectly good man if he'd just be himself and speak openly and stop being such a prat.'

I know she was only being nice about him because she was happy to have the pills all ready to go. Who knows, maybe she'd already taken one or two.

I wrote to the vicar with my sister's blessing.

Dear Reverend Derek,

You may have noticed that I have not been attending church. The reason for this is that I'm questioning organized religion and can't stand all the idiots in church. I still pray but privately in my nightie at bedtime.

Added to which, I've heard that due to my divorced status I need the Bishop's permission to take communion and that has made me feel quite rejected. It's imperative that I evaluate God in my life. If you have time one day, please could you drop in to openly and naturally discuss the God and church aspect with me.

All good wishes,
Elizabeth Vogel

And delivered it by hand. The vicar knocked on the door the very next day and was invited in for a cup of coffee. He took it milky.

I saw this as a sign of his keenness on our mother, though my sister thought not. She explained that vicars always rush round to anyone showing even the slightest flicker of interest in God these days before they change their mind again. She, my sister, had begun to lose her faith around that time, having just reached the age of doubting everything. And according to her, half the world was teetering on the brink of disbelief because of the Beatles and the kind of pills our mother was taking.

Whatever the reason for his speedy response,

54

the vicar appeared and, to our amazement, they seemed to have sex that very day. And from the noises the reverend made he either really liked it or it was physical agony. This began an affair that lasted thirteen days. He never stayed longer than an hour and always insisted on talking about spirituality and so forth and she'd always drift off during that part. We didn't always see him because we might be at school, but I kept tabs on it via asking our mother plenty of questions.

'Did that vicar come round?'

'Yes.'

'How long was he here?'

'An hour-ish.'

'That's not long for discussing God.'

'He's got the rest of his flock to see to.'

'What did you talk about?'

'God mostly.'

'Was it nice, having him to visit?'

'Not particularly.'

Soon the vicar's wife called and she and our mother had a heated discussion which included the vicar's wife saying, 'Hang on just a minute, *you* invited *him*.'

To which our mother responded, 'No, I did *not*.'

Which was both true and yet not true, and my sister and I saw the flaw in our system. We cringed and looked at each other, expecting the vicar's wife to produce the letter I'd written to her husband, but she didn't, which was a huge relief and we both thanked God.

And the vicar didn't come round again. He'd been a waste of time and our mother hadn't taken to him. But, we had to admit, there'd been no play-writing at all during the fortnight of sex with the reverend. A short act appeared afterwards, though.

Rev. Hope: Why do you want to pray alone and not with the rest of the flock?
Adele: The rest of the flock are idiots.
Rev. Hope: I know what you mean.
Adele: I prefer to speak to God alone, in private.
Rev. Hope: Perhaps we could pray together.
Adele: Will God mind?
Rev. Hope: I'm sure he looks away when necessary.

5

Xmas was a busy time in Flatstone and entailed much more than the advent candle and clove-studded oranges of previous years. Our school became a hive of Xmas industry. There was the constant rehearsing of the school nativity play (*Mary Had a Baby*). And Xmas decorations to be designed, created and displayed around school. Xmas presents to be made for much-loved mothers and hard-working fathers. Turkey and pudding to be eaten at the Xmas lunch, letters to be written to Father Xmas — who apparently had an elf waiting to take them to the village hall ready for him to read at the Xmas Fayre. And then the special Xmas assembly where the headmistress would remind us that Xmas was *not* about presents, turkey or Father Xmas, but about Jesus.

The headmistress was neurotic when it came to Jesus, especially at Xmas when she worried that he might be ignored or eclipsed by other nicer features of Xmas. So much so that she got the vicar in. Reverend Derek appeared one morning at school assembly and spoke to us on the subject. We sang 'Away in a Manger' quite vigorously and then the vicar produced a sign with the word 'Xmas' written across it in huge capital letters.

'X,' he said, 'X-mas. How many of you write *Christ*-mas like this?' he asked, smiling, tapping the word.

A good few children put their hand up. I didn't put mine up, sensing a trick.

The vicar scanned the hall. His smile fell and his face turned stony. 'More than half of you,' he said.

He told us it was lazy and insulting. 'Do you not see how lazy and insulting it is, just to avoid writing five letters?'

He didn't know when it had started, but guessed it had come over from America, probably with rock 'n' roll. Whatever, Xmas was creeping in more and more and becoming almost normal. He himself had received two or three Xmas cards with 'Happy Xmas' scrawled inside and it saddened him to think that people *he knew* would insult Christ like that.

'Because, let's think about this, children, when you write X-mas, what's the word you're not writing . . . hmm?'

He gazed around the hall. Only about two children had their hands up this time and the vicar pointed to a boy called Daniel.

'You, what is it we're not writing when we write X-mas?'

'Christmas?' said the boy. And everyone giggled.

'Christ,' said the vicar, 'we're not writing *Christ.*'

There was something quite infuriating about that vicar standing up on stage tricking us into admitting we wrote Xmas and then saying what a lazy and insulting thing it was, when, for some of us, it was simply a way of not having to worry about how to spell it — my friend Melody, for instance, was usually a good speller but she often forgot the h, and even Little Jack, who was 'a precocious speller' according to his teacher, often missed out the t. The problem was, it was a seasonal word and therefore we hadn't had the all-year-round practice that you have with non-seasonal words such as Accommodation or Squirrel.

And there was that idiotic little vicar saying it was an insult to Jesus to write Xmas. I didn't think it an insult, I thought it common sense and wondered why the vicar didn't just talk about something ordinary like the miracle of his birth, instead of moaning about him being insulted in an abbreviation.

I have written Xmas ever since. And I try to never write the word fully out. I even say Exmas. Not to insult Jesus, but in memory of that idiotic little vicar.

Xmas Xmas Xmas.

* * *

And if I'm honest, Father Xmas had become more important to me than Jesus by then. It had nothing to do with the writing of Xmas and even if I'd written it as *Christmas* I'd still have been more interested in Father Xmas. The thing was, on Xmas Eve in 1968, when our parents were still married to each other and we lived in town, I'd heard him arrive in his sleigh on our rooftop.

A loud thump woke me as the sleigh landed and I heard the tinkle of sleigh bells as the reindeer tossed their impatient heads. And nothing since has quite matched the joy of hearing his boots clomping across the tiles to the chimney. I didn't expect to see him, or even *want* to see him, but hearing him was the most magical thing. Thinking about it now, I suppose if I'd heard Jesus — as opposed to Father Xmas — arrive on or near my house, I'd have been quite excited too, but it wasn't Jesus, it was Father Xmas and personal encounters are powerful things, as my sister knew from locking eyes with a policeman in a traffic jam and overly admiring the police for some while after.

The next morning (Xmas morning 1968) — sitting in our parents' four-poster — I spoke about hearing the sleigh.

'I heard Father Xmas land on the roof last night,' I said, mainly to our mother.

'You don't look very happy about it,' she said.

'I'm just worried it's the best thing that'll ever happen to me,' I said, 'and now it's happened.'

'It won't be the best thing, I promise,' she said.

'But what could be better?' I asked.

And our biological father came in and plonked a red and white box on the bed. And before we could begin unwrapping it, a puppy popped its head out (it was Debbie) and I suppose that should have been better and it was, in a way, but also it wasn't.

★ ★ ★

That year, our first Xmas in the village, there was a bit of controversy about who should be

Father Xmas at the Xmas Fayre. For the previous two years it had been Mr Longlady, the beekeeping accountant, him having stepped in for Mr Lomax, the Liberal candidate, who'd been incapacitated with an ailment that meant he couldn't sit on a church hall chair for sufficiently long to enact the role. But now, this year, Mr Lomax was ready to resume the position and had agreed a comeback with the vicar and negotiated a better chair.

My family didn't feel like attending the village Xmas Fayre and queuing for an orange from the Liberal candidate, partly because he'd seen an excerpt of our mother's play and partly because we had vivid memories of the glorious grotto at Fenwick's of Leicester from our time of being town-dwellers. Fenwick's being marvellous at Xmas. Mainly because of the amazing window displays and evocative Xmas music floating around. Also, the opportunity to try out eau de cologne and see the neatly folded woollen scarves on the way through to Santa. And then it actually being the real thing — as opposed to the Liberal candidate with a sore throat in a beard.

So, after a family conflab, we decided to go to Fenwick's instead, even though that would mean a thirty-mile round trip, a long wait in the queue and various spontaneous things our mother might suddenly do. What we hadn't bargained for was that our mother would drive into the street where we used to live and park just across from the arched gates of our old house. But she did. And we saw the Xmas tree in the obvious position in the glorious bay window, twinkling.

And Mrs Vanderbus's tree in a similarly pretty window twinkling back at it.

She switched off the ignition and, realizing we'd be there a while, I let myself look up to the roof where Father Xmas must have parked his sleigh, just above my room — my ex-room — some years before. And stupidly I tried to relive it. I'd made a rule when it first happened not to relive it too often so as not to wear out the feeling, but, looking up from the car window that evening, I found I had just about worn it out.

'Do you remember living here?' our mother asked us, staring ahead and exhaling smoke through her nostrils. I had my first experience of wanting to be sarcastic, but said instead, 'Yes, do you?' and she took that to be sarcastic anyway and gave me a look.

'Do let's call on Mrs Vanderbus,' my sister said.

'And the Millwards,' I added.

But our mother couldn't face it. She wasn't happy enough — they'd see that she was so much less now. Less of a person than she'd been when we'd lived here and we'd had pleasant folk all around us. Town folk who didn't mind everything so terribly and who had faults of their own.

And Mrs Vanderbus, being Dutch, would be honest and unafraid and say, 'Eleezabet, what have you done to yourself? You're so thin, so tired, oh my Got, you must get away from that evil willage.' And so forth. And the lovely Millwards would say, 'You look splendid, Elizabeth, the country air must be doing you a power of good.' And that would be worse.

'Do you remember I heard Father Xmas land on the roof?' I said, laughing.

'Oh yes,' said our mother, 'but it was just the aerial had fallen down and was blowing around.'

'Yeah,' said my sister.

'I know,' I said, but I hadn't known.

In Fenwick's later, our mother left us in the queue for Father Xmas and went to do some shopping, and when we got close to the end of the line I felt I couldn't go in and I let my sister and Jack go in without me. It wasn't the real Father Xmas — I knew there was no such person, I'd known for a while. Just as I'd known that the best, most exciting thing ever to happen hadn't actually happened — I'd just imagined it and clung on.

I sat on a toadstool at the door to the grotto and enjoyed the thought of the TV aerial blowing about on the roof. The new meaning to the old memory. And then, thinking I had about five minutes, I went to look at some gloves.

6

We loved to walk in the meres — a network of narrow lanes between the fields that farmers had trodden, ridden and driven into existence over the years. Wide enough for a tractor, just, they were perfect for ponies or walking children and edged with charming tunnel-forming trees and bushes from which things would dart and scamper. We liked playing in the streamy ditches that ran alongside and, because my sister loved farms and all farmy things, we'd peek into farmyards and little paddocks where baby things could often be seen.

It was the animals she loved, of course, and it slightly bothered her that the farmers didn't seem to like them that much. She noticed that farmers never stroked their little calves but would shove them aside as if they were nothing but a nuisance, and if a hungry piglet poked his little pink snout up, a farmer wouldn't smile or say, 'Hey, little fella,' he'd bash it on the nose with the bucket. My sister loved all animals and it was her ambition to see a family of hedgehogs in line — as you see on greetings cards. And she had a list of mammals she'd seen, like other people have lists of birds or trains. She'd spotted her first badger by the age of four and had been pleased to see it. She used to say that only people who loved animals should be allowed to be farmers and those who were indifferent might become a policeman or butcher instead and just have the one dog.

I stuck up for the unloving farmers, explaining that farming was a job and the farmer couldn't keep stroking the babies and being sentimental or he'd get nothing done and the corn would choke in the weeds etc. Farming was like being a parent: you might coo for a moment at someone's baby in a pram or a kitten in a brandy glass, but when it came to day-to-day life you just got on with it and if your kids came too close, you'd shove them out of the way and get on with whatever you were doing.

Anyway, one day in early spring my sister suggested a visit to Turner's Farm, a mixed sheep and cow farm. The main reason being that she'd heard that some early lambs had been born. But also she was wondering if we might add Farmer Turner to the Man List, him being a farmer and all the associated benefits. She was hoping of course that he'd turn out to be an animal-loving farmer. I was dubious on all counts, having seen him looking stern and overweight in a dirty vest. But we set off down the meres to investigate and on the way picked a bunch of catkins. Our mother liked to have these in a brown jug in the hall as a reminder to hang on because spring was on the way.

Near Turner's Farm we clambered over a dilapidated gate and noticed, across the field, a cow acting strangely. As we drew closer we saw that the cow, a young one, had its head stuck in a disused plough that had been left rusting near a gateway. Every few moments the cow would struggle and pull and her feet would scramble and churn underneath her but she'd stay stuck.

'If I could just turn her head slightly,' said my sister, 'it would come out.'

And that seemed true, for the cow wasn't as stuck as she thought. A slight turn and she'd be free.

We stayed quiet a while thinking and I saw the lush, herby grass the cow had been trying to reach under the plough, strands of it hanging from her muzzle. She struggled and churned again, stopped and let out a low moan.

'Help me,' said my sister. 'Let's try and get her out.'

My sister approached but the cow immediately became distressed and we decided to go to the farm instead and get Farmer Turner — who would reassure the cow before releasing her. We ran to the farmhouse three fields away, pelted into the yard and rapped on the door. A grim-looking potato-faced woman with one enormous hairy eyebrow stood with one side of her lip up and listened to our tale and sent us to a barn where the farmer stood winding wire around something. Sunlight was slipping sideways through the planked wall and he looked quite romantic with bare forearms on such a cold day. My sister told him about the young cow.

'If you could just turn her head to a thirty-degree angle,' said my sister, who knew her maths, 'she'd be right as rain.'

'It's number 81,' my sister called after him as he jumped into his Land Rover, 'the cow is number 81.' Because like me, in the still moments, she'd noticed the aluminium tag on the cow's ear.

Farmer Turner bumped and jolted out of the mucky yard and we ran behind, pleased with ourselves. In my happy little head I put Farmer Turner to the top of the Man List and smiled, thinking how thrilled he would be to swap the one-browed, potato-faced woman at the door for our sexy mother with her bone structure and see-through blouses. I jogged along with thoughts about a possible new life with this capable man at the helm — all the lambs for my sister and tractor rides for Jack and a happy family for me and Debbie. And number 81, tame and probably mine.

Breathless, we caught up, leant on the gate and waited to see some expert remedying followed by number 81 cantering away, indignant, mooing.

My sister turned to me. 'Man at the helm?' she said.

'He'd be perfect,' I said.

'I was thinking we could write to him . . . ' my sister began, 'and ask him for advice on manure . . . ' But before she could finish, we were rocked by the unbelievably loud crack of his rifle. I felt the noise through the metal gate, right up to my eyeballs.

The cow flopped immediately and hung by her head from the rusty metal trap. Only then did the farmer twist her head the necessary thirty degrees and let it drop. For a moment she looked like a dead stag in some old painting with oversized dentures and folded-over neck. The farmer kicked it straight and a clearish liquid poured from the cow's open mouth, ran down the hard mud and made a tiny steaming lake where our catkins lay.

We trudged home in silence. I tried to speak to my sister to say, 'How awful!' or something, but all she would say was, 'Look out for catkins, Lizzie.'

And then, having picked a new bunch close to home, I held them out for her to inspect. She took them and looked at them and then flung them down and walked quickly on. I didn't catch up because seeing someone try not to cry is one of the saddest things to see. I lagged behind and looked for catkins.

★ ★ ★

Our mother kept Dr Kaufmann's little pills with her purse in the fruit bowl. She took the stated dose and apparently felt better and calmer. My sister said we shouldn't make anything (too positive) of this calmness because people who take pills often act out the effects they are expecting to feel and in the case of these particular pills our mother was certainly expecting to feel calmer.

'So, it could all be an act?' I said.

'Sort of,' said my sister. And added, 'It's early days.'

Overall, she didn't seem that much better to me, just sleepy, like a darted bear that can no longer object or maul. She occasionally got the giggles if anyone said 'cheeks' or 'crumpet' but there'd always be a short delay and she'd soon forget what it was that set her off, by which time we'd be laughing at her laughing and she'd say, 'What are we laughing at?' and we'd all stop. It was nice to be laughing, though.

Our mother continued to write the play, but less so and only after she'd read to us from *The Hobbit*, which seemed to go on for years, and if she'd reached the necessary level of inebriation, which was usually around 8.30 p.m. The necessary level lasted only a short while, then she'd be too drunk and simply listen to music, though very quietly. Rachmaninov, who resembled her father-in-law as a young man with his nice mouth and dark eyes, or Bob Dylan, who looked like he might be from *The Hobbit*.

With our mother in this reduced and carefree state and without Mrs Lunt's daily toilings — mopping floors, heaving great baskets about the place and replenishing the Dairylea — our new home soon became horribly untidy and chaotic. We left the shutters at the front of the house half closed — we didn't want anyone seeing in too clearly.

Instead of ignoring the situation like any normal children, my sister and I got involved and gleaned from a tattered booklet how to use the washing machine — we felt it imperative as things were piling up and we were re-wearing dirty clothes out of the Ali Baba. But the booklet was from a Hoovermatic deluxe twin-tub and our machine wasn't a Hoovermatic deluxe or a twin-tub, so it was partly guesswork. We found a basic cycle that whirled everything around in warm water for a few hours and stuck to that one.

We had mishaps — a few catastrophic. Twice the door was left open, once when a corner of a towel was trapped and once when it was just not closed, and the boot room flooded. Those times of flood were the worst times because so many things got wet and spoiled, including a runner in the hall that had been woven by twenty-one girls for twenty-one days and had cost twenty-one rials — each girl earning one precious coin. We flung it over the line for a few days. It dried out OK but it went and stayed stiff and smelled like a wet dog for ever after. We felt guilty about the twenty-one girls, their hard work ruined.

Worse by far, though, was the second flood and the resulting ruination of the balsa-wood boxes that our mother's father had brought for her from India. Especially as he had died just a short while before the second flood and she hadn't even said goodbye. Mind you, she'd never really said hello either as he'd been at war when she was born. And when my sister asked if he had died peacefully our mother replied, 'Yes, he ceased upon the midnight with no pain.' Which meant he had been put to sleep by a doctor as if he were a poorly pet because it was the kindest thing, and came from Keats.

Anyway, the warm soapy water from the second flood washed away the beautiful hand-painted elephants, ladies, birds and so forth from the Indian boxes. And caused the sides to buckle and swell and when we tried to rescue them the staples popped off and they collapsed into a smudgy heap.

And we did an awful thing. We put the spoiled boxes into rubble bags and put them out for the bin-men and never said a word to our mother about what had happened. We thought she'd never notice. We knew it unlikely that she'd ever again go into the boot room now she was taking Dr Kaufmann's helpful pills. And I don't think she ever did. And later it occurred to me just how very bad it was. Not us causing the flood or hiding the broken boxes, but that she'd never again think about them or remember them or wonder about them. Even though she'd loved them so very much.

The full impact of Mrs Lunt giving us up dawned on us gradually in that boot room, as did the full horror of doing laundry. Mishaps continued and it became very stressful. Many items of clothing came out ruined — hard and small or the wrong colour or matted, or twisted like lengths of ancient rope, discarded rags washed up on beaches.

Then there was the drying of it. The hanging it on the line for all to see or on the two wires strung across the boot room. The smell of it when we didn't get to it in time or the weather was humid.

And then there was the ironing. It was dreadful how crumpled everything looked and how depressing the crumpledness was — it being such a sign. A thousand little creases, not a few deep and straight ironed-in lines, but the chaos of the crumple, like wayward microscopic worms shouting, 'No one cares any more, make us wards of court.'

I decided one particularly crumpled day to 'do' the ironing: (a) I had to get rid of the creases for our ventures into public (school) and (b) I remembered the aroma of hot linen from Mrs Lunt's daily ironing drifting around the house as a happy thing, and therefore I thought that in doing the ironing I'd be killing at least two birds.

'Where's the iron?' I asked our mother.

'The iron what?' she yawned.

'The actual iron, for ironing things with?' I asked.

'It's gone awol,' she said.

She often said things had gone awol and I was never sure what awol meant. I thought it meant 'nipped out of a left-open gate' because the thing that most often went awol was our Labrador. And her going awol meant she'd nipped out of a left-open gate.

I found the iron eventually in a big cupboard that wasn't anyone's business except the daily help's. But since we had no help it became my business and my sister's. It contained the iron and the ironing board and some soda crystals and buckets, brushes and a small mangle, folded tablecloths and other things of that sort.

Getting the ironing board up was a job in itself and I knew why Mrs Lunt, at the old house, had ironed a few items every day, including pants and tea towels, to legitimize the leaving up of the board. Doing it was awful too. Not as bad as the other aspects of the laundry but bad all the same. First of all, if the iron was hot enough to make any inroad on the creases it soon began sticking to the clothes. I melted a hole in a favourite nightie and made an iron-shaped brown mark on a T-shirt. I ironed a bit of my own exposed stomach and twice the iron fell to the floor and once a bit of it broke off as a result.

My sister came to look at me and said I was doing more harm than good. I mentioned the smell of hot linen and the sense of well-being and she said it smelled to her as if a blacksmith had gone berserk burning horse hooves and wasn't at all pleasant.

My sister and I saw first-hand how utterly terrible housework was (laundry being particularly horrific) and that it was never-ending and tyrannical. We went to our mother and asked how she thought we might cope now she was semi-conscious much of the time. She explained that she herself was temperamentally unsuited to housework and laundry and always had been — even before the pills had kicked in. And hearing there was such a thing as temperamental unsuitability to it, we realized we were probably afflicted in the same way and felt a bit better about everything. Of course it's a shaming thing to look back on, but there it was.

And all of a sudden we realized that Mrs Lunt was obviously suited to housework and saw her in a new light — as capable, strong, unusual — and felt wretched and stupid for letting her go without more of a fight. Our mother sympathized with us but said there was no easy solution. Helps like Mrs Lunt were thin on the ground in villages and, like the Brownies and Scouts, had waiting lists as long as your arm and you had to swoop whenever one came free and try to engage them before anyone else got there. There was a story of an elderly lady on her deathbed having to endure people knocking on the door, swooping for the daily help.

We knew of only one available woman in the parish. This woman had a card in the newsagent's. This woman, Audrina, was good at cleaning apparently but was also a spirit medium — a fact advertised on the same card. We mentioned Audrina to our mother but she didn't want a spirit medium hanging about at our house doing laundry. We didn't know what a medium actually was — my sister thought a prostitute but I thought something to do with ghosts. I strongly suspected I was right — our mother wouldn't have minded a prostitute hanging about doing laundry.

Anyway, our mother said we should just try to pull together as a team and, if the worst came to the absolute worst, we'd have to go to the Three Sisters in Malby and buy some new T-shirts and pants. We should have told her then about the water-damaged rug and Indian boxes — to indicate the worst had already come. But we didn't, thinking what's the point of going on tranquillizers to cheer yourself up if your daughters keep delivering really sad news? So we let sleeping dogs lie.

With all this in mind my sister wrote to Mrs Lunt.

Dear Mrs Lunt,

You are so right — petrol has shot up in price. Some say it will soon be ten bob a gallon in old money. But we are finding it difficult to keep up with all the laundry and housework here. It would be an enormous help if you would reconsider your decision to leave and actually start coming again. You don't have to come every day, just two or three longer days would probably be enough and use less petrol than coming every day.

The thing is, Mrs Lunt, I am temperamentally unsuited for housework (and it turns out so are the girls) whereas you are 100 per cent suited. Plus it's imperative to have it done, especially the laundry which has piled up like Mount Sorrel.

Please telephone Lizzie or myself if it's 'yes', otherwise just forget I ever wrote.

I hope you are well.

Yours truly,
Elizabeth Vogel (Mrs)

Mrs Lunt didn't telephone and the house got more and more messy. Also, no nanny would come to live with us in the village either, even though they'd have had their own bathroom, a little telly, the use of a Mercedes and a minimum of two ponies to choose from. The nanny agency sent two candidates in taxis to view us but both hated the idea of having to drive the Mercedes such a long and windy way into town for a film or a new bra, and they didn't even ask our mother what the salary was (and that said it all).

After all those years cooped up with amber-eyed Moira and her predecessors, it was nice to be free to go where we wanted on our own and not have to do what the nanny wanted us to do, such as play endless games of Who Am I? and drink Nesquik. Though it did occur to us that a nanny might have usefully contributed to the laundry effort.

We wandered freely around the village and peeped into car windows to see if any dogs had been left inside. We chucked hard apples into the pond, sat in the pear trees and visited fierce-looking bulls, and we looked for Debbie, our dog, who kept running away. Not *away* away, but just enjoying the freedom of no one shutting the gate.

7

My sister and I started going to London on our own on the train, with a bit of cash and a *Whizzer and Chips* for me, and whatever book my sister was reading at the time. Ruby Ferguson or Gerald Durrell.

Our trips to London began because although our mother was happy with the pills overall, she soon realized she couldn't get quite enough to keep up with her feelings of loneliness and misery. And she'd started taking slightly more than the stated dose. Plus she needed a different kind in addition, to help give her that bit more vim. Dr Kaufmann would not prescribe any more pills, however eloquent and reasonable our mother's requests for more. It would have been wrong.

So much for my sister's worry that they might make her feel 'too better' — they soon weren't making her feel better enough. 'It's like having over-diluted Ribena,' our mother explained. 'It's almost worse than having no Ribena at all.'

And we knew exactly what she was talking about.

In order to get more pills, our mother had to go to London to get topped up by a doctor who turned a blind eye. This was OK for a while, but soon she got sick of going all that way and once had a breakdown (in her car) halfway home and had to call our father's chauffeur, Bernard, and

77

he'd given her snooty looks in the rear-view mirror all the way home, and later our father had rung and accused her of upsetting Bernard and giving him snooty looks and said she needn't think she could cadge a lift again.

Anyway, that incident put the tin lid on the London trips and she got herself into a panic about getting enough pills — thinking she might have to hang around outside a library in the dark or something horrible and do a deal.

My sister wondered if our mother might take on Audrina, the available help who was also a medium, to go and hang around outside a library once she'd done the laundry but our mother was against this idea. It being her belief that you should only break the law yourself and not get others to do it for you.

So my sister and I told her we were more than happy to go to London for her. I amended it quickly to 'happy to go' (thinking that being 'more than happy' might be the same as being 'more than welcome' — i.e., not). She was very grateful for the offer but said we were far too young to be going to get pills in London on our own.

★ ★ ★

The train was inky blue with a yellow nose. I'd been expecting it to roar into the station and screech to a halt like a car might, but it didn't. It rolled in ever so slowly with a face like a sad puppy and little wipers on the two side windows blinking. It had come from Sheffield and wasn't going to remain for long in the station, so we had to jump aboard quickly and get settled in our seats. I loved it. The tickets, the station, the smell, the noises, the mysterious other people, the lurching rhythms of the forward motion and the tiny little toilet. We bought ourselves tea and toast from the buffet car and actually would both have liked our tea a bit less milky, but you can't have everything, and the toast was utterly perfect: darkly grilled, buttered to the edges and sweating in its napkin.

London was approximately two hours away and Dr Gilbey's rooms were on Devonshire Place — a short taxi ride from St Pancras station. On our first trip, my sister decided to take a detour via London Zoo. She'd planned it all along but she dropped it on me as a surprise as we waited in the taxi rank.

'Shall we go to London Zoo?' she said.

'I don't think so, we don't have time,' I replied.

'We do,' she said. 'We don't need to be at Devonshire Place for two and a half hours.'

'I'm not sure,' I said.

'Well, I'm going to the zoo,' she said. 'I'll meet you at Devonshire Place later.' And of course that was that. I mean, you don't just walk round London on your own when you're ten and you don't even know the place.

I honestly don't remember much about the zoo that first time, except Chi Chi the giant panda. There was a long notice on an information board about Chi Chi. We read that Chi Chi displayed all the symptoms of chronic

79

loneliness, and yet had confounded bear-breeding experts when she refused to mate with the only available male, An An, who'd been brought over all the way from Moscow Zoo in a crate especially for that purpose.

And my sister had said, 'Hey, just like Mum and Mr Lomax.' And we'd laughed.

Mainly I remember that my sister loved being at the zoo and was utterly captivated by certain young animals and seemed to want to gaze at them for ever.

And when it was time to leave the zoo and go to Devonshire Place, she complained that we'd not seen half of it and begged for another ten minutes which turned into twenty and then, when we did finally leave, lots of other people wanted to leave too and there was a very long line at the taxi rank. I suggested that I pretend to be very ill and ask to jump the queue to get to a hospital. But my sister is less deceitful than me. We did ask to go to the front, our reason being that we needed to get to Devonshire Place to get our mother's pills. No one felt it a good enough reason to let us jump in and everyone ignored us, looking away and pretending to chat, but looking at us again when we turned away. We stood at the end feeling foolish. It was just like being back in the village.

We decided it would be quicker (and less embarrassing) to walk, so we did and we ended up lost and then very late. When we finally arrived at Devonshire Place the enormous shiny door was shut and didn't have a real knocker, only an ornamental knob bang in the middle. My sister rang the bell and rang and rang. I looked around.

The street — or should I say the 'place', since it was a place, not a street — was a row of very tall terraced houses each with its own identical set of black-painted railings, the same set of windows (smaller and less impressive the higher you went up, so that the top windows were just rectangles of grubby glass), the same large black front door and door furniture. The houses were identical except for one, halfway along the terrace, whose paint was beginning to peel and whose window box contained browning geraniums, petals from which were dropping into the cracked paint and bleeding their browny-red juice into the cream, making it all unkempt and messy.

Dr Gilbey's, like the rest, was pristine. Its window boxes were festooned with tiny lime-green spheres and frondy leaves in different shades trailing — but tidily — onto the hard deep ledge. I felt sorry for the odd one with its geraniums, its neglect highlit by the uniform smartness of the rest. But thanked God it wasn't Dr Gilbey's. That would have been awful.

My sister pressed the bell again and then held her finger there until a woman put her golden head out of an upstairs window.

'We've come to see Dr Gilbey. We're late, we got lost, but we're here now,' my sister shouted.

'The consulting rooms are closed, I'm afraid,' the woman called.

'But we've come from Leicester on the train,

all the way, just to get our mother's pills,' my sister shouted up.

'Dr Gilbey can't see anyone now, you'll have to make another appointment,' the woman shouted back.

'Please, can you ask him to just chuck the pills down to us? We can't go home without them, she's had a terrible time, she's split up with our father and everyone in the village hates us and the doctor in the village won't give her any more pills, please, please.'

I decided (judging by the look on the woman's face) we were getting somewhere with the pleading, so I joined in.

'Please, *pleeease*, this is the only doctor in England who will give her any pills,' I called up, and for some reason I burst into tears and stayed looking up. Even my sister was shocked and looked round at me as if I'd made a terrible mistake.

But the door buzzed and as we walked through the inner door the woman was trotting down the pretty stairs, her golden hair immobile. She ushered us into a white waiting room and established our identity.

'Wait here, girls,' she said, and paused in the doorway to ask, 'Can I get you a glass of orange squash?'

'No, thanks,' said my sister, at exactly the same time as my 'Yes, please.'

She came back with one tall glass of squash on a tray and a bulging paper bag. My sister handed over our money envelope and took the bulging bag.

'We went to the zoo by accident,' I blurted.

'By accident?' said the woman, smiling.

'Well, we went there deliberately but stayed too long by accident,' explained my sister.

'Don't you have a zoo in Leicester?' she asked.

'Well, there's Twycross Zoo, which is very good, but it's right over the other side of the county,' I said, 'and we wouldn't get over there.'

'Added to which, London Zoo is world-renowned,' said my sister, who always had such wonderful things to say.

'Yes, it is,' said the woman.

'But Twycross Zoo has the PG Tips chimps,' I said.

'Ah, that's where they're from,' said the woman.

'Yes. They're real chimps,' I said, proudly.

And then we were back out on the street with our package and we hailed a taxi to St Pancras station and got on the five o'clock Sheffield-bound train with a hundred other people who mostly got off along the way. I'd left my *Whizzer and Chips* down the side of my seat on the outward journey, thinking, stupidly, we'd be returning in the same seats. To be fair, though, on boarding for the return journey I realized my mistake straight away and didn't show myself up by looking for it.

'Don't tell about the zoo,' my sister reminded me at Kettering.

I'd bought a tiny giant panda for Little Jack from the gift shop with 'From London Zoo' printed at the base in gold.

'Can't we just tell Little Jack?' I asked.

'God, no, he's the last person to tell. He'll

make a mountain out of it one way or another and his teacher will be round worrying Mum — just keep your mouth shut.'

I was one of those people (still am) for whom doing a thing was all about the telling. What was the point of going to a world-renowned zoo if you couldn't tell people you'd been to it? If you couldn't mention that Chi Chi the giant panda hadn't been allowed into the United States due to her being a Communist panda. That she'd ended up in London and had refused to mate with the available male even though she was lonely and had a centrally heated enclosure. Because all she wanted was to be back at home in China eating bamboo and mating with another Communist panda.

What was the point?

My sister and I were (are) very different in that respect. For her, it was the being there and the seeing the rare, exotic and dangerous animals, and once we came away it was over with and packed away with her other thrilling memories. Whereas I don't want to be thrilled unless I'm allowed to tell the story of it.

★   ★   ★

When my sister and I phoned from the coin-box at the railway station to say we were back in Leicester, our mother was very pleased to hear from us. We'd been longer than she had expected and she had got it into her head that we'd run away like her second cousin, Margot Fenton-Hall, who'd gone to London aged fourteen in

1950-something to be measured for ballet shoes at Frederick Freed's and had never come back — only sent a note to her parents saying, 'I'm not coming home, don't look for me.' She hadn't even been to Frederick Freed's for the shoes and wasn't seen again by her parents until she appeared on telly years later playing a motel secretary in a soap opera. Our mother's aunt and uncle wrote to Margot (now with a new name), care of the programme, begging her to get in touch but she never did and they had to endure seeing their daughter on the telly every week on a dreadful programme that they hated — and not even on the BBC — which was vexing. But they couldn't bear not to watch. Our mother doubted the actress playing the secretary actually was the second cousin. Which was much sadder than it actually being her, I thought.

Our mother was glad to have us back from London anyway, and relieved that we weren't going to end up on ATV, which she thought would be a wrong career choice for both of us. She always imagined my sister would become a vet — if she could just overcome her fear of science experiments — and that I would be a teacher or a writer. She had no idea what Little Jack might become but felt sure it would be something 'extremely important'. That's what she said but Jack probably didn't believe she really thought that. I didn't.

8

While we'd been in London — staying too long at the zoo and crying in Devonshire Place and getting pills — Little Jack had been scheduled to visit our father, on his own — a thing none of us liked. And it hadn't gone to plan.

Little Jack liked our father but going to his new house with his new wife and baby was always somehow awkward. It was the kind of awkwardness that overwhelmed things or gave you a headache. Mainly, it was the baby. Firstly, the baby was very popular with its parents. He had blond hair with brown eyes, which must have been an unusual combination because they never stopped saying how lovely it was in a baby.

'Look at that blond hair with those brown eyes,' they'd say.

And that was irritating but, more importantly, Jack claimed that the baby didn't like him. Jack's problem with the baby had started during a visit Jack and I had had together a couple of months before. It had been Sunday lunch and Jack had said he wasn't hungry. He'd pushed his food around the plate and just scooped the odd mouthful and chewed it for ages and our father had said Jack must use his cutlery properly.

This annoyed me. I thought that if you decide to leave your children, fine, but you don't then have the right to stop them scooping in the

European way just because you don't choose to scoop.

I was so annoyed I spoke up on the subject.

'Dad,' I said, 'it's the modern way. If we ate like you, pronging one pea at a time, we'd look like idiots at school. Everyone scoops nowadays.'

Our father did a small head bow. 'Thank you for your contribution,' he said, and told an anecdote about a brilliant genius overlooked for promotion due to being known for his poor table manners. And turned his attention to Little Jack.

'Jack, you must eat your peas and carrots.'

And no sooner had our father uttered those words than the baby started saying 'more' — meaning he'd eaten all *his* peas and carrots and wanted some more. We'd never heard him speak a proper word before, so we couldn't just ignore it, and the rift between Jack and the baby began.

And our father's wife, with a look of pride, spooned a few more peas and carrots into his little bowl of semi-mushed-up lunch. And the baby gobbled them up, staring at Jack, and asked again for more.

I had my own crisis at that Sunday lunch table. I say crisis, though it was more of a philosophical meandering. I asked myself how it was that our lovely tall father had suddenly become the husband of a new woman and the father of a whole separate new baby who could already say 'more' and outdo Little Jack on the veg front. I gazed at the blond-haired baby. What would it make of us, I wondered, as it matured, its half-siblings arriving every month or two and

87

eating a roast dinner (badly) and being tutored in table manners and being irritable about it? The baby was sure to grow into a table-manners expert and to be well rounded with our proper and fussy ex-father as its man at the helm. As these notions floated around my mind I felt a surging wave of sadness for this little half-brother of mine. Imagine, I thought, having someone's ex-father as your own and having to see the unruly cast-offs for Sunday lunch every three months — it would be horrible, surely, and really annoying. I felt sorry for him and hoped to God that our new man at the helm (when we'd secured one) didn't come with anything of that sort. My heart sank at the thought of some discarded old daughters and a son turning up for lunch and forgetting the manners he'd taught them in his previous life. Scattering crumbs and chomping at our kitchen table while we were trying to enjoy a new happy life with home-made pineapple fritters and whatever our man at the helm liked to eat.

Anyway, back to that Sunday lunch: it really did seem that the baby was rubbing it in for Jack. I don't know what age babies usually start doing that kind of thing, but this baby seemed to be saying 'I love vegetables,' which was hard on Little Jack because he had previously been our father's only son and now he was relegated to being 'one of his sons', and added to which he only liked pie and now this new baby could eat a better lunch than Jack even though he hadn't even walked yet.

So that's how it always was — awkward, not

enjoyable, and a baby-Jack rift. And as a result, on that day (the day my sister and I had been in London), on the journey to our father's house, on his own in the chauffeur-driven car, taking advantage of a stop at Bagshaw Bridge service station, Little Jack absconded and Bernard had had to leave the Daimler on the forecourt and run after him. Bernard had searched high and low, on foot at first, then cruising slowly round the streets in the Daimler, and eventually he'd gone back to our house and had to tell our mother that Jack had absconded. Our mother thanked him for his trouble and said that Jack was home safely and watching telly.

That night, waiting in the Chinese takeaway, our mother recapped the events of the day. First, Debbie had nipped out of the open gate and stolen a christening cake from Merryfield's bakery, and then Jack had run off, and as if that wasn't enough, my sister and I had been in London far longer than expected and Debbie had passed raisins on the slabs all day long.

'What a day!' she said.

'What a day!' she said again, puffing away in the waiting area. And it turned out she could say 'What a day' in Greek, Latin and German, but that it didn't always mean the same exact thing — i.e., 'What a day' in English meaning 'What a strange day' but in the other languages you had to add the word 'strange' for it to make sense. The lady at the counter told her how to say it in Mandarin.

To be honest, it all got a bit much, her saying 'What a day' in all these languages and dwelling on it like that, but I can't deny it had been the strangest day.

★   ★   ★

It wasn't long after that strange day that Mrs Iris Longlady called round to firm up on the vague tea invitation she'd issued when we'd first moved to the village. Because people never called round we weren't used to being called on and we weren't sure what to do, so we just stared at her. She didn't mention the tea invitation for some while, and started her visit with a complaint about one of our ponies having stepped on her daughter Melody's foot on a public highway. Our mother sympathized but quickly related a story about Little Jack being stung by one of their bees and swelling up like a balloon.

Things must have equalled out then because Mrs Longlady launched into a full-blown chat. Our mother's lack of interest must soon have become obvious, though, because Mrs Longlady switched her attention to me and held my eye while she rambled, mostly about her twin daughters. We knew the twins already from school. One nice-ish, one less so. Melody (nice) and Miranda (less so). In fact, Melody and I had developed a secret little friendship. Secret for her because her mother disapproved of our mother and our not having a man at the helm. Secret for me because my sister and I officially disliked the Longlady girls. My sister didn't know Melody and just lumped her in with her less nice twin, Miranda, whom she did know.

Melody and I often met up on the way to school and at going-home time we could quite reasonably walk home together, coming from the same classroom and being almost neighbours. Also a secret and known only to the Longlady family and me was that Melody was a latchkey kid on Tuesdays because her parents were occupied out of the village and Miranda had sporting commitments. I would often sneak into Melody's house for half an hour, or she might sneak home with me and look at the ponies, which was how come our Shetland pony had stepped on Melody's foot. The thing is, anyone horsey knows how to react to being stepped on, with a push at the shoulder before the pony bears weight, but a non-horsey person doesn't and therefore sustains an injury. Melody, being non-horsey and only knowing about bees, got a bruise on her foot. That's when we invented the story about meeting unexpectedly in the lane to explain it.

Mrs Longlady asked me if I could tell the twins apart. I knew she wanted me to say that I couldn't, but I could, easily, so I didn't say anything. She then asked our mother if she could tell them apart and our mother very sweetly said no, she couldn't, which was kind because she'd never even seen them. My sister spoiled it by saying she could tell them apart and explained that one was fatter in the face and had bigger teeth.

Mrs Longlady claimed forcefully that the twins were identical and definitely from the one egg. Her emphasis on this and the distinction of the single egg made such an impression on me that when, around that time, we had the *Facts of Life* film at school and saw a diagram in pastels of an egg and were given full details of the miracle of conception and the strange phenomenon of twins, I saw that innocent illustrated egg as Mrs Longlady's egg (containing the embryonic Melody and Miranda) and I saw the illustrated sperm, penetrating and fertilizing the egg, as the sperm of Mr Longlady the accountant. As if they were the prototypal and original sperm, egg and embryo — which was quite disturbing and sick-making and made it all much worse than it might have been if I'd been able to think in the pastel abstract. Or about cattle, as my sister had.

I told our mother that I couldn't get the Longladys' egg and sperm out of my head. Our mother wished I hadn't told her that. She put her hand up to her mouth and told me to go and read *The Beautifull Cassandra* by Jane Austen. Apparently the thing about Jane Austen is, it shoves unwanted thoughts aside and replaces them with contemplative ideas and musings that are of use and beauty. It turned out I was too young for Jane Austen, though, because *The Beautifull Cassandra* didn't manage to shove the Longladys aside, except that the unusual double-1 occupied me for a moment — thinking it looked wrong.

Anyway, when Mrs Longlady had said all she'd come to say and finally seemed to be leaving, she said, 'I just popped round to say come to tea tomorrow at three. I'm baking today, so make sure you're hungry.'

★ ★ ★

We arrived at Orchard Corner the next day at three. Mrs Longlady looked down the street. She asked when our mother would be appearing and we said she wouldn't be appearing and Little Jack said, 'She's gone to bed.'

And Mrs Longlady said, 'Well, *really*!' and left Mr Longlady to run the show.

The twins appeared with their hair in matching plaits. My secret friend, Melody, didn't give away our friendship and was almost as mean as her less nice sister, Miranda, but probably only to hide that she liked me.

Miranda had been moved up a school year due to being cleverer than children of her own age (this really boiled down to the fact that she'd memorized the eight-times table and was tall for her age). Hence she was in my sister's class. But, alas, after being moved up it turned out that she wasn't quite clever enough for the next year up, after all. Like when a certain size of shoe is a bit too tight but the next size up is a bit too big — she was between the two years (cleverness-wise) and she knew it. So, after being moved up, Miranda felt she had to cheat or copy to stay afloat. She needn't have worried, though — you can't move a kid up a year and then humiliate them by moving them back down again. They might get teased and go into a downward spiral and end up less-clever when they'd started out cleverer-than-average.

93

At the tea the twins seemed to dislike Little Jack, Miranda especially, and stared at him when he tried to speak, which he soon stopped doing. And though they were a bit hostile towards him, I'm ashamed to say that at that point my sister and I were slightly captivated by Miranda, the less nice twin. Mainly because she strode about with tall confidence and slanged inventively. Melody, as mentioned before, also seemed less nice in that context and seemed to go along with her sister on everything, including not liking Jack. But fair enough.

When Little Jack picked up a little toy penguin, for instance, Miranda shrieked at him, 'Hands off my penguin, you little tealeaf.' And when Jack almost jumped out of his skin Melody laughed and Miranda said, 'He's a jumpy little dingbat, isn't he? What's up with him?'

And Melody laughed again.

Miranda said her name meant 'must be admired' and somehow that rang true, because however horrible the conduct, on one level it was somehow impressive. That's how bullying works, I suppose. We should have stuck up for Jack more but (a) it was funny seeing him being called a gritty little pug and (b) we didn't want her to start calling us inventive names. She had already called me 'Miss Muffet' just because I sat down. And laughed at my frog puppet which I'd brought especially, thinking they might like it.

When Mr Longlady called us in for tea Miranda said, 'Damn it.' And Mr Longlady had rather crossly asked her not to swear. We thought it odd. We had no idea that damn was a swear

94

word and also we wondered why he'd not objected when she had shouted out, 'Cunty balls, cunty balls,' as she swung on the swing in the garden.

Perhaps he hadn't heard.

Miranda was confusing — warm one moment, crushing the next. She praised the loveliness of our house and got us talking about its loveliness, but then spoiled it by saying that people in the village hated us for living in it. Little Jack, having been protected from this kind of talk due to his age, took it to heart and asked why people in the village hated us, and Miranda said, 'Ah, poor little mongoose, they don't hate you, they hate your mother.'

And Little Jack said, 'No, they don't.' And looked really sad.

And Miranda said, 'Of course they do,' in a really caring way, and patted his arm like a nice teacher and poor Jack didn't know whether to feel better or not.

Later, at the tea table, Miranda told us that she had a special secret name for us. She asked us to guess what it was. We said we couldn't guess.

'Do you give up?' said Miranda.

'Is it the mongooses?' asked Little Jack.

'No, that would be silly,' said Miranda.

None of us spoke. 'Do you give up?' she asked.

'Yes,' we said.

'OK,' she said, 'I'll tell you. It's the cunty balls.' Which annoyed me because I'd had a feeling it was going to be that — only I didn't say in case she laughed at me, which she would have if I'd said it. You just couldn't win.

At tea we had tinned peaches and custard with hundreds-and-thousands sprinkled on top. Mr Longlady kept referring to it as trifle — which it wasn't — and Miranda advised us not to have too much or we might puke up. There was no sign of the baked goods advertised the day before by Mrs Longlady.

I looked at the two Longlady girls across the tea table. They really didn't look identical; they only looked, to me, slightly similar — as if they were ordinary sisters or cousins. Miranda had thin lips — barely any lip at all on the outside — and you could always see how well she'd cleaned her teeth, or not. Whereas Melody had plump, juicy lips and you could hardly see her teeth at all. Plus Miranda was taller than Melody and her ears poked through her hair at the sides.

I always felt sorry for Melody constantly being called 'identical' to Miranda with her thin lips. It's a wonder she didn't beg her parents to stop saying they were identical. I could see that Miranda, on the other hand, was keen to be presented as identical to Melody, who was quite reasonable-looking, comparatively. Miranda would often say, 'No one can tell us apart.' And you'd see Melody looking fed up.

Before we'd properly finished, Mr Longlady had had enough of Miranda's trying behaviour and cleared the table. We sat around the table for a few minutes with Miranda pontificating, when some music drifted in. It was a soft, slow violin with an insistent piano underneath. We all of a sudden went quiet and began to listen. And then, to our astonishment, Miranda began to cry, not sniffling and tears but the paced, empty sobs of a fake. My sister and Little Jack knew it and stared at her coldly. Melody, however, was terribly affected by her sister's performance and began to cry for real, producing tiny chokes.

'Whatever's the matter?' Melody cried through her little chokes.

Miranda wouldn't say for some moments.

'Is it the music?' Melody asked.

It wasn't the music, though. Apparently it was Bufo, my frog puppet, which she'd laughed at not twenty minutes before. Now she was cradling it and gazing into its eyes.

'It's practically identical to the one my grandfather gave me for my birthday when I was six,' she was finally able to say. 'Just before he died . . . and it . . . it got lost,' she sobbed out.

I wanted to snatch Bufo away from her, but it would have seemed callous.

Bufo actually belonged to our mother. Her father had brought him back from a faraway place at the end of the war when our mother was only tiny (possibly along with the Indian boxes we ruined during our laundry misadventures). He'd brought curious things like bullets and animal teeth for her older brothers and illustrated playing cards and marbles with strange colours running through. But for our mother he'd brought a work of art. A polished wooden frog puppet with beautifully intricate jointed legs and bulging eyes that moved. Our mother had wanted to call him Frog but her father had already named him Bufo, and though he wouldn't have minded the change she kept it as Bufo.

'May I keep him for a day or two, Miss Muffet?' Miranda said, looking at Bufo and touching his eyeballs. '*Pleeease*.'

'He belongs to our mother, really,' I said, looking at my sister, imploring her to put a stop to it.

'I shall cherish him and guard him and I shan't let anything bad happen to him, I promise, Miss Muffet, I swear on my own mother's deathbed.'

I absolutely did not want to let her have him, but my courage deserted me and I found myself thinking perhaps it wouldn't hurt and that she would surely be nicer to me if I said yes. But I knew it was wrong and that I should say no. Bufo was all our mother had left from her father, since my sister and I had destroyed the Indian boxes.

My sister got up and spoke to Miranda. 'You can borrow Bufo for a very short while, that's all,' she said. 'Not for long.'

Miranda looked at me and smiled triumphantly.

'Thank you, Miss Muffet,' she said with a shrewish smile, and waved one of Bufo's little front legs. 'Goodbye, Miss Muffet,' she ventriloquized on behalf of Bufo.

Mr Longlady reappeared then and said it was time for us to go home, so we did.

9

So we got on with life and other things and had regular, though not frequent, pill trips to Devonshire Place in London. The woman Julia, who'd looked out of Dr Gilbey's upstairs window when we'd first gone and given me the orange squash, seemed pleased to see us each time and offered us more squash and mysterious little biscuits of a type we'd never seen before — dark, crisp and sugary but not much to them, so that you couldn't help taking another and another and another until there was nothing but a dusting of the fine rusty-coloured sugar on the pretty plate and sometimes, as we left, I would run my finger through that. So nice were they that I could almost taste them as we alighted from the train each time at St Pancras.

My sister and I enjoyed our London trips and looking back I think they were quite educational. We took detours to important places such as Madame Tussaud's before going on to collect the pills from Devonshire Place. Collecting the pills became a minor little thing at the end of a day out. We became good at hailing a taxi as we walked along pavements and took turns walking backwards at busy times. And we learned not to panic if it seemed we were running late, because you didn't have to wait at a taxi rank, you could hail one almost anywhere (unlike a bus or a train). We (eventually) realized we were expected to give the taxi driver approximately 10 per cent more than the fare, money-wise.

My sister asked a nice-seeming driver what we might be doing to make previous cabbies swear at us when they set us down. The nice-seeming driver was appalled that we didn't know about tipping and explained the whole system. We tipped him and he said, 'Take care, gels' in the London style, which was a bit different from the driver before who'd called us a pair of fucking bitches. The rule was: 10 per cent unless you have loads of luggage, then 15 per cent, or 20 per cent if you're foreign. Which I have always adhered to since.

One time we approached Dr Gilbey's office on Devonshire Place on foot and from a different direction, having been to see the Wallace Collection nearby, which we'd heard about from our mother who described it as 'a most romantic and sensual collection'. My sister and I hadn't realized it was going to be a picture gallery and were expecting a small zoo.

On this day we were after a bowl of soup before calling for the pills. We were hungry and running early for once (the Wallace Collection being quicker to look at than the two hours we'd allowed) and we found a small café with high stools along a window-ledge and went inside. The menu was quite unusual to our eyes. My sister said it must be Spanish because of all the unusual things chalked up on a blackboard, including osso buco and a sandwich with pimientos. That and the shiny black hair of the waiters. But they did have cheese on toast and they did have soup (oxtail), so we had one of each. And shared and wished we'd just had two soups, the cheese on toast being like nothing we'd ever seen before — except candle wax — and the bread hardly toasted at all. We learned that Heinz soup is a safe bet in a strange café.

In other words, we learned bits about London (taxis = tipping), about art and culture (Wallace Collection = picture gallery) and about life in general (Heinz soup = safe).

One time, on the outward journey, we were stopped by a nosy and bored policeman before we'd even got on the train at Leicester station and we told a white lie to get rid of him quickly. And that turned out to be the wrong thing to do, though not as wrong as telling the truth would have been. It would have been better to have told darker lies (such as we were meeting someone off the train) or not to have been in the situation in the first place. We told him we were going to London to see our father (which was half untrue). My sister had hidden the pill and zoo money down her sock just in case we got searched.

The policeman didn't like our attitude, not that we'd been rude but my sister had told him not to worry about us and that had made him worry (it's always the way), and he asked us to accompany him into an office just off the platform where he made us answer a whole lot of questions about who we were, the purpose of our visit, how old we were, what we were up to. The policeman looked for our number in the telephone directory but it wasn't listed because of our mother being female and he thought we were fobbing him off with false identities. Then he realized we were claiming to be the children of Edward Vogel of H. Vogel & Company and he obtained our telephone number a different way via Charles Street and rang our home. We heard his side of the conversation with our mother.

'I've got two juveniles here going off to London by train. Are you aware of this, madam? . . . I see, and you're consensual with that, are you, madam?'

While this conversation dragged on, the clock ticked and time went by and I realized our train was on the platform. I pointed to the clock on the office wall and then to the doorway but the policeman closed the door with his toe.

He frowned, phone to his ear, listening to our mother.

'Well, that is curious, madam. The older one has stated to me that they're meeting with their father at St Pancras station in London.'

I tapped his arm. He looked away. 'I see, madam.'

We missed the train. I heard it pull away and I began to cry.

The policeman said, 'Your mum wants a word.'

My sister took the phone.

'Yes. We've missed it,' she said. 'Sorry. OK, so shall we come home?'

We caught the next train but had to skip the zoo.

★ ★ ★

My high hopes for the pills were eventually dashed and I had to agree with my sister that all the pills in the world couldn't stop our mother from being sad and writing her play. To be honest, it seemed as though the more pills we got, the more acts appeared.

So it was time for the next man on the list. We'd set our hearts on a very nice man called Phil Oliphant who lived in the village and loved horses, whom I may have mentioned before. My sister had met him by accident when looking for a new pony for herself, and he'd been the perfect mix of nice, handsome and horse-loving and even had wrought-iron gates on his driveway with a horse-head motif.

But we were stalling on Phil Oliphant because (a) he was too good to mess up and (b) his name was Phil, but mainly (c) our mother wasn't ready for a new man encounter with it being spring, her worst season bar winter, and a time when she hardly wanted to leave the house, let alone have sex with a horse-lover.

We resorted to interacting with the play, listening to new scenes, listening again to old scenes, listening to edited scenes and acting it out. We even wrote some poems to sprinkle in amongst the drama. One of mine was a true story about a lost guinea pig who had run down a rat hole and hadn't come out again, even with a parsley lure. It was awful, awful, awful. Three awfuls.

Our mother knew how bad I felt because I was usually very brave and good at dusting myself down and marching on, but this guinea pig thing had made me feel dreadful because I blamed myself. Our mother said that bad things of our own doing are the hardest type of bad thing to get over. She knew this — most of the bad things in her life having been her own fault.

Our mother said that writing a poem about it might help. It didn't help because it got me thinking about what might have happened (inside the rat hole), whereas before writing the poem I was just sad to have lost the guinea pig and blamed myself for letting him run away. And that showed me how powerful poems can be. In a bad way. And I suppose, if I'm being fair, in a good way too.

Our mother called poems 'pomes', whereas we said 'po-ims'. That irritated me almost as much as the sadness they caused. Anyway, we soon got sick of the plays and the poems and we became reckless. We'd always said we'd avoid inviting our schoolteachers to have sex with our mother because it could get awkward — in fact it was one of our two golden rules. But in desperation to break the play cycle my sister sent an invitation to a young man called Mr Dodd, Little Jack's teacher.

He was young. So young, he wasn't even married — just engaged. We knew Mr Dodd wouldn't make a very good husband for our mother (he was a teacher, her worst type of person, plus a bit of a sissy), but we needed to do something to cheer her up and he did have a sweet face, being Spanish on his mother's side, and linguistic skills. And we needed a rehearsal in the run-up for the attempt on the very nice and pony-loving Phil Oliphant.

Dear Mr Dodd,

Please would you come and talk to me about Little Jack's stammer. I gather there's not much to be done except to be patient and not get angry, but I want to make absolutely sure I'm doing all I can as his only visible parent. It is imperative to help all we can.

Please come one evening and we can discuss over a drink of wine, whisky or squash (your choice).

Yours,
Elizabeth Vogel

Mr Dodd called in later that week and the visit went much better than we'd dared to hope. After a brief chat about speech therapy, and two glasses of whisky plus the availability of a plate of cheeselets — which they didn't touch — they seemed to have sex in our mother's sitting room in front of the fire. We peeped through the French windows. Mr Dodd definitely had his trousers at least down and maybe right off.

It turned out badly, though, in the long run because he only wanted to do it the once and she kept pestering him — by telephone — to come round again and became very upset when he didn't and wrote a play about it. Not the usual one act, but a whole long drama in the Rattigan mould. Poignant and cringe-making.

Mr Ladd: I didn't mean to give you the wrong impression.

Adele: You gave me the impression that you were a nice person.

Mr Ladd: I'm engaged to be married.

Adele: You didn't mind being engaged on Friday evening.

Mr Ladd: I couldn't resist your beauty after you'd given me all that whisky.

Adele: I'm a bit worried about Little Jack's stammer.

Mr Ladd: Jack doesn't have a stammer.

Adele: What? You think I invented my own son's speech impediment?

Mr Ladd: I don't know.

Adele: (*calls loudly*) Jack, *Jack*, come in here, will you?

It was disappointing that Mr Dodd — who was meant to prevent the writing of the play — caused such a concerted bout of writing. But it taught us an important lesson and we never again had anything to do with teachers.

Soon afterwards, just as our mother was beginning to feel better about Mr Dodd not wanting to have sex with her again, our gardener, Mr Gummo, came to speak to her in confidence. He'd heard some 'nasty rumours' and didn't feel comfortable with knowing and not telling her about them etc. Mr Gummo was one of those people who always have to do the right thing — however brutal and upsetting. And then, as if to make up for it, he created a beautiful rockery to cover an unsightly manhole in our front garden that she'd been asking him to do for ages and he'd always refused, for sensible reasons. He planted miniature alpine saxifrage and thrift among a scattering of craggy rocks and said it was meant to resemble Switzerland in the springtime. Our mother was utterly thrilled with it and said it was worthy of Chelsea.

It went against Mr Gummo's better judgement — to cover a mains drain like that — and he made it clear to us that access might be needed at some point in the future and that would mean hurriedly removing it and we all accepted the fact. Our mother gave him a pay rise for doing the rockery, for overruling common sense in the name of beauty and, I suppose, for telling her about the nasty rumours and not minding. We added him to the list.

PART II

Charlie Bates

10

The summer eventually came and we at last had some warm days and were just beginning to plan our approach on Mr Phil Oliphant when suddenly, one afternoon, when the heat had shimmered above the slabs and our mother had roasted all day on her two-position recliner, a man arrived. A man not on the list, not from our village, unbidden by letter and totally out of the blue.

He was a plumber, apparently, though not the boiler-suited kind with an interest in the whys and wherefores of a leak or finding the right pipe, but in a narrow-trousered suit, tight round the backside and with gaping pockets.

Our first sight of him that late afternoon, he was standing at our five-bar gate, sun behind him, pretty much a silhouette.

''Scuse, love, has a dog just run in here?' he called.

And even though a dog definitely hadn't — or we'd have known about it from Debbie, our Labrador — our mother, shiny with Ambre Solaire, called from her lounger, 'Come in and have a look around.'

'What breed is it?' I asked, wanting the facts.

'It's one of them spotty Dalmatians,' he said, his eyes scouting. 'Belongs to a woman down the road. I've gone in to fix her boiler, and the bugger's run out.'

And, I thought, There's no Dalmatian living round here.

It's a thing any dog-loving child would know — whether or not a spotty dog lived nearby. He'd have been better off saying this mythical dog was a Collie-cross or Jack Russell. The glamorous breed choice gave him away. But no one in my family noticed things like that — actually, Jack might have, but he'd been inside with his train track — and I kept it to myself.

Charlie Bates specialized in boilers and pest control and said the two often went hand in hand.

Of course we didn't find the spotty dog, but Charlie Bates left his headed paper just in case we heard anything or our mother ever needed any advice on his specialist subjects. The headed paper was thin and the lettering flat and smudged. It read as follows:

CHARLES W. BATES
Plumbing and pest control at your convenience
Tel.: Hilfield 337

Later, our mother kept tapping his printed name with her polished but natural-looking fingernail and, when she'd drunk enough but not too much, she rang him and asked him to come over and check the boiler.

'I was wondering about fumes,' she said, 'you know, with the children.'

My sister and I looked at each other open-mouthed. Resentful and cross. He wasn't on the list and had no right turning up like that.

The problem was, we were to discover later, he looked like Frank Sinatra — though it must have been when Frank was gnarled and the whites of his blue eyes were bloodshot in the mornings and yellowish all day.

★ ★ ★

Charlie Bates took one look at the Potterton. 'It's giving out fumes left, right and all over the fucking place, love,' he said, and he wondered how we were all still alive. He drank a glass of Bell's and gritted his teeth on the swallow as if it disgusted him and talked her through the options ('I take it, chuck it, get you a new one — or I walk out of your life for ever').

'What's wrong with it?' my sister asked.

He ignored her.

'Yes, what actually *is* wrong with it?' our mother asked.

But Charlie had no interest whatsoever in discussing the workings of anything or explaining what might be right or wrong with a thing.

'It's fucked, sweetheart,' he said.

Then, the very next day (another hot one), with a tiny papery cigarette sitting on his lower lip, Charlie Bates heaved the Potterton out of its cubbyhole, walked it on its corners across the kitchen to the back door and up the ramp on to his trailer. It was like watching a handsome man dancing with a fat lady out of politeness. Still no boiler-suit. His tie loosened and his smart shirt dark at the armpits.

Then, with a whisky-laced cup of coffee inside

him, banging a broom and shouting, 'Geddout of it, you bastards,' he chased a couple of homeless rats out of the kitchen that had apparently been nesting behind the boiler.

We all turned away, too squeamish to even look. Perhaps there were rats, perhaps not. That's the thing, I told myself later. If you won't look at a thing, how can you know if it's real or not? and I vowed to hold my nerve in future.

Our mother waved her hands about at the idea of rats, screamed and tiptoed around in her stringy bikini top, slopping coffee. 'Oh my God, Charlie,' she said in her posh voice. And sidled up to him for a scaredy half-hug.

A replacement boiler, rather smaller with rust patches, was fitted for the price of well over one hundred pounds cash of our mother's money. As she counted it out into his cracked fingers, she looked right at him. 'Come to dinner, Charlie Bates,' she said.

'What? Me, here, dinner, when?' he said.

And she said, 'Whenever, tonight, tomorrow, or we could go out.'

And with us three watching, they held each other's eye and made an arrangement to dine at Wong's the following Friday.

'Wong's, then. I'll pick you up,' he said, and my sister and I looked at each other again. And that was that. It would probably go wrong at Wong's or beyond, but he was definitely a little blob of happiness at least, if not more.

★   ★   ★

114

A few days before the date at Wong's we drove into town. Our mother had to go to Steiner's on Horsefair Street to have her hair looked at and possibly trimmed. She always liked to see Geraldo at Steiner's, him being by far the best stylist in the whole of Leicester and the East Midlands. He'd won awards for his methods and results. He did men and women and didn't prefer one over the other except that he loved the kind of long hair you most often saw on women. If ever Geraldo were unavailable our mother would try another day. Steiner's had an appointment system, but our mother wasn't the appointment type when it came to her hair. Or anything much.

An appointment with Geraldo was more than just a trim, even if you were only having a trim. And that was all our mother ever had — an inch and a half off the ends. We often went to Horsefair Street with her because there were other things to do in the vicinity such as go to the dentist or the shoe shop or the theatre. And we loved to watch Geraldo trim our mother's hair, so it suited us.

Geraldo would start by brushing her hair vigorously with his eyes closed and then he'd throw handfuls of it up into the air as if it were money he'd just found unexpectedly in a chest in a cave on a beach and then he'd pick up a single strand, and he'd look at it, turning it over and over and up to the light, and rub it between his fingers, listen to it and smell it, and then he'd ask her how she was, how her love life was, how we were and ask her how her menstruation was and was she drinking plenty of wine and she'd laugh and say she drank whisky and he'd tut at her with his finger.

Our mother liked Geraldo because he loved long hair like hers — long hair on a pretty, thin face with no make-up. Basically straight but with a slight wave to it on the ends. Geraldo didn't only love long hair, he *respected* long hair. He had long hair himself and had it parted very far to the left so that the fringe came over his brow in a straight line and looked like a skull wrap.

Anyway, that day, just before the date with Charlie, we were at Steiner's and our mother was in Geraldo's chair for a trim, and he had asked her how she was and thrown the hair about and all of a sudden he put down his comb and said he needed a moment before he commenced the cutting, and he went away into a back room for some minutes while our mother had a cup of coffee.

'What's wrong with Geraldo?' I asked her.

'He's just sensitive,' she said.

The receptionist butted in. 'Geraldo knows your mother's hair intimately and something he's seen today has bothered him,' she said, and she passed us a packet of digestives which were very dry without a drink with them but no drink was offered.

Our mother became agitated at this uninvited intervention from the receptionist.

'What do you mean? What has he seen?' she asked.

'It could be anything — it might be a sign of dehydration or split ends,' said the receptionist,

116

looking at her own fingernails.

'You don't think he's seen grey, do you?' said our mother, and she leant forward and peered at the hair in her reflection.

Then Geraldo came back.

'Geraldo,' our mother began, 'what's the matter? What have you seen?'

'I want to cut you a feather cut,' he said and, as if he'd said something much worse, he hid his face behind his hands and peered through his fingers, waiting for a response.

'No!' our mother said very quickly, then, 'No, I can't, my hair is my trademark, it's all I've got. It's all I've got except for my plays. It's the thing I love most in the world apart from the Indian tea boxes my father brought back from Ceylon, and I don't even know where they are.'

Geraldo sat down on the floor in front of her salon chair and bridged his fingers. He was Italian and that's the Italian way of saying, 'Stop being silly'.

'If a woman has something and it's all she has and she protects it and cherishes it and her life is going nowhere,' said Geraldo, getting louder, 'then she must throw away that thing. Chuck it away. It is my belief that the thing, this beautiful long hair, is holding you back and you cannot go forward and find peace until you have cut it off.'

My sister and I were very interested in this line of reasoning and were pleased to see that she softened a bit. Her head went slightly to the side, which showed she was at least listening.

'What does a feather cut actually look like?' she asked.

117

Geraldo leapt to his feet, swung her round to face the mirror and held up parts of her hair. He angled her face to look in different ways.

'So, Eliza-*beth*, it's choppy like this and razored and spunky and it's saying, 'Hey, here I am!'' and he laughed and she laughed and we laughed at the thought of our mother's hair saying, 'Hey, here I am!'

She was about to agree to it, and had begun to say, 'Oh, all right, then,' when Geraldo showed her some pictures of people with the feather cut.

'Look how smart, how cheeky, how now!' said Geraldo, pointing to whoever it was in the pictures.

And then she said, 'Oh, I don't know, Geraldo. It sounds terribly nice and I understand the theory behind it, but I think I need time to consider it. Maybe next time?' she said.

'Yeah, sure,' he said. And he swung her round and got started on the one and a half inch trim. I picked up the feather cut pictures. They were all of the same man from *Monty Python*.

At home later, we saw her looking at herself in the glass a few times and holding up bits of hair. Then she took a pill and went to sleep.

The next day she told us of a dream she'd had. A bird had flown down and started pecking at some seedlings and the seedlings had grown very suddenly and become bigger than the bird. She saw it as a sign that we should go back to Steiner's and see Geraldo about the feather cut. She rang and made an appointment, which was most unlike her and showed just how imperative the feather cut suddenly was.

'What do you think, Lizzie?' our mother asked.

'About what?' I asked back.

'The feather cut,' she said.

'Oh, I think it looks very modern and nice,' I lied.

'Do you like it?' she said.

'Yes, definitely,' I said, 'I love it.'

We went into town again and left the car near Victoria Park, and on the walk down we called in at the museum and threw coins into the fishpond and looked at the giraffe and the mummies. We called in at the printer's for the new headed writing paper and cards that our mother had ordered months before and hadn't had the heart to collect. The printer was a bit cross about it and asked what she thought the shop would look like if everybody left it six months before collecting their order.

'I'm sorry, I just haven't had the heart,' she said, in a wispy voice that seemed to take the wind out of the man's sails, and he apologized for sounding unkind. I took note of the technique and thought we could have added the printer to the list of men if only he wasn't situated fifteen miles from our home.

Then we went to Steiner's to see Geraldo. My sister and I were worried and excited at the same time (both of us, both things) about the pending feather cut. Worried because we'd seen how ridiculous the *Monty Python* man had looked with it and yet excited because it was something new and worrying.

'OK,' said our mother, 'let's see how this style looks, then.'

And to my shock, I was ushered into Geraldo's chair. Although I was horrified, I felt I could hardly object, having been so positive about it when our mother had asked me earlier, and anyway I was speechless.

'Such a clever, clever idea,' said Geraldo, laughing, 'to try it out on the kid first.'

I was gowned up and shampooed and, before I knew it, Geraldo was chopping into my hair with some kind of razor-comb. I felt the blade slicing and from the corners of my eyes saw great chunks of hair falling to the floor. I glanced at my sister. I saw a look of deep concern on her face, as if watching a disaster in slow motion and powerless to stop it.

It didn't take more than a few minutes. Our mother stood by the chair and held her hand over her mouth for the duration.

'Ta-da!' said Geraldo as he unveiled me. He spritzed me with some hairspray and preened me a bit, then said, 'So, whadayou think, Elizabeth?'

'Oh my God!' she said. 'No, I couldn't possibly have that done to me.'

I looked very different, startlingly so, and ultra-stylish with the feather cut. But I was ten and lived in a small village and stylishness didn't get me anywhere. I looked like a grown man from a pop group — Rod Stewart or someone of that ilk — whereas before I'd looked like the author Anaïs Nin with her prim Edwardian face.

At playtime the next day at school a boy said I looked like a hairy ape with my new hair. I didn't look anything like a hairy ape but I knew what he

120

was getting at, and I wondered dismally what Miranda Longlady was going to make of it. What clever description she'd come up with. And then, feeling worried about that, I remembered Bufo the frog puppet and that she hadn't given him back, and I felt angry instead, which was better.

11

Our mother's date with Charlie Bates at Wong's seemed to have gone well, partly on account of its 'no chopstick promise', and was the start of many dates.

There was nothing much to do in the village for a loving couple. Charlie hated the pubs on offer except for the Piglet Inn and he couldn't go there with a lady. So she and Charlie would drive all the way into town at night in Whisper, his white Saab. To Winalot's in Lee Circus, where Charlie would play cards, win or lose money, and our mother would sit on high stools looking nice and drinking Bonny Doons. Going out in town meant they were always out late. For a start everything closed later there, and then there was the sex to be had in the car on the way home which, according to the *Facts of Life* film, could take up to thirty minutes, and then the drive home after that.

Meanwhile, alone at home, we'd be making Ritz and Primula sandwiches and watching anxious dramas and horror films and then, too scared to go to bed, we'd wait in the porch, which was where Debbie, our Labrador, slept and we'd crowd around her, Little Jack actually in the wicker basket beside her, the smell of her warm paw-pads comforting him.

My sister would be wondering if our mother and Charlie might settle down soon and not go out so much and if they might get married. And if the village would then think more highly of us (or less badly) with him at the helm, in spite of him being the least popular plumber in the area. And I'd be trying to work him out. Often the image of his mouth would pop into my head, as if it might hold a clue. The lower teeth, like a row of shutters lightly ajar, and one upper incisor, standing sideways-on to its neighbour, which, to my artist's eye, was a fully opened door into his mouth. I wondered how his teeth had come to that — I imagined it was due to fighting and being repeatedly punched and the teeth being knocked almost out but firming up again in slightly the wrong place. They seemed to be a warning, those misaligned incisors. But nobody else saw them. They were too busy looking at his blue and red eyes.

Little Jack would eventually fall asleep beside Debbie, and my sister and I would keep each other awake with comments and chitchat, and then we'd hear them arrive home and crowd them at the door saying, 'Did you have a nice time?' etc., Debbie's tail banging on the radiator, and Charlie would say, 'Fuck off, you lot.' And we'd scuttle off to bed.

I have to admit Charlie did make our mother happy some of the time. Which doesn't sound much but it was an improvement on her being unhappy all of the time and it was the whole point of everything. She had a new sense of adventure and we got continental quilts for our beds (not Jack, though, he wasn't ready) and made a huge mural on the hall wall with pop star heads, Smirnoff bottles and other bright images from the *Observer* magazine.

We even had a few trips to Kenwood, a large open-air swimming pool with an ice-cream shop. It was a favourite thing for all of us and a huge treat. Debbie wasn't allowed in, though, nor any dog, so maybe that was why in spite of us all loving it we didn't go very often. Anyway, the pool was marvellous and cold and frighteningly deep. A great expanse of rippling blue edged with hot slabs. Our mother was a terrific swimmer and would always dive straight in, swim like mad, climb out glistening with chlorinated droplets and then flop down onto a towel and sunbathe as if dead and presumably enjoy being looked at in her bikini pants with her top undone as it always was — to avoid strap marks in her tan.

You might imagine there'd have been oppor-tunities to top up the Man List at the pool (especially with our mother so much on show), but not so. For a start, it was too far from home and any man would have had a long journey to our village for dates. Plus the men always looked undesirable. Being wet making them look spivvish, which was fine in the 1950s but by the 1970s was a bit off-putting. Plus they were almost naked and sat around looking furtive with water dripping off their chest hair and you couldn't help imagining all sorts of unpleasant-ness. And anyway, we had Charlie in the frame.

Our mother wasn't quite so happy on the many evenings Charlie didn't come over and often reverted to play-writing. And even though he hadn't been on the list or properly vetted, my sister and I agreed that, though less than ideal, Charlie was better than nothing. For now.

⋆   ⋆   ⋆

Our father phoned to invite my sister and me to stay a night. Little Jack wasn't invited as a punishment for having bolted from the car the time before when the chauffeur stopped for petrol.

'No, thanks,' I said, speaking for my sister and myself, because in those days visits to divorced fathers' houses were awkward and to be avoided.

'Oh, but it would be lovely to see you both,' he said, sounding genuinely disappointed, 'especially after last time.' Meaning the time before Little Jack had bolted, when we had cancelled at the last minute due to me having a rash and them not wanting me to infect the baby.

'The thing is, I feel awkward with Vivian and the baby,' I said, thinking honesty was the best policy and knowing that any other objection would just be solved.

'I see. Well, why don't we have lunch in town on Friday instead?' he said. 'Then it'll just be us . . . I'll send Bernard to collect you.'

I was pleased in the end that this had cropped up as it occurred to me that spending some time with our father (a proper and intelligent man with manners and nice teeth) without the complications of his new family would give us the opportunity to assess Charlie against him. I suspected it would throw Charlie's failings into

125

sharp relief and that we'd see him for what he was — i.e., not quite up to the job of man at the helm.

When Friday came I chivvied my sister to get ready, but she said she was busy. And said she wouldn't go to Fenwick's dining room even if she wasn't — it being so utterly snobby and full of old grannies eating slowly with clunking great knives and forks. I begged her to come and I'm ashamed to say I cried at the thought of the journey in the Daimler followed by lunch in Fenwick's alone with our father and all that cutlery. But she said she wasn't going and that was that.

It was a prospect so dreadful — the being alone with a parent, apart from everything else — that I revealed my illegal friendship with Melody Longlady (albeit only to our mother, who was good at being understanding about that kind of thing and not telling) and asked if I should invite her along to act as a buffer. Our mother advised me strongly against it, reminding me that an invitation might put Melody in an awkward position and then *she* might need a buffer.

So I asked our mother to insist that my sister came with me. She said my sister had every right to not want to go (because, in all honesty, who would?) but agreed that she might have made her intentions known a bit earlier.

'Why not take Little Jack with you?' our mother suggested.

'He's banned because of running away — remember?' I said.

'Oh, just take him,' said our mother.

'But what if he runs away again?' I said.

'Hold on to him,' said our mother.

'It's a long journey,' I moaned.

'You'll manage,' she said.

Soon I had Jack on the dog lead and he was really annoyed and pully, like disobedient dogs sometimes are. I explained calmly and in the style of my teacher, Miss Thorne, 'This is what happens to little boys who run away from their father's chauffeur.'

Bernard arrived and wasn't at all keen to carry Little Jack as a passenger after the last time, but I showed him the restraining device.

'If he bolts off, he's on his own,' said Bernard.

'He won't be able to,' I said, holding up the plaited leather leash.

We got into the back of the car and drove the short distance to Bagshaw Bridge service station. I can explain now why Bernard the chauffeur always liked to fill up there. It was because the manager had fitted a device to the fuel nozzle that made it stop flowing when the tank was full and a little latch so that the nozzle could rest on its own. This freed the attendant up to do other little jobs such as clean the windscreen or check the water, which he did quite happily for free. Bernard knew of no other service station in all of England that did this. Though in the USA — where he had lived for many years as chauffeur to a Congressman — helpful attendants with nozzle devices were the norm. Bernard considered this country of ours to be a backward-looking little dump and the drivers here idiots, happy to put up with insufficient oil checks and smeary windscreens. That's why he liked going to Bagshaw Bridge service station and ditto why he liked collecting us for my father (if you didn't count little kids running off).

Knowing it was Jack's getaway point last time, I held on quite tight for the duration of the stop and watched for signs. But once we were on the road again, Little Jack fell asleep and lay right down with his head on my leg and it was like having a real dog with me. Soon the collar flopped loosely over Jack's shirt and I chomped on pear drops to ward off carsickness. Bernard puffed away on his cigarette and switched on the radio.

'Your dad doesn't like the radio going when he's on board,' said Bernard.

Then the radio started talking about the Apollo missions and he quickly switched it off.

'Don't you like space?' I asked, and he said, 'No, not really, can't be doing with it.'

We pootled through suburbia, or, as Bernard called it, the sprawl, and I stared out of the window.

'Two houses, two garages, two houses, two garages,' said Bernard. 'If there's one thing I hate it's the sound of a garage door clanging up-and-over. Whatever happened to wooden garage doors that open in the normal way?'

What a strange thing to hate, I thought, and wondered if I'd care about such things at his age, which was roughly forty, I reckoned.

When Bernard dropped us outside Fenwick's of Leicester on the corner of Belvoir Street, he told us to go straight up to the fourth-floor dining room and say we were to meet Mr Vogel, and he ruffled Jack's hair and said, 'Still with us, Fido?' and Jack let out a loud bark and Bernard jumped out of his skin and called him a little bastard and drove off.

Little Jack wouldn't let me take the lead and collar off, and every time I tried he barked. He insisted on moving through Fenwick's on all fours, sniffing at things as we went. People stared at us and looked worried. I acted normal. In the lift an old woman said, 'No dogs allowed,' and Jack barked at her.

My father was there in the dining room already and was all smiles (he even commented on my new dramatic hairstyle) until he looked down and saw Little Jack. He told him to get up. Little Jack gave him a quizzical doggy look and barked. Then my father was furious and tried to wrestle the collar off him. Jack growled and bit my father's hand and scampered under a table where a couple were having roast of the day. The couple lifted the tablecloth to look at him and he started yapping like a terrier. My father bobbed down and tried to take hold of Jack, but Jack snarled and bit him again. The couple called the waitress and Jack snarled at her too. In the end my father dragged him by the lead and bustled him into the lift and apparently gave him a bloody good slap.

Then Bernard was whisking us home and we'd had no lunch and I told Bernard all about it. Bernard said it was the absolutely funniest thing he'd heard all year. He banged the steering wheel with his palm and said he was going to dine out on it. Him mentioning dining out got us on to the subject of dining out and I asked if we could stop at the Golden Egg for something to eat. Although Bernard had a new respect for Little Jack, he didn't quite trust him and couldn't be held responsible. Jack made a few high-pitched barks and I translated that he promised not to run away. In the end Bernard stopped at the Travelin-Man and got us an egg-and-cress roll each and a Kit Kat between us. And Jack stopped being a dog and said thank you in English.

My sister was 100 per cent jealous that she'd missed out on seeing Jack snapping and biting and barking, so we re-enacted the whole thing and she laughed so much she did a bit of wee and our mother asked us to do it again and she laughed too. It was a great day for Jack. I don't think he was ever the same again. Knowing you can make an impact on people you want to make an impact on without even speaking or changing your jumper.

Our father telephoned later to discuss Little Jack's behaviour. I heard our mother say, 'Well, what do you expect?' and then, 'I'll ask him to telephone you, if he wants to. It's up to him.'

Then we had a family conflab about Jack phoning our father.

Our mother was very reasonable and support-ive of Jack, but she did say she thought Jack should probably phone, bearing in mind he had bitten our father twice, and then we all started laughing again.

Jack did phone. We all stayed quiet so we could hear him on the phone, but we only heard this:

'I don't know.'

'I know.'

'I don't know.'

'I know.'

'All right, then.'

'Bye.'

After all that excitement and fun, my sister asked me how Charlie had compared against our father, and though I hated to put a spoke in the wheel I reported that, compared with our father, Charlie seemed like some kind of lunatic.

'Double damn,' said my sister, and I agreed.

★　★　★

Charlie said he couldn't fully relax in our mother's sitting room the way it was. It was too austere for his taste. He disliked the bare wood floors and the white walls. It reminded him of a whitewashed barn at the centre of an awful experience in his life. His awful times had usually occurred during the war or just before it.

'You need something a bit darker on the walls and a bit of soft,' he said, meaning cushions, I suppose, and curtains.

He went on to describe a marvellously soothing and sumptuously romantic wall colour especially devised and produced to promote relaxation in adult lounges.

'It's called Rendezvous,' he said. 'It's meant to capture the street-lit sky as seen through a New

York bar window at night.'

Or something along those lines. Our mother seemed to like the sound of it and cocked her head to imagine the scene.

'It's pricey, but if you want a relaxing lounge to relax in properly, then you need to do something with these bloody walls,' he said, 'and Rendezvous would suit marvellous.'

'It sounds lovely,' said our mother.

'It's hard to source, that particular colour is, but I'll see what I can do, and you can get that idiot handyman of yours in to slap it on,' said Charlie.

And so Mr Lomax arrived plus two large white cans with 'Ronday-View' penned on the lids. And no sooner was the sitting room blacked out with the darkest paint you can imagine than Charlie announced, 'You need a piece of Axminster down to finish it off.'

Our mother didn't agree to that, though, being a hater of carpets, but she did agree to a smart rug, which Charlie provided promptly for fifty-five pounds. And some large fluffy cushions for another twenty.

Soon Little Jack had qualms. He looked out of the window a lot, frowning, and stammered more on the k and m and said things such as, 'Charlie's making our world so dark.' I of course had my own qualms about Charlie. But Little Jack having qualms made more of an impression on my sister. She worried when Jack worried because in spite of never being told anything, he seemed to have a sense of what was underneath and behind everything. Having Little Jack was like having two brothers really. The boy who knew and detected everything and looked out of windows worrying, and the ordinary little boy who wouldn't take his coat off and had a George Best lampshade.

My sister, still being largely pro-Charlie, gave Little Jack a project to help soothe his qualms and stop his worries getting out of hand and to give him a sense of purpose. She told Jack of the old saying 'Know Thine Enemy', and though she didn't know why exactly and wasn't sure Charlie even was our enemy as such, Jack was very excited about having a solo project and set about knowing him via asking him lots of questions.

Jack had soon gleaned all sorts of information pertaining, including that Charlie had lost a finger and a half in the war, his own fault, not a bomb or a gun but a rusty catch on a door. He couldn't eat spaghetti because of something that had happened in Italy. He'd never in his life eaten a banana and was allergic to a certain kind of tree — a fir or a pine — he couldn't be precise, only that he came out in hives in certain weather with a certain tree. He didn't believe in God, a thing that Jack found troubling to begin with, but not as troubling as the fact that the concept of outer space made him feel sick. And apparently he couldn't even imagine the planets or hear their names without feeling queasy. It reminded me of Bernard the chauffeur and his Apollo phobia. Finally, he didn't like German people but liked other types, especially Americans.

It was all very helpful in knowing Charlie and

kept Jack feeling involved. I, however, was more interested in what our mother actually saw in him, so I addressed my questions to her. The main thing seemed to be — according to our mother — that he'd taken to us.

'What do you love so much about Charlie?' I said one day.

'Well, he's taken to you lot,' she said, 'and that's the main thing.'

It wasn't the main thing at all, but thinking about it, there was just enough truth in it — it seemed that in his rough way he did like us. He found us amusing and liked to amuse us and I can't tell you how nice that was. And even though one man seeming to like us didn't compensate for a whole entire village thinking badly of us, it was very nice and perhaps explains why we tried so hard to like him.

12

The kids at school were terribly upset by the news and walked around in gloomy disbelief. The news was that O'Donnell's funfair was cancelled due to an attempted murder.

My sister and I weren't all that bothered about the cancellation of the fair and were actually quite pleased about the attempted murder. Firstly, we'd had no experience of O'Donnell's fair and therefore didn't know what we'd be missing, but we did like it when anything bad happened in the village, as long as it had nothing to do with us (and since the murder was only attempted and not committed). Looking back, it seems a bit schadenfreudey and mean, but you have to remember the village didn't like us.

The reason for the fair being cancelled was that Mr Clegg, on whose land the fair always took place, had committed attempted murder. He'd shot his wife, then run away along a canal bank. It was almost a double-death because Mr Clegg flung himself into the water to drown, but it turned out to be no deaths as the wife was only grazed and Mr Clegg was fished out of the canal before he had time to drown by four members of the ornithology club who were hiding out in the bushes because someone claimed to have seen a very rare egret in that spot. And even if the ornithologists hadn't been there, there was a group of civil engineers working on a very long

135

canal tunnel adjacent to the plunge point who would have fished him out, only the ornithologists got to him first. There was also a dog walker and a farmer nearby.

That was the thing about this village: you couldn't do anything without a whole bunch of people knowing about it. You couldn't even jump into a canal to drown yourself without people queuing up to jump in and drag you out. The village was furious about the shooting, not only because of the cancellation of the fair but because it ended up on the *Nine O'clock News* read by Richard Baker and put the village in a bad light. The village blamed the wife for being provocative and wanting too many material things when the poor husband was only on an overlocker's wage in spite of living on a farm.

While I'm on the subject, other bad things happened around that time, including a spate of gate-liftings which infuriated the village and ended up in the papers (the village still reeling from the non-fatal shooting). Mrs C. Beard said what did you expect in a recession, but took the precaution of chaining her two gates together so that anyone lifting one gate would have the other to contend with.

The village hated being in the news for anything other than dog shows and so forth. And hated anything that happened at night and gate-lifting always happened at night. One night, our own gate was lifted and we were thrilled and our mother refused to ring the constable because she thought he should have better things to do with his time and if he didn't he might write a play. Ours was one of the few gates to be actually stolen, most being lifted and left to the right of the gate opening. Ours, being pure timber, was taken away and probably used as firewood. We had to have another immediately due to Debbie and this time got a tubular metal one which was very cold to sit on and a bit clangy.

★   ★   ★

The thing about having siblings is you can find yourself dragged along their paths and tangled in their worries and prejudices — which often seem more reasoned than your own, especially if you're unsure of a thing. And so it was with me and my clever, open-eyed big sister.

She in turn was often unduly influenced by Little Jack's childish inklings and qualms. But then Little Jack tended to be easily fobbed off by me. It was a circle of anxiety, manipulation and reassurances. And never more than over Charlie Bates, about whom we were quite happy to change our minds overnight and back again the next day, with my sister leading the charge and me towed behind thinking more or less what she thought and Little Jack running to the front and then to the rear. After a week of disliking Charlie, he might suddenly show us how to sneak up on someone from behind, say a soldier you wanted to kill or just anyone you wanted to scare the shit out of. And how to open a locked door with two library cards Sellotaped together or a fish slice or anything hard and flat. And that might cause my sister to say, 'People aren't either

137

goodies or baddies, they can be a mixture of both.'

And then, a week later, he might teach us how to make a *decent* cup of tea, which was not as easy as we'd imagined because you put the milk in after the teabag and not with it, which made it hard to judge the colour/strength. And how to make a decent Whisky Mac, which was exactly as easy as we'd imagined, using bottle lids (four parts ginger wine to one part whisky). And that might cause my sister to say, 'He's no good. He's a chancer, a bad egg, and once an egg has turned it's bad for ever, a leopard can't change its spots.'

Consequently, one minute we'd be vowing to get rid of him and then we'd like him again. And then he'd suddenly stop coming round and we'd worry like hell that it was all over. And then he'd turn up and ask for money and if I wasn't careful I'd remember that he was a liar and that his toolbox was three-quarters empty and he'd been stripped of his gas fitter's badge and that he couldn't speak eloquently. Not even as eloquently as Mr Lomax, and Mr Lomax was hardly eloquent. But I'd stay behind my sister and push these things out of my mind.

Our mother was no help. She was fully in love with him and no amount of patchy behaviour on his part altered that. We made suggestions about other eligible males but it was as my sister said, 'It's tough to topple the incumbent,' which she'd heard on the telly regarding something to do with the news.

Then something big happened. It was all to do with O'Donnell's rescheduled funfair which had

138

come to Mr Clegg's land after all — his wife having not pressed charges and his solicitor being able to show how nice he usually was when not provoked and how remorseful (trying to drown himself).

* * *

We asked our mother if we could go to the rescheduled funfair. She was writing a play and listening to Beethoven's Pastoral Symphony and kept putting the needle back to the big build-up at the start. Charlie hadn't been over for a while and the play was bilingual and about a broken-hearted woman running away to Holland to grow tiny edible vegetables.

Adele: I geen Nederlands spreken.
Man: You must try.
Adele: I have grown one hundred little lettuces.
Man: But to no avail.
Adele: Ik ben gegroeid 100 stuks.
Man: Laat me tellen.

We asked again about going to the fair and she mistook it for an invitation to come with us and said funfairs made her sick — a thing I find I've inherited in adulthood — and she put the needle back to hear the Beethoven build-up again. After it had settled to the strings, we changed the nature of our request and asked for money. She was still unable to focus and in the end we helped ourselves to a one-pound note from her purse, which lived in the fruit bowl.

My sister and I thought we'd kept the fair secret from Little Jack. We didn't want him tagging along: he was too little and would need a degree of looking after. We skipped off down the road. Soon Little Jack was calling out a word from his babyhood (which meant: yes, no, what, goodbye, hello, wait and help), something like 'Nur', and running to catch up with us. Him saying 'Nur' was annoying. He must have been seven by then, but he reverted to 'Nur' because he wanted to remind us that he was the youngest and little. We didn't fall for it, though, and we were cruel to be kind.

'You can't hang around with us,' we told him.

'We just want to be two girls at a fair,' I said, as if that was the most reasonable thing in the world, like saying, 'We just want to breathe.'

But he didn't care. He just wanted to go to the fair — as you do when you're his age — and he followed us.

So we arrived at the fair just as the sun was going down and soon the dark night showed up the hundreds of on-and-off coloured bulbs and it was wonderful. My sister and I shook Little Jack off almost immediately. Something caught his eye and we walked quickly on. Then we ate candy-floss and went on a sickening ride, linked arms and laughed and spent our one pound. But soon we'd had enough of the smell of spoiled grass and braised onions.

At home, all was dark. Only Debbie was there (pushing her food bowl around on the stone floor with her nose to remind us she'd had no supper). Our mother was out. Beethoven was

140

quiet though the disc, still revolving, crackled eerily. And there was no sign of Little Jack whatsoever. We trudged back to Clegg's to look for him. We bickered and the night was ruined.

The fair seemed sinister now. The coloured lights looked like ordinary bulbs roughly daubed. Soft muddy ruts tripped us, a laughing Elvis fell into my sister and made her cry, and harsh voices rang around in the dark. We looked everywhere for Little Jack. We called 'Jack' and 'Jack' and everyone seemed to be laughing at us. So we went home again, hoping and praying we'd find him there.

Our mother was home. She was upset because a pot of stove-boiled coffee had melted a great hexagon in the middle of her new fireside rug. And she'd scalded her arm trying to rescue it. A smell of singed hair and burnt coffee heightened the sense of something being wrong.

'Is Little Jack home?' we asked.

'He was with you at the fair,' she snapped.

We looked upstairs and then in Debbie's basket in the porch and in places he couldn't even be — like the bread oven, which he couldn't fit into. He wasn't anywhere. It had got very late and we assumed he was dead and that if we went back to the fair we'd find his little body slung across one of the dodgem cars being buffeted and spun, surrounded by laughing people and the clumsy Elvis.

Those minutes were dreadful. I felt sick. It was all our fault, like it had been with the guinea pig and the rat hole, and I began to imagine how I'd get through the rest of my life knowing I'd abandoned my brother and let him die at the fair just so I didn't have to be in a three, with a kid. Our last memory of him being that stupid word (Nur). How could my sister and I ever be happy again, knowing what we'd done?

In desperation and against my sister's wishes, I rang Charlie's telephone number. 'We've lost Little Jack at the funfair at Clegg's,' I told him.

Charlie met us at the gate by Clegg's and we set off to look for our little brother properly. Charlie stood in his suit, relit an already smoked cigarette and gazed around with squinted eyes. He seemed to block everything out — all the Elvises and noise and flashing lights. He turned quickly to a row of wagons, flicked the cigarette aside, got down on to his hands and knees and crawled underneath a wagon opposite the Pot o' Gold, with its fluffy prizes hanging from the panelled roof. A moment later he came out with Little Jack under him, like a baby elephant under its parent.

We crowded round Little Jack for a moment and Charlie walked away. We all ran after him, me dragging Little Jack by the hand.

'How did you know where to find him?' I asked.

'I put myself in his shoes,' said Charlie.

We saw then what an asset a brute like Charlie Bates could be — for the odd moments of extraordinary peril — and he edged ahead of my sister's beloved Mr Oliphant. We tried to thank him for helping us and saving Little Jack, but he told us to fuck off home. We hinted that we'd like a lift — our house being almost a mile away

— but he zoomed off in Whisper, his white Saab.

Little Jack was too tired to walk quickly. His cloth animal was gone and he was scared of the dark. I piggybacked all three-stone-seven of him — with his jaggy elbows and legs — all the way home. I was so happy to have him back, I didn't care. I vowed out loud in front of my sister that I would never let her or Jack down again. I'd do my utmost to keep them safe and happy. My sister told me to shut up and walk faster. In the end she stomped off ahead.

We didn't want our mother waking in the night and not properly knowing Jack was found, so I started to write her a note:

Dear Mum. Don't worry about Little Jack. He's not lost — he's home. PS I hate fairs too now.

She half woke while I was writing and she mumbled, 'Did you find Bufo?'

'Bufo?' I whispered.

'Bufo, my little frog.' And she went to sleep again, leaving me with a guilty feeling that ruined the happy-ending aspect of the night. I couldn't believe that after having the initiative to phone Charlie and then carrying Little Jack all the way home and being considerate in not waking our mother, I should be rewarded with a poke in the eye and the reminder that I had outstanding obligations vis-à-vis Bufo.

I lay in bed furious. I made a silent but solemn vow to get the frog puppet back and to punch Miranda Longlady in the face. Not that I ever would punch her in the face, but you fantasize about such things at that age when tired.

★ ★ ★

Everything suddenly went against me. I knew I ought to get Bufo back as we were way past the three-week maximum imposed by my sister, plus our mother had mentioned him. But like always, when you're the lender, you feel selfish asking for the thing back.

My sister was unhelpful in the extreme. She said, 'Oh Lizzie, don't tell me you've not got Bufo back yet.'

This reminded me what it would be like not to have a sister.

And I said, 'You know I haven't got him back yet.'

And she said, 'Well, you'd better sort it out.'

And I said, 'Could you help?'

And she said, 'Just ask Miranda Longlady for him back — God, what's wrong with you?'

So next time I saw Miranda I asked her, in a straightforward manner, for the frog puppet back and she responded, 'Frog? What frog? Oh, *that* frog, your little puppet thing, yes, I'll get it back to you forthwith.'

Then every time I saw her after that, she'd point at me and say, 'Frog'. And never did give it back to me. So I decided that if we were ever to get Bufo back, I'd have to get into the Longladys' house and simply take him.

I came up with the following plan for rescuing Bufo. I made sure I walked home with Melody

144

on her latchkey day, which was Tuesday when her mother was at *Lecciones Espanioles*, her father was on his way to the Charles Keene College for his advanced accounting class, and Miranda was at sports club. And then I'd ask if I might pop in to see the Sindy fashion house she'd been telling me about.

Although Melody was nice, she had some minor defects. Mainly that at only eleven years old she already had silly adult preoccupations. For instance, she always commented on how much things cost and dabbed herself like mad if she dripped anything down her clothes at lunch. Also, she gossiped constantly about her family, inane things, as if they were of great interest to me. Such as how her father always kept an umbrella on the back seat of the car for use in sudden downpours. As well as more unusual things such as the fact that her mother had to keep her pubic hair trimmed right back to prevent the sensation that insects were creeping up her legs in bed.

A suitable Tuesday came and Melody and I reached Orchard Corner — which was the name of the Longladys' home, it being on a corner and having assorted fruit trees in the garden — and I asked if I might pop in. And Melody said, 'Of course.'

It was an added bonus that I got to see Melody in full latchkey mode, a thing I always liked. Approaching the house, she'd look around to check that no one could see her, then fumble down her collar for the front-door key which was on a string round her neck, hanging under her vest. The string was that bit too short, though, and she'd have to bob down to keyhole height to give herself enough string to work with. I always wondered why she didn't just take the key-on-a-string off.

'Wouldn't it be easier to just take it off?' I wondered out loud that day.

'You never ever take your door key off,' she said importantly, 'it's the number one rule of having a door key.'

Inside, Melody said she was starving. She tore off her coat and taking something from a wooden dish, placed it on the sideboard and halved it dramatically with a cleaver. In a different story, this might have been a worrying image. It was a pomegranate and, rather than worrying, it was puzzling — a person claiming to be starving, then eating fruit seeds painstakingly with a pin. She pushed the other pomegranate half over to me. I said, 'No, thanks,' suspecting it might be more ornamental than edible.

Then she showed me the Sindy fashion house, which was Sindy in a polo neck and shorts and surrounded by more clothes on little home-made mini coat-hangers in a cardboard box. It was pathetic really, but I said how great it was, obviously.

'The box came with the tiles for the new shower-room,' she explained.

'Oh,' I said.

'We're having a shower-room built,' she said.

And then I heard about Mrs Longlady's shower unit, which was being installed in what had been a fourth bedroom. Melody tried to tell me the reasons for its installation, but I really needed to get on with finding Bufo before the other Longladys got home.

'Mum can't have baths . . . poor thing,' said Melody, grimacing.

'I'd love to see round your house,' I said. 'Why don't you give me a speedy guided tour while we chat.'

So Melody showed me around upstairs and told me the intimate reasons for Mrs Longlady's incompatibility with baths and the necessity of the shower. I looked as closely as I could without it seeming that I was looking for something. There was no sign of Bufo anywhere. And I'm afraid I left Orchard Corner without him.

I didn't come away empty-handed, though. I had the knowledge that Mrs Longlady couldn't take baths due to unwittingly sucking up the bath water and it seeping out again afterwards for the rest of the day and this causing wetness and all sorts. And that she'd tried bathing at night, but it wasn't much better and she'd needed an incontinence pad in the bed.

At home I told my sister that I'd tried and failed to rescue Bufo, and she'd changed her tune. She said I was making a pointless fuss because our mother had absolutely zero interest in Bufo. I reminded her that Bufo was our mother's last remaining memory of her beloved father. My sister contradicted me and mentioned the lock of hair.

'There's the lock of Grandpa's hair,' she said, 'with the poem in the frame.'

I'd forgotten about the gruesome lock of hair

that our mother's mother had cut from his dead head just after he died and wrapped in a cigarette paper. Our mother had been horrified at the time, but had taken the thing anyway and later at home set it down in a little glass dish. We'd all had a look at it and found it a bit morbid and horrible. Our mother contemplated it with a glass of whisky and inevitably started writing a poem about it, focusing on the way the hair grease had turned the cigarette paper translucent.

The poem was called 'Murray's Superior Pomade' and it mentioned Bufo, now I think about it.

Always Murray's Superior in its orange tin
You didn't like to mix things up
You loved celery in the mornings with salt
    and gin
My Latin frog and your springer pup

Always flattened, so neat, mousey, still
Obedient, waiting, combed
I only knew it oiled
It may have been wavy left alone

The poem seemed to be saying that his hair was always neat and well behaved. My sister said it was about a spaniel dog, not his hair. Whatever, it was written beautifully in looping brown ink on yellow paper, illustrated and framed with the lock of hair behind the glass.

In spite of my sister and the existence of the

poem, I decided it was time to own up about Bufo — if nothing else, to get it off my chest — especially now that I could hide it behind the revelations about Mrs Longlady's pubic hair and seepage anecdotes.

13

Our mother told us she was pregnant. This was an enormous relief to me as it meant I didn't have to own up about Bufo, not yet anyway, and probably had a good year before I had to make another rescue attempt — with a baby on the way. Everything stops for a baby, I find. She seemed highly tense but excited and overall happy. In fact, this was the absolute happiest she had ever been to my knowledge — ditto my sister's — and it seemed I was justified in postponing Bufo's rescue for a while.

Our mother wasn't sure whether or not we'd realized that she and Charlie were intimate in that way. We did realize — my sister and I had seen the two of them. Charlie with his hairy bottom going up and down on top of her, as she lay on the rug in front of the fire, fast asleep. Just as we'd seen it when Little Jack's teacher, Mr Dodd, came round (as previously mentioned) and they'd done a similar thing on that same rug, only our mother had been wide awake that time.

'We must keep it a secret — we mustn't talk about it,' our mother said, meaning the baby, and immediately began reviewing her name choices.

'I think I'm going to call it Jack,' she said.

And my little brother said, 'B-but that's my name.'

And she said, 'No, it is not. Your real name is James. We call you Jack because I like the name Jack better than the name James. You'll have to go back to being James or start being called Jim or Jimmy.'

But my brother Jack didn't like Jim or Jimmy, so he stopped speaking.

'What if it's a girl?' my sister asked.

'Phoebe,' said our mother. 'But it won't be, it'll be a boy.'

'Is Charlie the father?' I asked, and she said, 'Of course he is.' But in such a way that meant 'probably' or 'possibly' or 'I don't know' or even 'no'.

We had to keep it absolutely secret. We weren't allowed to speak about it, even at home, just in case anyone was around. We had a secret code for it among ourselves. It was Bluebell the baby donkey. How silly — it makes me sad to write it — Bluebell the baby donkey.

We'd say, 'When Bluebell comes, I'm going to knit him a little jacket.' And Little Jack would frown. He wasn't looking forward to Bluebell the baby donkey arriving and having to switch over to being called Jimmy or Jim.

'Mother,' my sister said one day, 'should we perhaps start calling Little Jack 'Jimmy' now so we get used to it before Bluebell the baby donkey arrives?'

She said it to upset Little Jack even more. Isn't it funny how siblings do that to each other? Really, my sister's heart was breaking for Little Jack having to give up his name for Bluebell, and yet she felt compelled to poke

151

around in the pain of it.

The pregnancy was wonderful, though — if you didn't count Little Jack's reluctance to become Jimmy. It was, as previously stated, the happiest we'd seen her. And she confided in us that she experienced butterflies in her pelvis from dawn to dusk, which is one up from butterflies in your stomach excitementwise, and is a woman-only thing.

I longed to tell someone — well, Melody. It wasn't worth it, though, because however nice Melody was, she was only really interested in her own family and if I told her about this secret pregnancy she'd be bound to tell me some sickening secret of her own. I'd confided in her once before over a previous thing to do with our mother, only to have her blurt out that *her* mother had taken to wearing a loose kaftan with no underpants and sipping cider vinegar in a bid to combat moistness in her undercarriage. Remembering that and the bath thing, I decided against telling her anything that might in any way lead back to anyone's undercarriage, especially our mother's, which I always wanted to keep private.

Then, a few months into the pregnancy, our mother began to have a miscarriage in the middle of the night when Charlie was at home in his bungalow. It went on and on and there was endless blood and pain. My sister rang an ambulance and they took our mother on a stretcher. As they left the house I said, 'Don't drop her.' I said it so that our mother would hear and know that I cared.

And the ambulance man said, 'Don't worry, love, we never drop people on Wednesdays,' and gave me a reassuring smile.

Later, I realized with a panic that the ambulance had arrived at past midnight, meaning it wasn't a Wednesday at all, it was a Thursday, and therefore they might have dropped her. I let myself cry then, making out it was that silly worry, when really it was the whole unexpected horror.

At five o'clock in the morning my sister and I decided we'd make Mrs Lunt's pot-dots to cheer ourselves up, but it was harder than we thought and we gave up before the pastry dough had 'come together in a soft ball' and chucked it in the bin. So instead we rang a few people up, people we knew, whose numbers were in our book. We dialled and hung up as soon as they answered. The phone would ring and ring and then someone would say, 'Hello?' groggily, with a question mark. We fell about laughing at the groggy hellos. We almost wet ourselves. We even rang our dad and he did the funniest groggy hello. So we did him again but it made us sad the second time. So we decided to phone Charlie, but not to hang up.

A woman answered and said Charlie was asleep and was it an emergency. I said our mother had gone into the Royal Infirmary. There was a pause while the woman and I had realizations about each other.

'I'm sorry, wrong number,' I said.

'I hope things turn out all right, dear,' the woman said.

Then my sister cleaned up the dreadful bed and the blood-soaked towels and didn't even ask me to help — she let me lie on the settee with Debbie. She cleaned the kitchen and fed Debbie and at eight o'clock we got Little Jack ready and set off for school. He dawdled and cried and knew something was up.

'Is Bluebell here?' he asked, waiting at the zebra.

'Bluebell might not come after all,' said my sister.

'We don't know that,' I said, 'not for sure.'

'Bluebell's definitely not coming,' she said (to me).

The smell of pepper filled my nose, which usually meant tears would come. I'd got my heart set on Bluebell: he was real to me and hearing so definitely he wasn't coming — that he'd died — I felt my heart break, I really did. I felt a small but definite crack. But I did a couple of coughs and we crossed the road, all holding hands.

I upset my teacher that morning. She mentioned that I looked 'particularly unkempt' and I said I was sorry but our daily help had let us down.

'Could your mother not get off her backside?' she muttered.

'She couldn't, actually,' I said rather rudely.

'And why is that?' asked Miss.

'She's temperamentally unsuited to doing laundry,' I said.

We did needlework after that and my embroidery stitches took a bad turn. Miss, who was already cross, said she wasn't surprised by my sloppy stitching when our mother was such an irresponsible woman. Which I thought a coincidence, bearing in mind that our mother was — that very morning — at Leicester Royal Infirmary miscarrying an unknown man's baby. Maybe even Mr Dodd's. And Mr Dodd himself was just along the corridor, teaching Little Jack's class leaf-rubbing with wax crayons.

Our mother came home from hospital later that day. She was wretched and awkward, with bluish rings around her eyes. It was very embarrassing. She lay in bed moaning through clenched teeth and wouldn't look up from her pillow. She didn't cry as such, but moaned like an injured and forlorn animal in the forest. And my sister and I knew we had our work cut out.

★   ★   ★

What good does crying do?

None. Not unless you're prepared to cry very loud and in front of people. And we weren't.

OK, there was no Bluebell but, on the plus side, our mother bought a puppy to cheer herself up — a miniature poodle called Honey. Honey took our minds off Bluebell and did all the usual puppy things like shaking a teddy and being sweet with Debbie. It was a help in the happiness campaign, although fairly shortlived because our mother soon got fed up with Honey and stopped finding her delightful. For one thing, she whined and made a horrible noise when eating (like a starving rat), and for another, she had a dodgy leg which popped its socket every now and again and it made our mother feel funny. We liked her, though (Honey): she had a sweet character, was very loving and not aloof like another poodle we'd known (Katie).

Also, still on the plus side, Charlie reappeared and was romantic in his behaviour. Our mother asked why he'd stayed away for so long and he explained that he'd been so short of money he couldn't afford to pay anyone to do the plastering etc. on the two bungalow shells he was doing up, and that meant spending all God's hours doing it himself. Our mother was appalled that such a stupid thing had kept them apart and gave him three hundred pounds to take someone on immediately.

Later, I asked our mother if Charlie might be married. Not that I minded, just that it was as well to know these things.

'Men like him are always married,' she said.

'So will he stay married?' I asked.

Our mother explained that Charlie was stuck in a dreadful rut. And although he was keen to get out of the marriage, he was less than halfway through some major kitchen renovations he started in 1969 and felt he couldn't leave Mrs Bates until it was finished.

'Can't Mrs Bates do it herself?' I asked.

'She's not 100 per cent compos mentis since an accident with a train door,' she said, 'and she's like a limpet clinging on.'

'Can't Charlie just get on with it, then he'd be out of the rut?' I asked, meaning the kitchen.

Our mother reminded me that Charlie was

already renovating two bungalow shells and hardly had a minute. But was doing his best.

I was keen to solve this conundrum and irritated by the shortsightedness of the main players. 'Well, couldn't you get someone like Mr Lomax the Liberal candidate to fix the kitchen?' I asked.

Our mother didn't say anything for a while, but said eventually, 'I did lend him some cash a while ago to get it done, but he's so busy.'

★   ★   ★

One day our mother asked me to go to Charlie Bates's home — which was in the next village — and sneak a look at the kitchen renovations. It was a strange thing to ask me to do, but I did it.

'It's number 12, Bradshaw Street,' she said. 'Don't be seen.'

I went on my Raleigh Rustler. I could cycle no-handed by then (no other girl could). So I emphasized it by folding my arms across my chest. This gesture had the added bonus of making me feel purposeful, a thing I've always liked.

I arrived at Bradshaw Street and cycled past number 12 a couple of times. It was a pretty bungalow with a greenhouse-style porch at the front, full of leggy plants and old pots. I went round to the back and peered through the kitchen window. It was a state. No cupboards or sideboards, just bare breezeblocks, all lumpy with bits of cement. A trolley with a teapot and a tin of Marvel. I saw our old Potterton in the corner. I recognized its distinguishing features. And I saw her, Mrs Bates, with a short grey bob, in the next room, smiling at the telly and perhaps even talking to it.

'So did you see the kitchen?' our mother asked when I got home.

'It needs a lot of work,' I said.

'Sketch it out,' she said. 'I want details.'

'Why?' I asked.

'For Mr Lomax,' she said.

★ ★ ★

Our mother became impatient with Charlie regarding his half-finished kitchen renovations.

'I've a good mind to pay someone to go in and complete the work,' she said, testing the water.

'I thought you'd have got it sorted by now,' said Charlie.

The next day our mother told me to put on my lilac-leaf dress (it looked like hearts but it was leaves), brush my hair out nicely and put a little bow in Honey's head curl.

'Where are you going, all dressed up?' my sister asked.

'We'll be back soon — we'll bring chop suey — look after Jack,' was all she'd say.

And we got into the car and roared off. She told me she was going to face up to Mrs Bates and ask her to have mercy on her and Charlie's love. It made her cry a bit just saying it. And I was infected.

'Wow!' I said, full of pride.

'And offer her some cash to get off his back,'

she added. 'I wonder what she looks like,' our mother wondered.

The truth was she looked nice. Nice round face and a happy smile, even though she was on her own and had no one to smile at except the telly.

'Plug ugly,' I said.

'How do you know?' said our mother.

'I saw her that day I went spying on the kitchen.'

'Why didn't you say anything? Jesus!' she said, and glanced at me. 'Short or long hair?'

'Short.'

'Good,' said our mother. She drove one-handed while she arranged her own (long).

We arrived outside the bungalow and Mr Lomax (the Liberal candidate) was there in his van. Our mother spoke to him through the window.

Honey the poodle jumped out of my arms and ran around the candy-tufted garden, stopping every now and then to worry her hair ribbon with her front paws, like a curly rodent. Our mother knocked and Mrs Bates finally opened the door. Our mother began in a straightforward fashion.

'May I come in, Mrs Bates? I need to talk to you.'

We went in and were ushered into the living room. 'Come through to the lounge,' said Mrs Bates. Our mother winced at the word (lounge) and we all sat down. Honey took an immediate liking to Mrs Bates and vice versa, and though I'm sure Mrs Bates sensed it wasn't going to be a

159

joyful encounter, she fussed Honey and gave her a fig roll off a flower-shaped plate on the arm of her chair.

Mrs Bates told us about the tabby cat called Hilda she'd had for seven years. It had started out all right, but Mrs Bates said that Hilda had totally ignored her for the last five years until one day Hilda went to live with a man at the end of the street. I wondered whether, hearing that sad tale, our mother might have qualms about the message she was about to deliver.

'Dogs are more companiable,' said Mrs Bates.

'Companiable?' said our mother. 'Is that a word?'

'I think so, it means they're more of a companion,' said Mrs Bates.

'Oh, yes, I see, they are indeed,' said our mother.

Our mother offered Mrs Bates an Embassy. Mrs Bates took one and our mother flicked her lighter towards her. As Mrs Bates tilted her head for the little flame, our mother said, 'Charlie and I want to live together. He wants to leave you.'

Mrs Bates didn't seem surprised.

So our mother told how she'd accidentally married a homosexual, and that while she had absolute respect for people of all types, including homosexuals, she couldn't have remained married to him when he was in love with a Vogel's engineer from Ashby-de-la-Zouch. Mrs Bates frowned at the thought and Honey, who seemed to be struggling with the fig roll, swallowed.

Our mother went on that being alone with

three children had plunged her into such a pit of loneliness and driven her to drink such excessive amounts of Bell's etc. and take so many pills that she never knew what day it was. Then she'd met and fallen in love with Charlie. And life had changed for the better and she didn't feel the need for drink so much.

'And the pills?' asked the canny Mrs Bates.

'I'm weaning myself off them day by day,' said our mother, glancing at me. I knew this was true because I'd been to Dr Kaufmann's surgery with her and overheard the conversations therein.

'I don't want to hurt you. Charlie doesn't want to hurt you — it's the last thing in the world we want — but we are genuinely and fully in love,' our mother said in her nice voice.

The doorbell rang and Mrs Bates got up out of her chair to answer it.

'What do you think?' our mother hissed at me. But Mrs Bates was back before I could reassure our mother with 'Yeah, good.' Which was what I would've said.

'So, yes, you were saying?' said Mrs Bates, flopping back into a chair and patting her knees for Honey.

Our mother picked up the threads of her campaign. 'Charlie has explained the state of the kitchen and has told me he feels obliged to make it right before he can leave,' our mother began.

'Well, he ripped it all out years ago and never put it back properly like he said he would,' said Mrs Bates, pointing towards the mismatched Western-style swinging doors.

'Yes, well, I expect you know that I am in a

position to be able to help with the cost of putting it right and, to that end, I've brought a builder along,' said our mother, sounding like one of her own plays. 'Mr Lomax is outside now listening to Radio 2 in his van — he's happy to come in and assess the work needed to give you a brand-new kitchen.'

Our mother waited there to see how the land lay. I thought she might be over-egging it.

'You mean, to pay me off,' said Mrs Bates, twirling Honey's topknot in her index finger.

'Look, Mrs Bates — Lilian — be realistic, please. You know Charlie is going to leave at some point; if not now with me, it'll be someone else. Play ball now and you get your kitchen fixed.'

I hated that she said 'play ball' — it seemed so wrong. But she was doing her best and hadn't been through any training for this kind of thing.

'And make you feel better about taking him,' said Mrs Bates, smoothing Honey.

'It's life, Lilian. You win some, you lose some, and you just take some,' said our mother, 'so let's bring this builder in and you'll actually get something out of it — for crying out loud.'

'I suppose so,' said Mrs Bates, and I was sent out to beckon Mr Lomax in.

Mr Lomax came in, greeted Mrs Bates and began measuring up in the kitchen. I played solitaire with green marbles on a smooth wooden board while he worked and our mother sat anxiously and kept picking up the *Leicester Mercury* and putting it down again. Mrs Bates just sat there rhythmically stroking Honey, who'd fallen asleep with her teeth bared. Soon Mr Lomax reappeared and the atmosphere changed. He had Mrs Bates leafing through chunky files, picking pine-style finishes and handles. He said he'd construct the new units in his workshop and fit them along with a whole array of modern features the following Wednesday. The following Wednesday! Mrs Bates seemed quite pleased at that. And, all being well, he'd have it done in a day.

Mrs Bates showed flashes of real pleasure at some of Mr Lomax's further descriptions — the pan carousel, for instance, that could accommodate more than double the pans of a normal cupboard, the A-Z spice rack and the cascade effect on a glass door panel — and kept putting her hand up to her face to hide her smile. You could see it in her eyes, though.

Mr Lomax said he'd love us and leave us and went, and Mrs Bates was quickly back to her expressionless self.

'So we'll be off too,' our mother said. 'Are you happy with everything?'

'Yes, fine,' said Mrs Bates, not looking at us. She cuddled Honey, kissed her on the nose and then held her out to our mother.

'Why don't you keep her?' she asked.

'The puppy?' exclaimed Mrs Bates. 'But she's yours, and won't the children miss her?'

'They've got Debbie,' said our mother, 'and I can tell Honey just adores you.'

We drove home via the Red Rickshaw takeaway.

'You know what gets me?' our mother said.

'What?' I said.

'She's bloody ancient,' she said.

And then, thinking that happy thought, she smiled and tapped the steering wheel to the beat of imaginary music. Her idea to face up to Mrs Bates had been a good one and it was very nice to see her happy after the loss of Bluebell. The whole project had been clear-headed and purposeful. And she was the happiest I had seen her since the pregnancy.

'All's well that ends well,' said our mother, meaning sorting Mrs Bates's kitchen and dumping Honey.

'Well done, Mum,' I said, 'you're a genius.'

'Thank you, Lizzie.'

'Is Dad a homosexual?' I asked, as we waited for our order in the Red Rickshaw.

'They all are, if you're not careful,' said our mother. 'That's the challenge.'

The others were overly pleased to see us when we got home. It wasn't even late but they were both at the door with Debbie. And I saw how disheartening it must be to get home to desperate-looking children in the porch. It made me hate them and I vowed not to do that again.

14

It was Thursday, the day after the Wednesday when Mr Lomax the builder/Liberal candidate had been and fitted the kitchen units and fripperies in Mrs Bates's bungalow. And we were waiting for the next thing to happen, which was supposedly that Charlie Bates would be released from the marriage and would arrive at our house and start a live-in relationship with us.

Our mother and my sister were bags of nerves and couldn't settle. Our mother unusually optimistic, and my sister worryful as ever.

There were a few doubts on the horizon but I think we all truly believed that, once the kitchen was all done and dusted, Charlie Bates was contractually obliged to arrive in Whisper the Saab with a load of suitcases and a stuffed wolf (or something manly and unusual) and maybe a few presents for us. And we'd celebrate with Seven Stars Around the Moon — the Chinese feast for four people from the Red Rickshaw, but ask them to substitute the pork balls with a plain chicken drumstick (Charlie being funny with foreign food and the pork balls being pure blobs of fat in batter). Our mother looked in the lane for signs of Whisper's arrival, longing for a pat on the back from Charlie for her decisive and trouble-shooting action, followed by some 'So I said, then she said . . . '

However, by about ten o'clock that Thursday

my doubts became grave and I found it difficult to go along with the supposition any longer. As a rule our mother sat in her own sitting room with its special atmosphere, blazing logs and music, but on that day and for the next two she hung around in our 'playroom', chattering nervously and making little nonsensical plans. My sister and I watched telly and read comics and did our utmost to steer her off or ignore her, but it was difficult — she kept having thoughts and ideas.

'As soon as Charlie has moved in, we'll get a new fence around the paddock and make it like racecourse railings and we'll put duck eggs under the broody hens and have ducklings.'

My sister and I — working steadfastly at our origami at that point — nodded and changed the subject and then I accidentally made a paper duck.

'Look — a duck!' shrieked our mother. 'And just as I was talking about hatching ducklings. It's an omen.'

She didn't mean it — she was cleverer than that, but was befuddled by the mix of hope and fear and probably hunger.

'It's a cocked hat,' I said, bringing her back down to earth.

Mrs Bates's kitchen had been fitted, that much we knew. Our mother had driven past twice during the working day and sent me on my Raleigh Rustler towards the end of the afternoon. Mr Lomax's van had been there on all three occasions and you could hear drilling noises. After 5 p.m., our mother had telephoned

Mr Lomax, who'd said the work was complete save a couple of hinge caps for the new swing doors. And though she'd paid in full in advance, there was a few quid outstanding due to price increases and that he'd drop the bill in.

So Thursday slipped by, then Friday and Saturday, and we heard nothing from Charlie Bates. I won't even write about it, except to say our mother sat in her wardrobe for a while, in the space she'd made for Charlie's suits etc.

Then, on Sunday morning, I heard the front door's alarming buzz in a pause in the monstrous clanging of church bells. When I opened the door I saw Honey, our mother's ex-poodle, standing there by the ornamental barrel on three legs, the fourth at an angle — her hip out of joint.

I picked her up and clicked her leg back and dodged her licky face. She smelled of Mrs Bates's Tweed by Lenthéric.

'What does it mean, Lizzie?' our mother said, and before I could respond she repeated, 'What does it mean?'

She took Honey from me and inspected her, turning her over and around and asking repeatedly, 'What does it mean?'

My sister appeared. 'Oh my God, Honey's back, what does that mean?' Which wasn't helpful.

'Maybe Mrs Bates doesn't like poodles,' said my sister.

'Of course she likes poodles, they're her favourite dog — she's always dreamed of getting an apricot poodle,' said our mother, beginning to sound distressed. 'That's the only reason I got her.'

'Do you mean to say you got Honey to trade for Charlie?' my sister asked, a little sadness in her voice.

'Why else would I buy a fucking poodle?' our mother snapped.

We three all sat on the settee in front of our newest mural (cigarette adverts: Rothman's, Silk Cut and Gauloises).

My sister said, 'So it looks as though Charlie has returned Honey.'

'But why,' I said, 'when Mrs Bates clearly liked her so much?'

Our mother just watched and listened to our inane and skirting discussion.

'Why do you think?' said my sister, meaning 'Don't put the ball in my court.'

When I could stand the waiting no more I said, 'It's a sign — a sign that he doesn't want to go along with the plan.'

Our mother screwed up her eyes and you could see her throat moving in her neck.

'He's saying, 'Have your poodle back, it's over.' That's how I see it,' I said.

'Do you think he's saying that?' said our mother, and Honey jumped up on to the settee and our mother batted her off.

'Yes, honestly, I do,' I heard myself say. I'd never been an outspoken person before then, but it felt good being honest and direct.

'Ring him,' our mother said. 'Would one of you please ring him.'

My sister rang, which was very good of her.

But she was the eldest and it was the least she could do, seeing as I'd done everything else re Charlie Bates up to that point. All the cycling and spying and speaking.

'I'm ringing to find out why you brought Honey back,' my sister said into the phone.

'Yes, it does that . . . yes, but not very often . . . I don't *know*, perhaps it's a weakness in the breed.' My sister went on like that and our mother and I were puzzled and kept looking at each other and frowning.

Then she said, 'I see, all right . . . All right, I'll tell her.'

My sister got off the phone and told us that Charlie had brought Honey back because of the defective hip joint. Honey jumped up on to our mother again and this time our mother petted her.

'And he's unhappy about the Liberal candidate going in and tarting the kitchen up without his say-so, and — ' she said, with a pause ' — and it sounds like he has ended the relationship.'

Our mother didn't cry, but gazed into the middle distance and did some elaborate blinking and swallowing.

I'm ashamed to say I did cry, just a few tears, not for us or our mother, but for the kitchen that had been installed and the pan carousel and the whole clear-headed venture going unrewarded — it being all for nothing. And for Honey being dumped back with us, and our mother not even liking poodles, actually thinking they were ridiculous, but getting one as part of the

169

campaign. And for Mrs Bates, who had always dreamed of getting one.

'It's clear now,' said our mother, 'with hindsight I shouldn't have sent Mr Lomax in to do the kitchen. It was stupid, stupid, — but it seemed right at the time.' She lit a cigarette and exhaled through her nostrils and said, still gazing at a place on the wall (where a hairline crack made the shape of a honking goose), 'I'll know next time.'

My clever sister said some of her wisest words. 'Mum, I'm glad you got Mr Lomax to finish the kitchen. Now you know the score.'

And whatever the score was, she had lost. Anyway, she didn't cry or moan, the way she did over Mr Dodd or our homosexual father or losing Bluebell. She drank quite a lot and spilt a glass of Scotch and ginger on my painting (still life with dog bowl) and she reminisced about how great Charlie was and that he never sat down to urinate like other men did (against popular assumption) and that only well-endowed men can actually stand up, like the coalman, and produce a decent flow. And telling us this she began a historical play.

King (Jack): My daughter will choose her prince.
Prince (mother): No prince can urinate without
    a seat.
Princess (me): Pray elucidate.
Prince: He will spray and splash his silken stock-
    ings.
Princess: I want a prince who can urinate stand-
    ing but without spraying his garments.

170

Prince: There is not in this land such a
    prince.
King: Nor in any kingdom beyond.
Princess: Then I do not want a prince.

★ ★ ★

Little Jack's new teacher, Miss Benedict (the
replacement for Mr Dodd, who'd left due to
nerves), rang for a chat to discuss Little Jack's
demeanour (that's what she said). Our mother
was too busy to speak to her at that moment in
time, so the new teacher called round in person
on her way home. They sat at the kitchen table
and my sister and I listened under the window.

'Jack has been very anxious recently and I
wanted to put you in the picture,' said Miss
Benedict.

Our mother hated it when people said things
like 'put you in the picture'.

'What picture?' asked our mother.

'About the donkey,' said Miss.

'The donkey?' said our mother.

'Bluebell,' said Miss.

'Oh, Bluebell the baby donkey,' said our
mother, wistfully.

'Yes,' said Miss, 'Jack has been quite
preoccupied about Bluebell's imminent arrival.'

'We're not getting Bluebell after all,' said our
mother.

'Oh, I see,' said Miss, jolting her head (in a
dramatic and sarcastic manner). 'And is Jack
aware of this change of plan?'

'I'd assumed so, but I'll speak to him and

make sure he's fully in the picture,' said our mother, and her voice gave way slightly.

'Are you all right, Mrs Vogel?' asked Miss.

'Yes, I'm sorry, I'm just — ' voice cracking again ' — just a bit sad about it.'

'About not having the donkey?' said Miss.

'I know, it sounds ridiculous, doesn't it?'

'No, not at all, I think I'd be disappointed too,' said Miss, suddenly sympathetic.

'That's kind of you to say.'

'Perhaps Jack has picked up on your feelings,' said Miss.

'Perhaps,' said our mother.

Miss Benedict said that our mother should feel free to drop into school and let her know of anything she thought might affect Little Jack. Any domestic disruption (such as nearly having a baby donkey but then not having one, for instance).

Our mother thought for a few seconds and told Miss Benedict a true thing about her mother, our grandmother (whom we hardly ever saw due to the fact that they disliked each other intensely and when we did it wasn't very nice except for the cakes). The thing was that our grandmother had splashed out on a pair of red boxing gloves for Little Jack, hung a punchbag in the garage and egged him on, in the hope that it would ward off any homosexual tendencies. Miss Benedict seemed deeply uncomfortable with that. She paused, then said, 'Well, do come into school any time to talk.'

'Thank you for calling in,' said our mother, nicely.

We crouched down and watched Miss Benedict drive away slowly in a brown Vauxhall Viva. Then popped up again to see Jack come out of the larder.

'Jack,' said our mother, 'you *do* know Bluebell isn't coming, don't you?'

Little Jack nodded.

Our mother stroked Little Jack's hair then, and he leant his head on her arm for a moment.

It was a bit embarrassing, but Jack seemed to like it.

15

The idea of the family reunion came to my sister at a family event. We rarely attended these, partly because we weren't often invited and partly because we hated them. But, for whatever reason, we *had* attended on this occasion.

Our mother had been very unhappy after all the Charlie stuff and nothing seemed to help. She'd been to Steiner's hair salon on Horsefair Street and Geraldo had taken three inches off. She'd tried a ponytail and white nail varnish, she'd donated some books to a library including *The Severed Head*, a play script with a rare signature inside, but nothing had made any difference.

We knew not to try to introduce Mr Oliphant yet, it being too soon after the Charlie/Lilian/Mr Lomax tangle, and we'd put the Man List on the back burner. And we were stuck for something to do, when we suddenly attended this family party. We arrived very late and missed whatever the thing was (the christening of a little cousin?) but arrived in time for the bit at the house for drinks and bits of bread and salmon and flaky pastry and nuts.

To be honest, it was a reversal of roles for my sister and me on that day. I could sense the antagonism towards our mother and felt dreadfully uncomfortable. My sister, on the other hand, was keen to get our mother back into the family fold. We stood to the side and talked quietly. My sister reminded me that I'd always thought of the family as ready-made friends who must surely have some affection for her deep down and as 'minerals to be mined', which I'd apparently once said but didn't sound at all like me.

I wasn't sure. 'Look around the room,' I said. 'Which one of them even likes her?'

Two women were talking about vegetables. One was saying she'd had a glut of runner beans and the other was asking if you had to blanch them before freezing and the first one wasn't sure. They were our mother's sisters-in-law.

'They like her,' said my sister, and she reminded me of two incidents in which each of the sisters-in-law had been exceedingly kind.

One of the sisters-in-law had come to stay for a night when our mother had driven (accidentally) off a bridge at midnight. I shan't go into detail except that this aunt-in-law had arrived and been so kind it was almost troubling. She'd cleaned the house from top to bottom and groomed Debbie with a shoe brush and said lovely, soothing things to us. When our mother returned, with a J-shaped scar on her forehead, the aunt had said, 'I don't know how you cope on your own, Elizabeth.' And it was the nicest, most supportive thing anyone had ever said to her and she had to swallow hard and look away to stop herself from crying with gratitude. Which was a shame, because it looked so rude.

The other sister-in-law had come rushing out to Shearsby Bath in her Hillman Imp when my

175

sister hurt herself falling off a pony. She could easily not have bothered but she did bother, even though it was miles away and petrol being so expensive and she had her own little children too. And she was nice and made nothing of her trouble. I seem to remember her buying us a round of Toffee Crisps on the way to the infirmary.

My sister reminded me, forcefully, that our well-established unpopularity within the family was a result of us having slipped out of the loop due to the divorce and not that they didn't like us as people.

'They just don't like what we've become,' she said, 'feral and manless.'

It was a vicious circle, she said, a circle that we just needed to break.

Plus there was an unmarried brother of a sister-in-law who was very practical and loved books and might do for the Man List.

In the end I consented to give it a go, but we agreed also that we would sidestep our maternal grandmother — a prickly woman, as previously mentioned — who seemed to like making people feel bad about themselves, which was easy with our mother who had failed at marriage, had two abortions and a miscarriage, a drink problem, an addiction to prescription drugs and who, for some reason that I can't explain, had a habit of storing stemware upside down in the cupboard — a thing which always infuriates the well-bred.

Then, just as we'd finished discussing and agreeing, a tipsy uncle or an aunt or a cousin in a group of uncles and aunts and cousins mentioned a pending holiday, saying, 'We're all off to Dorset.'

My sister butted in and asked, 'Oh, Dorset, lovely, where exactly?' and 'When?' and 'What's the name of your house?' and so forth, and the tipsy aunt or uncle or whoever told her all the charming details.

On the way home our mother said what cunts they all were. My sister objected. Our mother stuck to her guns and gave examples of their cuntishness. Little Jack joined in with our mother and said that an uncle had said nasty things about our father. 'What did he say?' our mother asked.

'That Dad was a bloody disgrace,' said Little Jack.

Our mother was furious then and we sped home. 'The fucker, how dare he!' she ranted, as we flew over the very bridge she'd driven off the year before and got the J-shaped cut.

'He only said he was a bloody disgrace,' said my sister.

'He shouldn't have said it in front of Jack,' snapped our mother.

Back at home, my sister told our mother that we'd been invited to join the group of uncles and cousins and their various offspring on the holiday — not really expecting her to believe it or be prepared to actually go to Dorset at such short notice, but to feel a bit better about them and have nicer feelings towards them.

But she did believe it and she was prepared to go and so, can you believe it, we went. We asked a lady at Merryfield's bakery (the only nice person for miles around, bar the doctor and Mrs C. Beard) to feed the ponies and she was delighted. And we asked Mrs C. Beard to have Debbie but she wasn't delighted, so we went back to the lady who was delighted about the ponies and asked her to have Debbie as well and, lo, she was delighted about that too.

'We've been invited, at the last minute, to stay in a holiday house with our family,' we told her, 'in Dorset.'

'Well, you don't want to miss out on that,' said the nice lady at Merryfield's. 'It's important to get together.'

And in our excitement, we sort of believed we had been invited too and it was the most wonderful feeling — to have been included — and we all felt marvellous about it. Our mother was cheerful as we packed and bought us new stripy beach towels from Woolco on the way, and I used deodorant for the first time in my life — Three Wishes 'Woodland Fern' — and the smell was glorious and fresh and I reapplied it when the smell wore off until my armpits were white.

My sister hated the cold strangeness of my aerosol and preferred Mum roll-on, the blue version, same as our mother. I would have loved all three of us to use the same, but I found the roll-on sticky and not so invigorating. My sister packed a camera that might have been Charlie's that she'd discovered in the garage, and Little Jack packed a torch and some tins of Scotch Broth which he loved at that time.

Our mother spoke to Mr Lomax, who had popped round to do an odd job, and he helped her look on a road atlas. Mr Lomax was a member of the Institute of Advanced Motorists (which meant he could turn on a sixpence and park in a shoebox) and he was able to give her lots of tips for driving long-distance: have plenty of coffee stops and if you find yourself nodding off at the wheel, rock back and forth vigorously and open a window, and if the worst comes to the worst, get one of the children to tap you repeatedly on the head.

Halfway there my sister and I had some feelings of anxiety and whispered to each other during a coffee stop. Suppose the uncles and aunts weren't pleased to see us? we asked ourselves. Suppose there wasn't room in the house? But we talked ourselves round. I think we said that once we'd arrived and settled they'd see how funny we all were and inventive and good at games and so on, and we'd have a breakthrough and all cook a communal supper together and we'd sleep on fluffy cushions in a sitting room with the tail-end of a fire in the grate.

Arriving in Dorset, we drove into the mossy gravel driveway (mossy gravel gone spongy with years and years of dropped pine needles) outside a square Georgian house standing in all-around grounds (the sort I loved and still do). In the time it took to see how utterly lovely it all was, our mother discovered it had not been an invitation at all but an embarrassing misunder-standing, and after seeing the puzzled and embarrassed expressions we went away again and drove the hundreds of miles home. No one spoke except for Little Jack, whose garbles were like an irritating tune that soon you don't even hear.

It was worse than Mr Dodd and Charlie and the vicar and the kitchen caper and everything. It was deeply shaming and my sister, for once, felt guilty. So guilty that she agreed with my long-held belief that she should join in with the play from time to time, and not begrudgingly but enthusiastically — just to ease the misery.

> Aunt F: Christ! It's Adele and the kids.
> Uncle G: What the hell are they doing here?
> Aunt D: They've turned up out of the ruddy blue.
> Uncle C: Not that bloody menace and her brood?
> Uncle G: Duck everyone, play dead.

The morning after our return from Dorset we had the embarrassment of going to tell the nice lady from Merryfield's bakery that she wouldn't need to look after Debbie or the ponies after all — we blamed an uncle's tonsils — and the woman was very sympathetic and said he should consider getting shot of them.

My sister wanted to come up with something lovely to help our mother get over the utter humiliation and the long drive. We started by making bread rolls with a great lump of leathery dough given to us by the nice lady from Merryfield's, who said there was nothing in the world better at cheering people up than freshly baked rolls. It reminded us of Mrs Lunt's similar claim for jam tarts.

We divided the dough into four, put them into the oven and waited for them to be cooked. The nice bready smell did its best to make us feel better and then, while they cooled, we went and sat with our mother in her bed. My sister read to us from some funny memoirs and was about to offer to do more of the play, when Little Jack rushed downstairs and back again with a letter and a leaflet that had come through the letter box. The letter was the bill from Miss Woods's shop and the leaflet was advertising the Summer Garden Party.

'Not another bill,' said our mother, looking at Miss Woods's letter, and then, 'Not another fair,' looking at the leaflet.

And then we all felt the need for the bread rolls. My sister said she might pop across for some raspberry jam and our mother said could we make do without the jam due to her having no money handy to pay the bill. And in fact, could we steer clear of Miss Woods's shop for the time being.

We had the bread rolls plain and discussed the Summer Garden Party. It was to be held on the first Saturday of the July Fortnight. It was going to be run as if the year was 1945 — its inaugural year. There were to be dog classes, terrier racing, a flower show, a white elephant and second-hand clothing stalls as well as a tea dance. There was even going to be condensed-milk toffees for prizes just as there had been in 1945 ('the prizes will be cash in appropriate amounts and toffee from a wartime recipe in the waxy paper of yesteryear'). Little Jack loved the word yesteryear but said it should mean the year before this current year, not the olden times in general which we insisted it meant.

The Garden Party reinforced my sister's feeling that we should dump Charlie Bates once and for all because it presented an opportunity to make a proper move on the much more preferable (in her eyes) Mr Phil Oliphant. My sister decided to enter Debbie in one of the dog classes in order to firm up our acquaintance with Mr Oliphant, seeing as he was to be the senior judge in all canine events bar the terrier racing. Her goal was to make sure he met and shook hands with our mother, who would be standing beside me to the left of the collecting ring. Men found it almost impossible not to fall in love with her once they'd shaken her hand — or so my father once said. So it was essential I was there to position her while my sister manoeuvred Mr Oliphant towards us as he exited the arena.

My sister was sold on Mr Oliphant and constantly reminded me of his attributes. And overall I agreed, Mr Oliphant actually being a nice man whom people respected. You have to be extremely respected to be one of the judges at the Garden Party. And, thanks to my sister going round to his house looking for a pony, we were sort of friends of his, acquaintances anyway. Also he was handsome in a well-dressed-farmer type of way, unlike Charlie, who looked like something out of an old film — always smoking and looking sly and like he was about to kill someone with a hidden gun.

On the day of the party it took us quite some time to convince our mother to even come to the show, let alone to place her in the hand-shaking position for the dog judge.

'I really can't be doing with it,' she said, sounding just like our old help, Mrs Lunt.

'The whole village — no, the whole parish — will be there,' I said.

Our mother groaned.

'It's going to be old-fashioned like the wartime of yesteryear,' I said, which was wrong again.

'Only a bit wartime-ish,' said my sister, 'but there's a flower show and Mr Gummo's showing his sweet peas and a rare alpine,' she said, proving it was worth listening to gardeners when they speak. Our mother was fond of Mr Gummo since he'd covered the manhole and not minded about the rumours, and it was clever of my sister to have plucked that out of her memory when everything I plucked was such a turn-off.

Eventually, it was the idea of seeing Debbie in the dog show that appealed to our mother, and she went to her room to get ready and reappeared in a flimsy dress whose pattern could have been the dancing shadows of a wind-blown tree — but might equally have been a coffee stain. She'd taken to wearing hats in public and that day wore a floppy one to suit the dress. And sandals which were so flimsy it was as though there was no sandal at all, only a thin leather string looping her big toe and heel. She looked a dream.

I was telling the truth when I said that

everyone in the whole parish of four villages would be at the Summer Garden Party. It was held every year in the grounds of Kneebone cottage hospital, which wasn't actually in the village and only did varicose veins, bunions and appendixes. Not knee bones, or anything tricky or potentially fatal, the only death in twenty years having been a lonely chiropodist in a window leap.

The dog show element was very much just for fun and not like Cruft's or anything where you had to take surgical spirit to the dog's paws and put Carmen rollers in their hair. There were various classes, the first being the Dog Most Like Its Owner, in which Mrs C. Beard's daughter, Charlotte, won first prize with their boxer dog, Minnie. Mrs C. Beard seemed thrilled, but Charlotte did not and she didn't want her toffees of yesteryear.

My sister entered Debbie in the All-rounders, which was open to all dogs and was 50/50 (beauty/obedience). In the starting line-up, Debbie snapped at a little brown dog called Teasel. It was unlike Debbie to snap and my sister said so to Mr Phil Oliphant when he came round doing his close-up inspection of the entrants.

'Debbie wouldn't usually snap,' she said, loud enough for the audience to hear.

Mr Oliphant suggested it might be the stress of the event and said Debbie was a lovely bitch in spite of the uncharacteristic snap. Then he went on to inspect Teasel and commented that Teasel looked like a teasel. Then he turned to my sister and said, 'Doesn't this little dog look exactly like a teasel?'

My sister nodded and agreed that Teasel the dog looked just exactly like a teasel, as if it was a good thing and amusing.

Mr Oliphant found nice things to say about all the dogs in the show, and of course Teasel won first prize.

My sister didn't mind not winning and wasn't surprised, especially after Debbie had snapped at the eventual winner (Teasel).

We stood at the rope, watching the last of the dog classes — the obstacle course with obedience aspect. My sister was delighted to report that Mr Oliphant had remembered her and had asked her if she'd found herself a pony yet.

'What did you say?' I asked.

'I said yes, I had found a pony called Sacha and he was very nice but that my sister, you, were now looking for a pony,' she said, beaming.

'But I'm not,' I said.

'I know, but I said you are and he said he'll keep his ear to the ground for us,' she said, wide-eyed and nodding slightly, 'and is more than happy to look at any pony we're considering and give it the once-over.'

'Why, though? I don't want a pony,' I said.

'Him and Mum — you know,' she said, exasperated, 'just pretend you do.'

I was losing faith in Mr Oliphant. First of all, he was just too nice, and also I'd seen him walking round the show in a straw boater with his judge's badge on and linking arms with a

185

woman. And as if that wasn't enough to put you off, there he was commenting that dogs looked like teasels when no one except him knew what a teasel was. My sister said he might've meant a weasel, but I thought he was just showing off knowing what it meant. I bet the owner didn't even know.

'I've seen him linking arms with a woman,' I said.

'That's only his wife,' said my sister. 'The marriage is on the rocks.'

'How do you know?' I asked.

'I just know, plus you don't walk round linking arms with a wife if the marriage isn't on the rocks. Linking arms is a sign, a very bad sign.'

'Then why do it?' I asked.

'Don't ask me, people just do it, it's desperate. It's instigated by the weaker partner,' she said. 'We did it in Science. It's animal behaviour.'

Then I had to go and fetch our mother and Little Jack so that we'd be in time to introduce her to Mr Oliphant. We watched the last few dogs run through fabric tunnels and sit down. That bloody Teasel won again, which was pretty annoying. Then the dogs and owners filed out of the ring, followed by Mr Oliphant, and my sister waylaid him as planned.

'Mr Oliphant,' she called. 'Mr Oliphant, I'd like you meet our mother.' And he veered off course.

'Hello, Mrs Vogel, how very nice to meet you,' said Mr Oliphant, as he took her hand gently in his.

Our mother looked so pretty with loops of soft

hair falling around her bare shoulders. Her sleepy green eyes looking so unusual and big under the floppy hat. She was by far the best-looking woman at the show — the pill-induced wooziness, and the light shapes in the dress pattern which moved like fluffy clouds in the summer sky, all adding to the general effect.

'This is the dog judge, Mr Oliphant,' my sister told our mother loud and clear. 'He's offered to help us find the perfect pony for Lizzie.'

'Golly, what a very kind dog judge,' said our mother. Mr Oliphant laughed as if she'd been joking, but I didn't see what the joke was.

So Mr Oliphant had shaken her hand and been a bit mesmerized by her and had seemed — for all of the moments it took — to be in love with her, but then the woman I'd seen him linking arms with waddled up and claimed him back. I could see what my sister meant: the marriage did seem to be on the rocks. The magical atmosphere created by our mother's prettiness, the sleepy sensuality brought on by a mixture of her nice eyelids and the pills, was washed away by this woman, like a bucketful of Jeyes Fluid dashed on to a grubby step.

'Phil,' she said, 'you're wanted in the committee tent.'

'Am I?' said Phil Oliphant, sadly.

★　★　★

My sister and I wandered off to see the small pets, while our mother and Jack went to see the

187

pork pies in a tent. Apparently there was a clever one with a layer of chutney under the pastry lid that Jack had read about in a leaflet. A few minutes later Mrs Frink from the hunt announced that the organizers were looking for help to get the piano up on the stage, as the Talent Show was about to begin.

Everyone flocked to the stage to get a good seat. The deck-chairs were soon all taken and my sister unfolded our rug again and we sat on it with Debbie in between us. Our mother and Little Jack failed to see us waving at them and stood on the other side of the stage, watching from behind a trestle table strewn with second-hand clothes, Little Jack nibbling the pastry off his pie.

The show began and two girls did a ballet routine called *Goose Pond*, which was meant to be like *Swan Lake*. Judging by its boringness, it probably was quite like *Swan Lake* and people started fidgeting. Then a boy sang 'Blue Suede Shoes' very quickly, which was slightly better than the ballet. Then a girl read a poem she'd written about a river flowing out to sea, which was easily the worst of the three.

Then a very small girl did a tap dance and burst into tears, which I didn't count, and two girls did a reasonable gymnastics routine with one-handed cartwheels and the splits. The audience enjoyed it until one of the girls couldn't get right down into the splits for the finale and it looked awkward and no one clapped. But overall, it was probably the best. So far.

Last, but by no means least, suddenly there

was Miranda Longlady. My sister and I were agog seeing her up there. She was smiling the smile of an entertainer (mad but professional-looking) and wearing a yellow dress and a bowler hat. She took her time in setting up the stage. And looking at her, it was as though the sun had come out — this was partly because Melody, her egg-twin, was shining a strong torchlight upon her, and partly because the sun had in fact just come out. After welcoming the audience to the show, Miranda brought out Bufo, our mother's frog puppet, from a little box. Bufo was shy at first and hid under Miranda's arm. She'd put a yellow ribbon round his neck to match her dress and the ribbon around her hat. I hated her.

She began, 'Ladies and gentlemen, let me introduce you to Freddie the frog.'

I glanced at our mother across the trestle table. She was very alert and open-mouthed. I felt very awkward. I felt embarrassed to see Bufo up there, as though he was my child or brother or something, and I felt ashamed that our mother would see him. Her being in no fit state to be seeing frogs from her childhood that I'd lent without asking.

Freddie the frog soon gained his confidence and bowed. The two of them performed a hysterical routine, with Mrs Frink accompanying on the piano (as she had with the *Goose Pond* girls and the gym duo). They finished with a short, flirty, comical conversation. Miranda had become an accomplished puppeteer and when they were done, the audience laughed and clapped and called out, 'More!'

189

Mrs Graham-Golding came on to the stage still laughing and clapping. Almost incapacitated, she had to lean on a chair while she got her breath back.

'Oh my goodness me. Oh dear,' she panted, 'that was wonderful, was it not, ladies and gentlemen? Thank you, Miranda and Freddie.' Miranda curtsied and Bufo waved. And everyone clapped again.

I looked over at our mother and we gave each other a long and wide-eyed stare. Then Mrs Graham-Golding appeared on stage again with her co-judge, Mr Frink from the hunt, to announce the contest winner. It was Miranda, of course, and Bufo, and she was called up to receive her little trophy and a bag of the wartime toffee.

I felt confused. My sister was clearly of the opinion that it had been a good result. My own overall feeling was of deep resentment and anger and jealousy and the feeling (yet again) that I wanted to punch Miranda in the face. I looked around and saw our mother step away from the trestle and waylay Mrs Graham-Golding in a similar fashion to my sister's waylaying of Mr Oliphant (determined and a bit abrupt). I jumped up from the rug, but by the time I'd got close enough to hear the conversation, it was coming to an end.

'I see, well, that is a shame. It's a tricky situation,' Mrs Graham-Golding was saying, 'let me see what I can do.'

Soon after that, the judge appeared back on stage. She apologized for asking for the audience's attention once again. 'Just before we commence with the tea dance, I should like to announce that Freddie the frog, joint-winner of the Talent Contest, was appearing by kind permission of Miss Lizzie Vogel and the judges have decided that Lizzie should be awarded some toffee.'

There was a ripple of applause and I made my way up to take the little paper cornet from the smiling judge.

Miranda stood close to the stage. 'What a freakish lot those Vogels are. First, they force the stupid bloody frog on me' — she turned to Melody — 'didn't they, Mel? And now they want my glory for that little idiot Lizzie.'

Melody nodded vigorously until Miranda smacked the top of Melody's head. And as I clambered off the stage, Miranda flung Bufo at me.

'Here's your frog back.'

I was happier than I had ever been. It wasn't the justness, the frog back or the toffee. It was that our mother had acted for me, for us. It was the look we'd given each other across the trampled grass and the warped trestles. And that we'd been thinking the same thing.

Later I said to our mother, 'Isn't she the bitter end?' which was the kind of thing she'd say, having been brought up in the 1950s.

Our mother nodded. I wanted more, though.

'I hate her, don't you, Mum?' I said.

'No. I don't hate her,' she said, 'but she is the bitter end.'

16

While we waited for Mr Oliphant to come good, I'm afraid to say a dispute arose regarding control of the Man List. I'd always known my sister was pretty much the boss, but I thought there was an understanding that we both had to agree before any man was added.

Mr Nesbit was an oldish man with a full beard who had apparently once lived in a section of our house. He often sat on the street bench almost opposite, sucking Nuttall's Mintoes, shouting out about the Suez Canal and inviting children to knock on his wooden leg.

Looking at the Man List one day, I was surprised to see Mr Nesbit's name had been added without prior discussion, albeit with a question mark. I knew only too well that men were a bit thin on the ground in the village and our mother was in need of cheering up after the disastrous attempt to re-engage with the wider family, but I was 100 per cent anti-Mr Nesbit. It was a notion too ludicrous to even discuss, but his name was there in blue pen so I had to.

'Why have you added Mr Nesbit to the list?' I asked, hoping it might be a different Mr Nesbit, a doctor in the next village or something.

'Why not?' she said.

'You mean to say it actually is *the* Mr Nesbit?' I said. 'He's virtually a tramp.'

'He's a war veteran, Lizzie,' said my sister.

'He's got mental problems,' I said.

'He's been through some trying times,' said my sister.

'Mum would never cope with the wooden leg,' I said.

'She'd bloody well have to get used to it,' said my sister, sounding very cross.

'It would be a disaster,' I said.

'We said we wouldn't rule anyone out,' my sister reminded me.

'I'm ruling Mr Nesbit out,' I said.

'Well, I'm saying give him a chance,' said my sister.

'No,' I said, 'he's temperamentally unsuitable for the helm.'

I felt uncharitable but very sensible. We couldn't have someone on the list who habitually shouted, 'Get off and milk it,' as we rode past him on our ponies. Plus, how could we work together if she could act in that unilateral manner? Not that I would have used those words at that time. Obviously.

'How would you like it if I added someone without your say-so?' I said.

'You can add whoever you like,' she said.

So I did. I added an equally undesirable man to the list — someone I knew my sister would never want at the helm. Someone on a par with Mr Nesbit.

Mr Terry the butcher was one of those cheerful, involved-in-the-village types who collected money for the Xmas decoration committee and donated pieces of meat and premium sausages to the Summer Garden Party.

'You've added Mr Terry to the list,' said my sister.

'Yeah, I know, he's nice. He's a redhead. Mum loves a redhead,' I said.

'He's a butcher, Lizzie,' said my sister.

'Is that bad?' I asked.

'I'm a vegetarian,' said my sister.

'You can't rule him out just because you're a vegetarian,' I said. 'He's a redhead.'

'Mum's a vegetarian,' said my sister, clutching at straws.

'No, she's not,' I said.

'How do you know?' she said.

'I saw her eat a chicken's leg on New Year's Eve,' I said.

'She was drunk and had forgotten about being a vegetarian,' she said.

In the end we agreed to delete both Mr Terry and Mr Nesbit.

I wouldn't really have wanted Mr Terry the butcher either. Not with our squeamish mother and all those bloody aprons, but I'd rather him than Mr Nesbit and his slogan-shouting and the leg propped up outside the bathroom door.

★　★　★

The pills our mother got from Dr Kaufmann and Dr Gilbey of Devonshire Place were a help, but the truth was that she remained basically unhappy without anyone grown-up in her life to have chats or sex with. I suggested she make friends with Mrs C. Beard across the road — for chats. But she wasn't keen, probably because

194

Mrs C. Beard seemed preoccupied with all the wrong things, such as the one-way system in the village and how increased road speeds might affect the duck pond. My sister suggested we buy a new yearling to 'school on', but our mother had had enough of ponies. I think she'd been put off by Robbie, our Shetland gelding, with all his minor ailments and his major one.

I felt let down by the pills: they'd not made enough tangible difference, only causing a hiatus in the laundry resulting in irreparable damage to most of our clothing. So I took the brave step of going to see Dr Kaufmann on my own. I felt we were grown-up enough to seek proper advice and stop groping around in the dark, and made an appointment in the correct manner — on the phone — and when the receptionist asked for a brief description of my ailment I said, 'It's personal,' and the receptionist said, 'I'll make a note to that effect.' So I said, 'It's not an ailment, but a worry.' And the receptionist said, 'Say no more, dear.' And sounded a bit like Dick Emery.

I could tell Dr Kaufmann was uncomfortable when I stepped into the surgery alone because he ran to the door and called his wife to come in. She rushed in and offered me two Smarties, which I thought odd — her being a doctor's wife and Smarties looking like pills. I refused them, just in case they were pills. Dr and Mrs Kaufmann obviously knew about things at our house and looked at me with knitted brows.

I explained that our mother was lonely due to having no moral support and asked him and his wife what we should do for the best. I was careful to look at them both in turn as I spoke, because our mother had taught us always to look at everyone in the group when speaking and never just the man, which one is prone to do.

Dr Kaufmann asked me why now, particularly, I had come for advice. I explained that my sister and I were a bit worried about being made wards of court. He said things really weren't that bad. We shouldn't worry about abstract things, he said, but try to help with the everyday.

'Such as what?' I asked.

'Such as making sure the whole family eats a meal every day,' he said.

And he seemed to think this — the meal thing — was the key.

Dr and Mrs Kaufmann were exceedingly nice and helpful and made me feel so much better. They made me realize that our mother wasn't the only adult who had pills and loneliness. And that sometimes even families *with* a man at the helm had problems. I could have cried with relief.

I didn't say a word about the extra pills we were getting from Dr Gilbey of Devonshire Place. I was tempted momentarily, knowing how cross Dr Kaufmann would be, not with our mother who was, after all, just a person on medication due to circumstances, but with Dr Gilbey, who was supposed to be a trained doctor with huge responsibilities. I imagined Dr Kaufmann getting the train with us to London and having it out with Dr Gilbey, swiping the tumblers of orange squash and little biscuits off the tray and scattering pills on to the floor as a

196

symbol of his anger and calling Dr Gilbey a disgrace, which is about the worst thing one man can say to another without swearing. I couldn't imagine Dr Kaufmann swearing.

* * *

I came away from the doctor's feeling much less worried and reported the recommendations to my sister and we decided between us we should begin a cookery spree — an idea proposed by me ages ago (if you recall) — and I took the moral high ground.

'I warned you about the underweight thing months ago,' I reminded my sister, 'and all you wanted to do was buy more foals.'

My sister was hurt by this and reminded me that it had taken her months to get me to care one iota about our poor abandoned mother and her state of mind.

So we truced, let bygones be bygones and straight away selected a few cookbooks to look at for ideas. We settled on *My Learn to Cook Book* by Ursula Sedgwick because it contained very attractive illustrations of eggs, pies and simple meals and offered clear and detailed guidance via a friendly cat and dog character. The recipes seemed very achievable as opposed to those in the other books, which appeared almost to be written in a foreign language plus had photographs, which were always off-putting as opposed to Ursula Sedgwick's jolly illustrations.

We made Quick Lorraine, which was basically egg and bacon pie except with the addition of grated Cheddar and ground-up peppercorns. The shortcrust pastry was the most difficult part, as it always is, but, using *My Learn to Cook Book*, it turned out great. Then, at tea, eating the Quick Lorraine, we got our mother reminiscing about her cooking glory days. And interwoven was the story of her marriage and its breakdown. Which was news to us.

She told us that, in the early years, she and our father had been a pair of trendy iconoclasts — eating one day at Cranks vegetarian restaurant in Carnaby Street with two baby girls in tow (my sister and me) and the next day, on a whim, they'd leave us with Jane the nice nanny and dine at the Savoy — where his parents kept a suite — and order room service omelettes with vodka and not even bother to eat them but rush out to a show at the last minute and have ice cream. They were free of convention in those days and our mother had loved that. Midway through the 1960s, however, my father was suddenly called back to Leicestershire to take over the family business. It was fair enough: he was in his mid-thirties and it was about time he did a day's work.

My father was impressively able to snap back into the man he was required to be, but our mother struggled. There was something wrong with her. She says it boiled down to the fact that she was so young, only twenty-something, and hadn't ever wanted or needed to be serious and proper, but I suspect it was more that she didn't like the man my father had snapped back into — the true, proper, educated him. To be fair, she'd fallen in love with and married the other version — a person who didn't really exist and had been going through a phase. And that must've been a bit daunting.

It was scary to think you could accidentally marry someone who was in a phase.

Our mother did her best to support him as a wife, and did OK up to a point, on the entertaining side of things with her cookery skills — the foundations of which she'd learned at her boarding school, where they taught girls everything they needed to know in order to be a good wife to a successful man (plus Latin and maths). And then honed the skills at home with Gwen, the family's inventive cook, who was interested in Italian and French foods — a rare thing at the time. Unless in Italy or France.

The dinners our mother produced during those years — between the iconoclastic years and the divorce and before she and he stopped liking each other — were as beautiful to look at as they were delicious to eat, and this was much appreciated by the many business guests our father had to entertain — especially the Americans, who were way ahead of the British in the ways of food apparently.

Our mother's meals often had a clever theme. It was something Gwen the inventive cook had taught her — make the food look interesting and your husband (or guest) will find you enigmatic beyond the plate. And that reminded me of a thing our sports teacher used to say about starting one goal ahead if you and your teammates all have your hair in medium-height

199

ponytails (as opposed to different heights/styles).

Our mother made sure that the meals she served were fascinating. For instance, a flourish of multicoloured steamed matchstick vegetables arranged as a rainbow above a hunk of grilled flesh was called Richard of York Gave Battle in Vain. I could picture it in my mind. Other dishes I could picture were the Tropical Aquarium — tiny savoury shapes in aspic, depicting fish with spinach seaweed. And Picture-frame Pie — which looked, from a distance, like a Cézanne — set with apricot gelatine in ornate pastry, sculpted to resemble the carved wood of a frame. Last one: inspired by Giuseppe Arcimboldo, a fruit and nut platter depicting an old man's swollen face with apple cheeks, a dappled yellow conference pear for his drunkard's nose and half-open Brazil nuts for eyes.

Her ramblings were quite interesting, but more importantly, they offered a perfect run-up to our suggestion for a cookery spree and, as soon as she stopped rambling, we begged her to cook for us and she was quite touched.

'Cook something for us,' we begged.

'No, I can't,' she said coyly, 'I've lost my confidence, foodwise.'

'We beg you,' we said.

'Don't beg,' she said.

'It's only us, Mum. It won't matter what happens. We're not even grown-ups,' said my clever sister, 'and no one will know.'

★ ★ ★

All that chatting and begging led to the risotto a couple of days later.

As our mother began to prepare her ingredients and equipment, my sister went out to groom her pony and teach him to count to three with his hoof, Little Jack read his book about Romans killing people and themselves, and I was left to supervise the risotto, which annoyed me. I was not interested in cookery per se and especially not in watching someone else cook special rice. Plus I hated being on my own with a parent (still do) and I didn't know what to say — whether to encourage, enquire or ignore, having had no experience of cooking or spectating it, except for the Quick Lorraine.

I must say, it *was* amusing, though, seeing our mother at the stove all aproned up and with a low ponytail. She really looked the part, which was odd in itself as I'd never before seen her looking the part — any part — except on a sun-lounger. She had her utensils laid out and the special rice ready beforehand, which seemed a good start, but no recipe book; the recipe was in her head, which seemed bad. She put oil and butter into a pan, added a whole lot of chopped onions and let them cook down while she boiled up some coffee. She then tipped the rice into the onions. It was going well and the comforting aroma of the sweating onions soon began to swirl around and, with it, a feeling of well-being.

She must have got bored then because she suddenly left the cooking area and started writing in her notebook at the kitchen table and swigging the coffee. It was a big kitchen, the table and cooker being at opposite ends. I went over for a peep at the notebook, hoping to see a recipe, but saw what looked like the beginning of a play.

Adele: I thought macédoine.
Roderick: (*irritable*) I asked for julienne.
Adele: But you know I'm afraid of the mando-
line after what happened.
Roderick: But it achieves uniform thickness.

Spotting that, I knew my place was back by the rice and onions — which were now whining softly in the pan and begging to be stirred. I didn't, though (stir). I knew, even at that young age, you don't stir someone else's pan, however desperate the situation. And that people who do are outrageous interferers and have no respect for the person whose pan it actually is. Gwen had taught our mother this years ago and then, when my sister unthinkingly stirred a pan of grated potato that was meant to be staying in one piece, our mother explained the rule to us.

I became a bit alarmed about the rice and onions — it looked as though it might be starting to burn. The onions and oil had gone to nothing and it was left to the rice to take the heat. The whole thing had taken a turn for the worse and a new sound was emitting from the pan, an agonized hiss, and the anxious smell of hot metal obliterated the comforting aroma of sweating onions. I decided I must speak out, and though I knew my interference would have an adverse effect on the project (and would make our mother hate me), I had to try to save the risotto. I guess this is the worrier's dilemma. Speak out and be despised, or live with devastation.

'Can rice burn?' I asked.

'No, not really,' she said, without looking up from her notebook.

I struggled on. 'Are you sure?' I said, in a dreadful high voice.

'About what?' she said, looking up now, annoyed.

' . . . that rice can't burn,' I said, and she sprang up and crossed the smoky room.

'Why didn't you tell me it was burning?' she said.

'I did,' I said.

'Jesus!' she said, and flung the pan into the sink. The kitchen filled with hissing steam and it was as though Stephenson's derailed Rocket had burst through the wall. The others appeared and asked what had happened and my sister looked at me, blamingly.

'You didn't stir her pan, did you?' she asked.

'No, I didn't,' I said. 'I'm not stupid.'

That was the end of the risotto. But happily it didn't put her off altogether and it wasn't long before she dragged out a huge, rather stained earthenware pot (given to her by Mrs Vanderbus, who no longer needed the capacity) and cooked a casserole of frozen chicken wings. The result was a soup of fingery bones and soft carrots in a soupy liquid — but quite nice and a success in terms of filling the house with the comforting aroma of stewing onions and not burning.

And she carried on for a while with

low-maintenance dishes, mainly stews in the earthenware pot and sometimes roasted fruits with demerara sugar and custard, and I just wished that one day Dr Kaufmann would peer in through the window and see the scenes of meal production and note how sensibly I'd taken his advice. Sadly, I have to admit that our mother didn't actually eat much of the food herself — just picking at it while she cooked — carrot coins and the odd spoonful here and there. The point was, though, that she was buying and cooking food and that was very good for the campaign to keep us out of the Crescent Homes.

17

Charlie Bates's non-appearance all this time should have been a relief to my sister and me, but after a while it wasn't. We could have done with him. We actually missed him and the way he made our mother feel.

It had been the same when we'd lost our father, who'd seemed nothing but a killjoy and table-manners tyrant, but then not having him at home with us had been disastrous, albeit gradually, like pulling at an irritating thread and accidentally unravelling your cuff, then your sleeve, then the whole jumper. After a short while we felt the lack of him and yet felt uncomfortable with him. The problem was, we didn't know him any more. Each day that passed we grew and changed, and every time we saw him he seemed settled more snugly into his new life. He even got a new dog.

My sister said it wasn't that having a man was good, but that not having one was bad. And that men were just irritants of one sort or another that you'd rather have than not. And it was that (the rather having than not) that explained all the unpleasant, crosspatch fathers you saw in armchairs and driving seats, and reading newspapers before anyone else was allowed. Women and children would simply rather have them than not — even with all their habits and bad breath — and that was the basis for the repeat pattern we were desperate to repeat.

Anyway, Mr Phil Oliphant hadn't shown any signs of popping in with news of a suitable pony for me, and since there was no one else on the horizon and nor did we feel inclined to scrape the bottom of the barrel and apply for the retired mechanic or the gardener quite yet, we said we'd do what we could to repair Charlie and our mother's relationship.

I know it doesn't make sense and I'm sorry, but that's life, I'm afraid.

My sister's recent reading led her to the conclusion that Charlie's love for our mother had 'fallen asleep' and just needed reawakening. This mostly happened in ancient marriages where one partner has gone to seed physically or mentally. Apparently love couldn't be awakened with the gentle opening of the window blinds or a cup of tea at the bedside, but needed a proper jolt — a metaphorical pulling off of the sheets and a dead leg.

My sister thought it through carefully and devised the following plan to reawaken Charlie's love. One of us (me) would go to the Piglet Inn and blurt out to Charlie that our mother was paired off with someone else. This news would be said as if blurted out without thinking and would make Charlie wild with jealousy and regret. I wasn't entirely sure what 'paired off' meant, so I double-checked.

'You'll just drop into the conversation that she's going out with Mr Lomax,' my sister said.

'Mr Lomax — really?' I said.

'It's got to be Mr Lomax,' said my sister.

'Not again,' I said.

'Well, why not? He's the obvious choice,' she said.

'Not the crab,' said Little Jack, with a bored person's very good memory for things from a long time ago. 'I don't like him.'

'Look, she doesn't actually have to *go out* with him. Charlie just needs to think she is. And someone just needs to mention it in front of him,' she said, with her hands up in a USA-style gesture meaning 'Come on, guys!'

'We just need to accidentally-on-purpose blurt out that she's having a romance with someone,' she said. 'Anyone would do . . . but Lomax is probably best.'

Jack's objections caused a brief discussion as to who the fake new lover should be for maximum impact, but we remained in favour of Mr Lomax as the reawakening conduit — him being a handyman of repute, a holder of the Confederation of Registered Gas Installers certificate and a Liberal, plus his alleged ability to sit through Shakespeare, if need be, which Charlie couldn't (having once said to our mother that he'd rather stick a pin in his eye than see *Hamlet* at the Haymarket).

The plan was that I would go to the Piglet Inn and buy two fleur-de-lys pies. And accidentally bump into Charlie. I had a few rehearsals and the following Saturday I mounted the Raleigh Rustler and went to the Piglet Inn. Charlie was there, which surprised me for some reason, leaning on the bar reading the racing paper. I tapped him on the elbow and he looked down at me and nodded.

'What are you doing in here?' he grunted.

'I've come to get two pies,' I said.

'Well, I've come to get drunk,' he said.

'Why?' I said.

'I ask myself the same thing all the time,' he said.

'You should try to cut down on it,' I said.

Then the barman asked Charlie what he was having and Charlie said he'd better serve me first — before I put the Piglet out of business with my prohibitionist talk.

'Two takeaway steak pies,' I said, and the barman went away to get them and that was my chance to blurt out the lie. But in spite of many successful rehearsals, when it came to it, standing there with the overwhelming stench of cigarettes and beery carpets and the sense that the whole room was staring at me, it was hard to deliberately blurt it out. It's easy to blurt things out naturally when you don't mean to and you shouldn't, but when you're *trying* to the time never seems right, then you wait too long, the perfect moment passes and then if you wade on and insist on blurting it, it seems 100 per cent deliberate (which it is).

Plus you can only drop something into a conversation if you're actually having a conversation, which you never are with Charlie — him not being a conversationalist.

Anyhow, I didn't manage to blurt it out. I paid for the two pies and said, 'Bye, then,' to Charlie and he looked at me with his red eyes and said,

'Bon appeteeto,' which was strange, him hating Italy so much.

I left the bar and went to get my bike. As I was leaving the Piglet car park, I saw Mr Lomax go into the bar. I waited a moment and then watched through the window from the roadside. Mr Lomax went to the bar. Then he and Charlie went together and sat at a little round table, like best friends, with their pints and what looked like pies. It was strange because when, previously, I'd mentioned Mr Lomax to Charlie, he said he knew of him but hadn't been introduced.

I cycled home, and though nothing awful had happened I was troubled by the thought that I could easily have been mid-blurt when Mr Lomax arrived. And that Charlie might, right this moment, be relaying the lie to Mr Lomax. I felt that panicky feeling you have after a stupid near-miss. At home I couldn't face telling the others that I'd failed to blurt out the lie about Mr Lomax, nor could I bring myself to say that Charlie and Mr Lomax were having a drink together like old friends, and maybe even a pie.

'Was he there?' my sister crowded me.

'Yes, he was at the bar,' I said.

'So what did you say?' she asked.

'I just let it slip that Mum was dating Mr Lomax,' I lied.

'Dating?' said my sister.

'Yes.'

'Did you say 'dating'?' she persisted.

'No, I think I said she's *going out with* Mr Lomax,' I lied.

'Good, 'going out with' sounds more modern and sexual. What did Charlie say?' said my sister, excited at the thought.

'He looked really furious,' I lied. 'His eyes looked sideways, like he was imagining it.'

Then, for some reason, my sister decided to bring our mother in on it.

'Lizzie has told Charlie that you're going out with Mr Lomax,' she said.

'What did you tell him that for?' asked our mother.

'To make him jealous,' I said.

'To reawaken his love,' my sister said.

'Oh?' said our mother. 'What did he say to that?'

'He was furious and jealous,' I lied, quietly.

Jack and I sat down to the fleur-de-lys pies and I put my troubled feelings to the back of my mind. But then around five o'clock that afternoon Mrs C. Beard came over and told us something that brought my troubled feelings back to the front of my mind. Mr Lomax's van had blown up. Mr Lomax wasn't in it, he'd been moving a radiator in Mr Terry's flat above the butcher's shop when the van, parked in Mr Terry's space behind the shop, suddenly and for no apparent reason blew up and caught fire.

My sister gripped both my arms.

'What?' I said.

'Oh my God! Charlie's tried to kill Mr Lomax,' she said, 'because of what you told him.'

'No,' I said, 'it was probably just a coincidence.'

'There's no such thing as a coincidence,' she

210

said. 'It's when things coincide.'

'Exactly,' I said, 'they coincide and that doesn't mean the two things were connected.'

'What two things?' asked our mother.

'Lizzie telling Charlie you're dating Lomax and Lomax's van being blown to smithereens,' said my sister.

'It wasn't smithereens, it's still in one piece,' said Little Jack, who'd somehow seen it.

'It sounds like a non-verbal message,' said our mother, seeming awfully pleased.

'I suppose so,' I said, 'or it might have been a coincidence.'

I looked at my little family all smiling and quite happy at the thought that Charlie had tried to maim or kill Mr Lomax — or at least blow up his van — and I realized then that I was the only normal one.

Just as I was assessing the different levels of madness represented by my family, the Longlady twins appeared at the door. It was unusual for them to call and I wondered if something bad might have happened. Like both their parents having been killed in a car bomb and them needing to move in with us.

It wasn't that, though. They'd had their ears pierced at Green's of Church Gate and now stood there with tiny gold rings in their ears, and though it was exciting and a talking point I saw how diluting a twin could be (if mismanaged) and decided an ordinary sister was probably preferable. I vowed that if I ever had twins, I'd separate them at birth and let them meet at mealtimes and by accident only, like other types of sibling, and not have them trolling around in matching pinafores and similar hair and sharing momentous moments. Soon after the piercing, though, Miranda had to remove her sleepers due to her lobes having gone lumpy in spite of being dipped into a saline eggcup before bed every night. Not satisfied with saying her earlobes had gone lumpy, Miranda announced she was susceptible to keloid scarring, which sounded more worrying and more interesting than Melody's perfectly healing ears.

★ ★ ★

Soon after the exploding van and the pierced ears, I was in the street. I'd thrown a sweet wrapper down and Mrs C. Beard came rushing out of her house to tell me to bloody well pick it up and dispose of it properly. It was rolling away in the breeze and she waited while I ran after it, and gave me a short lecture on what the world would look like if everyone threw Wig Wag wrappers down. And then asked me if I'd heard the news about the Bateses' bungalow. It was actually a Curly Wurly but she said Wig Wag, being originally from abroad.

I hadn't heard about the Bateses' bungalow and half expected to hear it had been blown up. Mrs C. Beard told me that Mr and Mrs Bates had moved out of their bungalow at 12 Bradshaw Street and into one of Charlie's other properties (presumably one of his bungalow shells). And that 12 Bradshaw Street had been sold to a young couple who'd got it at a renovator's price.

I liked Mrs C. Beard and didn't mind that she always told us off. But I didn't like the bungalow news — especially the bit about the renovator's price — and decided it would be best if our mother didn't hear about it quite yet.

I told my sister, though, and she was livid, especially the bit about the renovator's price.

'You know what that means, Lizzie?' she said.

'I think so,' I said, thinking she meant that Mr Lomax hadn't actually done the kitchen renovations. I struggled with the idea, as I couldn't think why he wouldn't have or what it meant.

'That Liberal candidate never did the kitchen, that's what I think,' she said.

We rode our bikes over to 12 Bradshaw Street to see for ourselves and snuck round the back and, peering in through the window, we saw the kitchen — the same cementy mess as I'd seen before. The backdoor window boarded, no cascade effect glass to be seen, no new cupboards, no pan carousel, and no A-Z spice rack. I felt sad for the second time over that kitchen and vowed never again to get emotionally involved with a room, especially someone else's kitchen.

My sister and I decided to wait a while before telling our mother. However, the very next day in the pharmacy, we heard Mr Blight saying to her, 'I see your friend has sold his bungalow, then.'

'What bungalow?' said our mother.

'Number 12,' said the pharmacist, and then he

said what I knew he was going to say, 'to a young couple. They got it at a renovator's price.'

'Renovator's price?' said our mother. 'But — '

'Come on,' my sister interrupted, 'let's get going.'

We walked home, our mother's mind ticking over, her hand softly, protectively at her throat and, I suppose, her heart slowly sinking.

Back at home our mother sat drinking coffee. 'Sold it to a young couple for a renovator's price?' she said. 'But it didn't need renovating. Mr Lomax renovated what needed renovating.'

'Mrs C. Beard told Lizzie they were a *retired* couple,' said my sister.

'Mrs C. Beard? What's she got to do with it?' said our mother, somehow missing two other points.

Later, she phoned Charlie, a thing she hardly ever did — if ever; well, maybe once. A woman answered and said that the Bateses had moved house and she didn't have their new number.

She rang Mr Lomax and asked some direct questions and said, 'I see,' a few times and after saying, 'OK, then, cheerio,' hung up.

'What happened?' my sister asked. 'Why didn't he do Mrs Bates's kitchen?'

'It's all right,' she said, 'Mr Lomax did the work, as discussed, but not in that property.'

'What?' said my sister. 'In what property, then?'

'In one of Charlie's bungalow shells. It makes sense,' said our mother. And she seemed satisfied with that.

214

* * *

Of course, my sister and I were now 100 per cent off Charlie Bates, not so much for blowing up Mr Lomax's van as for having the wrong kitchen renovated at our mother's expense.

Although surprised that he was capable of doing something as serious as blowing up another man's van, my sister seemed impressed that her campaign to reawaken Charlie's love had been so successful.

It was very difficult for me to join in a proper discussion or give my views on this subject, as it had all become like a story in a book you're not really concentrating on — where one of the characters has told a lie, made a mistake, opened someone else's letter in error or misunderstood something — I couldn't remember what was true and whether Charlie might have blown up Mr Lomax's van or not.

It gave me a headache and I vowed to tell only the truth, the whole truth and nothing but the truth in future — lies being a nightmare to manage. Anyway, it all happened or was lied about and understood or not, and then Charlie suddenly turned up at our house.

After seeming theoretically impressed by the van bomb, when she actually saw him in the flesh my sister came down hard against him and was most unwelcoming.

'You! What do you want?'

'I've come for a cup of tea with your mother,' he said, barged in and flicked his fag end out behind him.

He told us to put the kettle on and disappeared into our mother's sitting room. My sister told me to listen under the window while she made a pot of tea.

Charlie's voice was muffled, but I heard him ask if he could borrow an amount of money. I think it was a thousand pounds. It was either a thousand or a hundred, and the way he was speaking it was more than a hundred.

'It's a lot, I know, and you know I hate asking but . . . I'm in a bit of a fix,' he said.

'I'll try,' our mother said. 'I'll see what I can do . . . when do you need it?'

'Toot sweet,' he said, 'tomorrow at the latest.'

They must've kissed then because it went quiet, and then my sister knocked at the door and went in with the tea. She'd given him my Kellogg's Corn Flakes mug and I honestly didn't think he deserved it.

'What were they saying?' my sister asked.

'I wish you hadn't given him my mug,' I said.

Not more than fifteen minutes later, our mother called us into the sitting room. She and Charlie were having a minor disagreement.

'No, listen,' she said to Charlie. 'Shush, Lizzie won't mind, will you, Lizzie?' said our mother.

Charlie leapt up and said he had to get some cigs from across the road.

'Mind what?' I said.

'Popping over to sit with Mrs Bates for an hour or two,' she said.

'Why?' I asked.

'Charlie would like to relax here with us and take his mind off his problems for a while, but he

216

doesn't like Mrs Bates to be on her own,' she said. 'He's a softie at heart.'

'What problems?' I said.

'His bungalows and the indoor market coming to nothing, and his wife,' she said, and added, 'Lizzie, you're sounding rather unsympathetic.'

'Why me, though?'

'You know her from last time and she really liked you,' she said.

'Do I really have to?' I whined.

'We, as a family, have to give something back in return,' she said.

'In return for what?' I asked.

'For getting Charlie to ourselves for a bit,' said our mother.

Of course I agreed, just in time for Charlie to waltz back in with some Lloyd's Old Holborn and a paper.

'Thank you, Lizzie, you wonderful girl,' she said, and she gave me a hard little hug. 'Lizzie has said she'll pop over to see Lilian tomorrow to keep her company while you're here.'

Charlie gave me a look. A slightly disgusted look.

'I'm looking forward to it,' I said, and gave him a similar look.

★ ★ ★

The next day Charlie was at the table at breakfast time, which meant he'd stayed the night. I asked his advice on how I might entertain Mrs Bates.

'What does she like doing?' I asked.

217

'Don't ask me,' he said. 'Yakking, mostly.' And then he went across the road and got a different newspaper.

My few hours with Mrs Bates were fine and flew by. She was in a new bungalow and had things in boxes but nice curtains up. She sent me out to Baxter's to get some Walker's Ready Salted and a bottle of Hoyes' lemonade to have with the ham salad we'd be having for our lunch. Before we ate, she took ages over 'spot the ball' in the paper, tracing with her finger the way the ball probably travelled after probably being kicked by the player with his leg raised. Then put her ink crosses in a gentle arc.

Then, while we had the ham salad, she told me about a BBC2 documentary she'd watched the night before about a man who had committed a murder but possessed unusual maths abilities. The man had always known he was capable of violence — he'd flown off the handle at the drop of a hat since the age of two as well as doing tricky sums in his head.

After that Mrs Bates made herself a batch of what she called napkins (but I realized were sanitary towels) out of last week's Radio Times and kitchen roll. On one of them you could make out Jon Pertwee's face through the kitchen roll top sheet. She kept saying 'What a rum do' about the documentary and 'Poor chap', as if she couldn't get him out of her head.

Mrs Bates asked what our mother used, sanitary towel-wise. I said Kotex and Tampax, and Mrs Bates gasped, 'At those prices?' and I felt awkward at the relative luxury of our

218

mother's pads against Mrs Bates's home-made ones.

Mrs Bates was keen to show me her calligraphy writing set. I told her I was proud of my handwriting and she asked me to show her a sample. I wrote my name and address and held it up for her, but she'd gone back to 'spot the ball'.

When she'd done she opened the pages of her calligraphy writing book. She'd written out the words of a hymn. The writing was nice but a bit old-fashioned. She looked again at my writing and pursed her lips. For some reason no one ever complimented me on my nice handwriting. Mrs Bates obviously wasn't impressed and my teachers, who were always on at us about it, just ignored it. Mine was one of the neatest in the class. I don't mean to show off but it was nice. I practised it, doing nice loops (but not overdoing it) and having a perfect slant. I did find signing my name a bit of a challenge as I struggled with the double z and, annoyingly, Lizzie was the one word I couldn't dash off with a flourish. I had to go quite slowly and it was unimpressive to see. I started signing 'E. Vogel' to avoid the z's.

My sister's writing was unattractive. A horrible mix of upper and lower case that I'd read was a sign of schizophrenia. I told her about it being a sign of schizophrenia but she said she couldn't care less what it was a sign of and that it was *what* you wrote that counted, not the neatness (or not) of your writing, and she starting using even more capitals. I thought that reaction was probably a further sign of schizophrenia but kept it to myself. I didn't mention any of this to Mrs

Bates, but made sure I admired her calligraphy and then looked at the different nib widths on the special pens.

Finally, with approximately one hour to go, we made two plum pies against the clock. Mrs Bates always kept her rolling-pin in the fridge so it wouldn't upset the pastry and had a special method for pinching the pie edges so that fruit juice wouldn't leak on to the oven floor and burn. And when the pies were cool enough, I said goodbye and went home with a plum pie in a Co-op carrier hanging from my handlebars and promised to bring the pie plate back as soon as we'd done with it.

Back at home, I found my sister watching telly.

'I'm back,' I said.

My sister nodded and carried on watching telly.

'Where are the others?' I asked.

'Little Jack's in disgrace and Charlie's gone to the Piglet Inn for a pie,' she said, bored.

I felt a bit annoyed, to think that Charlie had been at the Piglet Inn eating pies while I was entertaining his wife (making pies). I found our mother in the kitchen, sketching a scene. 'I'm back,' I said, and she nodded too.

'So what was it like?' she said.

'Mrs Bates sent this pie,' I said, that seeming to be sufficient explanation.

My sister appeared then and they both stared at the pie, as if I'd plopped something alien on the table, and made faces.

'Doesn't anyone want any?' I asked.

Our mother stood gazing, trance-like, at the

pie, frowning and scratching the back of one leg with the other, and then lit a cigarette.

'Mrs Bates made it, and I helped,' I said.

I was crestfallen. I'd gone off on this mission and, to be honest, I'd expected some sort of hero's welcome on my return, especially as I'd come with a home-made pie with a no-lard pastry.

Our mother looked at the pie for a moment more, then picked it up and dropped it, tin plate and all, into the kitchen bin.

'What've you done that for?' I asked in a cry.

'I don't want you bringing Mrs Bates's food back here,' our mother said definitively.

'Why not?' I asked.

'It might be poisoned,' she said.

'What a thing to say — Mrs Bates wouldn't poison a fly,' I cried.

'She might poison Charlie, though,' our mother said.

I picked the pie out of the bin, grabbed the Co-op carrier, stormed out of the house and cycled over to Mrs Bates's.

'They didn't want the pie,' I said breathlessly, and handed her the carrier bag.

Mrs Bates looked confused, as if she was unable to understand what I was telling her, like a French person or a guinea pig. She just shook her head ever so gently and took the pie with both hands.

'Sorry,' I said, and suddenly felt like Mr Gummo, delivering bad news for all the wrong reasons.

221

18

One evening, soon after my visit to Mrs Bates, Charlie was round and he and our mother were having an altercation. A cheque she'd given him had bounced and caused major difficulties and embarrassment. It was meant to pay for some materials for his second bungalow shell and the non-payment had caused a cash-flow emergency and an interruption to the work.

'You'll have to ask your ex-husband,' Charlie was saying.

'I can't ask for any more,' she was saying.

'Say you need money for something for the kids,' he was saying.

And so the conversation went on in that vein.

In the end, our mother telephoned our father and asked for some money to take us on holiday. Our father must not have been feeling very generous. We couldn't hear his side of the conversation, but we gathered he was saying he couldn't keep sending money for holidays we never actually had. And seemed to want to know what the hell she was doing with all the money.

'It's everyday expenditure,' she said, 'the children are bloody expensive,' and she plucked things out of the air desperately: 'Lizzie went to Porlock with the school — that cost a fortune — and the ponies have had vet's bills, we've had to have a new bread bin etc.'

We didn't see this as a problem, more of a

bickering between our two already divorced parents. And when, a few days after this phone call, a caravan was delivered in lieu of holiday money and our mother was beside herself with fury, we thought it very funny and were secretly pleased Charlie wouldn't get his money. Also, and more importantly, the caravan, an Eccles Topaz, was most enchanting to my sister, Jack and me. It was second-hand but 'in pristine condition' and full of surprises inside with ingenious things and hidden cupboards and foldaway items. Our mother walked round it, said, 'The petty bastard,' and kicked it a few times.

The Eccles Topaz was very noticeable in our lane and of great interest to the neighbourhood. Anyone who walked past openly admired it: 'Oh, you've got a caravan,' and so forth. So much so, our mother considered camouflaging it with a net and leaves. And then, to make matters worse (for our mother), a man from Bagshaw Bridge garage arrived to fit a reverse periscope (a retrovisor) on to her car and extension arms to the wing mirrors. Our mother was livid and told the man to take his hands off her car, and the man said, 'Suit yourself,' dropped the paid-for parts on to the driveway and stomped off.

Then Mr Lomax, the Liberal candidate, was at the gate looking at the Eccles Topaz. Admiring its lines and actually patting it with his hand.

'She's a beauty,' he said. 'What are your plans?'

'I did not buy this caravan. It was given to the children by their father in lieu of money for a holiday,' said our mother.

'Well, the world's your oyster with a caravan,'

Mr Lomax said, and seemed to be of the opinion that a caravan was a jolly good thing, which made our mother even crosser.

Mr Lomax left and Charlie arrived soon after and surveyed the Eccles Topaz with a stony expression. Within a week it was gone again, plus the bits and pieces of the retrovisor and the wing mirror extensions, and we supposed Charlie got his emergency money after all.

Our mother was very anxious, we could tell. She smoked more than ever and left cigarettes burning in ashtrays and standing up on their ends and lit new ones and didn't even take a puff. In the end, she wrote an act for the play about the situation.

> Roderick: I'm sorry, Adele, I can't give you any more money.
> Adele: What about a holiday for the children?
> Roderick: I made some shares in your favour and you must live on the dividends.
> Adele: What about an impromptu holiday?
> Roderick: I have arranged for a nearly new Eccles Topaz to be delivered from Don Amott, King of Caravans.
> Adele: Well, I shall gift it to my lover, who will sell it through *Exchange and Mart*.
> Roderick: What about the much-needed holiday?
> Adele: A caravan does not equal a holiday, however pretty its name.

Miss Benedict turned up again to tell our mother that Little Jack had been refusing to take his coat off in the classroom. She seemed eager to have the interview over and done with as soon as possible, not wanting to risk any untoward turns in the conversation. They sat again at the kitchen table.

'I just wanted you to be aware,' said Miss Benedict.

'Of what?' asked our mother.

'Of the fact.'

'What fact?'

'That Jack has been refusing to take his coat off,' said Miss Benedict.

'Is it important?' asked our mother.

'Well, yes. If he's asked to take it off, he really should take it off,' said Miss Benedict.

'Perhaps it might help if you didn't ask him to take it off, then he could have it on without disobeying you?' said our clever mother.

'But the children all have to take their coats off inside,' explained Miss Benedict.

'Oh, I see,' said our mother. 'I'll speak to Jack about it.'

'Thanks, that would be helpful. I was wondering if you'd had any further thoughts about getting a baby donkey,' Miss Benedict said.

Our mother hadn't seen that coming and was silenced while her head decoded it.

'No, I haven't and I shan't,' said our mother, eventually.

Then Little Jack entered with his coat on and said hello.

'Hello, Jack,' said Miss Benedict.

'Hello,' said Jack.

Then Miss Benedict said goodbye etc. and left.

'Why was she here?' asked Jack.

'She was updating me,' said our mother.

'Did she take her coat off?' asked Jack.

'No, actually, she didn't,' said our mother.

We could have done without Miss Benedict coming round and harking back to Bluebell the baby donkey. It didn't do Little Jack any favours at all, only serving to remind our mother of a recent bout of unhappiness. It was a reminder to us, though, that busybody actions are often selfish at heart and mostly don't help the intended recipient. And coming on top of the Eccles Topaz and our father's refusal to cooperate, it resulted in a horrible play that went way back to our mother's miserable years at a cheap boarding school in Lincolnshire.

Miss Bruce: Adele Benson, you were seen wearing your gaberdine in the hall.

Adele: Sorry, Miss Bruce.

Miss Bruce: And do not be seen wearing any outdoor garment ever again inside the hall, form room or any other part of the school.

Adele: Yes, Miss.

Miss Bruce: Only a barmaid would wear a gaberdine inside.

Adele: Yes, Miss.

Miss: Are you planning to work in a public house, Benson?

Adele: I don't think so, Miss.

Miss: We shall see, shan't we?

After the demise of the Charlie Bates relationship, it was increasingly hard to know how to
herd our mother into happiness. I say 'herd'
because she was like a sheep who didn't seem to
understand the direction in which she should be
trotting. And would wilfully dart away from
guidance and not be nudged towards lovely, jolly
things.

She disliked food (the eating of it) and had
stopped cooking and she hated telly. She only
really liked rugged men, whisky and ginger ale,
poetry (especially love poems, annoyingly),
Shakespeare plays and sunbathing. And here we
were, two girls, both poetry haters and not
inclined to drink.

I put all her known likes into my head and
thought creatively and came up with what
seemed a brilliant solution — a Scrabble
tournament. Her and Little Jack in one team
versus my sister and me — thinking it might
overlap into poetry writing. My sister was
supportive of the idea and I took it to our
mother. She wasn't keen and just said, 'Ugh!'

However hard she tried (and she tried very
hard) to recover from the Charlie Bates thing,
she just couldn't.

'Are you still sad about Charlie?' my sister
asked her.

'Very,' she said. 'The thing is, no one likes me
and I've already had sex with two husbands in
the village.'

'And a teacher,' my sister offered.

'He was one of the husbands,' said our
mother, seeming to forget he was actually only

engaged to be married and not a husband, as such.

And then my sister started counting and wanting a true account of the husbands and I had to elbow her.

★ ★ ★

My sister and I decided it was time to make another, more concerted play for Mr Oliphant. He has popped up a few times before, I know. That's how it was with him. Here's a recap on why we liked him. He loved horses and was nice. He wore a cloth cap but in a well-dressed kind of way, and had nice jackets albeit farmer-style, and had a nice rounded lump in his trousers which, my sister explained, meant good underpants and the English arrangement of his male parts, bunched up, as opposed to the European way of having it all hanging down one trouser leg and looking lopsided. Plus hiding, she said, the obviousness of an unwanted arousal.

Also, Mr Oliphant's financial stability was reassuring. Quite often around that time bills would come through the letter box and our mother would run her hand through her hair and swear out loud and fling them in a pile under a paperweight.

Let me get something straight before we start the Mr Oliphant episode. I did not ever want my own pony. I liked ponies but I wasn't a true horsewoman. My sister was, though, and could speak to the horse with her seat and steer it with her voice. I knew I'd only ever speak with my voice and steer with the reins — and that's not what horses really want.

We had a couple of little ponies called Robbie and Bilbo in the paddock. Robbie was very fat and had laminitis and, though he couldn't be ridden hard, had to be walked daily to relieve his legs. And Bilbo had a bowel thing and had suffered a twisted gut after an undetected bout of colic before being rescued by a horse refuge and then rescued from the refuge by my sister. In addition to those two invalids, my animal-loving sister had her own pony for actually riding, as opposed to just caring for. He was a New Forest pony officially called Blaze, but she was trying her utmost to change his name to Sacha — after the French singer of 'Raindrops Keep Falling on My Head'. Her reasons for wanting to change the name being that he didn't actually have a blaze (the facial marking) and because calling a pony 'Blaze' was like calling a dog 'Rover' and she hadn't reached the ironic stage, aged only eleven. We all tried really hard to remember to call him Sacha and not Blaze.

My sister had acquired Blaze all by herself. She'd looked in *Horse & Hound* every week and the *Leicester Mercury* every day. And that was when she first met the well-known local equestrian Phil Oliphant. Mr P. Oliphant lived at the edge of the village and she'd popped in to see if he had any ponies for sale that might be suitable for her. Phil Oliphant had no pony for sale at that time but said he'd keep his ear to the ground for one. My sister had been pleased to know that she'd got Phil Oliphant's ear to the

229

ground on the search, because although he was a farmer he wasn't a busy farmer, he was the type of farmer who owns a lot of fields but has a private income from an old uncle and never has to do any actual work on the land except for building horse jumps and places where the hunt can pass through with maximum excitement. We all knew that Prince Charles had hunted across Mr Oliphant's fields and had fallen at one of his tiger traps — that's how challenging they were.

Eventually, and without the help of Phil Oliphant as it happened, my sister found herself a pony — Blaze. Then, like everything else, she wanted me to have a pony too so I'd be in it with her. I didn't want one. And apart from the awkward business of passing the war veteran Mr Nesbit and his embarrassing comments, I loved plodding around on our general family ponies and I didn't mind doing my bit towards the upkeep of them, but I was certain I didn't want my own. I'd seen how much work was involved and I didn't want the responsibility.

Months had passed since Mr Oliphant had said he'd keep his ear to the ground, so we decided it was time to give things a kick-start. My sister felt his name being Phil was a blow. We'd known one other Phil, Phil Smith, our father's lover from Vogel's — an altogether different type of man — and she worried that our mother might see it as a sign. I was much more worried that I'd end up having to have my own pony. But we both agreed that with all his land, his love of dogs and horses and all other things considered, he'd make a marvellous man

230

at the helm (or 'helmsman', as my sister had started to say). We went round to his house anyway to get the ball rolling.

He remembered us and we reminded him he was going to help us find a pony and then he remembered that too. My sister suggested we attend a horse and pony auction with him doing our bidding. I think she imagined Mr Oliphant in a bidding war with a cruel type of farmer, touching his cap for the perfect pony. I thought this a very risky strategy and thought it might result in me actually getting a pony. I'd seen this kind of thing in *Laurel and Hardy* and other shows, where the people don't really want the thing they're bidding for but end up with an oil painting or a grandfather clock when in fact they were just sneezing. And luckily Phil Oliphant felt the same, saying it would be illegal and that he might end up having to buy the damned thing.

'But my sister needs a pony,' said my sister, not giving up, 'and our mother isn't as experienced at choosing horses as you . . . we really need an expert equestrian.' And that's the thing about flattery, people don't notice anything else if you also say they're good-looking or experienced.

Phil Oliphant said although he couldn't do our bidding at auction, he'd be happy to give us his professional opinion on ponies we were considering, but only if our mother was all right with that.

We told him we'd find a batch of ponies via the ads and make appointments to see the most appropriate ones and see if he might be available to accompany us on any of the viewings.

That very afternoon we rang upwards of twenty pony vendors and made appointments to view two on the following Saturday. And then we invited Mr Oliphant along and he said he'd be delighted to come. When he turned up on the day, though, our mother said she wasn't in the mood to meet horsey Phil Oliphant, the dog judge, and said we should ask him to come back later. This was awkward, so we told him she'd got a lady's problem and could he come back in half an hour when she'd cleaned herself up. And when he called back, she was in the mood and had changed into a silk shirt. And when they said hello, it was as if they were already in love. Phil Oliphant's eyes flicked between our mother's nice smoky eyes and her nipples — until she folded her arms to shield them.

And so began a long and detailed hunt for a pony for me.

I reminded my sister a number of times that I did not want a pony and that I was going along with it only for our mother's happiness, and that once she'd got serious with Phil Oliphant, or engaged to him, we must stop looking and let me not have a pony.

My sister said, 'Of course, that's the plan. She's run out of money anyway, stop worrying.'

And hearing that, I stupidly stopped worrying.

Phil Oliphant definitely took to our mother and she to him and we went to see practically every pony who lived in the area. We scoured Derbyshire, Nottinghamshire and Cambridgeshire as well as our own county. We saw two more

Blazes, Conker, Ruby, Robin, Ruben and Zippy. We saw two very nice mares, both called Dana. We saw Eliza, Rosa and Petula, but our mother preferred geldings.

We saw a few yearlings which weren't broken in yet. We liked Rollo, a dapple-grey, but not Martha. My sister wanted me to get William, a light bay Exmoor, but Mr Oliphant preferred Snowball, except he showed signs of crib-biting.

It was funny to see our mother, who wasn't at all horsey and had very little experience buying ponies, being so picky and interested and pretending to look at their hooves and touching their fetlocks. Things were going well and towards the end of it I didn't even bother going along, saying I trusted my sister's judgement, and then even she stopped going and so it was just Phil Oliphant and our mother trotting these ponies along verges, looking at their teeth and asking country folk what was their rock bottom.

And they seemed quite happy for a while and often came home all fuzzy. In the end something must've happened between Phil Oliphant and our mother (my sister said he had dental crowns and didn't use tooth picks but I think he was just too nice). Whatever it was, he was suddenly off the case and our mother, without really consulting me, made a verbal agreement on the phone regarding a six-year-old bay gelding from a riding school a few miles away. I tried to object but she explained that only the quick acquisition of a pony would shake off Phil Oliphant, which was something she was suddenly keen to do. She didn't even listen to my side of the predicament.

We drove up to the riding stables and immediately saw a scruffy brown pony nosing around some rubbish bins in what was clearly a non-pony area. We went into the tack room to meet the owner and said we were here to view the thirteen-hand-high pony. The owner said, 'Oh, Maxwell, right, he's around here some-where.' And he whistled from the tack room door, then shouted, 'Come oi, come oi,' and banged a stirrup iron against the wall. The brown dustbin pony appeared and came rushing up to the owner — looking more like a dog than a pony — and the owner said, 'Meet Maxwell.'

'Why isn't he with the other ponies?' I asked.

'Maxwell does his own thing,' said the owner, or words to that effect.

Maxwell came sniffing round us and got his teeth round a tube of fruit Polos I had in my pocket. He pulled at them. The owner gave him a smack on the muzzle. 'You can't keep stuff in your pockets with Maxwell around.' He laughed and showed us the flappy mess that had once been a pocket at the front of his overcoat.

The owner said Maxwell was a real character, full of charisma, hilarious and always up to his tricks. I wasn't particularly pleased to hear that. Charisma and character are not all that desirable in a pony. You want them to be normal, trustworthy and good at zigzagging through poles.

I gave our mother and my sister pleading looks and said I really wasn't sure Maxwell was right for me — him being so charismatic etc. and me not really ready for my own pony. But, for their own separate but desperate reasons, both our mother and my sister wanted to acquire this oddball of a pony and before I knew it our mother had handed over fifty-five guineas — a guinea being slightly more than one pound in horse and livestock money — and Maxwell arrived by Rice trailer the next day with a saddle, bridle and head-collar. He was by far the cheapest pony we'd looked at.

So in addition to my other worries I now had a charismatic Welsh Mountain pony to look after day in day out, seven days a week, summer, winter, spring and autumn. He was twelve hands and three inches high at the withers. That was how come he was so cheap (that and his charisma), because ponies are sorted by the hand and half and Maxwell, at 12h 3in, was one inch too tall to enter the 12h 2in classes at gymkhanas and shows. This put him in classes with the likes of Sacha ridden by the likes of my sister and other dedicated horsemen and horsewomen. Not kids like me.

I didn't mind that much, pleased to never have to win anything. I minded much more about the everyday. The keeping this pony alive and not letting him die or harm anything or kill anyone. I suppose a bit like being a parent.

Although my sister was terribly disappointed that somehow we'd let horse-loving Phil Oliphant slip through our fingers, it was a huge consolation to her that I now had Maxwell and therefore as much on my plate as she had on hers (almost). In the first days of pony-ownership, I lost my cool with my sister and reminded her that I had never wanted a pony and that I'd only agreed to look for one so our mother could have sex with Phil Oliphant. And now Phil Oliphant was nowhere to be seen and I had this extra burden. A charismatic burden.

My sister wondered if we might add the riding school man to the list, him being horsey and handsome in a Heathcliffy kind of way, but I just yelled at her that she'd have to find a man on her own from now on as I'd be too busy. Also, that if the Heathcliffy riding school man came anywhere near me, I'd insist on his taking Maxwell back before I allowed him anywhere near our mother.

19

Debbie was ill with something and had to see the vet. The vet was called Mr Swift and I liked the name. My sister added him to the list, though in all the worry about Debbie we didn't go through the pros and cons properly, but my sister insisted he was probably a good candidate, being Oxbridge-educated and on a vet's salary. She really had started factoring the economics in by then, which added to the excitement somehow.

And though we were sorry for Debbie, we were amazed at how quickly after Mr Oliphant another possible expert helmsman had appeared. When you think of all the months with no one decent.

It turned out that Debbie had a suspected blockage. This was diagnosed because she kept being sick and trying to be sick and seemed lethargic. I didn't know exactly what a suspected blockage was, only that it was uncertain but might be somewhere between bad and very bad indeed.

Mr Swift was kind to us and said although it might be bad, it also might not be (not realizing that the word 'might' meant might and might not) and he said that we mustn't blame ourselves. I hadn't blamed myself until he said that, and I felt I had to clear the matter up. I asked him why he thought we might blame ourselves. 'What I mean is, you mustn't feel it's

237

your fault that Debbie might have eaten something that may have caused a blockage,' he explained.

'We don't blame ourselves,' I said, upset and wanting this cleared up in case of a fatality, and imagining going around with the weight of possibly, though probably not, being to blame.

'What I mean is that Labradors are greedy beggars and they eat all sorts of nasty things, and that can cause this kind of thing. And you mustn't think it's your fault,' he went on.

Mr Swift gave Debbie a dose of something and stroked her throat to make her swallow and told us to watch her very carefully. A couple of hours later there was a pile of used teabags on the lawn all in a sort of grassy foam. We'd forgotten to watch her, but agreed that this could have been Debbie's suspected blockage.

Our mother telephoned Mr Swift the vet and he dropped by that evening and looked at the teabags, which we'd left on the lawn where they'd been passed. He poked them with a slim stick and agreed with our supposition. 'These look as though they've been partially ingested,' he said, meaning that Debbie had eaten them and shat them out again.

He congratulated Debbie — who'd gone pretty much back to normal — with a vigorous neck rub, and had a drink with our mother in her sitting room and didn't leave until after we'd gone to bed and then they probably had sex — definitely, if I believed my sister, who said she'd heard evidence including Mr Swift groaning and saying, 'This is unbelievable.'

My sister kept me awake wondering what Mr Swift could have considered unbelievable.

'Do you think he means the sex is unbelievable,' she asked, 'or the *fact* of them having sex?'

'What do you mean?' I asked.

'Is it *it* — or the idea of it?' she wondered.

She was always wondering things like that now since starting at secondary school and doing a project on Knowledge. And since doing this course she seemed to be going backwards and always wondering and pondering on things that she'd have taken in her stride before.

'What would it be for you?' I asked.

'Oh, for me, the idea of it. But that's just me,' she said, 'I'm quite philosophical.'

Debbie had a series of trips to the vet's surgery after that. She had her dewclaws clipped and her various checks and even had her teeth cleaned. Our mother seemed very happy and bought us two rabbits called Benjamin and Bertie and they had a few trips to the vet too.

One day our mother called Mr Swift to see one of the ponies but she forgot which one was supposed to have a problem, so we had to make something up on the spot. My sister — being the imaginative one — said she'd seen Sacha limping. Mr Swift asked her to trot him along the path and felt down his pasterns, then he came in for a cup of coffee and our mother slapped him round the face and he roared off in his Volvo.

We questioned our mother and she said things were extremely bad but gave no details. She

239

wasn't referring to Sacha's leg — we knew that much.

★ ★ ★

From time to time that dreadful Farmer Turner, who'd shot the cow that was stuck in the plough, would yell at us from his mud-caked Land Rover and say Debbie had been near his ewe field. Debbie did have a tendency to roam the village but we couldn't imagine she'd be a sheep-worrier. She was such a lovely dog. Farmer Turner would say, 'That black bitcha yours as bin up near my top field an' I'm warning you if I see her set foot in that field I'll shooter no questions ast.'

This made Farmer Turner our sworn enemy. We couldn't imagine how, once upon a time, we'd considered him perfect and my sister remarked that that was the thing about love. He was a liar and a dog-shooter and he was fat and we used to hear his distinctive voice booming out of the Bull's Head of an evening saying aggressive things and laughing. I imagined him leaning back on a stool and I used to wish he'd fall off it. We three all worried constantly when Debbie was out — that she might accidentally end up near the ewe field and that Farmer Turner would shoot her. Our sensible mother said if we were that bothered, why didn't we ever shut the fucking gate.

He never did shoot Debbie, as such, but one day someone ran her over, picked up her injured body and chucked her into the ditch by the road and we put it down to him. It was almost a relief to have it over and done with.

A woman called Doris who always wore ill-fitting slippers shuffled up to us as we played. She was always shuffling around near our house and we used to laugh, carefully, at her snail's pace. She'd have been quite sprightly without the slippers — she had to shuffle to keep them on. Doris was the woman who, like Mr Nesbit, had apparently lived in one of the cottages that previously made up our house and apparently been evicted by force from it. She had a moustache above her wobbly top lip and you could tell from the dark hairs that her pale blue eyes had once been brown.

When she reached us that day we realized she wanted to tell us something, so we stopped playing and listened to her whispery voice. She'd seen a stricken dog in a ditch. 'It looks like your'n,' she whispered and lifted a wobbly arm, and added, 'By the paddock there, in that ditch runs along the road, someun's hit'n an flung it in, I reckon.'

We pelted, me already crying, and my sister planning ahead with every stride. We got to the ditch and there was Debbie half submerged, sides heaving and wet and her eyes looking frightened and pleased to see us all at once. My sister was down there beside Debbie in an instant, lifting her face out of the water and shouting instructions.

'Lizzie, go get Mum. Send her here in the car. You ring ahead to the vet, Mr Swift, the number's in the book under S for Swift,' she said.

'Jack, you go with her now and you get a big towel and come straight back, quick as you can, Jack, all right?'

We watched my sister wiping Debbie's face with her sleeve. 'Go on, hurry!'

As I ran I planned how I'd word it. Our mother needed things simple and clear. I needed to avoid any ambiguity or irrationality — our mother loved to ask penetrating questions to undermine authority and upset assumption. But there was no time for that.

I stood in front of her. She was scribbling in a Silvine spiral-bound notebook. I saw the word 'imperative', which cheered me and jumped off the page and into my mouth.

'Mum, Debbie is seriously injured. It's imperative we get her to the vet,' I said.

Through the window I saw Little Jack running along, tripping himself up on a huge sand-coloured towel — the largest (the so-called 'bath sheet') of a set of top-quality Christy's Soft Sensations that our mother had bought from Fenwick's of Leicester to replace those lost when a crate had gone missing with some of our linens on the day we moved and the lorry brought the tree bough down and cracked the listed arch and so on.

'She is very injured in the paddock ditch,' I told our mother.

'What's wrong with her?'

'I don't know, but it looks bad,' I said. 'We need to get her to Mr Swift.'

'No. Not Mr Swift, I am *not* going to him,' said our mother, staring at me as if I'd said

242

something outrageous.

'But Mr Swift is our usual vet,' I said, 'he knows Debbie, he saw the teabags on the lawn — remember?'

'I am not going to Mr Swift,' she said. 'You'll have to find an alternative.'

I leafed desperately through the phone book and scanned down the list of veterinary surgeons (surprised at the spelling of veterinary) and came to a Mr Nightingale in Longston.

'Mr Nightingale in Longston?' I checked with our mother.

'Another bird,' she said. 'Where is he?'

'24 The Parade, Longston.'

She closed her book. 'Come on, then,' she said.

'Shouldn't I ring ahead?' I said.

'Never ring ahead,' she said.

Then she and I arrived at the ditch and saw Debbie wrapped in the sand-coloured Soft Sensation bath sheet and my sister sitting in three inches of ditch water talking into Debbie's bedraggled ear.

Our mother clambered down into the ditch. 'Oh baby,' she said to Debbie, 'what have you been up to?'

And she took the sand-coloured bundle softly on to the shelves of her arms. I offered my arm down to pull my sister up. Then we all helped our mother out of the ditch.

'OK, Princess Debbie Reynolds,' said our mother, using Debbie's official kennel name, 'let's get you to 25 The Parade, Longston.'

I didn't correct her, because it was the thought that counted.

My sister sat in the back seat next to Little Jack with Debbie across her lap, and I sat in the front but was turned facing them all the way.

'Have you seen the injury?' our mother asked.

'There's a lot of blood on her left side and I think she's a bit crushed. It might be her ribs.' My sister's voice let her down then and Little Jack began to cry. My sister questioned our mother's route.

'Why are you going through Hilfield?'

'Mr Swift isn't available today, we're seeing a Mr Starling,' she said.

'Nightingale,' I corrected.

Soon we were there at 24 The Parade. I held the door open and our mother carried Debbie in.

'We need to see Mr Starling — it's an emergency, I think she's been hit by a car,' said our mother to the veterinary receptionist.

'Mr Nightingale,' I said.

'Of course,' said the girl. 'Come this way.' Our mother followed the girl and placed Debbie in a shallow container on a table and stroked her nose.

'It's actually Mr Swift in surgery today. I'll get him right away.'

Our mother swore under her breath.

The nurse heard and looked sympathetic. 'Don't worry, he's a wonderful veterinarian.'

Mr Swift was very caring and nice and made no sign of acknowledging the unbelievable thing that had passed between himself and our mother. And our mother held up well too. He wanted some time with Debbie and asked us to wait in the waiting area. We waited. We were too sad to pick up a magazine, but I read an article over a woman's shoulder in which a milkman is crushed to death by his own float and yet an eight-stone woman is imbued with power and lifts a truck off her young son. It seemed terribly unfair (on the milkman). After about fifteen minutes Mr Swift appeared at the door of the surgery.

'Mrs Vogel, would you . . . ?' and he gestured her to enter the treatment room.

We followed her.

Mr Swift wondered whether it might be best for us to wait in the waiting area but our mother said Debbie was our dog and if we were big enough to have a dog, we were big enough to hear whatever he had to say.

'Debbie's injuries are serious and complex and, as you suggest, most likely the result of a road accident. She's suffered trauma to her chest and left hind leg.'

'Can you save her?' our mother asked.

'I can try. The leg looks straightforward and the ribs should mend with rest, but there's something else. Has she been in water?' Mr Swift asked.

'Yes, she was found in a shallow ditch,' our mother said.

'Hmm, thought so. Her breathing suggests the early stages of pneumonia,' he said, 'and that complicates matters a bit.'

'Can you save her?' our mother said.

'I can try, if you want me to,' he said. 'The other option is to put her to sleep.'

245

'What's best for Debbie?' our mother said.

'It's hard to know, but I would like to try and save your dog,' said the vet.

'Very well,' said our mother.

And then we spoke about various treatments, operations and so forth and we went home leaving Debbie there at 24 The Parade in a critical condition.

That evening my sister and I glued ourselves to the telly. And Little Jack wrote a mature letter, which made us very proud. He even asked how to spell 'definitely'.

Dear person who ran over our dog,

You are a cruel person. First you ran our dog over, then you chucked her into a ditch to die. Or maybe you thought she was already dead. I would like to run you over. I would not chuck you in a ditch because you are too fat to lift. So I would just keep running you over until I knew that you were definitely dead. Everyone in this house hates you. And I bet we're not the only ones. I feel sorry for your kids and dog.

From,
Jack Vogel

The next morning we rang the veterinary surgery at eight on the dot and heard the news that Debbie had pulled through and had even wagged her tail at the nurse. We heard just how much against the odds it had been and we all cried and our mother said, 'Let's all promise to be better.' Which none of us really understood then. But I do now.

Debbie made a slow recovery and was always a bit wonky after that, and one eye bulged a bit and she didn't live as long as she might have had she not been chucked in that ditch, but she survived and that was the main thing. Debbie surviving against the odds that time was a real boost to morale, as things like that can be, unless they're a downer, and we felt quite blessed.

And just to round it off, Farmer Turner came round and produced the letter that Little Jack had posted through his door on the morning after the accident.

'I didn't hit your bitch. If I wanted 'er dead, she'd be dead. I don't want 'er dead. I'd prefer you keep 'er safe on yer own property and the reason she's not dead is because I ant seen 'er in the ewe field. But I will shoot 'er if I see 'er there and that's all I can say.'

So we weren't so sure after all that it was Farmer Turner who ran Debbie over. In fact we thought it must've been a real accident and that maybe Debbie toppled into the ditch herself and that made us feel better too. And Debbie didn't roam quite so much after that, anyway. She preferred to stay on our property. Maybe she understood what the farmer said. And we added him to the list again but only briefly, saying we didn't want anyone who wore a vest and had a gun.

We wrote to Mr Swift, the vet, thanking him for saving Debbie's life. Our mother was keen that we should and she was quite particular about the wording ('You were most sensitive'). I felt it unnecessary — he was just doing his job after all. None of us thought to write and thank Doris the whiskery old lady in the slippers who had saved Debbie's life just as much as the vet had, but that's the way the world is (vets being thanked and old ladies being forgotten) and who knows if she'd have liked that kind of thing.

I don't know what became of the Christy's Soft Sensation bath sheet. My sister said she thought the nurse would have taken it home as a perk of the job, it being so luxurious and almost brand-new.

Writing about the Debbie situation reminds me how good our mother was when bad things happened. It always came as a surprise, her being so rubbish at the ordinary everyday things. She was especially good when *really* bad things happened or people died, not so much the practical stuff but the other often-neglected stuff such as actually going to see the bereaved. Crucially, she knew not to run away or to pretend it hadn't happened. She knew that you should immerse yourself in it.

When her granny choked to death on a Lucky Black Cat pendant made from Whitby jet that had fallen into some rice pudding, she flung herself at her mother and showered love upon her. And even though she disliked both her mother and the granny, she was there at Kilmington pouring Scotch on the rocks, lighting two cigarettes at a time and saying what a good eye Granny had had for scarves. When the

248

husband of a family friend suddenly just died for no reason one night and didn't come down to breakfast, she zoomed over there in the car and said things about the deceased that no one else would even think of saying. He was so kind. He was such a considerate driver. He had such a sensitivity for Beethoven, and other things that seemed far-fetched, but the friend didn't mind because the person had died and needed bolstering.

Sadly, though, when her own father ceased upon the midnight with no pain, her goodness in a tragedy failed her. She was like a useless little pebble on a riverbed. She hadn't been expecting the death and had some bad feelings about it. She got it into her head that her mother and the family doctor had been a bit hasty in the helping. It was a shame because she'd always been the person who knew how to behave and how to make the bereaved feel better, but suddenly there she was saying the very worst things and reminding her family what a menace she was. My sister and I tried to steer her into normality — e.g., 'Come on, Mum, don't say stuff like that' — but she shook herself free metaphorically and raged down the telephone, 'If he was so fucking ill, why didn't you telephone me to come and say my farewells?' and her mother had said, 'I thought you'd be too drunk.'

20

My pony Maxwell turned out to be nothing but trouble, as I knew he would. I don't want to write too much about him as I'm planning a whole book (all about him) and he should only have a bit part in this one.

In the beginning he behaved in such odd ways that I was genuinely afraid of what it all meant. He was an attention-seeker, an escape artist, a thief, and so utterly selfish it wasn't true. He wasn't like any ordinary pony and it was typical of me to end up with him.

If I rode Maxwell when it didn't suit him, he would do his best to knock me off by walking or trotting very close to a tree or a wall. And when I learned how to lift my leg to avoid being hoicked off, he would fake a stumble and put his head down so that I might topple off the front, and when I got used to clinging on to the pommel and holding myself on until he'd corrected himself, he'd roll over. But that was only if he didn't fancy a hack out. To be fair, he sometimes *did* fancy a hack out — however, on these days he'd always return home exactly when he wanted to and when the moment arrived he'd simply turn round and trot me home.

He was much better behaved with my sister on him because she was a proper horsewoman and didn't mind using the crop on him. I wasn't a crop-using type and Maxwell knew this. It got so that I couldn't go out riding with my sister because she would get so cross with Maxwell that she'd snap a twig from an elder tree and give him a whack. And so if he saw her ready for a hack, he'd refuse to accompany her, knowing he'd get a whack.

As far as this story is concerned, we got into trouble for taking Maxwell upstairs. Our mother hadn't been at home when it happened. We didn't tell her exactly what occurred but she found out. When she knew the main details, she became like any normal nasty mother and made us clean out the hen house as a punishment (a job that Mr Gummo would usually do) and it put me right off the hens and almost off eggs. It seemed unfair because we *didn't* take Maxwell upstairs as such, he just came when we called — we never really thought he would. He came up because he was such an unusual pony. An unusual pony that our mother had insisted on buying — that I had never wanted in the first place.

I tried to explain this to our mother, but she hated long sentences and judged you on the first few words.

'We didn't take Maxwell upstairs, as such,' I began, and before I could add the rest she'd accused me of trying to tell her black was white.

That day had started out OK. Our mother had gone to a hospital appointment in a taxi — Denis the retired mechanic's Ford Zodiac. She hadn't wanted to drive herself because she didn't want to have to drive home again afterwards because she was having a pregnancy

251

terminated. Mr Oliphant was the father (and in my opinion should have done the driving) and had apparently been mortified to hear about the pregnancy as he already had four children with his wife, that awful clingy woman we'd seen at the summer fair who kept linking arms with him even though the marriage was on the rocks.

Our mother said that had made it doubly disappointing (that we could behave so stupidly while she was out of the house having a horrible procedure and was utterly miserable and sad).

This is what happened.

She'd gone off in the retired mechanic's Ford Zodiac and we'd gone to play on her four-poster — a thing we loved but seldom got the chance to do, her being in it so much. From the bed we could see through the open balcony doors that Maxwell had escaped from the paddock and was in the garden, nosing around, as he often did. We called him in the style of his ex-owner at the riding school ('Come oi, come oi') and to our astonishment and delight we soon heard him clopping up the interesting staircase. And he appeared at the doorway of our mother's bedroom and walked smartly across the polished boards. I liked him then, for a moment, his big brown eyes full of wonder at the new place, his chestnut lashes tinged black at the tips. He was a handsome pony, I can't deny it. Much handsomer than Sacha, who was grey and a bit wishy-washy.

Unfortunately, once fully in the room, he stepped on a rug, skidded slightly and became fretful. In this state, he stepped on the draped bed-curtain, which began popping off its brass rings, and a section flopped down over his head. In all the head-tossing that followed, our mother's walnut dressing-stool broke in half and clattered to the ground.

Maxwell then clip-clopped into the landing and that's when he looked out of the window. He let out a loud whinny and bashed at the mullioned panes with his muzzle. The window rattled and banged and miraculously didn't break. Mr Lomax the Liberal candidate happened to be in the street posting his manifesto at the time and he looked up with a most unhappy expression.

My sister and I ran down the stairs and called Maxwell to follow. But he just stood at the top of the sweeping staircase, trembling and pawing the ground like a nervous little bull.

'Come, Maxie, come,' called my sister. But he wouldn't. He just whinnied and pawed.

'Come on, you bastard,' I called, feeling desperate and responsible and resentful and thinking how I always knew something like this would happen (him being an unusual and charismatic pony).

My sister said, 'Swearing at him won't help.' She went away and came back with a bucket of nuts, which she rattled. 'Come, Maxie, come,' she coaxed.

Suddenly Mr Lomax was there in our hall with us with his light tan boots on.

'Keep back,' he said, 'in case it jumps.'

'He won't jump, he's a calm pony,' said my sister.

253

'He's a Welsh Mountain,' I added, 'he can turn on a tap with his hoof.'

Then it became clear that Mr Lomax was something of an expert on pony psychology.

'Ponies can go most uncharacteristic when they're in a strange environment,' Mr Lomax said. 'I doubt he'd have the wherewithal to turn on a tap in his current state, he's gone semi-insane because you've let him look out of an upstairs window.'

'Is that bad?' we asked.

'Bloody right it is. Never let a horse look out of an upstairs window, that's my advice to anyone who likes bringing them indoors,' said Mr Lomax. 'If you have to bring them in, then you must draw the curtains beforehand.'

Mr Lomax said we were in a highly problematic situation, and in an ideal world four men would escort Maxwell down backwards with a twitch on his lip and, failing that, he should be sedated. My sister said she was anti-twitches and Mr Lomax said they were perfectly humane if applied to the lip, though never the ear. The two of them argued about twitches for a while, and then Mr Lomax asked my sister to fetch something with which to blinker Maxwell (if she didn't object to a blinker). She fetched a bikini top, thinking it was the right shape. Mr Lomax ushered us to a safer area within our hall and we all looked up at Maxwell, who stood sweating above us. Mr Lomax crept up the stairs and reached round to tie the bra over Maxwell's eyes. But before he'd finished the bow, Maxwell leapt the first flight of steps, crashed through the banister to the parquet below and lay there with his belly heaving. Neither my sister nor I dared approach him. We just stared, not breathing, like we had with an injured wood pigeon the day before.

I imagined, briefly, dragging Maxwell's body out of the hall by the hoof, through the front door and into the street, realizing it would be the only way, and was just imagining Mrs C. Beard rushing across to admonish us about littering, when he was up on his feet again. He looked around, shook himself and walked slowly through the kitchen, out of the back door, and began cropping the lawn with his six-year-old teeth.

'Jesus,' said my sister.

She thanked Mr Lomax for his help and he gave her a couple of Liberal Party posters to put in the upstairs windows.

Our mother ended up staying in the clinic for a night and our grandmother arrived to stay with us. When she saw the wrecked banister she asked how it had happened, and we told her Maxwell had done it. She was confused about who Maxwell was but didn't admit it or ask for details. She just shrugged and tutted and tried not to look at it. We sorted out our mother's bedroom except for the broken stool, which we hid in a cupboard.

Then when our mother returned we said that Maxwell had barged into the banister by accident. Our poor mother was too tired and sad to even think about it but rang Mr Lomax from her bed and of course he knew all about it and the truth came out. As so often, my sister and I hadn't thought it through.

'Mr Lomax tells me you brought the fucking pony up here!' said our mother, suddenly more awake.

'Not as such,' I began to say. And that's when she got cross and we ended up cleaning out the hen house. I was dreading Mr Lomax turning up and giving a full account of the event, but luckily he rang back and insulted our mother by asking for a cheque upfront and waiting for it to clear in the bank before he began the work. Either that, or cash. And our mother told him not to bother and that she'd arrange for someone else to come.

Neither my sister nor I have ever forgotten the rule about horses and upstairs windows and I've never had one inside since. Nor that an overnight stay might be required with a pregnancy termination.

21

The Longladys were going to America for a whole fortnight for the holiday of a lifetime. And to see a seriously ill relative of Mrs Longlady's who lived in Boston. Melody was beside herself as she had always longed to see Boston in the fall. I wasn't sure what it meant to see Boston in the fall, except it meant seeing Boston.

Mr Longlady wasn't going on the holiday and wouldn't be seeing Boston because, according to Melody, he'd seen an American film about a psychopathic American truck driver that had given him recurring nightmares, plus it was one less airfare and someone to hold the fort and feed the bees.

It was coming up to the time of the USA trip when our mother began to tell us how things were looking financially (quite bad). It was a strange and curious thing that as recently as 1970 Vogel's, the business, had been given the Queen's Award for Industry and was used as a business case-study and had sponsored a new department at the university. But by 1972 parts of it were in serious trouble and, sadly for our mother, the bit of the business that she had shares in, Vogel Machine Parts (VMP), was in the deepest trouble. So much so, the dividends were not forthcoming. Added to which her savings had been very much used up on bills she didn't even know she had. Such as enormous bills from Miss Woods's shop.

One particular bill from Miss Woods's shop was ten times what our mother was expecting. And she did what people do when they get a bill of that kind: she asked for a breakdown. Seeing it itemized caused her to take an intake of breath so sharp it was like a skidding car.

'Cold cuts,' she said. 'It's pound after pound of cold cuts.'

'What are 'cold cuts'?' I asked.

My sister took the itemized bill from her and looked. Then she said, 'What are cold cuts?'

'Ham,' said our mother. 'Pound after pound of ham.'

'And lots of this, look,' my sister pointed. 'What is that?'

'Tobacco,' said our mother. 'I shan't be angry, but have any of you been getting ham and tobacco from Miss Woods's shop?'

We said we definitely hadn't. But she'd known it wasn't us before she asked.

'How can he have eaten so much ham?' she wondered aloud.

'He did like ham,' said my sister.

'But pounds and pounds of it?' said our mother, shaking her head in dismay.

We'd stopped having anything ham-like a long time ago after my sister spoke to a young woman who worked in the VG store and said that unless you can see what part of the body the meat is (e.g., leg or wing), then it's probably all the stringy bits, nostrils and lips and so forth, all mushed up.

But we'd hated the hams even before that.

258

There were three types: the traditional ham leg, rolled in gingery breadcrumbs that looked like the ham from *The Tale of Two Bad Mice*. The haslet, tweedy-looking and unashamedly made from bits and bobs and lips and sinew, along with porridge oats. Finally, and worst of all, tongue — the whole tongue, from far back in the throat, deeper than the mouth, and that was truly grotesque. Miss Woods would heave these monster meats between the chiller cabinet and the slicer, holding them against her body like great fat babies.

In addition to the usual reasons for hating the hams (the appearance, smell and death of the pig), I hated the influence they seemed to have over the people of the parish. Old ladies would walk from outlying hamlets to get the haslet, and old men would buy just one slice of something for a lonely lunch and walk back the very next day to get another. Housewives bought a selection for the whole family's sandwiches for a week.

Miss Woods's shop was never ever empty. You never walked in and had to wait for her to come in from the back. She always had people queuing for the hams. She didn't even boil or cure them herself. She got them from the same place that the Co-op and VG got theirs, from Gormond's the catering butcher. But people still liked to queue for it and watch her wrestling with it and carving it.

It irritated me that the ham was so popular when it was nothing special and that so much of it was on our bill when we hated it. My sister reminded our mother that she should seek advice from her accountant about the bills and so forth. My sister knew the parlance because we'd acted out an informative little play on the subject our mother was working on. I'd played our mother and our mother had played my father (albeit only telephone voiceover).

> Roderick: (*on phone*) You have shares made in your favour and you must manage them and live on the dividends.
> Adele: I'm not au fait with finance and invest-ments, as you well know. You are torturing me.
> Roderick: You must manage your affairs.
> Adele: There seem to be no dividends forthcoming. I'm in dire straits.
> Roderick: You must see Mr Box, your accountant, and hopefully fiscal confidence might ensue.

And then in a later scene my sister had played the accountant, Mr Box.

> Mr Box: Do you not read your statements of advice, Mrs Bird?
> Adele: I do, Mr Box, but I'm not always fully up to grasping the meaning.
> Mr Box: The spending of the money is easy, Mrs Bird, the understanding and managing of it are a requirement.

And our mother, directing, had said, 'Mr Box is much less jolly than that. Play him as a bit of a bully.'

So we knew from the play that things were not only bad but that our mother was uncertain about the shares, afraid of the accountant and therefore uncertain as to the direness of the straits. None of it came as a shock. It was just a new thing to be thought about.

And I did think about it and, just like Sherlock Holmes, a recollection came to me, very clearly, from the time that I'd searched in the Longlady house for Bufo the frog. I'd noticed a thing I hadn't been looking for at the time, a seemingly unimportant detail, and filed it away in my mind for later.

And it was this: I'd noticed that Mr Longlady had been working on a sideboard which was doubling as a desk — albeit a narrow, long one — in a hallway, his actual office having been given over to make a shower room for Mrs Longlady. Mr Longlady had been working from a battered old textbook called *The DuPont Method of Business Accounting* or *Return on Investment the DuPont Way* or something along those lines.

I told my sister this recollection and suggested that we should add Mr Longlady to the list. Not intending that he should become the man at the helm, or have grown-up conversation or sex with our mother, but to help her understand and manage her finances via his accountancy training and get her out of the financial pickle that she was most definitely in. Especially as Mrs Longlady was going to be off the scene on the holiday of a lifetime seeing Boston in the fall.

My sister reminded me that Mr Longlady had

actually been on the list since the list began and for exactly such an occurrence. Which was very true when I thought about it, I just hadn't noticed him — that's how unnoticeable he was, even on the list in blue pen. Anyway, the letter went like this:

Dear Mr Longlady,

I would be exceedingly grateful if you could spare me a few minutes to discuss some shares I've had made over in my favour from my ex-husband in lieu of maintenance. I really need an accountant and would prefer one who has studied the DuPont method. Even if they don't know that much about the DuPont, just a smattering of under-standing would be impressive. Please call in for a drink and a snack one day, preferably tomorrow while my children are at school and your wife has gone on holiday.

It is imperative that you don't tell your wife. I suspect that your coming to my house would be seen as high treason — in spite of her offering your services when we first moved to this village.

Yours sincerely etc.

Then one day when three of the four Longladys were safely away seeing Boston and we were waiting to see if he'd call in, our mother came into the playroom looking perturbed and holding the letter we'd sent to Mr Longlady.

'What's that?' my sister asked, knowing full well.

'It's a letter from me to Mr Longlady,' said our mother.

'What are you writing to him for?' asked my sister.

'I'm not. I have never written to Mr Longlady, but he just called to show me this. Someone has written to him purporting to be me,' she said, and explained that someone, she couldn't think who, had written to Mr Longlady, alluding to our private family matters.

'What does it say?' I asked.

My sister read the letter with a tone and expression of puzzlement.

'I don't understand,' my sister said.

Our mother boiled up a pot of coffee and tried to work out who could have or would have written such a letter and why. She got an extra cup out for Mr Longlady, who was apparently due back any minute after feeding the bees.

'It does sound quite like me,' she said, meaning the letter, 'but older and more formal.'

Mr Longlady appeared at the door and they settled down to a cup of coffee.

'I'm sorry,' said our mother. 'I am so embarrassed and can't think who'd do this.'

'Not at all,' said Mr Longlady, 'it's just malicious lies.'

'Well, the letter is quite right about the shares. And in fact it's pretty much accurate in every way. I don't know why but they seem to have dried up.'

And then they started discussing the situation.

'I'm ashamed to say I'm hopeless on the whole money thing,' said our mother.

'It can be tricky,' said Mr Longlady, sounding nothing like the bullying Mr Box. 'If you like I'll look at your paperwork and advise, if I can.'

Mr Longlady was there all day and even had lunch with us and because, like every other man I've ever known, he was a huge fan of omelettes, we had omelettes with cheese and Ryvitas. And he read some paperwork and went home, taking more paperwork with him. He was back again the next day with his thoughts.

There was never any question of his becoming the man at the helm. The accounts were too important for one thing, but also he had very clearly advertised a crop of mouth ulcers and a recent chesty cough during which he'd lived on Veno's Lightning Cough Cure.

Mr Longlady was most alarmed by the state of our mother's financial affairs. There was no money whatsoever coming in from our mother's shares, he said. He suggested she speak to my father urgently. Our mother explained that she didn't like to ask for any more money, especially after the Eccles Topaz incident, which had been humiliating in the extreme. Mr Longlady said she must clarify the financial situation as a matter of urgency. He sat again at the kitchen table with his shirt sleeves up, reading more pieces of paper and tapping his finger on lines of numbers on the statements from the bank. And wondering where it had all gone. After a while he said, 'Mrs Vogel, I think there are some documents you aren't showing me.'

And our mother admitted there were.

'Everything points to the fact that you have mortgaged the house in order to pay some of your debts,' he said.

And she had. She broke down then and Mr Longlady was very kind and said she wasn't to blame etc. The problem was this. Somehow our mother had very little actual money and had never actually had much, only shares from which money dribbled out and kept her going. Shares in this and that, she had sold; and shares in the other thing, she had sold; and shares in Vogel Machine Parts, she hadn't been allowed to sell due to them being her divorce settlement in lieu of maintenance. The VMP shares, though, were in a part of the business that had barely chugged along for years and had never been up to much, and now that the other parts of the business were suffering in the recession and unable to help VMP, VMP was down and almost out.

In spite of all her mixed experiences — in having a mother who disliked her and going to an unimaginative boarding school, getting expelled for being imaginative, being coaxed into marrying an iconoclast — our mother was unprepared for anything unusual happening and, like others of her class, it hadn't occurred to her that anything untoward would or could happen. She'd mortgaged our house to help Charlie complete his bungalow shells and when the VMP money dried up our mother was suddenly, literally, without money.

Mr Longlady came again on and off

throughout the following week and went through files and files of papers and even spoke to the bank on our mother's behalf and gave her options. He said one option was to remortgage and use the capital, and another option was to sell and buy a less expensive property. Our mother nodded. Then, suddenly, he had to go and collect his wife and children from the airport.

She thanked him. She actually said he'd gone above and beyond and that she couldn't thank him enough and gave him a tube of Bonjela that she'd picked up while getting her prescription made up. After he'd gone our mother sat for a moment with her head dramatically in her hands.

'Are you going to remortgage?' I asked, really to remind her of the key part of Mr Longlady's advice.

'I've already done that,' she said, 'I just didn't show him that paperwork. I think we'll have to sell up, which is pretty much the same thing, except you have to move out.'

★   ★   ★

In the middle of the Mr Longlady accounts episode, everyone got into a tizz when Little Jack's claim that he couldn't hear with his eyes shut became a proper worry. It was something he'd been claiming for some time. For instance, when our mother read to us from *The Hobbit* my sister and I would doze off, lulled by her boozy slurring voice (even she was lulled by it), but Little Jack would sit staring at her as she read.

'Snuggle down,' she'd say, 'close your eyes and imagine.'

And he'd say, 'But I can't hear with my eyes shut.'

So when there was a minor little fire in the omelette pan one day and Mr Longlady witnessed it and shouted that we should all evacuate the house as a precaution, we called and called and Little Jack just lay on the settee rotating one foot, most definitely awake but unhearing, and Mr Longlady — who was wrestling with a tiny fire extinguisher — said, 'Is he deaf?'

And eventually my sister threw a beaker of water through the hatch and he leapt up.

'I couldn't hear you,' he said with a stammer, 'I had my eyes closed.'

And when our mother was in Diggory's Kitchen Cave the following week, replacing the egg pan and looking at pretty glassware that she suddenly couldn't afford to buy (clear goblets with coloured stems), the new seriousness of Jack's claims suddenly dawned and we dashed out of Diggory's to consult Dr Kaufmann by phone (as it turned out).

We drove home with my sister doing hearing experiments on Little Jack and trying to catch him out. The thing was, though, with Jack you had to admit it seemed as though he was always right. And, more importantly, he didn't make stuff up.

We weren't going to be allowed to come to Dr

Kaufmann's for this unusual consultation unless we swore to be quiet and good, because laboratory conditions might be needed in order to test him. In the end, though, we were only there a minute as Dr Kaufmann simply referred Jack for a hearing test at Leicester Royal Infirmary. He actually telephoned the unit and got an appointment there and then for the following week.

★   ★   ★

When Melody Longlady came back to school after the USA trip, she'd prepared a little talk for the class entitled 'My Trip to the USA'. She hadn't prepared the talk in order to show off, but because Mrs Clarke had said she must after having a fortnight off school gadding about in America while the rest of us had 'done test after test and endured the mundane'. Mrs Clarke was our teacher for the new school year and she was as lovely as Miss Thorne had been mean. Full of enthusiasm, but a stickler for hard work too.

I was glad to have Melody back, us being secret friends and her being very handy for the walk home. And the whole class was agog to hear the USA talk. Not because we were that interested in someone else's dream holiday, but it was always interesting when some poor person had to stand in front of the class and give a talk and you felt that mix of intense sympathy and fascination.

When it came to giving the talk, Melody was quite shy and just read out a stream of things that none of us could take in, or even hear properly, about Boston and New York being on the east coast of the United States of America and having such and such population. At the end, Mrs Clarke thanked Melody for the factual account and suggested we follow on with a question-and-answer session in order to get a more personal response. It was clever and thoughtful of Mrs Clarke to suggest the Q&A because it suited Melody and she really got into her stride and told us some interesting things.

I can still remember the first question and answer because it made such an impact on me.

Mrs Clarke: So, Melody, what most impressed you about America?
Melody: The friendliness of the American people.

Melody expanded on this theme and told the class that at the start of the trip the Longlady family had felt rather anxious about all the smiling and friendliness and people saying hello to them and asking how they were doing. Unused to such warmth, for the first few days they really hadn't known what to make of it, and had worried more than once that someone was about to shoot them dead.

There had only been one person on the entire trip who'd acted disgruntled and that had been a small man who'd said a nasty thing about Northern Ireland and Melody's mother had come back at him with Vietnam and then they'd had to hurry along to avoid a deterioration. They soon got used to the immense kindness and niceness and started to enjoy it and then, arriving back in Britain, they'd found everyone utterly cold and rude by comparison.

'Has anyone else got a question for Melody about America?' asked Mrs Clarke.

I put my hand up.

'Yes, Lizzie.'

'Was the food nice?' I asked.

Melody seemed thrilled that I'd asked that and launched into a list of amazing food experiences they had had. Starting with Day One, when they'd arrived at the hotel and been exhausted — or to use the American, 'pooped' — but not particularly hungry, and decided to ring down for room service rather than go out for a proper dinner. They ordered beef sandwiches and tea to have in front of *Abbott and Costello*, which was on permanently.

They'd been expecting a few dry triangles with a dish of mustard and maybe some lettuce. But what arrived was half a cow's worth (each) of succulent roast beef slices, a basket of salted crisps, exotic leaves, tiny tomatoes, avocado slices and melted cheese, all on a silver tray with a variety of mayonnaises and mustards. And the tea wasn't just a simple cup of tea, but pint glasses of a sweet orange liquid over crushed ice, mint leaves and lemon slices. The description reminded me of our mother's pre-split dinners.

The class gasped at the idea of half a cow each and Melody continued with further tales of American food items being bigger and nicer than they expected.

I walked home with Melody after school. I asked (out of politeness) after the dying aunt they'd visited in Boston — whether she'd died or was still hanging on — and it turned out they'd not seen the aunt because she'd gone on a water-colour painting course that coincided with their trip.

I told Melody how much I'd love to emigrate to New York, for the food and the friendliness and the general excitement.

'I wish my family could go and live in America,' I said.

'I don't think your family would work out over there,' said Melody.

'Why?' I asked.

'You have to be absolutely normal and you can't act strange or unusual, they don't like it. You might get shot,' she said.

So I dropped the fantasy of emigrating and went off Melody a bit too.

22

Little Jack had, some months before, entered a national competition to win a bicycle. He'd answered a few questions about bicycle safety with ease, saying how you had to be aware of the brakes and use hand signals for turning and so on, but had struggled a bit with the tie-breaking slogan as slogans weren't his thing, so he asked our mother. And she came up with this:

> Whether bread, eggs, milk and cheese,
> Steak, mince or a lean pork chop,
> Beans, lettuce, spuds and peas,
> For freshness visit your Co-op.

She just said it without even having to think about it. But Jack didn't like it. 'It's too long, it's a poem. They only want a slogan.'

And then Jack himself came up with 'The Co-op — your fresh friend'.

It was good, but he'd never have come up with it had our mother not mentioned freshness in her poem.

Anyway, we'd forgotten all about the competition but it turned out that freshness was indeed the key, and we found out that week (the week of the accountancy realizations) that Little Jack had won a prize. Jack couldn't go himself to receive the prize because you had to be over eighteen to enter the competition, so our mother had to attend the ceremony and be publicly awarded one of three possible prizes (a bike or one of two hampers, one with assorted cheeses and pale ales and one with chutneys, jams and preserves).

The people who turned up to witness the grand giving away of the prizes by a local councillor seemed upset when our mother was awarded the bicycle and her slogan was praised for its simplicity and for mentioning freshness. One old lady actually shouted out, 'That woman's got a nerve entering a competition to win a bicycle — she could afford ten of them.'

And no one clapped as she wheeled it past. A man from the *Herald* and a woman from the *Mercury* took a few pictures of her scurrying away and I felt a bit sick. The faces of the little crowd ranged from bored to disgusted. And when we got to the safety of our back garden our mother dropped the Raleigh Superbe, put her fluttering hands up to her face and stood a moment like that. We all stood still as if to respect her. Then, just as she was recovering, Mr Longlady called round to ask how things were going, accounts-wise. Our mother put the coffee on and they sat at the kitchen table.

'Well, Little Jack won a bicycle,' she told him, 'so it's not all hardship.'

And then the door buzzer sounded again. It was Mrs Longlady this time and, hearing her voice, Mr Longlady slipped into the utility room.

'Congratulations on your luck,' said Mrs Longlady.

'It wasn't luck — it wasn't a raffle,' said my sister. 'It was a competition.'

'Well, congratulations on your skill,' said Mrs Longlady.

We waited a while for Mrs Longlady to speak. But she didn't and for a while neither of them did. Our mother understood the power of silence and knew that the desperation to fill a gap with words could put one at a disadvantage. Anyway, Mrs Longlady must also have known about the power of silence and was on that occasion stronger and annoyingly our mother cracked first. To be fair, she had just gone through the humiliation of winning a bike that no one wanted her to win and wheeling it away from a hundred scowls.

'So, how can we help you, Mrs Longlady?' said our mother reluctantly and putting herself at a disadvantage.

'I was wondering what you planned to do with the Raleigh Superbe,' said Mrs Longlady with a satisfied sniff.

'In what respect?' asked our mother.

'Well, I assume you won't keep it, and thought you might want to find a charitable solution,' said Mrs Longlady.

'No, I plan to keep it for the time being,' said our mother.

'I am surprised,' said Mrs Longlady. 'I'd have thought you'd want to give it to someone needy.'

'Yes, I might give it away,' said our mother.

'May I ask to whom?' said Mrs Longlady.

'To my son Jack,' she said, and gestured to Little Jack.

'But I meant for charity,' said Mrs Longlady. 'You know the village thinks it bad form you entering the competition at all.'

'Does it?' said our mother. 'Why?'

'Because you have so much and it was a chance for someone else to win something.'

'Well, thanks for calling,' said our mother. And she ushered Mrs Longlady to the door and closed it behind her with a slam.

Mr Longlady came out of the utility room, red in the face.

A different man might have taken our mother in his arms and kissed her on the mouth. But Mr Longlady's hands were as shaky as our mother's had been earlier and he looked as if he might be sick.

★   ★   ★

The day of Little Jack's hearing test at the Royal Infirmary came round. Our mother shuddered at the thought of Leicester Royal Infirmary because of all the babies — dead and alive — she'd either had or not had in that place, and all she could think of was either holding a baby or not and being desperate for a cigarette and wanting to phone someone but not knowing who and realizing there was no one to phone. And the memories and the prospect mingled and she was good for nothing but writing a play. Which she did, called *The Navy Nurse*, about a senior nurse who wears a navy dress.

My sister said, 'I'll take Jack to the hospital, Mum.' And I said, 'And me.'

And the three of us went into town on the bus, all through the little villages and lanes, and we sat at the back and ate a bag of kali fishes that we'd got at Miss Woods's, with cash, before the bus came.

It seemed a waste of time just to test out Little Jack's loopy hearing/eyesight mix-up, and it was an utterly boring day except for the bit where Jack had to wear enormous headphones and press buttons if he heard a buzz. My sister and I couldn't stop laughing at his serious little face and his slight starts every time the headphones buzzed and his eagerness to do the thing properly. The audiologist asked us to wait outside. Afterwards, she came out and said she'd write to our mother with the results. She seemed a bit cross with us. I hated being thought badly of, so I said, 'I'm eleven and my sister is twelve. We didn't mean to be nasty, we're just making the best of things.'

'I don't care if you're six and seven, your brother was undergoing a serious testing procedure and you were laughing at him.' And she strode away down the corridor. I was momentarily distraught and considered running after her, but didn't.

Some days after, the results came through saying Jack had perfect hearing, and though we weren't surprised, we were relieved. Then our mother asked if he'd closed his eyes during the test and he stupidly said he hadn't.

Our mother rang Dr Kaufmann and reminded him that Jack's hearing was only a problem if he had his eyes closed and could he please make another referral for Jack with that in mind. And a few days later an appointment came through for

Little Jack to see a paediatric counsellor. Our mother rang the consultant's number and demanded an explanation. 'Why, though?' she kept asking, and 'But what is it you're looking for?'

And our mother and my sister went to Dr Kaufmann and asked for an explanation from him. He was quite direct, apparently, and said something along the lines of Little Jack might *think* he can't hear with his eyes closed and he might think it so strongly that he's making it seem as if it's happening by cutting himself off aurally.

'So what if he does?' asked our mother deeply concerned.

'It might mean Jack is anxious about something,' the doctor said.

'Could it be *The Hobbit*?' my sister asked.

'It could be a number of things making him feel anxious,' said the doctor, 'and it might help Jack if we knew what it was. If anything.'

Our mother reluctantly agreed to see the counsellor but didn't in the end. She told Jack to keep his fucking eyes open and told us to go and shake him in case of fire. And we went to the Copper Kettle for a new egg pan. Which was twice the price of Diggory's but closer and had ample parking.

★　★　★

Then Charlie turned up like a bad penny. He asked to borrow money. Our mother said she didn't have any; she said it wearily and with a

277

sadness in her voice. Not so much sad at not having it as sad that he was here again asking.

I'm weary writing about it, I think, because her weariness comes back to me. Charlie asked imploringly and with much energy. She said she really didn't think she could help, she was waiting for a little money to clear in the bank for tax and rates that were overdue. She even repeated some of the stuff Mr Longlady had explained.

Charlie came up with possible ways and means of releasing money but she said no, she really couldn't help, and told him she was in dire financial straits. She told him that a man from the council had called at the house about the arrears on the rates. And about Miss Woods from the shop and the bill and how it had been all ham and rolling tobacco.

She said, emphatically albeit calmly, that she couldn't get any more money because our father's business was going broke bit by bit, and that although she'd only ever known being rich, she now had to start being poor. This was all said with such an air of finality and authority that my sister and I could hardly believe our ears when Charlie continued asking and saying that if she could just find a way to help him, he'd be able to wriggle free of Mrs Bates and be with her, properly and for ever. He took her two hands in his and said, 'Please, love, please.'

Our mother still said no, she couldn't help. Eventually she raised her voice. 'Look, Charlie, you've had all I've got, and Little Jack's going deaf with the worry of it. Now, please go.'

He left, slamming the door, and she was upset. We crowded round her and didn't even pretend we hadn't been listening.

★ ★ ★

A day or so later he phoned from a phone box and whatever he told her, it sent her into a spin.

'I can't get that amount in one go, there's a daily maximum,' she said, 'but I'll be there with what I can get today . . . I'll get more tomorrow . . . OK, where are you?'

We all had to get into the car straight away. She drove like a mad thing into town, parked on Horsefair Street, where no one else would dream of parking, and launched herself at a man closing the outer doors of the Midland Bank. She begged him to let her in. And he did.

She returned to the car moments later and she drove fast, heading south out of town, until we got stuck behind someone in a pink car driving extremely slowly. The pink car kept slowing down as if the driver might be looking for a house number or something. It was an unusual colour for a car and my sister wondered if it might be a prostitute's car and her slowing down to flash her naked body at pedestrians. Our mother became so impatient she roared round the pink car, overtaking on the wrong side, driving over a few front gardens and through some small shrubs.

My sister screamed, 'God, Mum!' or something, and our mother explained that she'd had no option and that the driver of the pink car had just proved the well-known fact that driving too slowly was far more dangerous than driving too fast.

'Where are we going?' my sister asked.

'Wharf Way,' said our mother.

Wharf Way was an industrial area on the edge of town where you might go for a new exhaust pipe or to chuck something unwanted into the canal.

'Why there?' asked my sister.

'Because Charlie's in danger, they're going to hurt him if he doesn't pay his debts,' said our mother, dissolving, and my sister knew to leave it there.

We got there and she parked overlooking the canal, and we sat quietly for some time while she rifled through her bag. The still, dark water made me feel cold. It turned out that we'd arrived very early for whatever we were there for.

'Hell, we're early,' she said.

Cigarette smoke was building up in the car and no one would agree to have a window open.

'It's cold,' said Jack.

'But I can't breathe,' I said.

'Oh, shut up, can't you,' said our mother. She looked at her watch. Then she smoothed out a scribbled note.

'Oh God, I think we're in the wrong place.' She gazed out of the window and then at her note and then her watch. 'Nevis, Nevis, Nevis,' she chanted — and then looked at the note again. I got out of the car and leant on the bonnet. It was so cold and windy, I was about to get back into the car when my sister got out.

'This is insane,' she said, and the wind blew so hard we leant into it and laughed.

'Get in,' our mother shouted at us.

'No, it's too smoky,' my sister shouted back.

'Get in, I want to be ready to go,' our mother shouted from the car window.

'Go where, though?' shouted my sister. 'What are we doing here?'

We carried on leaning into the wind and in the distance I saw the word 'Nevis' emblazoned on the side of a building and was about to point it out to our mother when she drove off, leaving us standing there. My sister and I looked at each other for a moment in disbelief. It was a dreadful place to be left, the awful water behind us and the wind wrapping our hair round our faces, and I felt quite panicked. I pointed and we ran, battling the wind, towards the Nevis building.

Things take an unpleasant turn here, I must warn you.

We got to Nevis and walked around it. A temporary giant For Sale sign had blown down and was careering around the empty car park and then a metal bin rolled towards us and I felt under attack. It seemed sensible to go into the building through the little open door.

We entered an enormous open space. The vastness and the sudden calm were difficult to adjust to. It was empty except for a few boxes and quite a lot of litter in the corners. On the steeply vaulted ceiling, which was at least twenty foot high, were lines and lines of tubular lights but only one line was illuminated. And except for the noise of the debris being blown about outside there was just a faint electric hum. I investigated a small flight of stairs and found myself on a mezzanine ledge. My sister followed and, seeing shadows, we stopped.

Fifty yards ahead, behind a low partition, stood Charlie Bates in a sort of kitchenette and Mr Lomax, pouring water from a kettle into a mug. We quickly bobbed down behind a tower of boxes. We were about to see a fight in a kitchen. Another fight in another kitchen. This one, in the Nevis warehouse kitchenette, was going to make the egg-water throwing skirmish of 1970 seem almost quaint.

Anyway, Charlie was leaning on the sink, Mr Lomax was sipping his hot water from a Derby County mug. Charlie was angry with Mr Lomax. It was difficult to hear Mr Lomax's side of the conversation because of the wind outside.

'I've had to do everything,' he said, 'every single fucking thing.'

Mr Lomax looked at the floor and said something inaudible.

'Right from the start, it's all been me,' Charlie shouted. 'I've had to go there and lie and lie, and you ponce around reading maps and patting the horse — this one was supposed to be yours,' said Charlie.

Mr Lomax looked ashamed.

'Well, she'll be here in a minute. I need to look like someone's set the boys on me,' Charlie said, 'so you'd better smack me up a bit.'

Mr Lomax said something we couldn't hear.

'Come on,' said Charlie, 'punch me in the mouth.'

Mr Lomax slapped Charlie softly on the face. 'What the fuck was that?' said Charlie, furious.

Mr Lomax slapped him again, harder this time, and Charlie slapped him back.

'Don't slap me, punch me, c'mon,' said Charlie, and slapped Lomax again. 'You got to punch me' — he pointed to his mouth — 'in the mouth.'

Mr Lomax punched Charlie in the mouth. Charlie staggered back and touched his lip.

'That's better,' he said. 'Again.'

Mr Lomax lashed out feebly a few more times. Charlie looked at his watch and then inspected himself in the mirrored splashback of the Nevis kitchenette. He roughed his hair up and agitated his clothing.

'D'you think I'll do?' he said.

Mr Lomax said something inaudible and Charlie said, 'Do I look roughed up?'

'You look fine,' said Mr Lomax.

Charlie looked at himself some more in the tiles, sighed dramatically and picked up a metal spatula from the drainer. He took a deep breath and began hitting himself across the face and head with it, again and again. He grunted and yelled as he did it and then grabbed a small breadboard and began beating himself around the head with it.

Mr Lomax looked away, put his knuckles to his mouth and whimpered. Charlie picked items off the draining board and hit himself with them and threw them down. At last, Mr Lomax lunged forward, flung his arms around Charlie and shouted, 'That's enough.'

And they slumped against the sink together, breathing heavily. Mr Lomax sank to the floor. Charlie looked again in the mirrored tiles. He laughed. 'Ha, 'smore like it,' he said thickly, and blood bubbled in a line across his handsome mouth.

Mr Lomax got up and, looking as if he was going to fall down again, leant against a wall.

'Go to the car, I'll meet you round the back.'

Mr Lomax didn't move.

We heard a car, it was Gloxinia. I recognized the squealing fan belt. Charlie looked out of a window slit.

'OK, here we go, El Indio,' he said, and looking at Mr Lomax he groaned.

Charlie left by the fire exit. Mr Lomax wiped his face and neck with a J-cloth and followed.

We watched as the fire door clanged shut and ran on tiptoe to the door, peeped out and saw Charlie limp out across the pointless lawn. Our mother stood there beside the car. I couldn't see much and the buffeting wind made it difficult to read the body language. But I saw the hand-over-mouth gesture of horror and I saw her scrabbling in her bag for the money.

My sister picked up a broken umbrella from the warehouse floor and was suddenly running towards them. I tried to follow, but the door swung back and knocked me to my knees. Looking up I saw our mother cradling Charlie and suddenly my sister lashing out at him with the skeletal brolly. Our mother screamed and danced Charlie out of reach, but my sister jumped on his back. Our mother grabbed my sister from behind, but she kicked out hard and caught him on the side of the head and Charlie limped away into the dark like an injured animal.

Our mother tried to run after him but my sister caught her and held her. The two of them were crying like something out of a police drama, their wind-blown hair all tangled together.

'We need to get out of here,' I said, but the wind caught my words and no one heard.

'We need to get out of here,' I tried again, and they still stood there. 'Get into the car, we need to get home,' I screamed, and I must've sounded authoritative then because we all got in and our mother started the engine. Little Jack was lying across the back seat, asleep, and I had to shove him along.

'Can you drive?' I asked our mother.

'Yes,' she said. She wiped her face with her sleeve and drove us carefully home.

⋆ ⋆ ⋆

At home Jack went to bed early with hot chocolate and my sister asked our mother twice if she'd like us to ring Dr Kaufmann. And after a while my sister asked again and then just rang Dr Kaufmann. He arrived and spoke to our mother for seventeen minutes and then left. On the way out he spoke to my sister and me.

'It's very hard when people don't behave well, especially when it's people we trust,' he said. 'Be very nice to her.' And we agreed we would.

The thing was, though, I wasn't (very nice to her). I felt cross and disgusted and that she was nothing but an idiot. So I just ignored her and took money from her purse in the fruit bowl and hung around outside eating sweets. If it rained, I did piano practice to drown everything out. After a day or two, I felt guilty and sorry and back to normal.

I went and plonked myself down on the sofa in her sitting room. She was sitting on the floor reading papers, ghostly with white, dry lips and looking as if she'd been in the bath too long or had died.

'Sorry,' I said.

'You shouldn't be sorry, Lizzie,' she said, and touched my head.

And then because I was back to normal it was my sister's turn to be nasty and she stayed away and tutted at everything our mother said and took money from her purse etc., but just for one day, luckily. Then, when she'd got over her unkindness, the three of us had a family-size packet of KP nuts and talked things over.

Although she looked like someone out of a horror film, our mother seemed quite calm and sensible. 'Well, I've completely messed everything up,' she said, 'and I've been stupid and blind . . . and now we have to think about the future.'

It occurred to me at that point, and not before, that she was about to say, 'And I'm very sorry but you will have to be made wards of court.' My sister looked stricken and I took that to mean she thought the same as me.

But she didn't, she was only worried about the ponies. 'Well, we can't keep *four* of them,' our mother said, 'we've got no money.'

My sister put her face in her hands and, however sad it was for her, I realized then that everything was going to be all right. We'd got no money. That was all. It was the norm — everyone had no money. That was the point, wasn't it? We'd had money when no one else had. Now we were going to be like everyone else. Or even more so, one of the underdogs. That was how I saw it and it was like a weight lifting.

My sister wanted to know if our mother might get the police on to Charlie for cheating her. Our mother said that Charlie hadn't committed any crime in law, only one of the heart, and the heart didn't count for much in the law unless it was murder.

'I could murder *him*,' said my sister.

We had a tea break and then moved on to more practical things, and our mother said she would do her best to sort things out and my sister wondered whether our father might be able to help.

'No, he can't help,' said our mother, and then she couldn't really talk any more, she just wanted to get drunk and go to bed.

'Why don't you write a play?' my sister asked.

'I need to think about getting the house ready to sell,' she said. 'Tomorrow I'll give Mr Lomax a ring and get him in to fix the banister.'

My sister and I left the room.

'Does she know about Lomax?' I asked.

'No, I didn't tell her,' said my sister.

'Should we tell her?' I asked.

'No, definitely not. We should let her ask him to come and fix the banister,' said my very clever sister, 'and see what happens.'

Mr Lomax came and fixed the banister. He turned up the next day and did a marvellous job and had a little go at other things too and when our mother asked for the bill, he said not to worry, she could pay him another time.

And after he'd gone we admired the fixed banister and the way he'd smoothed the dents in the parquet flooring and the lovely job he'd done on the slate floor.

'What a lovely fellow,' said our mother and, feeling better about mankind, went and wrote some of her play.

Later that evening we had the misery of acting it out. It was the trickiest bit of drama we'd ever attempted and quite draining. My sister insisted on playing herself (her being quite brave and heroic and saving us a couple of hundred quid, if not more) and because our mother was playing Charlie, the two of them had to choreograph a brutal stage fight — the result being Charlie dies from a bruise on the brain. It took ages to get the final kick right because my sister couldn't get her leg high enough to reach his 'greying temple' and in the end they had to turn it into a punch. Also, our mother kept changing Charlie's deathbed speech from 'I'm sorry, Elizabeth' to 'I do love you, it's just that I'm a rogue.'

I was playing our mother (as usual) and I swear to God I saw the whole vile situation clearly for the first time. Even though I'd lived right through it. That's how brilliant she was at writing plays.

*   *   *

At some point, soon after the Charlie fight, Mr Gummo had been clearing up the wind-blown garden and our mother had gone out to offer him a cup of coffee and he'd said what he always said, 'No, thank you, Mrs V, I'm happy with my flask.'

Our mother took her mug out anyway and told Mr Gummo she was going to have to let him go. He had to sit down on the garden bench and seemed to be blinking back tears. Our mother explained it was beyond her control — money was tight and due to be a lot tighter. Mr Gummo had of course heard rumours. The subject of the rumours he'd heard concerning our mother had only ever been about the financial situation within the business, and not about s-e-x as we'd assumed. Our mother poured her heart out to him and told him how stupid she'd been and that she should apologize to everyone for the mess she'd created.

'I should apologize to his wife,' she said.

'*Wife?*' said Mr Gummo. 'Charles Bates isn't married.'

'He is,' she said.

'No,' said Mr Gummo, assuredly, 'really, he's not a married man.'

'But Lilian?' said our mother.

'Oh, *Lilian*,' said Mr Gummo, with a sniff. 'Lilian's his mother.'

289

After a brief pause our mother took it well, she even laughed. Mr Gummo didn't see the funny side, though, and he stayed solemn.

'What a world we live in, Mrs V,' he said. 'Thank God for fauna and flora.' And they sipped their coffee.

He'd got all sorts of things coming up out of the ground over the coming months that he'd be very sad not to see, he said, in particular some alliums and Mexican daisies, whose seeds he'd collected from a wall and sown the spring before. That was the thing about gardening, the garden isn't about today but about tomorrow (his words), and he wondered if he might come and see how things were doing from time to time.

Our mother said of course he might and that she'd recommend him wholeheartedly to the new people. Hearing that she was planning to sell the house, Mr Gummo wondered if he might just keep the garden looking its best while she tried to sell the house and be *in situ* when the new owners took possession.

'Yes, I see,' said our mother, 'you mean as a sitting tenant, as it were?'

And they agreed that he'd keep the beds ticking over and the lawns nice, and tidy the laid hedge etc. and very much exist in the eyes of any buyer.

PART III

A Wholesome Endeavour

23

The Man List was looking very sparse when suddenly two new doctors came to the village. It wasn't that Dr Kaufmann was leaving, just that the village had trebled its population due to two housing estates being tacked on and joining up with various little hamlets that had been quite remote before. The village therefore needed more doctors to look after all the extra sick people and their sick children.

My sister and I got the news about these two new doctors from Mrs C. Beard, who told us that one of the doctors was quite handsome and almost divorced and the other was going to be a lady and probably best avoided unless you had a lady's problem. My sister and I focused on Dr Norman (the man doctor).

'A man, divorced, experienced, and a doctor!' I whispered, as we walked away from Mrs C. Beard.

'We'll see,' said my sister, resenting him, in her usual irrational way, for suddenly appearing in the village and not being on the list.

By accident of fate we were the first people in the whole village to meet the new man doctor in his professional capacity, which gave us a head start on anyone else looking for a husband. We'd gone to see Dr Kaufmann with an annoying cut on Little Jack's elbow, only to discover that Dr Kaufmann had had to dash off to a severed finger and the new doctor — who was just literally moving that day into a temporary dwelling — had rushed over to the surgery to cover.

Dr Norman cannot have heard how awful and irresponsible our family was because he was extremely nice and not at all suspicious. Unless, like Dr Kaufmann, he'd decided to ignore our bad reputation and be nice to us in spite of it. Anyway, seeing how new and nice he was, my sister gave me a nod and a look, which I took to mean he'd gone onto the list (mentally), and because Jack was being very brave about the cut we were able to chat as if nothing was happening.

So, as Dr Norman affixed the stick-on stitches, I jumped straight in.

'Have you got any children?' I asked.

'Yes,' he said, 'one son, aged nine.'

'Do you ever see him?' I asked.

'Yes, every other weekend — in fact he's staying with me this weekend.'

There was a small pause and my sister's eyebrows went up.

'Do you want to bring him to our house to see the ponies?' she said.

'And our tree house,' I said, thinking any normal nine-year-old might prefer a tree house.

'And my Romans,' said Little Jack.

Dr Norman smiled and said, 'Well, that's a very kind offer, I might well do that . . . if Mum has no objections.'

He looked at our mother and she said, 'That would be splendid.'

'What's his name?' I asked, meaning the nine-year-old son.

'Well, I call him Tuppence,' said the doctor, with a little chuckle.

We strolled home, Jack in a bandage, and all had our say about Tuppence's name.

'Tuppence?' said my sister. 'What a name!'

'It's just a pet name. His father probably came up with it,' said our mother, being fair.

'Yeah, like Shrimp, Litlun and Freckles,' I said, naming the three cute American brothers in my story.

'But it seems such a pitiful amount,' said my sister, 'financially speaking — I mean, tuppence? — that's 2p.'

'No,' said Little Jack, 'tuppence is less than 1 new p.'

'Oh yeah, OK, well, what can you actually get with less than 1p?' said my sister. And my two siblings sounded all cynical and critical and seemed to have been infected by the village — wanting to attack a newcomer for something as innocent as a nickname.

Dr Norman was living in one of the newly built chalet-bungalows behind Dr Kaufmann's that were actually designed for old people and had a rail along the garden path and nothing to trip up on. He'd rented number 10, but it hadn't been quite ready, so he was in number 16, which was really meant for a lady (who wasn't quite ready herself).

Mrs C. Beard heard we'd seen Dr Norman and came across the road and gave us extra information that she'd gleaned. One, that Dr

Norman had had to leave his ex-marital home in a something of a hurry after he and his wife had started being unreasonable with each other. Plus he needed to be on-call to fulfil the obligations of the new post. Also, that he had a girlfriend who had previously been a patient, or maybe a nurse — either way, it had a whiff of not being entirely above board. And two, that the lady doctor was helpfully called Dr Gurly.

That afternoon my sister wrote to Dr Norman.

Dear Dr Norman,

Please come round for a cup of coffee or tea (or whatever you prefer) so that we can welcome you to the village properly. Feel free to bring your nine-year-old.

Yours truly etc.

I objected to the letter, saying he was probably already coming round on Saturday with the nine-year-old.

'He'll cancel Saturday,' she said. 'He had no intention of coming and was very careful not to commit.'

I corrected her. 'No, he said he was coming.'

My sister corrected me. 'He said, 'I might well do that,' which means he probably won't.' As well as being philosophical, she'd also become quite analytical and kept noticing what people said and was getting more like our mother every day in her understanding of what they actually meant. In fact, since being at secondary school, my sister had started thinking about things in a very inconvenient way and had stopped believing anything anyone ever said, unless they were crystal-clear and didn't touch their face when they said it.

There had been some talk of enrolling her at a better school than Flatstone school, but this better one was in town and private and our mother was anti all that and, in the end, our father wasn't all that bothered.

Dr Norman did cancel on Saturday, or rather he just didn't come, which was what my sister had expected. And we decided to give it a few weeks and then send an invitation involving the nine-year-old. However, the new letter was not needed, because soon after that first meeting with Dr Norman he became our lodger for six weeks while he waited for his chalet to become ready. This came about as a result of Dr Kaufmann's suggesting it.

Our mother was glad of the prospect of cash for dinner money and cigarettes (it had come to that), but at the same time she was anxious about the reality of it in the week prior to his moving in. She asked us to get the house in a fit state for a lodging doctor while she jostled with the play and her accounts. She said cleanliness was probably important.

My sister went round with the hoover on an extension lead and did such a good job that the bag filled up twice with dog hair and other bits. I did the kitchen, including the cutlery drawer which had become chaotic and full of things that shouldn't have been in there, such as bits of macaroni, feathers and horse stuff. Little Jack got the doctor's quarters tidy and made a display of Subbuteo players along the tallboy in the bedroom. Later, I donated my bedside lamp and we made his bathroom pretty with a potted spider plant which had so many babies dangling, it was like a variegated shooting star. Plus a bar of Knight's Castile and some Radox bath salts in case he liked having a soak after a hard day's work.

The evening Dr Norman arrived we invited him to dinner as a welcome gesture, even though it wasn't part of the deal. The deal was bedroom, bathroom, use of the playroom telly, the garden, washing machine and one shelf in the fridge. The welcome dinner was macaroni cheese and a mixed salad of radish and cucumber with a French dressing. The French dressing was 90 per cent vinegar due to a mix-up and the salad had become pickled, but it seemed deliberate and didn't matter because the macaroni went down well. We'd consulted *My Learn to Cook Book* for a nice dish but didn't have time to do anything from scratch, only poached eggs, and felt they wouldn't quite do. We used a packet sauce but added extra cheese to make it cheesy, and you'd never have known.

Seeing the table set for four, Dr Norman thought we'd forgotten about the welcome dinner, so we explained that our mother didn't have dinners. It was thoughtless of us to say that, knowing that doctors are generally keen on people eating, but it just came out and unfortunately he questioned her.

'What's this about mothers not having dinners?' he said.

'What's this about lodgers poking their noses in?' she asked back.

And that made it a bad start and I'm not sure he felt very welcome, and he went upstairs as soon as he could.

The following Saturday Dr Norman went out in the morning and brought Tuppence back to the house. Tuppence was small for his age and seemed younger than his nine years and was loaded with sherbet pips.

'Hello, Tuppence,' I called to him, and he looked furious.

'Say hello,' said Dr Norman to Tuppence, and he introduced us all by name.

'I'm not Tuppence!' said Tuppence. 'I'm Thruppenny now.'

'Oh, you've gone up a penny,' said my sister, and Dr Norman patted Tuppence on the head.

'Yes, he's gone up a penny, haven't you, Thruppenny?'

And Tuppence, said, 'Yes, I have,' with a little stamp of his foot, like a five-year-old, and we all hated him and had no idea what to call him.

On the whole, Dr Norman seemed to be sexually interested in our mother — either that or it was a habit of his to act flirtatiously and look at women's nipples. And for a short while she seemed interested in him too. But somehow all the sexy nipple-looking and flirty chitchat seemed empty and cold and as though they weren't keen on each other. And, added to which, somehow my sister and I didn't even want Dr Norman at the helm. Yes, he was a doctor and knew not to say 'pardon' or 'notepaper', but he just wasn't the kind of man we wanted. He had a high-pitched laugh, which came out too often. He flapped his hands nervously around the ponies. Also, having Dr Norman at the helm would mean having Tuppence too (or Tanner as he would no doubt become) and we couldn't have stood it, we thought.

So after the enthusiasm in the surgery and the excitement at the prospect of his moving in, we were lethargic and just let Tuppence play with the Lego and ignored him while Dr Norman looked at our mother's nipples a bit more and had cups of coffee and laughed a lot. There were five minutes of drama when Tuppence climbed up into a pear tree, criticized our platform for not being a proper tree house, and then said he was too scared to climb down. Dr Norman could have regained some respect at that point, but instead he became anxious and wanted to call the fire brigade. I climbed up into the tree in my sister's running spikes to help, but Tuppence made such a fuss and wouldn't be helped so in the end I gave him a bit of a shove and he tumbled down quite safely into his father's flapping hands.

Later, having omelettes, Dr Norman asked if it would be OK if he brought his girlfriend, Penny, round.

'Do as you please, there are no rules here, as you've seen. Just do as you please,' said our mother, 'do exactly as you please.' She sounded cross in spite of her reasonable words and a bit like her own mother.

Before we'd finished our omelettes all up, Dr Norman seemed to have hiccups and kept holding his hand to his mouth and saying, 'Excuse me.' It went on for some time and we offered the usual procedural help and discussed amongst us the best methods for curing stubborn hiccups. Dr Norman declined all suggestions, including the tremendous shock which my sister put forward as an option.

'We could turn the lights off and do something shocking,' said my sister.

'We could throw a cushion at him,' said Little Jack.

Tuppence then helpfully explained it wasn't hiccups as such, but a rare kind of throat spasm where pockets of air get trapped in the folds of the oesophagus at times of stress and are released suddenly when the throat relaxes, causing a series of small painful burps. Our mother looked appalled and it put her right off him sexually (her being squeamish about anything to do with burps, sick or spit etc.). She looked nauseous and suddenly Penny the girlfriend seemed like a good thing.

★ ★ ★

Over the six weeks that Dr Norman was lodging with us there were many tiny mentions of our mother putting the house on the market, and at the same time Dr Norman grew to really like it and to feel it might be the ideal home for him and Penny and any kids they might have in the future. I thought this before Dr Norman actually did. And sure enough, when our mother finally decided she had too many debts and no money and selling up really was the only option, Dr Norman was first in the queue to buy it and he said how great it would be for him and Penny and any future kids.

Dr Norman brought Penny to see the house one day. Penny was young but had her hair in a bun and pale yellow trousers. They walked around the house, including the bits they wouldn't normally see, such as our mother's bedroom. I shadowed them, keen to hear their thoughts.

'How much do you think she'd accept?' asked Penny.

'She's pretty desperate,' said Dr Norman.

Dr Norman made an offer considerably less than the asking price. Our mother said the offer was a bit on the low side and Dr Norman said she could take it or leave it.

In the queue, right behind him, was Dr Gurly, the lady doctor who, we guessed, must have heard about the house from Dr Norman, there being no For Sale sign up. Anyway, Dr Gurly came to view the house with a friend called Sheela and a clipboard and they took detailed notes. They measured the height of the kitchen cupboards and asked if the interior shelves were height-adjustable — which they were — them being cereal lovers and cereal boxes getting taller and taller. Our mother left them to roam around outside and waited until they said how lovely the garden was and then told them about Mr Gummo.

Dr Gurly and Sheela were very friendly towards us and after they'd finished their look around said how much they liked the house and Sheela asked if we'd been happy living there.

What a question. In truth, we hadn't been very happy, but it would be unfair if that reflected badly on the house. The house, though less marvellous than we'd been led to believe at the outset, had been fine and hadn't demanded any attention. Its good points had never quite made up for the fact that it was stuck in the old heart of a jittery little village and not in a town. But it was a nice house, roomy and with a grassy paddock, outbuildings, view, beams and what-not. As the estate agent said, 'All the features you would expect from a superior dwelling', meaning gas-fired central heating, a downstairs lavatory and a view of the church steeple.

'In all fairness, the house has done its best,' I said, and that caused Sheela to look sad for a moment, so I looked at my sister who was perfect as always and patched it up with, 'Of course, we're sad to be leaving, but we can tell you'll be very happy here.'

And that went down very well and then Little Jack explained about our financial situation, which he was supposed to know nothing about, and it was slightly embarrassing.

Dr Gurly and Sheela then told our mother they would be making an offer, which they did, via the agent, and they offered the whole price and our mother accepted it and reminded them about Mr Gummo.

'What about Dr Norman and Penny and their future children?' I asked later.

'There are plenty of other houses around for them,' said our mother.

'Not as nice as this one, which has all the features you'd expect from a superior dwelling,' I said, and suddenly felt I'd said the wrong thing seeing as presumably we'd be moving to one of the less nice houses which wouldn't even be a superior dwelling.

The strange thing was, as soon as our mother had accepted Dr Gurly's offer, the agent, Golbert & Blick, put a For Sale sign up — when it wasn't even for sale any more. Our mother said that was the norm, and my sister said, 'What do you expect from an outfit who don't know how to spell 'windows'?'

'Spacious porch with original tiles and bottle-bottom windoes.'

And then, seeing the sign, other people wanted to look around, including Mrs Longlady and Mrs C. Beard, even though neither had any intention of buying it, but just wanted a little outing. Apparently that was the norm too and you just had to grit your teeth while they gawped at your sleeping arrangements and peered into your bathroom cabinet.

★　★　★

Then, in what seemed like a sudden move but probably wasn't, our mother made an offer on a two-bedroomed house on the Sycamore Estate. We knew where the Sycamore Estate was but had never been there. Our mother painted a vivid picture. She explained that the estate was a specially designed residential area with a whole lot of slim streets with modern semi-detached houses with garages or carports, saplings and nice bits of grass. It was near the senior school and handy for a parade of shops and a bus stop. She'd never been there either. It sounded ideal.

Dr Gurly and Sheela were very keen to prepare for their move into our house and one or other of them often drifted in between appointments to measure walls, windows and bits of furniture. Sometimes they measured things they'd measured before, thinking the original measurements untrustworthy. They were planning to put up a dividing wall in the kitchen to make an intimate dining room which they were going to fill almost entirely with a large dining table and have a low lamp hanging in the centre. They wanted a scrubbed kitchen table (about the size of ours) in the kitchen and a smarter dark wood table in the dining room for when they were entertaining their doctor and nurse friends.

Our mother planned to offer Dr Gurly and Sheela certain of the larger items of furniture and garden stuff at a price to be agreed — the Suffolk Punch, the four-poster bed (but not the mattress), the walnut wardrobe, the large settee in her sitting room, and other sundry items. Dr Norman came to see our mother to ask if she'd take a higher offer. Our mother said she'd accepted the asking price from Dr Gurly. Dr Norman seemed cross about it and offered a bit above the asking price. Our mother said she couldn't accept.

Dr Mann: Why have you sold the house to another doctor?
Adele: Dr Lady outbid you fair and square.
Dr Mann: But it's the perfect house for myself and Penny, my girlfriend cum patient.
Adele: It's also the perfect house for Dr Lady.
Dr Mann: She had no right outbidding me. Dr Lady's only a lady doctor.
Adele: She's two, actually.

24

We moved on a Friday with the help of Mr Lomax. Free of charge.

Mr Lomax was still a feature in our lives, even after turning out to be a partly bad apple. My sister felt sure he didn't know that we knew of his entanglement with Charlie Bates, and though it was tempting to a righteous person like her to make him face up to his misdeeds and general badness, my sister decided that his usefulness as a repentant odd-job man was too valuable to throw away on revenge and justice.

'But why's he being so helpful then, if he doesn't know we know?' I asked.

'*He* knows and that's enough,' she said. I still wasn't convinced, but I didn't mind because I didn't think he was all bad. I have to say, though, it felt wrong not telling Little Jack, who had sensed badness in Mr Lomax all along. It seemed unfair not to reward his intuition. I said so to my sister and she said people like him didn't need acknowledgement for their knowingness. If you know everything, you know everything and can't expect people to be constantly telling you that you were right.

The day started well. Everything was in boxes and lots of rubbish was in bags by the bins. Our mother kept reminding us there was very little space at Willow Drive and that we should only take what we absolutely needed or couldn't bear to part with. I packed my clothes and Monopoly and Scrabble, my collection of scrapbooks and a fan I'd got from Spain. We had eight trips to and fro on the move day in Mr Lomax's brand-new van.

Much of the big furniture did indeed stay in the house and became the property of Dr Gurly and Sheela — the scrubbed table in the kitchen, for instance, because it was too big, and other things too valuable to hang on to.

Let me describe our new house. It had two rooms downstairs. A kitchen and a lounge. Mr Lomax fixed a piece of chipboard up to make a bedroom for our mother in the smaller half of the lounge. The remaining bit of lounge adjoined the kitchen and became our playroom. We'd never had a lounge before and weren't sure what people had them for. Our mother, who'd previously winced at lounges, said a lounge was instead of a sitting room, only more for lounging in than sitting and usually smaller. Upstairs were two bedrooms, one of which had a pink and purple plaque affixed reading 'Lizzie's Room'. I can hardly put into words just how affected I was upon seeing this. I saw it as a sign that this was a most positive and perfect move for us, which I already thought. I apologized to my sister for her name not also being on the door — seeing as it was to be her room as much as it was mine and she said something that shook me.

'Well, you'll live here a good bit longer than I shall,' she said. And I thought about that for a moment — life without my sister. And I think I felt what Charlie and other men felt when pondering outer space and infinity and I was terrified by it. I didn't want to even imagine such a thing and my eyes stung and a smell of pepper surrounded me. Looking back, I was a bit all over the place, feeling first elated by the silly name sign, then devastated by a simple fact. It wasn't a reflection on the house or the room or the idea of my sister leaving in the future. It was just that moving house is a big thing and can upset your balance and cause havoc with your emotions.

To continue with the tour of the new house, there was a dampish bathroom with pale pink tiles covering the walls and dark patches where the carpet met the pedestal of the basin and the trunk of the toilet. And that was the whole house. The staircase was a ladder of chunky planks at such an abrupt angle that Debbie never ventured upstairs and the rest of us never went up or down without due care and holding the rope, which of course Debbie couldn't do, being a Labrador.

There were built-in cupboards and shelves around the place, including a cupboard that cut off a corner so that the cupboard was triangular and useless. The back garden was a lawny yard with a rabbit's grave at the end. We knew this because the girl who'd lived there before had said so in a note. That it was buried there and had been called 'Bunny'.

That first night, before we'd unpacked, I heard my sister say to our mother, 'Lizzie's gone a bit weepy.' And I could have killed her because then I did cry and had to pretend to be getting my clothes out of a bin bag.

Our mother said, 'Is she? Perhaps I should go and get some chop suey.'

And my sister said, 'Or chips?'

Our mother went off and came back with the chips and we sat on the floor. Debbie couldn't settle and kept wandering around. She didn't have much space. There was no boot room or porch. There wasn't even a space big enough for her basket and nowhere for her to stretch out like a walrus and be alone. Even the garden was too small. There wasn't room to run or chase a bee.

Eventually, days later, when Debbie was still unsettled, we decided we'd have to start walking her and that seemed so strange. The 'having to walk Debbie' thing was a negative. Debbie hated being taken for a walk — I think she was embarrassed. We'd drag her down to a square of grass and she'd sniff around and go to the toilet and while we were there waiting for her to go, other dogs would turn up and do the same and all the dog owners would smile and nod.

Another downside to the new house was that it had no land, only the yard of lawn and rabbit grave. This was a problem for our two remaining ponies, Sacha and Maxwell (Bilbo and Robbie having been sold and therefore of no concern).

We should have sold them all. But we couldn't bear to part with Sacha and Maxwell. Our mother said there was no spare money, so we had to find some cheap grazing for them or they would have to go too. 'Where there's a will, there's a way,' she said.

The first thing we did was go to see Dr Gurly. We explained our predicament, which was that we desperately wanted to keep our ponies but we had strong feelings about farms and could we please keep them in their paddock until we found a nice farm with a kind and animal-loving farmer. My sister told Dr Gurly about the farmer shooting the cow in the plough and Dr Gurly said, 'Golly, how horrible.' I added that farmers hardly ever stroked their calves or piglets, but my contribution was badly timed and rather cut short Dr Gurly's sympathizing over the shot cow, so I added the greasy-feathered crows hanging by their feet from boundary wire as a warning. And all the drowning, castrations, branding and baby mice. And Dr Gurly started laughing. Dr Gurly had the kind of confident manner that enabled her to laugh at things that weren't funny but might be a bit exaggerated.

She apologized, though, and said she didn't mean to laugh and it all sounded quite horrible and she couldn't bear the thought of us ever setting foot on a farm again. She was joking but not against us, just enjoying our stories, and said that as far as she was concerned we could keep two ponies in the paddock, but only as a stopgap with an eight-week limit and she didn't want the 50p per week. But she would like to check with Sheela first. Which she did later and then phoned to say it was fine but not for too long — because she wanted to get a go-kart. And go-karts and ponies don't mix.

We found the Sycamore Estate to be a magical place. The little houses lining the curved streets

311

being just like the triangle-topped squares Jack arranged beside his train track. And ditto the little trees dotted about and bits of picket fence. The Sycamore Estate was neat, cosy and small. The houses were either very similar or exactly the same. Some had been tampered with to give them the edge — such as a name etched onto a slice of wood.

Ours was number 28 Willow Drive and had no extras.

It was understood on the Sycamore Estate that things were as they were. If your house was prettified with fake Swiss shutters or black iron door furniture in the medieval style, then very good. If, however, yours was a bit rickety — say the lounge window was boarded up after an accident or a row, or the garage door dented after a bump — that was OK too. There was no sense that you were expected to enhance anyone else's life via your house or behaviour.

We were tucked away and no one saw us except the other Willow Drive dwellers. No one was there unless they lived there (and I'm not counting anyone who lived there), so no one was there. No one heard what we were saying, only estate people and they didn't mind us and we didn't mind them. No one walked past on the way to church and no one gazed in. No one parked outside to go to the Co-op or the doctor or the butcher or on a country walk. It was as though we no longer lived in the village.

No one on the Sycamore Estate had much more than anyone else except the occasional few who'd built extensions over the garages, but those people were admired for that little bit extra and not thought badly of and they usually had four children or a fourth on the way and that was their excuse for the extra room.

As I say, a few had fake shutters in the alpine style and some had medieval-style door furniture. One or two had knobbly glass in the front door and some had tarmacked over the nine foot of lawn at the front to fit another vehicle off the road. Some had a dog, many didn't.

No one took any notice.

★   ★   ★

After doing a few sums, my sister — who was getting to be a bit of a maths genius — showed our mother that even in the cheaper house and with a new attitude our finances weren't going to add up. She made a sum of the money needed for the mortgage, rates, bills, dinners, school uniforms, newspapers and extras (such as sweets, wine, whisky and cigarettes, dog food) and the total of that, minus the forecast amount from the few active shares, was a pretty big number.

'What about the money from selling the house?' I asked, not that I needed to know, but just clarifying for our mother and to remind her it had gone.

'That money went partly to the bank for the mortgage and partly to other people who needed money, such as Miss Woods for all the ham and tobacco, and the council for the rates and various others,' said my sister.

Our mother's family weren't doing so badly in the recession, mainly being in the professions as opposed to business and having a healthier mix of shares than our mother, who never bothered to learn about investments or thought to ask for advice. She could have asked them then for financial help (perhaps she did, I don't know) but our shortness of money was not going to be short-term, it was going to be for ever, unless something unusual happened such as winning the pools or 'spot the ball' and our mother didn't even do those things. So if her family *had* helped with money, they'd have had to keep on helping and helping and helping (like a charity that tackles the wrong end of a problem) and that would have been wrong and embarrassing. So in the end our mother decided there was nothing else for it.

'There's nothing else for it,' she said.

'What?' my sister said.

'I'll have to get a job,' said our mother.

'A job?' said my sister. 'God, what will you be?'

'I can't *be* anything,' she said, 'I didn't ever train to be anything. I'll have to *do* something.'

Jack began to cry at the thought of her doing something new that he couldn't imagine. 'What, Mum?' he sobbed. 'What will you do?'

'I don't know yet, Jack,' she said with a sigh. 'We'll see. There is one thing, though . . . '

'What?' we all said.

But she didn't answer. Her eye had been caught by a Vacant Situation in the *Mercury*.

'There you are,' she said, tapping, ' "Drivers

314

Wanted'. I can drive. I'm a good and experienced driver with a clean licence.'

'What was the one thing?' I asked, because it had sounded important and might be better than being a driver. But whatever it was, she'd forgotten it now she'd seen that Drivers were Wanted and her face had broken into a smile which included her eyes.

The driving job was the only position that appealed or seemed suitable (factory and nursing auxiliary jobs seeming a bridge too far) and she ringed it in pencil and composed a perfect letter of application to Snowdrop Laundry Services.

It wasn't long before she heard back and was given the date for an interview and we put her through the mill in rehearsal, her last interview having been for boarding school when she was eleven.

'Give me a practice run,' she said. 'Put me through the mill.'

'What is your favourite thing about driving?'

'How long have you been driving?'

'Have you ever driven a van before?'

'What jobs have you ever done before?'

'Have you ever run anyone over or had a crash?'

And my sister, who herself had attended a recent interview at the paper-shop, asked the most probing question of all: 'Why do you want this job?'

To which our mother answered, 'Because I have a family to keep and I'm in debt up to my neck.'

My sister advised her against that response, saying she needed a better reason than that in order to make herself seem perfect for the job.

'You should say you want a new challenge,' she said, 'otherwise it looks as though you're just doing it for the money.'

★ ★ ★

In between the application and the interview Dr Gurly and Sheela invited us for dinner. Dr Gurly rang one evening and said, 'Who am I speaking to?' and I said, 'It's Lizzie Vogel,' and she laughed so I knew it was her, it being the same laugh as when she'd laughed about the horrible farmers.

'Hello, Lizzie. It's Jill Gurly,' said Dr Gurly.

And I said, 'Hello, Jill,' and we had a little conversation.

Then she said, 'I'm ringing to see if you'd like to come and have supper with myself and Sheela on Friday night, after you've done the ponies.'

And I said, 'Me?' and Dr Gurly laughed again. 'All of you,' she said.

We'd never before, ever, been invited anywhere for dinner — or lunch or breakfast, come to that (not counting two weddings). Not all of us together, all three kids and our mother, as a family. Never. So we were overly thrilled. It was a bit like the time we were invited to go to Dorset except that this time the invitation was 100 per cent real and out of the blue and definitely not a misunderstanding or a lie.

How strange it was to be there in our old

house (which actually still felt like our house since it was brimming with our furniture and even a picture Little Jack had painted of a boot stuck up on the side of a dresser). But it was extremely nice. Everything was.

First, the niceness of Dr Gurly and the kindness of Sheela, who, it turned out, was a doctor too but not in the ordinary sense and who knew the audiologist who'd been so cross with us at Jack's hearing test. Sheela described her as an old bag with no sense of humour. After a bowl of onion soup which was very dark in colour and tasted slightly of toffee, we had a big cheesy bread thing with olives on top and all sorts of bits of vegetable which were both raw and slightly burnt at the same time. And with that, a great big wooden bowl of leaves and chives. Then there was a chocolate mousse, which was one of the nicest things I'd ever eaten.

'I hope the food is all right for you,' said Dr Gurly.

'It's the nicest meal I've ever had,' said our mother, which was probably true because there were only nice people in attendance and no one worrying about table manners and no meat and hardly any cutlery to speak of. Also, she hadn't had that many meals — as such — since being divorced. Just peanuts and fruit.

'The garden is beginning to come into its own,' said Dr Gurly, and that gave our mother the opportunity to say, 'Just you wait — soon there'll be Mr Gummo's alliums in the beds and Mexican fleabane all over the paths and steps.'

And it was a lovely thing to be able to say and

all because we had been invited and she had remembered about them.

'I want to get him to put in some blackcurrants,' said Dr Gurly.

'Yes, and to clear away access to the drains, which have been covered over the years,' said Sheela.

The three women drank a bottle of rosé wine in the fat bottle and then another and were tipsy and amusing and our mother told Sheela that she was probably about to start a full-time driving job and therefore desperately trying to reduce the prescription medication she was taking. Sheela stopped being tipsy and went into professional mode, which was the right thing to do.

'It's great to hear you're trying to reduce your medication. Well done. Are you doing it in conjunction with your GP?' Sheela asked.

'Yes, sort of, yes, I am,' she said. 'I was wondering,' our mother went on, 'how long it will take until I start feeling normal.'

'Normal?' said Sheela. 'You mean functioning without the medication?'

'Yes,' said our mother, 'normally.'

'As a rough guide, I always say it will take as long to normalize as you were taking the medication,' Sheela said. 'So if you've been on them for a year, you'll need a year.'

'Like the reflection of a mountain in a lake,' said our mother.

'Well, yes, that's a poetic way of putting it,' said Sheela.

'Anyway,' said Dr Gurly, changing the subject,

'Sheela and I wanted to get you all here and have a meal and say a huge thank-you for letting us buy your lovely house.' And she raised her glass and we raised ours.

And Sheela said, 'And you must come and see us whenever you like. You are very welcome.'

And Dr Gurly said, 'Here's to Maxwell.' And I didn't ask why she said that, I just knew he'd done something odd and didn't want any details.

And I realized that moving from the lovely house was the best thing we'd ever done. In moving from that house, we were welcome there, more welcome than we had ever been even when we'd lived there. I think it was the first place we'd ever been welcome. And the mousse had been the nicest thing I'd ever eaten and Sheela the nicest person and our mother was going to be back to normal in around two years. Like the reflection of a mountain in a lake. It was a lovely evening and we walked back to the Sycamore Estate in the dark.

'That was nice,' said our mother.

'Are they Libyans?' asked Little Jack.

'I think they are,' said my sister.

We wondered if they'd ever ask us again, seeing as we'd eaten everything all up and our mother had talked about her pill problem. And just to put the icing on the cake, they did ask us — they rang up about a fortnight later and said they were doing a curry and did we want to come over. I don't need to write about that because it was nice again and in the same sorts of ways and we were getting used to being welcome and that in itself was nice.

The day of our mother's interview at Snowdrop Laundry Services dawned and she got dressed in sensible clothes, apart from her sandals. My sister criticized them.

'What?' said our mother.

'Your feet don't look like they belong to a van driver,' said my sister.

In the end she wore a pair of Mr Gummo's shoes, which were only one size too big and had accidentally moved house with us. And she went off looking like a van driver from head to toe.

The Snowdrop depot was on the Soar Banks industrial estate, some eight miles from our home. She attended at 10 a.m. and was gone for two hours plus. When she got home, she was no longer the mother we'd always known, though I can't quite say why. She was just different, like a toddler who's been to nursery for the first time or a boy who's been in front of a magistrate.

'How did it go?' my sister asked.

'I don't know,' said our mother, taking off Mr Gummo's shoes.

'That's the thing,' said my sister, 'you never do, unless it goes badly.'

'They're going to let me know,' she said.

And then, at our insistence, our mother described the whole thing in detail with lots of 'he said/I said'.

She'd had twenty minutes' worth of talking with a man called Mr Holt, who was the traffic manager. Mr Holt had barely looked at her, and although he'd asked 'myriad difficult questions'

— including some on the subject of driving — he'd not asked that most probing of questions, 'Why do you want this job?' It seemed to be understood that it was for money.

Then Mr Holt had handed her a road map and said, 'It's Friday afternoon, you're in Malby. You need to get to Markfield. How are you going to get there in under an hour?'

And she, being OK with a map and a straight talker, said, 'I'd curse the person who planned the routes, then go via Enderby.'

'You're low on fuel in Loughborough and need to get to the Red Lion in Rothley,' he said. 'Where would you fill up?'

'I have no idea,' she'd said. 'I tend not to let myself get low on fuel.'

After a few more map-reading and route-planning questions, Mr Holt had handed her over to Miss Kellogg, his deputy, who'd asked her to park a Leyland van while she watched with a clipboard. Our mother reverse-parked it beautifully but Miss Kellogg had asked her, 'And how do you propose to open the back doors?'

Our mother hadn't been able to answer — only, 'I can't.'

Miss Kellogg explained that a van driver's back doors are his number-one concern. 'It's a case of 'Can I get things in and out of my doors?' and you never reverse-park unless you're done for the day,' she said.

Then, after Miss Kellogg, she had another session with Mr Holt. He asked her to drive him to the County Arms and back in the same Leyland van. And when they got back to the

321

depot, she didn't reverse-park but went into a space nose-in.

'Why didn't you reverse her in?' Mr Holt asked.

'I thought I'd leave access for the doors,' she said.

'Do it again, reverse in, we're done for the day,' said Mr Holt.

So she did and, wanting to keep the van neatly tucked in and in line with the other parked vans, she bumped the wall. After that, Mr Holt spoke again, at length.

He told her she'd broken the law twice during the test drive, once when she'd turned into Canal Street — it being a no-right-turn junction — and once when she'd moved off on an amber light. Also, she'd failed to apply the handbrake on the small incline turning into the County Arms and had held the van on the clutch-bite.

This was the most serious of the three mistakes and a van driver's Golden Rule, because although it wasn't exactly law-breaking, in the sense of the Highway Code, the engine on the Leyland vans couldn't withstand that kind of abuse on a daily basis.

'These vans are over two tonnes in weight, they want to roll back. You must never hold them on the clutch,' he said. 'Do you understand?'

And then he'd said, 'If you work for me and I have to get your clutch fixed, you'll have some explaining to do — are we clear?'

Mr Holt described the job. The main thing seemed to be just getting it done and the van not breaking down, particularly not on account of the clutch, and if a driver could achieve that, the rest was easy. The worst thing — the thing to be avoided — was that the customer would be dissatisfied and switch to another laundry — God forbid, Advance Towel Services, who were their main rival with towels.

'Who is your main rival with boiler suits?' our mother asked, showing great interest.

'Our main rival there is modern fabrics and washing machines and people doing their own.'

He told her the job was all about driving all over the county to shops, pubs, clubs and hotels, delivering and changing towels in toilets. Automatic roller towels, Turkish rollers, flats, tea towels, dust-mats and boiler suits. There were five set routes for each day of the week and each van had a driver and a boy. The driver and boy were expected to empty the dirty laundry at the end of each day and load the van ready for the next.

All in all, our mother seemed quite inspired by the interview and indeed the whole event and the marvellous concepts such as being done for the day and the bun stops, the payload and applying the handbrake, which she'd only ever used for parking and now knew it had this other crucial role.

Then, after her detailed telling of it, the phone rang and it was Mr Holt saying she had got the job if she wanted it just as long as she gave him her word that she'd use the handbrake. To start the following Monday at 8 a.m. She accepted and hung up the phone.

'I'm a van driver,' she said, and we celebrated with a little dance around her.

25

Our mother found waking up in the morning very difficult indeed and felt sick and miserable. Especially as it was dark and cold — two of her worst things. She'd set her alarm for 7 a.m. to give her thirty minutes to wake up properly and have coffee. It wasn't that she'd never *been* up at that hour, just that she'd never had to *get* up.

The first morning my sister and I dragged ourselves out of bed an hour early and my sister went down to our mother's room to make sure she was up. She wasn't, then she was. Once we'd heard her clanging about, we went down in our nighties to offer support. We'd planned to make eggy bread to give her a good breakfast but, seeing us, our mother was extremely grumpy and didn't want our support and was actually horrible to be with, much worse than usual, which was a bad start and disappointing.

'Who put that fucking kettle on?' she yelled, as it started its slow, whining build-up to the boil.

'I was going to make you a cup of coffee,' said my sister.

'Do it in the thing,' our mother demanded, meaning her coffee boiler. 'I can't stand the powdered.'

Then before the thing had the coffee ready, our mother made herself a powdered one and my sister stomped back to bed. And our mother was cross that she'd upset my sister.

'Jesus Christ, why do you have to bother me, even at this hour?' she said.

'We thought you'd like some company,' I said.

'When have I ever wanted company?' she said.

So I stomped off back to bed too. And soon we heard Gloxinia's engine revving and then trailing off as our mother drove away for her first day as a van driver at the Snowdrop Laundry.

'She's gone,' I said to my sister in her bed.

We said how much we hated her and hoped she'd get the sack and so on. Then we fell asleep and then we were up again having Weetabix and, to make things worse, Jack had to have his with Blue Band and some diabetic jam I'd stolen from my father's house because the milkman had skipped us.

When we got home from school, my sister said we should all tidy up the best we could and have everything nice for when our mother came home because she'd be shattered. We agreed and my sister started to make a macaroni cheese but found the milk never had come. So she switched to macaroni with tomatoes and cheese and Little Jack — lovely Little Jack — ran all the way to the shops on his own and bought a bottle of milk.

When we heard Gloxinia pull into the drive we all lined up, like the kids from *The Sound of Music*, and our mother surprised us by coming in the back door. We followed her into her bedroom.

'How was it?' asked Jack.

'Unbearable,' said our mother. She took off Mr Gummo's shoes and flopped onto the chesterfield which was in her bedroom and had become her bed.

'Why?' I asked.

'It just went on and on and with endless little things you have to do,' she said.

'Like what?' we wanted to know, but our mother was too tired to speak and just waved us all away and lay with her eyes closed for a while. My sister made her a cup of coffee and then she had a bath and went to bed and we didn't see her again for the rest of the week, except for the odd moment when she came in and dished out chicken legs and tubs of coleslaw.

She'd started buying the chicken legs from supermarkets on her travels and giving them to us in a bit of kitchen paper for dinner. I quite liked them but my sister obviously didn't, her being an ongoing vegetarian, and she thought we looked all caveman-like eating them with our hands and would have preferred we'd tackled them with cutlery, but our mother said not to make any washing up now she was working. Our ex-father's lectures on the importance of table manners had made an impression on my sister and she'd begun to sound like him.

'You'll never get a promotion if you eat like monkeys,' she told us, not that we knew what a promotion actually was, even though we'd had the same grisly warning plenty of times.

Our mother had a two-week probation period at Snowdrop Laundry, during which time she had to arrive bang on time and be shown the ropes by Miss Kellogg, the deputy. Miss Kellogg, who'd done a small part of the interview, was quite nice but very particular about every little detail and munched on porky scratchings, which was worse than our sister having to see us gnawing on chicken legs because Miss Kellogg would often get a pig's bristle stuck between her teeth and have to pick at it with a corner of her fag packet.

After the two-week period, though, our mother was free of Miss Kellogg and the porky scratchings, and in charge of the van and the van boy — the very nice and hard-working Deano. Also, she was able to chuck Mr Gummo's canvas shoes into the hall cupboard and switch to her own shoes. The van driver's job entailed driving to various venues across the city and county, as previously discussed, and exchanging dirty roller towels for clean ones in the toilets and cloakrooms. The best part was the bombing around in the van with the radio on or talking about plays (which Deano could do, up to a point, having studied English Literature A-level for a year) and the worst part was the actual going into the toilets. The men's toilets especially, being the worst bit of the worst bit and a bit of a shock to our sheltered mother.

She hadn't had much experience of men's toilets, having attended a girls' boarding school and then marrying and only really knowing our father and Charlie Bates, both of whom had obviously been quite fastidious in the toilet, standing or sitting, and either never dripping or splashing or, if they did, wiping it quickly up so she never saw. Now it was beginning to seem as though they weren't the norm, and the norm being to pee all around the toilet, splashing every part of the fixings and floor while scratching the pubic area and shedding hairs. To make it worse, it didn't look as though the splashings got wiped up very often, and they would congeal into syrupy orange droplets. Our mother's flip-flops became untenable (her word) and she decided to go back to Mr Gummo's Dunlops.

Once she'd got used to it and settled down in spite of the early mornings, the grumpy killjoy of a boss and all that urine, she quite enjoyed it. She seemed to have just enough fun with the van boy during the driving part to make it bearable and ditto the banter of the van drivers during the laundry-sorting part. She didn't enjoy the three calls she had in our village but got used to them quickly enough, and Mr Terry the butcher was always very pleased to see her and I thought it funny that after rejecting him man-at-the-helm-wise on account of his blood-soaked aprons, there she was every Thursday tiptoeing across his sawdusty floor and heaving seven of them into the van plus a smeary roller and two tea towels.

No one at Snowdrop minded that she was posh, they actually liked her for it and found it charming and funny, and no one made hurtful comments about Vogel's — what a disgrace they were going bust and so many people losing their jobs. They managed to avoid the subject by talking about other things, such as the news and funny customer stories.

She never liked the chaos when she got home, though, and still hated the kitchen. On the plus side she had neither the time nor the inclination for writing the play.

26

The Sycamore Estate was a better place for us to live and a relief. On the estate we were unremarkable and nothing to worry about. Plus we were latchkey kids, though we had no actual keys on string round our necks because we never actually locked the door, but, essentially, no one was at home when we got in from school and that was the important factor.

It would be wrong of me, though, not to mention that, however nice it felt being unremarkable, actually having no money was very bad indeed and caused an immediate and ongoing drop in standards, which in turn resulted in a dip in self-esteem for me because it turned out I hated having dirty hair and sitting in the launderette and being hungry.

The new house was fragile and, in spite of being relatively new, bits of it came away, things broke and didn't get fixed. Handles, knobs, doors and windows slipped, cracked and came off in your hand. It was cold to the touch and damp in parts, and even though there was so little of it, we couldn't keep it clean or tidy or warm and the hoover band snapped.

The laundry situation in the new house made previous difficulties seem charming. In the early days of the Sycamore Estate — there being nowhere to hang washing to dry (no boot room, not enough garden for a line and no space whatsoever) — we'd take bin bags full of wet washing to the launderette in an old Silver Cross pram, put a pound's worth of 10ps in, leave it tumbling and more often than not return to find the building locked up. When that happened we'd have to dash back the next morning before school for our pants and stuff. Then, one day, to make matters simpler, the washing machine made a grinding noise and conked out and we stopped worrying about it so much and just wore our clothes longer between washes. Being deliberately grubby seeming so much better than the worry of having nothing to wear. Ditto when the hot water tank became temperamental and our baths were lukewarm or we'd got no soap left, we just had fewer baths. I used to wear a pom-pom hat to hide my grubby hair, which made it worse but hid it. My sister used Batiste dry shampoo when she could get hold of it and bit the bullet when she couldn't and washed her hair under the cold kitchen tap. It doesn't sound so awful, but my sister and I were just getting to an age.

In addition to the launderette, the ponies (now an inconvenient mile away) had to be attended to and the shopping had to be done in dribs and drabs, and then the cooking and eating without the luxury of a big kitchen full of helpful old ingredients and no Miss Woods across the road with a tab. We couldn't remember how things had got done before, but we were sure they had. We concluded that our mother must have done a lot more than we'd realized. And now she was at work from 7 till 7 and was not to be disturbed after that with anything more than light conversation and good news, nothing got done without us doing it. And we didn't.

Our pets had to be got rid of. Our mother begged us to understand it was imperative. The rabbits, the guinea pigs, the cats and Honey the poodle had to be re-homed. We couldn't accommodate them any more. We had no space, no money and no time, she said. She didn't count Debbie, thank God. I think I'd have run away if she had.

'This is the first sensible decision I have ever made and I'm sorry it's a very sad one,' she said.

She stood in front of us in our new hallway and said, 'I beg you to understand,' and when my sister's face went bright red and crumpled and her mouth let out a creaking noise, our mother began to shout. I think she'd planned to shout all along. It was the kind of situation whereby some shouting is essential.

'Do you think I'm happy about this?' she shouted. 'Do you think my heart isn't breaking?' etc.

We had to accept it and our poor, newly sensible mother had to get the pets into boxes and make the trips (rodents first, then felines and then Honey) and take them to wherever you take pets that you've finished with that are still perfectly fit and well.

Very soon after that day, we received a circular from the Guides and Brownies inviting us to an open evening with talks, displays and assorted snacks. The letter said that if we were considering joining we *must* come along to hear about the organization and all the adventures and activities on offer, as they were looking for new recruits and had second-hand uniforms available.

The Brownies and Guides letter coincided with a low point. Our father, who didn't exist for us except for occasional awkward little visits, was suddenly all over the newspapers in reports of redundancies and family feuding and factory closures. We'd lost our pets — a thing too awful to think about — and, however devastated we felt about it, we never discussed it and pretended it hadn't happened. Our mother was never at home unless it was after work and then she'd be too exhausted to speak. Our one remaining pet, Debbie, couldn't make it upstairs. There was no God, according to my sister, and only idiots believed such nonsense. And most of the time, my sister was angry or worried. There was no hot water and the front door had warped in its frame to such an extent that the postman plopped the bills through the gap. And Little Jack's stammer was getting so bad, I dreaded him speaking. The Brownies finally contacting us should have been a good thing; instead it felt like a cruel joke.

Then, on top of all that, the telly broke. We turned it on and off and twiddled the knobs. There was no picture, only a yellowy haze and lines going up. The sound was still working, so we knew it wasn't anything to do with the plug. So we sat down and listened, hoping to hear something jolly that might cheer us after the Brownie letter. Nothing jolly came on. Just the news that Chi Chi, the giant panda at London Zoo, had died.

★ ★ ★

I woke up one day with a peculiar feeling. As if someone or something was lying on top of me and I couldn't budge the weight. There was nothing there, but I couldn't shift it even so. Eventually I got out of bed and sluggishly went about my business with the weight in front of me — it was like walking into a strong wind. I told my sister about the heavy weight and, telling her about it, I must've started crying. She said, 'Don't worry, Lizzie, we all have that feeling from time to time. Just totally ignore it.'

I did my utmost to ignore it and fend it off. On the way to school I bought a packet of Cherry Tunes with my dinner money, thinking them better for morale than my usual ten No. 6. But they didn't help for long, and at school the feeling crept back and tears began trickling down my cheeks. Though apart from the sluggishness, I really felt quite normal and not upset.

My teacher, Miss Munroe, was annoyed about it. Mrs Clarke wouldn't have been. But we didn't have Mrs Clarke any more, we had Miss Munroe.

'What's the matter?' she asked.

'Nothing,' I said, 'I just feel sluggish, as if I have a heavy weight bearing down on me.'

'There must be something more than feeling 'sluggish',' said Miss Munroe, squinting at me.

'I don't think so,' I said, wiping my eyes.

'There must be,' she said.

And this awkward conversation went on for a few minutes.

'Well,' said Miss Munroe, 'I suggest you go and wait in the girls' cloakroom until either you stop crying, or you work out what's wrong.'

I was in the girls' cloakroom all morning. Miss Munroe sent Melody Longlady in just before playtime to see how things were going.

'Miss Munroe wants to know if you're still crying?' asked Melody.

I looked in the cloakroom mirror. 'Yes,' I said.

Melody made a sympathetic face, a flat smile with sad, blinking eyes.

And then I asked Melody if she might be able to cry as well. But she didn't think she could cry. I only asked because, when she'd given me the sympathetic smile, it really looked as if she might have been about to cry. But apparently she hadn't.

At playtime, a few girls looked in on me. Some were very kind. Later, Melody came in again and told me I was to go and see the headmistress. I knocked on her door and she said, 'Come in.'

She asked me what I'd come to see her about. I said I thought it was because I was crying.

'What are you crying about?' she asked, and looked up from her desk like a doctor.

'I don't know,' I said. 'It's nothing.'

'There must be something. No one cries for no reason,' she said.

I apologized and said I was fine, and that actually I thought it was quite funny and a bit embarrassing that I'd been crying for so long.

334

But nothing I said offered a pleasing explanation and she seemed to be as annoyed as Miss Munroe.

'Look, Lizzie,' she said, 'can you please just tell me why you are crying, so I can get on with the important things I need to be doing? Hmmm?'

'I'm not really crying exactly, tears are coming out, that's all. Maybe I have an allergy,' I said.

I went back to the cloakroom for the rest of the day and read a book, which I had to keep wiping.

Then, at home, I stopped, and when our mother got home later she told me that the school had phoned the Snowdrop Laundry and asked her to make contact. Which was all she needed on top of all the chaos. Our mother had phoned the school in the late afternoon and spoken to the headmistress.

'What did she say?' I asked, mortified.

'She said you'd been upset all day and wouldn't tell them why,' our mother said, annoyed.

'I wasn't upset,' I said, 'I told them I wasn't.'

And the conversation went on like that. I won't bore you with it. I gave our mother the whole story, starting at the beginning with the heavy weight.

'I woke up with a great weight on me,' I said.

'Oh, the weight,' said our mother, suddenly understanding. 'It's the pig.'

'The pig?' I said.

'It's about a pig kind of weight, isn't it?'

'Yes, it is, a young one,' I said, 'a young pig.'

'The pig arrives when one's feeling fed up. He turns up first thing in the morning and pins you to the bed.'

'Why?' I said.

'To make you think, to make you cry and make you see,' she said, 'and when he visits, he's just trying to help. You must make him welcome and he'll soon be gone.'

'Why is it a pig?' I asked.

'A pig is so much preferable to an anonymous bag of corn, don't you think?'

Our mother explained her encounters with the pig and the ways in which the pig had helped her and she said she was extremely proud of the way I'd handled the pig.

Anyway, the pig has visited only once since then. And when it did, I made it welcome and carried it around until it trotted back to its sty.

★ ★ ★

The next day, after the crying, our mother said I could have the day off school to recover from the pig's visit and have a day with her on the van. It was a nice mix of excellent, revolting and annoying.

I had to share the front seat with Deano the van boy, who smelled of sour milk and had a painful spot on his neck. Our mother never closed her sliding van door, neither did Deano, and they careered around town half in and half out.

They ran here and there clutching roller towels, dashed into yards, garages and pubs, and nipped in the back entrances of shops, cinemas, clubs and offices, with rollers, mats and tea towels. They spoke politely to traffic wardens and other van people. They fixed dodgy towel dispensers and pulled their jumpers over their faces for the smelliest calls. And they sang with the radio and ate cheese cobs and swigged pop from the bottle. Our mother was marvellous. I'd never seen her like it. So busy and efficient and engaged.

At the White Horse Deano was chased by a dog and at the Black Dog our mother was chased by a horse. Later, the cook at the Granary tearooms gave me a Scotch egg when I nipped in with the towels. And it went on like that until, at the Fish & Quart, a woman told our mother that the Snowdrop depot would like her to get in touch immediately, and the bubble burst.

We went to a phone box. Our mother rang and spoke to Mr Holt. He'd heard she was carrying a young passenger (me) and wanted an explanation.

'It's my daughter Lizzie,' our mother said. 'Eleven and a half . . . She's had the day off . . . She's not ill, she's just miserable . . . All right . . . Yes, all right, I will . . . Yes. I will. I understand, yes,' she said, and hung up.

I had to wait out the rest of the route in Brucciani's in Church Gate (right near Green's, the jewellers, where the Longlady twins had got their ears pierced) and drink frothy hot chocolate and eat buns and read my book until they finished and picked me up. Back at the depot, we were greeted at the gate by Miss Kellogg, who said she'd help Deano with the unloading and so forth and that I should keep a low profile. Our mother was to go straight to Mr Holt's office.

Driving home, I asked how it had gone with Mr Holt.

'He's nothing but a miserable old bastard,' said our mother.

'Did he tell you off?' I asked.

'Of course he did. God, I hate that man,' she said, 'he's a bloody nightmare.'

It occurred to me then that Mr Holt might go on the Man List, but on reflection I decided the line between love and hate was on this occasion just too thick, and I didn't even raise it for discussion.

However much of a nightmare Mr Holt was and however annoyingly my day on the van had ended, I felt better. Better about the pig and better about everything else too. Better about our mother being gone from the house all those hours and our clothes being smelly. The Snowdrop Laundry had cheered me up and I couldn't wait until Little Jack and my sister had their turn on the van and could see and feel better for themselves.

★   ★   ★

At some point after that, Gloxinia died and was sold for parts to a man who fixed up old Mercedes and for weeks afterwards people would say, 'Where's that lovely old Merc of yours?' and our mother would say, 'She lives on.'

338

Our mother had to buy a new car. It had to be cheap but reliable and she took advice from Miss Kellogg, the deputy at Snowdrop (known as Deputy Dawg). Miss Kellogg knew a man who sold used but reliable family vehicles and we ended up with a Hillman Husky from Ray's Reliables, which was certainly cheap but turned out not to be very reliable and caused no end of trouble on the roads, stalling and not steering true when our mother pressed the brakes etc.

Miss Kellogg felt responsible for the poorness of the Husky's performance and put in a word with Mr Holt and our mother was given special dispensation to borrow her Snowdrop van on Fridays and keep it for the weekend. It wasn't usually allowed, but a blind eye was turned for her in view of the bad advice from Deputy Dawg. This meant she'd drop Deano the van boy at home before the last two calls and then drive home in Sofie (which was the name she'd given the Snowdrop van), the downside being that she and Deano the van boy would have the unloading and loading to do first thing on the Monday. Still, this was better than relying on the erratic Hillman Husky. We loved having Sofie the Leyland van, registration SOY 731F, parked outside our house with its snowdrops on the side and showing clearly we were part of a wholesome endeavour.

One Saturday morning our mother suddenly said she had to nip out and did anyone want to go with her. In the end Little Jack went and sat beside her in the van boy's seat.

They were back an hour later and we couldn't believe our eyes.

They'd had a haircut each and no longer looked like themselves. Jack had had a crew cut and it made him look like a new person after all the years of sticky-out curls and a fringe in his eyes. He looked like Action Man. Our mother had had hers chopped to the shoulder, bluntly as if with an axe. It hung in clumps, darker now, and with the fringe cut in you could see her eyes and brows. She looked like a girl on a ranch with lots to do.

The pair of them stood and let us gaze at them.

'Did Geraldo do it?' I asked.

'I can't afford Geraldo at the moment,' she said. 'We went to Durex Tony's.'

Tony was a man in the next village who cut hair in a grubby cubicle next to a sock factory and sold Durex and cigarette lighters. He had a picture of a half-man half-horse on the wall and was rumoured to have an illegally rude tattoo on his torso. Little Jack claimed that Durex Tony gave him a cigarette to smoke while he cut his hair with a shaver. But our mother said it was a lollipop.

★　★　★

On the Saturday afternoon after the haircuts, we decided we should go to Wistow Fields and let Debbie have a decent run. Debbie hardly got runs now, since we didn't have a field of our own, and she hated traipsing the pavements on

340

the lead and without a lead she was liable to go awol.

Our mother had settled quite well at Snowdrop by then. She hated it and hated the early mornings and the horrible bossy man in charge, but she was showing signs of not feeling quite so miserable.

'You're in a good mood,' my sister said that Saturday.

'I am, actually,' said our mother, and I studied her.

She'd been battling with the pills, battling the urge to take them and the misery she felt without them, and with help from Dr Gurly she was beginning to have the odd day of feeling vaguely OK with just a minimum of pills. And we hadn't been to London for months.

We three clambered into the Snowdrop van at around 4 p.m. with a packet of almond slices and some bottles of Sola Cola. My sister sat in the van boy's seat with Debbie at her feet. Jack and I jumped up into the mesh bunks and sat atop loads of grubby laundry and our mother swung herself up into the driver's seat. The drive that day to Wistow Fields was honestly one of the best quarter-hours of my life. Our little family (plus Debbie) unified somehow by the lumbering great van, her growling engine — top speed 35 miles per hour — our mother's left arm, bare to the shoulder, heaving the ponderous gearstick around and her bare feet whacking the pedals, Georgie Fame singing 'I say yeah, yeah', and Jack and me rolling around in the fixed cages among the damp and soapy hand towels collected from seventeen pubs on Friday.

We were happy, all of us at the same time, and as we clattered over the cattle grid into Wistow Fields I wanted us to keep driving and stay moving and get eventually to some better place (like America, where people would ask us how we were doing, only nearer). But we slowed up and parked on a verge, tumbled out and ran around a bit.

Our mother kept her Grundig going and my sister switched to a home-made tape from the hit parade and suddenly it was the New Seekers, whom we usually hated but joined in with. And we stayed there, singing songs we usually didn't like and eating the almond slices, and Debbie rolled in fox poo and we had to force her into a brook and our mother lay on a line of dirty Turkish roller towels and swigged from a Schweppes bottle and puffed away on Embassys and told us funny things about the Snowdrop lot. How supportive and amusing they all were. How they'd all had their own ups and downs. We heard again how Miss Kellogg had lobbied for us to be allowed use of the van and how she'd shouldered the blame for the Hillman Husky from Ray's Reliables. We also heard the story of how the smell of bacon had brought Miss Kellogg back from the brink of suicide in 1970.

'How?' my sister asked.

'Well, she was feeling suicidal and suddenly the aroma of sizzling bacon drifted in through her bedsit window and she realized, in the nick of time, she was more hungry than suicidal,' explained our mother.

We were all thrilled to hear about the bacon saving Miss Kellogg's life. Our mother said she herself had never felt suicidal and couldn't imagine such a thing. Which was nice to hear, and Little Jack said that if he ever got suicidal, he'd just do a load of daredevil things until he was either cheered up or killed.

Interestingly, the revelation about Miss Kellogg and the bacon rescue took us dangerously close to the subject of ham, which we usually skirted around and avoided (it leading to the subject of Charlie), and it's funny that although we had no reason to ever mention ham or cooked meats, the subject seemed always to be lurking along with other things we didn't want to mention like pets, baby donkeys and Dorset. But somehow, there on Wistow Fields that Saturday afternoon, with the sun low in the sky and droplets of Sola Cola on our moustaches, it had been OK to come close to the subject of ham. In other words, we were recovering.

After a while the day started to end and the Grundig started to slur and we were just thinking of heading home when I saw a look of great anxiety cross our mother's face. I thought it might at least be a herd of angry bulls or something that could do us great harm, but it was just a man.

A man striding towards us, quite ordinary, hands in pockets.

'Who's this?' I asked.

'Shit,' said our mother, 'shit.' And she scrambled to her feet and patted her hair.

'What's going on here?' asked the man. Brown

trousers, thin belt, long sideburns, sleeves rolled up.

'We just came out for a run around,' said our mother, looking crumpled.

'Pick these towels up,' he said, gesturing at the towels lying on the grass. He went to pick up the Schweppes bottle but she intercepted it. Then he swung himself up into the van.

'How did you get all those children here?' he called from the van.

'Two went in the cages,' she said.

Although the man didn't seem aggressive or even particularly angry, our mother was a bag of nerves. He was icy and machine-like and we guessed it must be Mr Holt (the boss) and we edged away so as not to witness our mother being told off. Before long, our mother told us all to get into Mr Holt's mustard-coloured Austin 1100, which we did, and he drove us home. All four of us plus Debbie.

After dropping us at home Mr Holt walked all the way back to Wistow Fields, on foot, to collect the van, drove it back to our house, got into his car and went.

'What was he so cross about?' I asked later on.

'He's just a miserable bastard,' our mother said. And she kicked the door to her room, thinking about him. She didn't kick it very hard, but her foot (bare) made a hole in it. I have to say, the kick wasn't much more than an angry gesture, but the hole looked like something awful had happened and I really wished it wasn't there.

Our mother was upset for the rest of the

weekend and dreaded going back to Snowdrop on the Monday morning. So all the excitement of the new manly haircuts and the niceness and unification of the van ride and the not minding thinking about ham came to nothing. I was furious with Mr Holt and felt sorry for our mother. My sister felt the exact opposite and said that our mother was to blame for being irresponsible, for taking a mile when she'd been given an inch, and mostly for being drunk in charge of the Snowdrop van.

Monday morning came and she was gone by seven. I meant to worry about her all day but I forgot until I got home and saw her there at 3.45, which was much too early.

'What happened?' I asked. 'Were you sacked?'

'No,' she said, 'but the bastard gave me a verbal warning.'

It sounded bad. 'Verbal?' I said. 'Is that bad?'

'Not as bad as written,' she said, and I still wasn't sure.

'Why are you home so early?' I asked.

'I was suspended without pay for the day,' she said.

She said Mr Holt was a bastard again and that she was ashamed and that she couldn't do the job and all sorts of rambling stuff. Mainly that Mr Holt was making life hell for her, being picky and horrible.

'Could you have a pill?' I wondered. 'Would it cheer you up?'

'Oh Lizzie, I don't want to, but I do want to. But I really don't want to.' And she poured herself a drink instead.

27

Soon our father called to take us for the day. It seemed that Bernard had been let go and he was doing his own driving in an automatic Citroën with an interesting suspension action. He didn't come into the house but tooted outside in the street and sat at the wheel, looking uncertain. We drove the forty minutes or so to his side of the county without saying much, the rattle of his onyx ring on the vibrating gearstick mesmerizing and annoying at the same time, and I think it was that that made my sister pull the side of my hair. There was no other reason for it.

We started having a tussle in the back seat and pulling each other's hair. It was unusual for us to be fighting like that and I was offended at her starting it. It seemed too intimate a thing for our father to witness; nevertheless, I fought hard and actually made her cry, which was horrible. The startling thing was that our father completely ignored us. He didn't look at us or say anything, only turned to Little Jack next to him and reminded him to notice the car's suspension.

'You'll feel the car lowering when we come to a stop.' Or something.

When our fight had completely finished he asked us how we were enjoying our new house.

'It's very small but fine,' said my sister.

And when we arrived at his house we found he had moved too. He was surprised we didn't know but concluded he'd forgotten to tell us or our mother had. His new house was a good deal less grand than his last, though not quite so small as ours and still managed to have all the features you'd expect from a superior dwelling, plus his housekeeper was still going round with a cloth and pegging things out on the line.

'I hear the firm has gone bankrupt,' said my sister. I marvelled at her use of language. The Firm.

'Well, yes, there have been some problems,' said our father.

We had the dreaded Sunday lunch, albeit at the kitchen table, and the baby who was a bit older by now wasn't all that well behaved and therefore didn't make Jack seem inferior, and the newer baby was of less interest to everybody, being the second and a girl and brown-haired.

My sister brought up the subject of our mother's job and said how much she was enjoying driving a Leyland van all day long and running into pub toilets five days a week, and after sounding quite interesting it went on too long and seemed pointed. I was cross with my sister. First, the unprovoked hair-pulling in the automatic Citroën, then the below-the-belt account of our mother's work. I wondered what was the matter with her. But then, as if in answer to that, I blurted out something truly awful. I didn't plan to and as I began it seemed like plain old chitchat, but as soon as it was out I realized it was nothing less than heartbreaking.

'People keep saying you're evil and bad,' I said

to my father, between mouthfuls of the roast dinner.

My father didn't wince, he just said, 'I am sorry you're having to hear that kind of thing. It's very unfortunate. I really am very sorry.' And his wife let her knife and fork clatter onto the table and looked at the wall.

'It doesn't bother me,' I said, thinking that made it better.

I didn't steal anything from the house on that trip. I usually took a pot of jam or a tin of mandarins. There was less on offer and I didn't feel it fair or right now the firm had gone bankrupt. But I did smoke in the bedroom and finish a bottle of lemonade that was meant to be for all of us.

Back at home my sister exaggerated how small and ordinary our father's new house was, to make our mother feel better, but then accidentally mentioned Mrs Penrose and our mother pounced on it.

'They can still run to a maid-of-all-work, then?' she said.

'Yes, but to be fair he hasn't got a chauffeur any more,' my sister said, and then realized how silly it sounded and we all laughed.

★   ★   ★

Our mother settled down at the laundry after the verbal warning and got back into the swing of being a Snowdrop driver, Mr Holt remaining a fly in the ointment, though. If he hadn't been there our mother would have found the getting up and going every morning so much easier. He was a stickler and seemed to notice every detail and to be actually on the lookout for mistakes and problems. If she was a few minutes late, he'd tap his wrist at her. If she unloaded in the wrong bay, he'd make her load up again and move the van. If she and Deano were back early, he'd give them an errand. One day a customer had rung to say a roller towel had jammed only moments after our mother had installed the clean one and left. Mr Holt made her go out to the customer and unjam it.

Once she'd found a dozen clean folded tea towels in the van and realized they'd left a customer without his correct number. They'd been halfway home when the discovery was made and decided to leave it until the next day. Back at the depot, Mr Holt noticed the tiny pile of hidden towels with his eagle eye and sent her back into town. When she put up a reasonable argument for dropping them in the following day, he simply waved her on and said, 'Wedge. Thin end of.'

It really seemed as though Mr Holt picked on her especially, that was the galling thing. One morning he stood in front of the van as she pulled out of the depot. He waved her down and told her to get out. Then he sent her home to change into sensible footwear. He insisted on all van drivers and boys taking a lunch break at a certain place on whichever route they were on and would check to see if they had indeed had a stop. Our mother said this showed he was a fascist.

The absolute worst of it was that none of her colleagues at the Snowdrop would complain about Mr Holt. No one seemed to want to say how picky and petty he was, and as far as she could tell, the rest of the workforce seemed to think his management style perfectly reasonable. They weren't friends with him or anything, except after work hours when he might chuckle at a joke or make an ironic observation; he was a popular, albeit distant, boss.

She told us that if she'd been able to get it off her chest, moan about him or slag him off, it might have made things easier, but she couldn't and apologized for 'bringing it home with her'. I didn't mind, neither did Little Jack, who suggested putting a picture of him on the dartboard, but that seemed too drastic. Our sister did mind. She told our mother she was part of the workforce now and the workforce needed leadership. And it was natural for someone from her background finding themselves suddenly in a subordinate role to resist and that she needed breaking in like a young horse. And that was probably what Mr Holt was doing, hence it seeming as if he was picking on her.

One day Deano the van boy called in sick and Mr Holt took his place on our mother's van. It was the worst day of her life, worse than all the court appearances, drugged-up hellish days in bed, school days, you name it. Mr Holt had sat in the passenger seat all stony silence, glancing at the dash as our mother drove the route and used the handbrake whenever possible. When our mother got home she needed two Disprins and a hot whisky to shift a day-long headache. The day had seemed like a week, she said, and we told her that was exactly how we felt after going to our father's and that it wasn't Mr Holt's fault (nor our father's), just the tension of the situation. Of not being able to relax.

We wanted details of the day. Mr Holt had insisted on a proper stop for lunch and the two had had to sit and eat a cheese and chutney cob together and he had chewed very slowly. He'd made her refuel before returning to the depot. He'd made her drop new price sheets off at every stop and, worse than anything, he chatted to the customers who knew him and he asked how things had been, customer service-wise.

'Didn't you chat amongst yourselves?' my sister asked.

'A bit,' she said. 'I told him why I'd taken the job at Snowdrop.'

'I hope you didn't say for the money,' said my sister.

'I said I'd taken it because we'd been derailed,' she said.

'*Derailed?*' we said.

'Catastrophically knocked off course, but that now I was taking control.'

'Taking the helm,' I said.

'Well, I didn't say that, but yes,' she said, and went to phone Deano.

★ ★ ★

My sister knew about my friendship with Melody by then and was quite understanding

352

about it. The two of them had a mutual though lopsided respect for each other. My sister liked Melody but was slightly contemptuous of her attempts at prettiness and ladylike ways. Melody's admiration of my sister, however, was unconditional. I expect it was because mine was (unconditional) and things like that rub off. I wasn't constantly advertising my sister's virtues or anything, but had said the odd thing that would have struck a chord with Melody. Such as her trying to save a duckling's life and her having the guts to snitch on a dinner lady who called a girl with a lazy eye 'Nelson'.

Our friendship came under some strain around the time of our move to the Sycamore Estate, though. It was nothing to do with our not being neighbours any longer, but my early grapplings with the semantics of fashion accessories coincided with Melody's handbag-usage phase (and her wearing of a beady necklace which she claimed played down a veiny sternum). Somehow the handbags and beads signalled she wasn't going to shape up as a friend. The final straw (metaphorically speaking) was a fabric bucket with bamboo hoops for handles, which Melody suddenly had with her at all times. What made me most sick about it was her habit (out of necessity) of frequently saying to me, 'Can you just hold my bag a moment?'

This was because she couldn't perform any two-handed task while holding it, due to the hoops being too small in circumference to be slipped up on to the shoulder. So, time after time, I'd be left holding it while she fiddled with her shoelace or gate latch. It wasn't as if the bag ever had anything worth carrying in it either, such as a Wagon Wheel or a penknife. I could tell this by the weight — it was, for all its stupid bucket-size, light as a feather. It was, like so many women's things, like a clumsy prop for a fancy-dress costume.

It sounds harsh, I know, but I had just realized that opting for anything sensible in the way of bags, shoes, trousers (even books and hobbies) marked you out as a tomboy (even if you weren't a tomboy as such), and although being a tomboy was thought by adults to be marvellous, it was a problem when it came to other children. Other tomboys might admire you but would often want to compete in tomboyishness, and that meant possibly having to fight them or having to jump off a roof or watch them dissect a wasp without minding.

Non-tomboys would not admire you — they'd think you were heading in the wrong direction and were either a lesbian in the making, which seemed a bad choice, or too lazy to make the effort for womanhood. I suppose they had to think these things in order to justify their own inconveniences and encumbrances. But back then it all felt like a trap.

Anyway, Melody had the womanly bag — and was looked up to by other budding women in spite of her childish clothes and veiny sternum — and she seemed happy. One day, it came to a head. Melody said, 'Could you hold my bag for a sec? My necklace has slipped round the wrong way.'

And I said, 'No, I bloody couldn't . . . Why the hell do you carry it around with you anyway?'

'It's my knitting,' said Melody, sounding shocked and hurt.

I said I doubted there was any knitting in the bag and that she just wanted to look like a budding woman. Melody adjusted the beads with the bag between her knees and shuffled quickly away and I was furious with myself, as you are when you do things like that. It felt like an ending.

* * *

Grocery shopping was a trial. Our mother was OK sending us to do it a bit at a time and the system where we nipped across the road to Miss Woods's when we needed something had suited her down to the ground. But self-serving a trolley-load of groceries and toilet paper in a brightly lit space had got the better of her enough times that we knew to avoid doing too much in one go. However, now she was a full-time worker it seemed sensible to stock up in one big weekly shop.

Our mother had settled well at Snowdrop and I was over my episode with the pig and my sister was over the Brownie letter and Little Jack even seemed to be speaking more easily and our mother was well into the reflection of the mountain in the lake. My sister and I had been discussing the Man List and wondering if it was time to recommence with the quest to find a man for our helm. So, one Saturday afternoon, sailing up the A50 in the unreliable Hillman Husky, our mother said, 'Shall we call in at Woolco and do a big shop?'

With all these very positive things in mind, we thought it would probably be fine. And we said yes. Because while a failed big shop was always depressing and upsetting, a successful one was to be celebrated for all the obvious reasons — mainly that we could have fried eggs on toast and Debbie could enjoy Pal for active life or Pedigree Chum or whatever was on offer and we'd have a whole week with no worrying about margarine or Weetabix.

Anyway, we went and loaded a trolley with essentials and the odd treat. Things seemed to be going well and it looked as though we'd get through it when suddenly our mother said, 'No, I'm unequal to this, it's too much — come on, I have to leave.'

And, as usual, my sister protested. 'We need this stuff, Mum,' she said.

'I can't do it,' said our mother, 'I've got to get out of here.'

'But, Mum,' said my sister, 'we're almost at the tills.'

The two of them argued briefly, but in the end we left the trolley by the soap powders and came home via the Red Rickshaw with 'no beef savoury feast for 2', which is what we always did on these occasions. On the way home my sister made a very clever observation.

'We always go to the Chinese takeaway if we leave the shopping,' she said.

'That's because it's always nearly supper time

and we've no food,' said Jack.

'That's what I'm saying,' said my sister, 'it's always that time in the afternoon.'

'So what?' I said.

'It's a classic low time for middle-aged women and people with mental illness,' said my sister.

You might think our mother would've been pleased to hear that and feel a bit better about it all, but she wasn't and told my sister to stop talking such a lot of utter crap. And then, just as she said that, pulling into our little driveway we saw the most amazing and beautiful sight — a cluster of carrier bags huddled by our front door. A family pack of Andrex, a tray of Pal for active life, and a family-size box of Daz automatic. It was our shopping, the exact shopping we'd just abandoned at Woolco.

Our mother was astonished and stood and stared down at it. She looked up the street and then down the street. I thought for a moment she was going to be angry. But she was simply amazed.

'What do you think it means, Lizzie?' she asked.

'I think it means someone saw us dump the trolley,' said Jack.

'Yes,' agreed our mother.

'And they took the trolley to the tills and paid for everything and brought it here,' I said.

'That means they know where we live,' said my sister.

'But they can't have followed us. We stopped at the takeaway,' said our mother.

'They know us,' I said.

'It's like *The Railway Children*,' said my sister.

'Oh my God, it is,' said our mother.

And we all got teary at the thought.

As soon as we'd finished our Chinese we unloaded our lovely shopping. It had been so long since we'd had the luxury of unpacking so much, Little Jack couldn't stop listing everything, 'Cornflakes, Sunblest, Mr Fresh, medicated Vosene, Knight's Castile, Jacob's, Germolene.'

And no stammering.

'Robinson's, Bird's, Fairy Bentos,' he sang.

'Fairy Bentos,' said my sister, 'what's that?' and she took the thing from Jack's hand.

It was a round tin containing a steak and gravy pie with flaky pastry. It wasn't ours; we hadn't put it in our shopping trolley. We decided it had been added by our benefactor as a special treat, and if we hadn't just had the 'no beef savoury feast for 2' from the Red Rickshaw we might have cooked it up.

We tried to imagine who it might have been. Our father? Grandmother? The vicar? Charlie? Mr Lomax? Mr Oliphant? Mr Longlady?

★ ★ ★

The next day I was shocked to see Melody Longlady at the door. Bagless. We were no longer anything like neighbours (and after the disagreement about the bag, not even friends) and her being there at the door meant she'd come all the way to the bottom part of the village and then ventured into the Sycamore Estate and looked around for our house. Plus she was wearing a

358

maroon tracksuit and no beads.

'Hi, Melody,' I said.

'Hi,' said Melody.

'Have you been on a run?' I asked.

'No, why?' she said.

It was a bit odd and formal like that for a while until I invited her in and we went into our part of the sitting room. We hadn't sorted out a settee yet, but there was a bouncy little Zedbed that we all sat on to watch telly. I flopped down and Melody flopped down beside me. I couldn't turn the telly on because it had gone yellow.

'How's the new house?' she asked.

'It's great,' I said.

Melody looked as though she had some really bad news to tell me. Someone had died or she'd seen her father in the nude. But it was only the surprise of seeing how everything was, the general situation, the state of the house, hearing about the pets. I hadn't wanted to tell her about the pets but had no choice when she'd gone round the back to see the guinea pigs and found only a few earwigs in the hutch. I asked her if she was OK.

'It's just seeing you here, and the pets all gone,' she began, and listed the negatives. Of course I could quite see what she meant and it must have been a bit of a shock, but I reassured her that the pets had been re-homed and were happier than ever with lots of bored elderly people giving them titbits or on farms chasing rats. And that we were really happy too, living down there.

'It's so near the chemist,' I said.

I remembered our kitchen full of food from the recent shopping miracle and offered Melody a glass of Nesquik and an orange Club, to cheer her up, which she accepted.

'Will you ever regain your former status?' she asked.

'Probably not,' I said. 'Our mum wasn't trained for anything except living the way we did and so she's driving a laundry van.'

'I know, we've seen her in the van,' said Melody. 'She must absolutely hate it.'

'She doesn't hate it, but it *is* work and that's never that nice,' I said.

'Is she in the van now?' Melody asked.

'No' — I pointed to the chipboard partition — 'she's the other side of that, asleep.'

Melody frowned and then she said something, the likes of which I had never heard and it had such a profound effect on me, it was all I could do not to cry into a cushion.

'My dad,' she whispered, 'thinks your mum is the most amazing woman he's ever met, selling up and getting that awful van-driving job.'

I did the thing that people do when they want to hear a good thing twice.

'What did he say?' I asked, and settled back on the Zedbed to hear it all again and, knowing Melody, expected it verbatim, but she surprised me with an elaboration that was even better.

'He said he didn't know many women who'd grab the bull by the horns and go out to work all hours,' she whispered, 'and not hang around waiting for handouts.'

I felt a bit humbled. There I was forever

moaning about the village and all its inhabitants and their handbags, and here was Melody in her tracksuit. She'd come to visit and been affected by our riches-to-rags slippage and even passed on a wonderful compliment and done nothing but good. It was like our friendship coming true and I was and still am immensely grateful.

When she left, I said, 'It was really nice of you to come all this way.'

And she said, 'I came yesterday as well but you were out.'

And, thinking about that for a moment, I made the assumption that it must have been Mr Longlady who'd bought our shopping for us and felt a bit disappointed.

'Oh, was it you who brought our shopping round?' I asked.

'No, but I saw the man dropping it off,' said Melody.

'Did you? What did he look like,' I asked, holding her elbows, 'the man?'

'He had brown hair and glasses,' she said, as if that was enough.

'Did he come in a car?' I asked.

'Yes, a yellow one.'

'Mustard-coloured?' I asked, high-pitched.

'Yes, mustard-coloured,' said Melody.

I knew then. It had been Mr Holt.

Then Melody fiddled around in her pocket and handed me a bundled-up woollen thing which turned out to be a knitted green hat with a lumpy yellow sun.

'I knitted it for you,' she said.

I put it straight on my head so I didn't have

the embarrassment of looking at it.

'Wow, thanks,' I said.

'That's OK,' she said.

'Did you knit it before or after our fall-out?' I asked.

'Before and after,' she said.

Then she said she had to go and left. I called from the front door, 'Thanks for the hat and thanks for coming, Melody.'

And she called, 'Oh, by the way, I'm trying to shorten my name, to Mel.'

'OK, Mel,' I said, and it suited her.

When my sister got home I told her everything. Starting with the shopping and it being Mr Holt.

'Mr Holt!' she said, and her eyes looked from side to side and she rolled her gum frantically between her front teeth as she thought about the implications.

'We mustn't tell Mum,' she said.

'Why not?' I said.

'He did it secretly and I think he knows best,' she said.

'Better than us?' I asked.

'Lizzie,' she said, with a face of great importance, 'I think he might be it.'

'It? God!' I said, not knowing what to think.

I told the rest of the news about Melody. How nice she had been and about the wonderful compliment from Mr Longlady, and knitting me the hat, coming all this way, being sad about the pets and worrying about the whole move thing.

'A truer friend no one had,' said my sister, which, put like that, sounded poetic but might have been a bit sarcastic.

We talked in bed that night for a long time. We agreed not to say anything to our mother about Mr Holt and that we'd just let nature take its course. We talked and talked but fell asleep before we'd finished.

★　★　★

Early one morning when I was still in bed, I heard our mother cry out in surprise. I thought perhaps she'd made another hole in another door or a handle had come off. Then I heard her on the phone.

'I'm going to be late,' she said into the phone, 'I might not make it in today at all.'

And then she talked some more but incoherently and tearful and I knew something terrible must have happened. And it had.

I was frightened of what I might find but eventually went to see. It was still dark outside and, because the bulb had blown in the hall, she was down there, with a bicycle lamp flickering, cross-legged on the floor with her head resting on Debbie. I thought she'd had a nervous breakdown and was just wondering if I should call the police or make some coffee when the door knocked softly and, being broken, it opened on its own and Mr Holt was suddenly there, framed, in his big coat with the early dawning light behind him and the birds singing in the young hedges like something out of *Snow White*.

Our mother shuffled aside to let him in and then gave a gasp as she saw me on the stairs. And she told me, right in front of him, that Debbie had died. I didn't want to believe it and genuinely thought I might be dreaming. It seemed very likely, bearing in mind that Mr Holt was there in a ginormous coat and my sister and I having decided that he was our future man at the helm, plus all the tweeting birds and the dreadful news about Debbie. It was too much and too strange to be real. So I just sat down on the stairs and hugged my knees to see what would happen.

'What do you plan to do?' Mr Holt asked.

'You don't plan at a time like this,' said our mother.

Mr Holt stood there and our mother looked up at him and said, 'I'm not sure you understand just how sad this news is.'

Mr Holt glanced up at me. 'I understand,' he said.

He said he'd go and open up the depot and come back as soon as he could. 'I want to help you with this,' he said.

When he had gone, she looked at me and said, 'What did he just say?' and I just nodded, meaning he had said the thing she thought he'd said.

Then there were a few awful minutes when the others came downstairs and had to hear the news. Debbie had died on her cushion in her corner and had looked very peaceful, our mother said. None of us had heard any barks, so we concluded she'd ceased upon the midnight with no pain and of natural causes. We were too sad to act sad. So we had a slice of Battenberg and a cup of tea and then Mr Holt was back and we couldn't wallow with him there, as we had to be on our best behaviour.

'Would you like a cup of coffee?' my sister asked.

'No thank you, love,' said Mr Holt.

Mr Holt asked what we wanted to do with Debbie. We all said we wanted to bury her in the garden and mark the grave with a stone memorial, but Mr Holt said that wouldn't be possible, the garden being too small. His suggestion was to have her cremated at the vet's and get on with life.

We agreed — none of us really wanted her out there next to that old rabbit called Bunny. Mr Holt lifted Debbie, wrapped in a blanket, into his car boot and we all set off to the vet's. When we got there Mr Holt placed her on a table and that was it. And Mr Holt drove us home again and went.

A few days after that Mr Holt came round with a piece of stone. It was the size of two house bricks and beige. It was Debbie's gravestone, not that she had a grave as such.

'What words do you want on this?' he asked.

Jack, who was usually good with words, came up with Debdog, which wasn't up to his usual standard and sounded idiotic.

'Debbie, the greatest dog in the world?' I tried.

'Too long,' said my sister.

'Debbie the dog?' said Jack.

'Too childish,' I said.

'How about Princess Debbie Reynolds?' said our mother. 'That's her kennel name.'

And however real and official it was, it sounded so utterly wrong for Debbie that none of us could respond until Mr Holt said, 'PDR would be cheaper, and means the same thing.'

'Yes,' we all said, 'PDR.'

'Perfect Dog Rests,' said Jack, but we all ignored him, it being a bit strange.

And when, a few days later, we saw the brick again, it had PDR carved into it in capitals. The chiselled letters were multifaceted and shadow-filled, so that they seemed not to be indented but standing out. It was an optical illusion, maybe a deliberate feature of the carving method. Whatever, it looked very beautiful and sombre and therefore perfect to commemorate our wonderful Debbie.

We held a stone-placing ceremony and put it in the garden as you do with memorials, and it looked rubbish (like someone had just dropped a large brick on the ground while passing through), but no one said anything aloud. We all said secret things to Debbie in our minds. I thanked her for her support and apologized for the time I put her in the wheelbarrow.

Mr Holt didn't want to join in with us. It was our business and he didn't want to see all the blubbering and nonsense, plus he said he'd spent enough time faffing.

The awfulness of Debbie's death cannot be described. Nothing helped.

28

By the time we'd added Mr Holt's name to the Man List, he was already coming round twice or three times a week and watching *Call My Bluff* on a portable Philips he'd lent us. And having dinners on the Zedbed — a pie or something and a tin of marrowfat peas — and then he'd do a few jobs and go home again to his flat in town. One Sunday he'd been round to sort out our warped front door and he asked why on earth we kept going to the launderette when we had an automatic washing machine in the house. We told him it was broken. He doubted it. He looked at it a while, then showed us how to approach a problem logically.

'The first rule is, you have a good look at it,' he said, switching the socket on and off and on again.

'OK,' we said.

'And try to work out what's wrong,' he said, trying to rotate the drum clockwise.

'OK,' we said, bored already.

'Then you might sort it out,' he said, trying to rotate the drum anticlockwise.

He explained that with consistent correct usage machines didn't usually go wrong. But in the unlikely event that something did go wrong, a little bit of common sense and rational thinking might give you a clue as to the problem, then you'd have a hope in hell of fixing it and, saying that, he leant into our Electrolux and plucked a hair-clip out of the drum.

My sister and I agreed that Mr Holt's general goodness and his extraordinary kindness over Debbie and his lending of the telly had earned him the right to skip the full vetting process. He was a proven animal-lover (within reason) via the headstone and he certainly liked telly, especially brainy stuff like *Mastermind*, which was still quite new and exciting then and we all loved it when Magnus Magnusson said, 'I've started so I'll finish.' And he suited Little Jack down to the ground with his interest in *The World of Facts*.

Mr Holt's philosophy was that there was the world and there was you and you had to find your place in it and hold your course and that you had to respect yourself.

To begin with it was as though he spoke in riddles or a whole different language — let your mother and I sleep on it, we'll see, perhaps, I'm not sure about that, I'll have to look into it, that's for us to know and you to find out, none of your business, get a good night's sleep, do it again and do it properly. It wasn't, though, it was discipline and due care, plus modesty and a lack of hyperbole, a refusal to overegg any puddings, gild lilies or say a job was done when it was shoddy. It was his way and we just weren't used to it.

And although we soon realized he was the best of all the men we'd ever had on the Man List (including the very nice Mr Oliphant), he did sometimes seem a million miles away from us in everything he thought and did, and we did occasionally wonder whether we wouldn't ultimately disappoint each other. My sister, for instance, had a horrible feeling that he might be one of those people who insist on solving every problem and cannot be satisfied with just talking through and moaning about a thing. We'd seen people like it before (problem-solving fathers) and thought it the one thing that would be unliveable with.

So it was decided that he'd have to undergo one simple test. I was to go to him with a dilemma rather than a problem — dilemmas being that bit more tricky than problems — and see how he responded. My dilemma (a real one) concerned my pen-friend.

This was the dilemma and how I presented it. Many of my classmates at school had exciting Spanish and French pen-friends (arranged by the school) called Olga and Maria who lived in mountainous areas or in Paris, but my own Rebecca Bellamy-Briggs lived in the north of England (I got her via *Pony Magazine*). The thing was, Rebecca had written to say she no longer wanted to be my pen-friend. Which suited me because I'd been thinking the same thing and was keen to move on (to a Spanish or French one, with future exchange visits in mind). The dilemma/problem aspect being that Rebecca's 'breaking off' letter had contained a letter from *Georgina* Bellamy-Briggs, the horse-loving older sister of Rebecca, introducing herself as my new pen-friend.

Georgina Bellamy-Briggs wrote that although Rebecca was sick to the back teeth of hearing the same old things about my peculiar life, she (Georgina) found my letters very amusing and would therefore be taking Rebecca's place as my pen-friend. She then ran straight into a pen-friend letter and said all the things a pen-friend would. She told me about her beautiful mare, Dido, and their goat and its two kids called Hepzibar and Nancy. So there was the dilemma: should I go along with the switch from Rebecca to Georgina? Or should I decline the offer and be free to seek a Spanish (or French) one?

I told him the whole story and while I spoke he held his newspaper down so as not to inadvertently look at it. When I'd finished, I asked for his advice. He was flummoxed and scratched his head to prove it. He remained silent for so long I thought he'd forgotten the story.

'What do you think?' I said, and recapped, 'Should I go with Georgina or not?'

'I don't know, love, I think you'll have to work that one out for yourself,' he said, and went back to his paper.

Which seemed a perfectly reassuring response.

★　★　★

Mr Holt and our mother swapped life stories slowly. And she passed on snippets. He was from East Anglia originally. He was thirty-three years old but seemed older because of his authoritative manner and disciplinarian ways and wanting things just so. He was self-sufficient emotionally due to being the only child of elderly parents, and never made a fuss unless witnessing laziness.

My sister and I wondered what on earth our mother had told him about herself. I mean, him, a hard-working disciplinarian and her, *her*. But whatever it was, they grew closer.

My sister broached the subject one Saturday morning.

'Does Mr Holt know all about you and all your pills etc.?' she asked.

'Yes, he does,' said our mother, 'I told him.'

'And was he OK about it all?' she asked.

'Yes, eventually. The two of us are going to tackle it together,' said our mother.

'So are you together as a couple?' asked my sister.

And they were, somehow. Though they had very little in common — only a love of cricket and a sense of the absurd. Soon he moved out of his flat and into our broken little house. He didn't bring much with him, only a few clothes, books, tools, a mattress and a can of WD40.

Our mother spoke to us about the new situation. She warned us that it might take some getting used to and that occasionally Mr Holt would seek solitude and we mustn't take it personally (or go bothering him), just that he would want some time to himself and might listen to the radio in the bedroom. She warned us that he wouldn't allow us to be slipshod and that we may as well save time and energy and just do things properly in the first place.

Mr Holt had a few words with us about the new situation too.

'You might have noticed that I'm here quite often,' he said.

We said we had noticed.

'Was it you who picked up our shopping at Woolco and brought it round for us?' I asked, wanting this outstanding mystery solved while we'd got his attention.

'I don't know what you're talking about,' he said.

'We thought it was you because of the tinned pie that was definitely not in the trolley when we left it,' said my sister.

'Yes,' said Jack, 'we've noticed you like that type of pie.'

'Oh,' said Mr Holt, and gave himself away with his expression of surprise.

He continued his words about the new situation, 'So you'll have noticed I'm here quite often and I suppose it's none of your concern really, but suffice to say your mother and I want to make some kind of life together, with you three, and I hope you're agreeable.'

We nodded and waited. And he told us that if we were (agreeable) he'd like to throw in his lot with us and see if it might be possible to stretch to a slightly bigger house, though nothing grand, just an extra bedroom.

'What's 'your lot'?' asked Jack, sounding manly.

'My savings, my WD40,' he said, but only because he had it in his hand at the time, 'and myself, of course.'

'What are you saving up for?' asked Little Jack.

'I suppose I was saving for a new car,' he said,

'but I've had a change of mind.'

So Mr Holt became the man at the helm. And to begin with, he was exactly the same as he'd been with our mother in those first months at Snowdrop: a nightmare, a stickler, a killjoy, an eagle-eyed fusspot. He'd come home with a dustpan and brush and say, 'Right, now there's no excuse for not sweeping up.' He'd ask why so much laundry was building up (we knew not to mention our temperamental unsuitability to it), and he'd insist we polish our shoes every week, pointing out that he would have been *ashamed* to leave the house with scuffed shoes — there was no excuse for it (unlike a worn collar or worn-down heels which a person might not be able to help). There was polish in the Cherry Blossom tin and two good shoe brushes. He seemed to believe that self-respect, or a lack of, centred around the shoe shine, or not.

I'm not going to pretend our mother was happy, but she was OK. Neither can I pretend Mr Holt was overly nice (he wasn't), but he was with us and he'd open the door if someone rang the bell, which doesn't sound like much but was. He spared us from the things that weren't our concern but told us what we needed to know, and though he had a temper he mostly was able to find his dignity before things got too unpleasant.

He cared about us and cared about the future and with that in mind gave us the shreds of self-respect that my sister had talked about all that time ago when I was overly optimistic about the pills. And I admit now that the self-respect

373

felt wonderful compared with the pills.

★ ★ ★

I wish I could have ended this by saying that we didn't need a man at the helm.

Our mother taking the helm herself and coping brilliantly all alone would have been a powerful finish. The thing is, no one *can* cope alone, not *really* alone. All those brave people who seem to do things solo actually have people in the background who love them or at least *like* them, wishing them well and worrying about them, saying kind and encouraging things and giving them a helping hand now and again. Our mother didn't have quite enough of all that until Mr Holt appeared.

At the time of his joining our family we'd have liked it if Mr Holt had been a bit jollier, let us off the hook occasionally and given fewer verbal warnings, but now, looking back, of course we can see it was imperative that he held tight — and insisted on properness, thoroughness and respect — or we never would have toed the line and things might not have worked out.

There has been much water under many bridges since then and more tales to tell, but you'll be glad to hear that Mr Holt is still there with our mother — albeit in a different house and us all gone — at the helm and keeping things shipshape. I don't know if any of us has ever properly thanked him for what he did, for that first can of WD40, for giving up that new car, and for doing without his solitude.

You could say Mr Holt had been hiding in plain sight. He was there, doing the right thing from the day they met at the interview. But, being unused to such types, we mistook him for a bully and so did she. The frightening thought is how easily we might have missed him. And had Debbie not died, we might never have put him on the list. But cast him and let him remain in the wrong role and locked antlers with him.

Equally, she might not have gone for the driver's job, or not at Snowdrop. And that would have been terrible because, whatever you might say about us and the inevitability of people like us ending up as we had, there was no one else in the world like Mr Holt. No one.

I used to wonder when exactly did she fall for him. And I think it must have been the day she'd called him from the phone box near the Fish & Quart and he'd been concerned about me being on the van. Back at the depot she'd had to speak to him. He'd been so kind and worried about her and about me. She hadn't told me that at the time, because it hadn't felt like kindness at the time. It had felt like criticism and rebuke.

And when she'd said, 'What else could I have done with her?' he'd said, 'You could have taken the day off.' And she'd told him, 'When you're in my situation you don't want to be at home,' and he'd been so affected by that he'd looked right into her eyes and said, 'I wish I knew how to help,' and that had been that.

When had he fallen in love with her? Easy: the moment she'd walked into the depot. More importantly, he'd known he was *right* to love her

Afterword

The Man List

Mr Holt

~~Dr Norman~~

~~Mr Swift — vet~~

~~Charlie Bates — plumber~~

~~Mr Gummo — gardner~~

~~Farmer Turner~~

~~Reverend Derek — vicar~~

~~Denis at the garage — too old?~~

~~Bernard — chauffeur~~

~~Mr Lomax — Liberal candidate~~

~~Dr Kaufmann — doctor~~

~~Mr Dodd — teacher (avoid if poss)~~

~~The coalman — too far away?~~

~~Mr Longlady — accountant and bee lover~~

~~Mr Oliphant — posh farmer~~

~~Our father~~

Acknowledgements

Special thanks to my mum, Elspeth Allison.

Thanks also to John Allison, Patrick Barlow, Victoria Goldberg, Stella Heath, Victoria Hobbs, Peter Humm, Mary Mount, Mark Nunney, Jon Reed, Jeremy Stibbe, Paul Stibbe, Tom Stibbe, Keith Taylor, Mary-Kay Wilmers.

We do hope that you have enjoyed reading this large print book.

Did you know that all of our titles are available for purchase?

We publish a wide range of high quality large print books including:
Romances, Mysteries, Classics
General Fiction
Non Fiction and Westerns

Special interest titles available in large print are:
The Little Oxford Dictionary
Music Book
Song Book
Hymn Book
Service Book

Also available from us courtesy of Oxford University Press:
Young Readers' Dictionary
(large print edition)
Young Readers' Thesaurus
(large print edition)

For further information or a free brochure, please contact us at:
Ulverscroft Large Print Books Ltd.,
The Green, Bradgate Road, Anstey,
Leicester, LE7 7FU, England.
Tel: (00 44) 0116 236 4325
Fax: (00 44) 0116 234 0205

WHAT WAS PROMISED

Tobias Hill

Post-war London: Children run wild on East End bombsites, while their elders strive for better lives in a country beggared by victory. Clarence and Bernadette Malcolm have come five thousand miles in search of prosperity, but find that the Mother Country is not at all what it was promised to be; Solly and Dora Lazarus, too, are strangers in a strange land, struggling to belong even as they try to make sense of their past; and Michael and Mary Lockhart take with both hands all that the world owes them, whatever the cost. In the street markets and tenements of Bethnal Green the three families live and work together in uneasy harmony, until Michael shatters the balance between them, his hunger for betterment changing the courses of all their lives over decades and generations.

REMEMBER ME LIKE THIS

Bret Anthony Johnston

Four years have passed since Justin Campbell's disappearance, a tragedy that rocked the small town of Southport, Texas. Did he run away? Did he drown in the bay? As the Campbells search for answers, they struggle to hold what's left of their family together. Then one afternoon, the impossible happens. The police call to report that Justin has been found in a nearby town, and he appears to be fine. And though the reunion is a miracle, Justin's homecoming exposes the deep rifts that have diminished his family; the wounds they all carry that may never fully heal. When a reversal of fortune lays bare the family's greatest fears — and offers perhaps their only hope for recovery — each of them must fight to keep the ties that bind them from permanently tearing apart.

THE CHILDREN ACT

Ian McEwan

Fiona Maye is a leading High Court judge, presiding over cases in the family court. She is renowned for her fierce intelligence, exactitude and sensitivity. But her professional success belies private sorrow and domestic strife. There is the lingering regret of her childlessness, and her marriage of thirty-five years is in crisis. Now she is called on to try an urgent case: for religious reasons, a beautiful seventeen-year-old boy, Adam, is refusing the medical treatment that could save his life, and his devout parents share his wishes. Time is running out. Should the secular court overrule sincerely held faith? In the course of reaching a decision, Fiona visits Adam in hospital — an encounter which stirs long-buried feelings in her and powerful new emotions in the boy. Her judgment has momentous consequences for them both.

DAUGHTER

Jane Shemilt

Jenny loves her three teenage children and her husband, Ted, a celebrated neurosurgeon. She loves the way that, as a family, they always know each other's problems and don't keep secrets from each other. But when her youngest child, fifteen-year-old Naomi, doesn't come home after her school play and a nationwide search for her begins, secrets previously kept from Jenny are revealed. Naomi has vanished, leaving her family broken and her mother desperately searching for answers. But the traces Naomi has left behind reveal a very different girl to the one Jenny thought she'd raised. And the more she looks, the more she learns that everyone she trusted has been keeping secrets . . .